WILLIAM

SHAKESPEARE'S

—— THE ——
JEDI DOTH RETURN

STAR WARS

PART THE SIXTH

WILLIAM
SHAKESPEARE'S

THE
JEDI DOTH RETURN

STAR WARS

PART THE SIXTH

By Ian Doescher

INSPIRED BY THE WORK OF GEORGE LUCAS
AND WILLIAM SHAKESPEARE

QUIRK BOOKS
PHILADELPHIA

Library of Congress Cataloging in Publication Number: 2013945949

ISBN: 978-1-59474-713-7

Printed in the United States of America

Typeset in Sabon

Text by Ian Doescher
Illustrations by Nicolas Delort
Production management by John J. McGurk

Quirk Books
215 Church Street
Philadelphia, PA 19106
quirkbooks.com

10 9 8 7 6 5 4

FOR BOB, MY DAD, WHO NE'ER CUT OFF MY HAND.

FOR BETH, MY MOM, WHO NEVER WED MY UNCLE.

AND FOR MY BROTHER ERIK, WHO NE'ER TRIED

(AS LEIA DID) TO KISS A BROTHER'S LIPS.

DRAMATIS PERSONAE

CHORUS

LUKE SKYWALKER, *a Jedi trainee*
GHOST OF OBI-WAN KENOBI, *a Jedi Knight*
YODA, *a Jedi Master*
PRINCESS LEIA ORGANA, *of Alderaan*
HAN SOLO, *a rebel captain*
CHEWBACCA, *his Wookiee and first mate*
C-3PO, *a droid*
R2-D2, *his companion*
LANDO OF CALRISSIAN, *a scoundrel*
MON MOTHMA, *leader of the Rebel Alliance*
ACKBAR AND MADINE, *rebel leaders*
WEDGE ANTILLES, *a rebel pilot*
NIEN NUNB, *a rebel pilot*
EMPEROR PALPATINE, *ruler of the Empire*
DARTH VADER, *a Sith Lord*
JERJERROD *and* PIETT, *gentlemen of the Empire*
JABBA OF THE HUTT, *a gangster*
BIB FORTUNA, *Jabba's man*
SALACIOUS CRUMB, *Jabba's fool*
BOBA FETT, *a bounty hunter*
THE MAX REBO BAND, *Jabba's palace musicians*
EV-9D9, *a droid in Jabba's service*
RANCOR, *a monster in Jabba's service*
THE RANCOR KEEPER, *its owner*

REBEL PILOTS, TROOPS, EWOKS, GAMORREAN GUARDS,
JABBA'S COURTIERS, BOUNTY HUNTERS, IMPERIAL TROOPS,
SCOUTS, OFFICERS, COMMANDERS, CONTROLLERS, GUARDS,
ROYAL GUARDS, *and* SOLDIERS

PROLOGUE.

Outer space.

Enter CHORUS.

CHORUS   O join us, friends and mortals, on the scene—
            Another chapter of our cosmic tale.
            Luke Skywalker returns to Tatooine,
            To save his friend Han Solo from his jail
            Within the grasp of Jabba of the Hutt.   5
            But while Luke doth the timely rescue scheme,
            The vile Galactic Empire now hath cut
            New plans for a space station with a beam
            More awful than the first fear'd Death Star's blast.
            This weapon ultimate shall, when complete,   10
            Mean doom for those within the rebel cast
            Who fight to earn the taste of freedom sweet.
            In time so long ago begins our play,
            In hope-fill'd galaxy far, far away.

ACT I

SCENE 1.

Inside the second Death Star.

Enter DARTH VADER *and* MOFF JERJERROD.

VADER   Cease to persuade, my grov'ling Jerjerrod,
               Long-winded Moffs have ever sniv'ling wits.
               'Tis plain to me thy progress falls behind
               And lacks the needed motivation. Thus,
               I have arriv'd to set thy schedule right.   5

JERJERROD   Aye, we are honor'd by your presence, Lord.
               To have you here is unexpected joy.

VADER   Thou mayst dispense with ev'ry pleasantry.
               Thy fawning words no int'rest hold for me.
               So cease thy prating over my arrival   10
               And tell me how thou shalt correct thy faults.

JERJERROD   I tell thee truly, Lord, my men do work
               As quickly as each one is capable—
               No more is possible for them to do.

VADER   Mayhap I shall find new, creative ways   15
               To motivate them.

JERJERROD   —Lord, I'll warrant that
               The station shall be operational
               Within the date and time that have been set.
               Upon my honor I may make such claim.

VADER   The Emperor, however, doth not share   20
               Thine optimistic attitude thereon.

JERJERROD   But, Lord, he doth expect th'impossible!
               I need more bodies to fulfill this task.
               If I had but a hundred able souls
               To work alongside those already here,   25

'Twould be far simpler to complete the work
And make this Death Star ready when 'tis due.

VADER   Thou wilt have opportunity to ask
The Emp'ror for these further workers, for
He shall arrive upon the Death Star soon.   30

JERJERROD   [*aside:*] O news that fills my heart with utter dread!
[*To Darth Vader:*] The Emperor himself shall come
                               here?

VADER   —Aye.
Displeasèd is he with thy thorough lack
Of progress on this station incomplete.

JERJERROD   Our efforts shall be doubled instantly!   35

VADER   I do hope so, Commander, for thy sake—
The Emperor is known for being less
Forgiving than myself. Pray, is that clear?

JERJERROD   It is, Lord Vader, perfectly. Thy words
I hear and shall obey. With gratitude   40
I praise thee for thine honesty herein.

                           [*Exit Moff Jerjerrod.*

VADER   The scene is set for this, the final act.
I shall destroy the rebels, one and all,
And turn young Luke, my son, unto the dark.
It is the role I play, my destiny—   45
The grand performance for which I am made.
Come, author of the dark side of the Force,
Make me the servant of thy quill and write
The tale wherein my son and I are seal'd
As one. Come, take mine ev'ry doubt from me,   50
And fashion from my heart of flesh and wires
A perfect actor: callous, cold, and harsh.
Let this, the second Death Star, be the stage,

And all the galaxy be setting to
The greatest moment of my narrative: 55
The scene in which the Empire's fight is won
Whilst I decide the Fate of mine own son.

                                       [Exit Darth Vader.

SCENE 2.

The desert planet Tatooine, at Jabba's Palace.

Enter C-3PO and R2-D2.

C-3PO   Again, R2, we are on Tatooine.
                I would not e'er have ventur'd to return
                Unto this place most desolate and wild,
                Except that Master Luke hath sent us here
                Upon an errand. Yet I know not what   5
                Our message is, but only that I should
                To Jabba of the Hutt deliver it.
                O place most barren—I have miss'd thee not.
R2-D2   Beep, squeak?
C-3PO   —Indeed I am afraid, R2,
                And so shouldst thou be, too, for Lando of   10
                Calrissian and brave Chewbacca ne'er
                Return'd from here.
R2-D2   —Beep, whistle, squeak.
C-3PO   —Be not
                So certain, R2, for if thou didst know
                But half of all that I have heard about
                This Jabba of the Hutt—his cruelty, how   15
                He tortures innocents, and all the beasts

He keeps to do his will—belike thou wouldst
Short-circuit.

R2-D2   —Hoo.

               [They approach the door of Jabba's palace.

C-3PO   —And now we have arriv'd.
But art thou sure this is the place, R2?
Mayhap 'tis best if I do knock? [*He knocks.*] Alas,   20
There's none to see us in, so let us go!

Enter GUARD DROID *on the other side of door.*

DROID   [*aside:*] Now here's a knocking, indeed! If a droid
Were porter of the Force here in this place,
He should have rust for lack of turning key.
I pray, remember the poor porter droid.   25
[*To C-3PO and R2-D2:*] N'getchoo gadda gooda,
                    einja meh.

C-3PO   My goodness! What foul greeting's this? [*To droid:*] R2-
                    D2wah.

DROID   —Haku! Danna mee bicchu.

C-3PO   Bo C-3POwah, ey.

DROID   —Ai waijay uh.

C-3PO   Odd toota mischka Jabba o du Hutt.   30

DROID   Kuju gwankee? Mypee gaza, ho ho!

C-3PO   Methinks they shall not let us in, what shame!
Still, well may it be said that we have tried,
For never would I give up easily
When sent forth on a task by Master Luke.   35
Yet we have tried and were refusèd here,
Thus, who could blame us for departing hence?
Let us depart now, aye, together fly!

　　　　　　　　　　　　　　　　　　　　　　[The door opens.
　　　　　O pity, it doth open and release
　　　　　Mine utmost fears. Now must we venture in.　　　40
R2-D2　　*[aside:]* My friend C-3PO was never for
　　　　　His courage known. So shall I lead, as e'er
　　　　　I have been wont to lead, into this place
　　　　　Although I too feel fear. *[To C-3PO:]* Beep, whistle,
　　　　　　　　　　　　　　　　　　　　　　squeak!
C-3PO　　O, R2, wait for me! O dear! We should　　　45
　　　　　Not rush, like fools, unto this scene. O my!

　　　　　Enter GAMORREAN GUARDS *and* BIB FORTUNA.

BIB　　　Tay chuda! Nuh die wanna wanga?
C-3PO　　　　　　　—O!
　　　　　Die wanna waugow. *[Translating:]* "We bring unto thy
　　　　　Dread master Jabba of the Hutt a message."
BIB　　　E Jabba wanga?
R2-D2　　　　　　—Squeak!
C-3PO　　　　　　　　　—*[translating:]* "A gift as well."　　　50
　　　　　[To R2-D2:] Wait, R2, pray, what dost thou
　　　　　　　　　　　　　　　　mean, "a gift"?
　　　　　Good Master Luke hath spoken not of "gift."
R2-D2　　Beep, whistle, meep.
BIB　　　　　—Nee Jab' no badda; ees
　　　　　Eye oh toe. Zah kotah amutti mi'.
R2-D2　　Beep, meep, nee, whistle, hoo.
C-3PO　　　　　　　　—He doth report　　　55
　　　　　That we are not to give the message to
　　　　　A soul, save Jabba of the Hutt himself.
G. GUARD 1　Grrf, mik.

C-3PO   —Pray, patience; he quite stubborn is
             When fac'd with matters such as these.
BIB   —Nudd chaa!
             [Bib Fortuna motions for the droids to follow.
C-3PO   R2, I feel a shaking in my core   60
             O'er this dread situation we are in.

Enter JABBA OF THE HUTT, BOBA FETT, THE MAX REBO BAND,
SALACIOUS CRUMB, LANDO OF CALRISSIAN *in disguise,*
and other members of Jabba's court.

JABBA   Ahho, nee jann bah naska ahho bah.
BIB   Kada no pase.
C-3PO   —Good morning.
R2-D2   —Beep, meep, squeak!
BIB   Neh bo shuhadda mana.
JABBA   —Ahh, shihu.
C-3PO   I prithee, R2, play the message now.   65
             The sooner we'll be on our merry way.
JABBA   Bo shuda!
R2-D2   —Beep, meep, whistle.

Enter LUKE SKYWALKER, *in beam.*

LUKE   —Greetings, O
             Exalted Jabba of the Hutt. Allow
             Me to make introduction unto thee:
             My name is Luke Skywalker, Jedi Knight   70
             And friend to Captain Solo, who e'en now
             Is in thy custody. I know that thou
             Art powerful, O Jabba, and that thy

Great anger t'ward Han Solo equally
Must pow'rful be. I seek an audience   75
With thy esteem'd and mighty personage,
To bargain for my friend Han Solo's life.
With thy vast wisdom we shall, doubtless, find
A goodly compromise that shall, indeed,
Be mutually beneficial, and   80
Allow both you and I to 'scape a more
Unpleasant confrontation. As a sign
And symbol of my honest will, I do
Present unto thee, as a gift, these droids.

| | They are hardworking, and shall serve thee well. | 85 |

C-3PO   Alas, what hath he said?

R2-D2   —Beep, whistle, meep!

C-3PO   Nay, nay! R2, I say, your message errs!
                 Our master never would betray us so!

CRUMB   O foolish droids, whose master fools them so!

BIB   [to Jabba:] Na maska bagweni, ees no Jedi.   90

JABBA   Ha ono wangee goghpah, ool.

C-3PO   —We're doom'd!
                 He will not bargain with good Master Luke.

JABBA   Nuh peecha wangee cogh pah, tong nam nee
                 Took chan kee troi. Ne Solo fah keechwa.

C-3PO   O, R2, look, 'tis Captain Solo, still   95
                 A'frozen in the carbonite.

R2-D2   —Beep, hoo!

CRUMB   A little more than dud and less than dead.

JABBA   Na pushka nab, de foghla pah nubin!

Enter EV-9D9, *a droid, as Gamorrean guards lead*
C-3PO and R2-D2 *to him.*

C-3PO   O what hath come upon my master Luke?
                 Did I offend him by some errant word?   100
                 Was he disturb'd by something I have said?
                 Or is this but a human's changing whim?
                 Belike I'll never fully comprehend
                 These people and their wayward, shifting ways.
                 One moment with my service is he pleas'd,   105
                 The next he sendeth me away in scorn
                 To serve the gangster Jabba of the Hutt.
                 Grant me thy mercy, Sir, I beg of thee—

Whatever my offense, O master true,
I prithee, do forgive C-3PO!   110

R2-D2   [*aside:*] What scenes of horror lie herein! I see
That droids are tortur'd here, fix'd fast upon
The rack and torn to bits, or burnèd on
The feet as though they were a piece of meat
Upon a spit. O terror to mine eyes—   115
And yet I know my master hath a plan.
Indeed, within my head I hold the light
That shall illumine our profound escape.

EV-9D9   New acquisitions, excellent. Thou art
A droid of protocol: say, is this so?   120

C-3PO   I am C-3PO, of human—

EV-9D9   —Aye,
Or nay shall serve.

C-3PO   —O. Aye.

EV-9D9   —Of languages,
How many dost thou speak?

C-3P   —Six million forms
Of speech I may claim knowledge of—

EV-9D9   —'Tis well.
We have not had a court interpreter   125
Since our great master anger'd was by our
Most recent droid of protocol, and had
Him thoroughly disintegrated.

C-3PO   —O!
Disintegrated? Fate most vile and cruel!

EV-9D9   I prithee, guard, this droid of protocol   130
May useful be. Take him and fit him with
A strong restraining bolt, and then return
Him unto our great master's chamber.

G. GUARD 2   —Mrk.

C-3PO   O, R2, do not leave me all alone!

> [*Gamorrean Guard 2 leads C-3PO*
> *back to Jabba of the Hutt.*

R2-D2   Beep, squeak!

EV-9D9   —Thou art a feisty little droid,   135
               But soon shall learn respect when thou dost serve
               Upon my master's sail barge. Thou shalt see!

> [*Exeunt EV-9D9 and R2-D2.*

C-3PO   [*aside:*] Within the court of Jabba now I serve.
               But O, what wretched things I see within,
               For when he loseth temper—which befalls   140
               Most frequently—thou mayst be certain it
               Doth mean the death of someone who is nigh.
               For lo, unto the rancor's pit they fall,
               Where such a massive terror lives that I
               Cannot bear watch, though all the courtiers here   145
               Do laugh and cheer as though it were a sport.
               The rancor cometh forth with growls and barks
               And catches up the poor and helpless soul
               Who, screaming in its terror, doth fall mute
               As rancor sinks large teeth into its flesh.   150
               The slaughter of the blameless! O, it is
               A vile and filthy service I fulfill.
               Grant me the patience to endure this time!

> [*The Max Rebo Band plays a song of*
> *tribute to Jabba of the Hutt.*

REBO BAND   [*sings:*] A gangster, aye, a gangster, O!
                   'Tis well to be a gangster.   155
                   A blaster ever by thy side,
                   A stately barge in which to ride,

A fair, young damsel to thee tied,
'Tis well to be a gangster.
A gangster, aye, a gangster, O!   160
'Tis well to be a gangster.
Full many servants lend thee aid,
More guards than a Naboo brigade,
And bounty hunters on parade—
'Tis well to be a gangster.   165
A gangster, aye, a gangster, O!
'Tis well to be a gangster.
The drinks all flowing fast and free,
A sarlacc pit not far from thee,
A rancor for thine enemy,   170
'Tis well to be a gangster.
A gangster, aye, a gangster, O!
'Tis well to be a gangster.

A blast is heard. Enter CHEWBACCA *and*
BOUSHH, *a bounty hunter.*

BOUSHH   Eyah-tay, eyah-tay, yo-toe.
C-3PO   —Chewbacca!
CHEWBAC.   —Auugh!
JABBA   Cheesa eejah wahkee Chewbacca—ho!   175
FETT   [*aside:*] The Wookiee hath been captur'd—e'en
            he who with my grand prize Solo once did fly.
            'Tis fortunate he hath to Jabba also been deliver'd.
            I only wish that I had been his captor, and reap'd
            the reward this bounty hunter surely shall receive.   180
            Even so, this Wookiee doth complete the set of
            smugglers for Jabba's merriment. Belike he too
            shall frozen in carbonite be, or mayhap be a
            supper for a rancor.
JABBA   Kahjee ta, droid.
C-3PO   —Aye, here am I, indeed,   185
            Thy worshipfulness.
JABBA   —Yu-bahk ko rahto
            Kama wahl-bahk. Eye yess ka cho. Kawa
            Na Wookiee.
C-3PO   —Bounty hunter strong and brave:
            The mighty Jabba of the Hutt doth bid
            Thee welcome, and shall gladly pay to thee   190
            The goodly sum of five-and-twenty thousand.
CRUMB   [*aside:*] No bounty hunter would be fool enough
            To take the first price offer'd, I'll be sworn.
BOUSHH   Yoto. Yoto.
C-3PO   —'Tis fifty thousand, and
            No less.

JABBA   [*striking C-3PO:*] —Ahh, uun yun kuss tah fiti pun.   195

C-3PO   Whatever was it that I said, Sirrah?
I did perform the function thou hast giv'n:
Precisely did I translate this one's words.

JABBA   Moonon keejo!

FETT   [*aside:*] This scamp had best beware, if
he would be a bounty hunter in the service of   200
great Jabba. It seemeth he hath little appreciation
for the famèd anger of the Hutt.

C-3PO   [*to Boushh:*]   —The mighty Jabba asks
The reason wherefore fifty thousand is
The sum demanded of thee.

BOUSHH   —Ay yo-toe!   205

C-3PO   The knave doth threaten us—he holdeth in
His hands a thermal detonator. O!

                                 [*Jabba's courtiers shrink in fear.*
                                Boba Fett takes out his blaster.

JABBA   Ho, ho. Kaso ya yee koli tra do
Kahn nee go. Yu bahn chuna leepa nah.

CRUMB   The Hutt doth call him fearless and inventive,   210
But never did invention make me fear
As this one's thermal detonator doth.

JABBA   [*to C-3PO:*] Kuo meeta tah te fye. Dah tee teema
Nye.

C-3PO   [*to Boushh:*]   —Mighty Jabba offers thirty-five,
And were I in thy place, I would accept   215
The deal. 'Tis better, as they say, to make
The peace than make us all in pieces be.
And truly thirty-five while living is
A sum more numerous than zero dead.

BOUSHH   Ya-toe cha.

C-3PO   —Praise the maker, he agrees!   220
CHEWBAC.   Auugh!
                         [Chewbacca is led away by Gamorrean
                         guards as music begins to play again.
LANDO   [*aside:*]   —This sad scene I witness with contempt:
           Another bounty hunter earns his sum
           For bringing in a harmless innocent.
           Now all is merriment and patting on
           The back whilst yet another's added to   225
           Their clan. A scoundrel's life 'tis true I've known,
           Yet never did I stoop so low as this.
           But still, I smile at what I here survey,
           For I know well this bounty hunter is
           No normal man—no normal man indeed!   230
           And his apparent prize—my Wookiee friend
           Chewbacca—is not as a pris'ner come.
           Bear thou this burden bravely, Lando, for
           The wait is almost over—soon the plan
           O'er which we took great pains shall come to pass.   235
           Be still, my scoundrel heart, with patience wait,
           For retribution comes in time, though late.
                                              [Exeunt.

SCENE 3.

The desert planet Tatooine, at Jabba's Palace. Night.

Enter BOUSHH.

BOUSHH   The silence of the night doth mark my work
           And like a gentle breeze sweeps o'er the air.

In stealth I move throughout the palace dark,
That no one shall bear witness to my acts.
Now cross the court, with footsteps nimbly plac'd.   5
Ne'er did a matter of such weight depend
Upon a gentle footfall in the night.
Put out the light, and then relume his light—
Aye, now I spy my goal: the frozen Han.
Thy work is finish'd, feet. Now 'tis the hands   10
That shall a more profound task undertake.
Quick to the panel, press the needed code.
O swiftly fly, good hands, and free this man
From his most cold and undeservèd cell.
O true decryptionist, thy codes are quick!   15
The scheme hath work'd, the carbonite doth melt.
Forsooth, 'tis done—within the silent dark
The greatest light doth sing within my heart!

> *[Han Solo melts from the carbonite*
> *and falls to the floor.*

[*To Han Solo:*] Relax thou for a moment; thou art free
Of carbonite's embrace, but thou dost burn   20
From this harsh hibernation malady.

HAN   I cannot see.

BOUSHH   —Thine eyesight shall return.

HAN   But where am I?

BOUSHH   —In Jabba's Palace you
Have been detain'd.

HAN   —Who art thou, voice severe?

> [*Boushh removes his mask to reveal Princess Leia.*

LEIA   The one whose heart and soul do love thee true.   25

HAN   O, Leia!

> *[They kiss.*

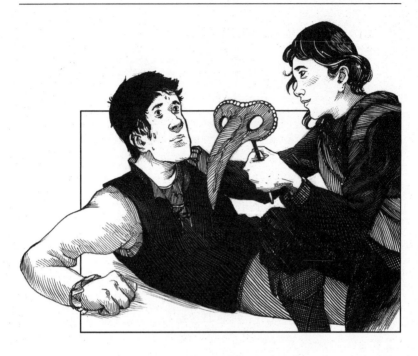

LEIA   —Come, and let's away from here.

Enter JABBA OF THE HUTT, BIB FORTUNA, BOBA FETT,
THE MAX REBO BAND, SALACIOUS CRUMB, LANDO OF CALRISSIAN
in disguise, and other members of Jabba's court.

JABBA   Ho, ho, ho.
HAN   —O, that laugh, it works me woe.
               'Tis too familiar in my memory,
               And like a chime from Hell's forsaken bells
               Doth ring most evilly within mine ears.   30
JABBA   Oofila mooga bos.
HAN   —Pray, Jabba, see:
               I was upon my way to pay thee back,
               And in returning happen'd on a course

                    That ran the other way. 'Tis not my fault.
JABBA   Achi pahbuk moonitnuh, Solo, bah.   35
                    Akingsah rebah bachmanah bakmah
                    Jaja weetnowah bantha poodoo, ho!
CRUMB   He shall be bantha fodder, O, 'tis true—
                    A Solo may make progress through the guts
                    Of banthas! Aye, my master's passing wise.   40
HAN   I'll pay thee triple, Jabba, thou canst not
                    Deny this fortune—be thou not a fool!
                              [Han Solo is taken away by guards.
JABBA   Nakko, kosleeya ni.
                              [Guards take Princess Leia to Jabba.
LEIA   —Now shall I be
                    His plaything? [To Jabba:] We have friends most
                                                  powerful.
                    Thou shalt, with all thy heart, regret this act.   45
JABBA   Bana madota, heah.
C-3PO   —Why were my eyes
                    E'er made to see, when such as this must be
                    Within my sight? I cannot bear to watch.
                              [Exeunt Jabba's court.

Enter HAN SOLO and CHEWBACCA on balcony, as their cell.

HAN   What fate is this? What curs'd, unearnèd path?
                    Within a minute rescu'd by my love,   50
                    Then taken from her unto this grim place.
                    How long was I in carbonite encas'd?
                    Am I an old man now, with graying hair?
                    What jubilant occasions have I miss'd?
                    What friends have died, or have been lost fore'er? 55

Hath our Rebellion disappointed been,
Or is it now fulfill'd with all success?
Because I do not know how long I've slept,
Or what transpir'd while I was frozen thus,
It seems my mind is sluggish to defrost.   60

CHEWBAC. Grrm.

HAN   —Yet another sound familiar, but
This one doth bring delight into my soul.
Chewbacca? Prithee, tell me, Chewie, is
It thou who art here with me?

CHEWBAC.   —Auugh.

HAN   —Sweet joy!
What bounty of affection do I feel   65
For thee, dear Wookiee. I cannot yet see,
But knowing thou art here doth warm my heart.
I prithee, give me news of all that is.

CHEWBAC. Egh, auugh!

HAN   —What sayst thou? Luke—a Jedi Knight?
What strange tomfoolery! Luke is but young,   70
Not made for rescues.

CHEWBAC.   —Auugh!

HAN   —Thou dost report
I have been gone a time but fleeting, so
Have all acquir'd delusions of some grandeur?
And what of Han? Have I been left behind?
O thought most base, O destiny unkind.   75

                                     [Exeunt.

SCENE 4.

The desert planet Tatooine, at Jabba's Palace.

Enter LUKE SKYWALKER.

LUKE   The time is now, the place is here, the man
              Myself, the matter: rescue of my friends.
              Be focus'd, mind; be settl'd, heart and soul.
              I enter unto Jabba's palace for
              One purpose and that purpose by itself: 5
              My friends to find and bring deliverance.
              Now to it, Luke, and earn the Jedi name,
              Not by thy might, but by thy calm and wit.

Enter BIB FORTUNA.

BIB   Yo mot tu cheep, do you pan Skywalker.
              Nuh Jabba mo bah toe baht too.
LUKE   —Nay, Sir.   10
              I tell thee: I shall speak with Jabba now.
BIB   Nuh Jabba no two zand dehank obee.
                      [Luke uses a Jedi mind trick on Bib Fortuna.
LUKE   Thou shalt take me to Jabba presently.
BIB   Naja takka to Jabba prekkenlee.
LUKE   Thou servest thy proud master well, and shall,   15
              In time, receive from him a great reward.
BIB   Eye sota y'locha. Ba chu noya trot.

Enter JABBA OF THE HUTT, PRINCESS LEIA, C-3PO, BOBA FETT,
THE MAX REBO BAND, SALACIOUS CRUMB, LANDO OF CALRISSIAN
in disguise, and other members of Jabba's court.

LUKE	[*aside:*] Say what is this? My Leia sparsely clad
	All in a metal-fashion'd suit? How strange!
	I did expect one of our company 20
	To be enclos'd in steel, but not like this.
C-3PO	At last, 'tis Master Luke to rescue us!
BIB	[*to Jabba:*] Nuh masta, gabba no pace Skywalker.
JABBA	Nah mass fa wong lee fah toon kay.
LUKE	—Thou must,
	Great Jabba, grant me leave to speak with thee. 25
BIB	Nuh Jedi modst be inco ee, baanah.
CRUMB	Old Bib but echoes what the man doth say!
JABBA	Ahh, ko ja vaya sko. Ees turo na
	Om Jedi mine chik.
	[Jabba strikes Bib Fortuna, who falls.
LUKE	—Let me be plain:
	Thou shalt with all expedience produce 30
	Both Captain Solo and the Wookiee, and
	Shall grant our safe departure from this place.
	'Tis this, and nothing more, I shall accept.
JABBA	Ya ku kacha ka puna ni sa. Ee?
LUKE	My Jedi powers may not work on thee, 35
	But still I shall take Captain Solo and
	His friends. Thou canst yet choose to profit from
	This plan, or be destroy'd. It is thy choice,
	But thou art warn'd: to underestimate
	My pow'r would bring about thy end at once. 40
C-3PO	But Master Luke, thou standest on—
JABBA	—Ban gon
	Wah she co, cah O Jedi. Cho kanya
	Wee shaja keecho, ho!
	[Luke uses the Force to take a blaster from a guard.

        Ah bahloosku!
       [Jabba presses a button that drops Luke and
         Gamorrean Guard 2 into the rancor pit.

CRUMB   Now shall we see the rancor rancorous!

     Enter RANCOR *into the pit with Luke and*
       the Gamorrean guard.

LANDO   [*aside:*] Alas, now Luke is thrown into the pit— 45
     His skill must see him through. My part shall be
     To give protection to the princess now.
C-3PO   For pity—now the monster hideous
     Hath come forth from his hiding place to sup.
RANCOR [*sings:*] They shriek at my mystique,   50
     My teeth they'll die beneath—
     A feast made for a beast,
     A treat that I may eat!
LUKE   What terrifying creature-thing is this?
     Ne'er have I such a ghastly being seen.   55
     But still these thoughts, for succor have they none:
     Be calm now, Luke, or else—sans doubt—you die.
G. GUARD 2 Squeal!
LEIA   —That poor guard shall be the first to fall,
     For he doth panic and is cornerèd.
     The rancor slowly makes his way t'ward him 60
     And sees his dinner spread before his eyes.
C-3PO   O wretched beast! He tears the guard apart
     With sound of breaking bones and crumpl'd flesh.
     One need not know six million language forms
     To understand the screams and sudden hush. 65
CRUMB   It shall be time to hire another guard!

RANCOR [*sings:*] The fat one now is flat,
        He growls within me bow'ls,
        And yet I'll not forget
        To source my second course.   70

LUKE   He turns in my direction, counting on
        His next delicious morsel to be ta'en
        E'en from my body. Aye, he cometh quick!
        This stick shall my protection be—we'll see
        If he hath appetite for wooded grains.   75

LANDO   [*aside:*] Luke now is in its grasp, but cunningly
        Hath bought a little time, and put a log
        Inside the creature's mouth. Fight on, good Luke!

LEIA   Well done, dear friend. Anon, make haste and flee!

RANCOR [*sings:*] The one doth quickly run,   80
        I'll catch him—down the hatch him!
        The stick's a nasty trick—
        His head shall be my bread.

LUKE   Now swiftly through the monster's legs I fly,
        For yonder, past the creature, lies a door!   85
        On reaching it, I shall make my escape.
                        [*Luke attempts to open the door.*
        Alas, but what is this? More bars behind
        The door!

C-3PO   —O Master, find another course!

LUKE   'Tis just the beast and I. But look, how he
        Doth come toward me through the very gate   90
        Whence first he came. If I could close the gate
        On him, he shall be slain. Aye, here's a rock,
        And there's the panel for the door's control.
        'Tis now or ne'er. I call upon the Force
        To guide this rock unto the very spot.   95

LEIA	His plan hath been reveal'd—O clever Luke!
	The rock he throweth straight and hits the mark—
	The gate doth fall, the rancor is destroy'd!
	O brave escape, O clever, daring Luke!
JABBA	Nuh toota ah! Gungsh Solo nuh Wookiee! 100
	Takootay noota bangass nuh baskah.
CRUMB	My master's plaything cunningly dispos'd—
	If Jabba shall not play, he'll make them pay.

Enter the RANCOR KEEPER, *as Luke is
taken back to Jabba's court.*

R. KEEPER	O that this too, too sullied flesh would melt
	Into oblivion, if I without 105
	My pet belov'd must live. O darkest world!
	O misery beyond compare to me.
	Already my beast's life doth play its part
	Within the tend'rest mem'ries of my brain.
	How well I do remember when the beast 110
	Was but a rancor pup. It was the runt—
	Was almost eaten by its mother cruel—
	Indeed, it had but little chance for life.
	Yet it was purchas'd as a novelty
	By Jawas who e'er seek abnormal things. 115
	I bought it from this band of Jawas, who
	Related to me all it had been through
	And chargèd me a paltry sum for such
	A worthy animal. Then did I raise
	It from its lowly start unto the grand 120
	And tow'ring hulk that now before me lies.
	How fondly I recall the playful nips

It gave me, which eventually turn'd
To bites that drew no small amount of blood.
I train'd it to be vicious, to enjoy   125
The taste of flesh and powd'ry crunch of bone.
Yet ever did it know its master true—
And never would it turn its anger fierce
Upon the one who lov'd it first and best.
Was ever rancor in this humor rais'd?   130
Was ever rancor in this humor won?
To think on it brings pain past all resolve.
O Fate, that ever I should see this day—
Now there's but little light left in this world,
For its bright sun unjustly is snuff'd out.   135
I shall away, and drown myself in tears,
Belike to live the sad remainder of
My mortal days upon this planet grave
Unfriended, unprotected, and alone.

                                                      [Exit rancor keeper.

Enter HAN SOLO *and* CHEWBACCA, *escorted by* GUARDS.

LUKE	O Han!
HAN	—'Tis Luke?
LUKE	—How dost thou fare, good friend? 140
	Thou art less cold than when I saw thee last.
HAN	The ice hath gone, but still the chill remains.
	But I am well enough, consid'ring all,
	And now we are together once again.
LUKE	'Twould not be miss'd. Such fun we have in store. 145
HAN	How is our cause?
LUKE	—The same as ever, friend.

HAN	That bad, indeed? And where is Leia?
LEIA	—Here.
	I am quite safe and, as of yet, unharm'd,
	But bound unto this wormlike lump of hate.
JABBA	Hagoy ooneetonuh.
C-3PO	—O dear! The great
	And high exaltedness, this Jabba of
	The Hutt, decrees that ye shall presently
	Be terminated.
HAN	—Just as well; I loathe
	A lengthy wait. [*Aside:*] The eyes may yet be blind,
	But 'tis relief to know the wit is well.
C-3PO	Thou shalt, therefore, be ta'en to the Dune Sea,
	And cast into the pit of old Carkoon,
	The nesting place of the all-pow'rful sarlacc.
HAN	As yet this Fate doth not so dismal sound.
CRUMB	[*aside:*] I lik'd him better when he was on ice—
	The frozen one hath quite a shrewish mouth.
	Belike the details of the sarlacc shall
	Give rest to his most flippant, prating tongue.
C-3PO	Within the sarlacc's belly ye shall know
	A definition new of suffering
	As ye are gradu'lly digested o'er
	A thousand thousand years. Thus saith the Hutt.
HAN	As I reflect, mayhap we should decline.
	I find I have no stomach for this feast
	Since it is we who shall the supper be.
CHEWBAC.	Auugh!
LUKE	—Thou wilt soon regret this gross mistake,
	For 'tis the last misstep thou e'er shalt make.

150

155

160

165

170

                 [*Exeunt.*

SCENE 5.

The desert planet Tatooine, at the sarlacc's pit in the Dune Sea.

Enter R2-D2 *on Jabba's barge.*

R2-D2   The end of this bleak scene is almost near,
               For I shall play the part of helpmate to
               My master true, securing freedom for
               Us all. No more shall Jabba terrorize
               The planet Tatooine, for he shall be   5
               Destroy'd before the double sun doth set.

Enter C-3PO, *bumping into* R2-D2.

C-3PO   O pardon me, I do apologize.
R2-D2   Beep, squeak!
C-3PO   —My R2, ah! What dost thou here?
R2-D2   Beep, whistle, meep, beep, nee!
C-3PO   —Well can I see
               That thou art serving drinks, but dangerous   10
               This place is. Soon they plan to execute
               Good Master Luke, and if we take not care,
               No doubt we shall be executed too!
R2-D2   Beep, meep!
C-3PO   —I wish I had thy confidence.

Enter LUKE SKYWALKER, HAN SOLO, *and* CHEWBACCA *with*
LANDO OF CALRISSIAN *in disguise and several* GUARDS
on balcony, as Jabba's skiff.

LUKE   [*aside:*] Here is the hour that ends in our escape,   15
Here is the moment Jabba sees defeat,
Here is the instant I have plannèd for,
Here is the battle grand: the skiff's the thing
Wherein I'll catch Han's rescue and take wing.

HAN   Methinks mine eyes have quite improv'd, for now   20
Instead of just a blur of dark I see
A blur of light. 'Tis almost pleasant. Ha!

LUKE   Alas, 'tis nothing here to see. I did
Once live on Tatooine, as thou dost know.

HAN   And thou shalt die here too. Convenient 'tis.   25

LUKE   Stay close to Lando and Chewbacca. All
Things shall end well, for I have plann'd it so.

HAN   So sayest thou. [*Aside:*] His confidence is such
               As I've not seen in him before; I know
               Not whether to guffaw or be impress'd.   30
                              [*Guards extend the skiff's plank
                                      and force Luke onto it.*
LUKE   The plank hath been set forth, and I shall walk
               Not unto death, but our deliverance.

        Enter JABBA OF THE HUTT, PRINCESS LEIA *bound to Jabba,* BIB
     FORTUNA, BOBA FETT, THE MAX REBO BAND, SALACIOUS CRUMB,
        and other members of Jabba's court below, on a barge.

JABBA   Koneetah!
C-3PO   —Hear ye! Victims of the great
               Almighty sarlacc: Jabba of the Hutt,
               His excellency, hopeth ye shall die   35
               With honor. Should ye wish for mercy now
               To beg, great Jabba of the Hutt shall hear
               Your pleas.
HAN   —Nay, 3PO! Say thou to that
               Vast slimy piece of filth bestrewn with worms
               He shall have no such pleasure out of us!   40
               Now that I am no more a markèd man,
               I shall most fully proffer my belief
               That Jabba is a horrid murderer
               Far worse than any I have ever known.
               Who here shall prove me wrong or argue, eh?   45
               'Tis right, good Chewie, I speak true?
CHEWBAC.   —Egh, auugh!
LUKE   Pray, Jabba, hear: I shall not ask again—
               Thou mayst free us, or be destroy'd anon.

So give us liberty or give thyself death.

JABBA   Ho, ho! Sabutah mayr.

CRUMB   —Aye, put him in!   50
No more of these fools' speech my ears would hear!

LUKE   [*aside:*] The scene is set. Pray, Lando, play thy part,
And R2, thou hast ever been most true,
Now fail me not in this most vital time.

R2-D2   [*aside:*] This is the moment; aye, this is the time.   55

JABBA   Koos nooma!

CRUMB   —Let the suffering begin!
I shall enjoy this show of pain and death.

LEIA   Alas, Luke jumps! But wait, he flips aright
Onto the skiff, and R2 hath releas'd
Into the air Luke's lightsaber! He has't,   60
'Tis his! O clever droid, with aim so true,
And clever Luke, devising such a plan.

HAN   The battle's here! Mine eyes see well enough
To know that now 'tis time for combat!

CHEWBAC.   —Auugh!

LANDO   Now, Lando, to thy recompense for all   65
That thou hast done! Betrayer shall become
The bravest fighter e'er rebellion's seen!
My courage here shall render payment for
The villainy I've tender'd in the past.

                    [*They battle, and many of Jabba's court
                    are thrown into the sarlacc's pit.*

JABBA   Ahh!

LEIA   —What role shall I play in this? I shall   70
Not stand aside and let them fight for me.
I am no fragile damsel to be sav'd,
But have, since I was young, fought for myself.

Thus, to my work: to slay the biggest foe—
Thou, Jabba, art for me and me alone!   75

FETT   I shall fly unto the fray, for no mere band of
rebels shall outwit the great Jabba of the Hutt.
They shall not easily defeat the one who doth
fill my coffers. Not, indeed, as long as Boba Fett
hath pow'r to live and breathe. To it!   80

[Lando fights with a guard and falls
off the skiff toward the pit.

LANDO   Alas, my friends, I fall!

[Boba Fett flies to the skiff.
Han Solo and Chewbacca fall.

LUKE   —Nay, thou vile Fett!
Thou shalt not have the best of us. A-ha!

[Luke strikes Boba Fett's blaster.

Thy blaster's now in twain by my lightsaber.

FETT   A hit, a very palpable hit! He hath torn my
blaster in twain with his lightsaber, but I shall   85
have him yet, and protect my great reward.
Go, ropes, and bind this rascal Jedi. Belike
Jabba shall further payment render when he
doth see the noble deeds done for his sake.

[Boba Fett binds Luke Skywalker with ropes,
but then is knocked down. Luke escapes and jumps
to another skiff, fighting the guards there.

LANDO   Han! Chewie! Can ye hear me?
HAN   —Lando!
CHEWBAC.   —Auugh!   90

[Boba Fett stands up and takes aim at Luke.

FETT   I have thee in my sights now, Jedi. Thou shalt
feel the pow'r of my rockets, and be no more.

CHEWBAC.   Egh!

HAN   —Boba Fett? What Boba Fett, and where?
                [Han Solo moves and activates Boba Fett's jets,
                         sending him flying into the pit.

FETT   Alas! The greatest Fett shall not die like this!
           O horrid Fate! Where is now my great reward?   95
                  [Boba Fett falls into pit and dies.

JABBA   Nuh oola koobah!

LEIA   —Those shall be thy words
           Most final! Now, the chains that bind me to
           This wretched lump of flesh shall be my hope!
           Whilst Jabba worries o'er the battle, I
           Shall throw the chains about his neck. Then, pull!   100
           Aye, pull—a princess' vengeance! Die, thou brute!
           Thou unsuspecting Hutt, I curse thy life!
           For all the innocent whoe'er did die,
           For all the noble souls thou didst torment,

	For all the gentle lives that are no more,	105
	For all the galaxy's injustice—die!	

[Princess Leia strangles Jabba of the Hutt. He dies.

HAN   Good Lando, thou didst turn thy back on me,
But thou shalt have a chance to earn thy due
Since Luke and Chewie tell me of thy shame.
Chewbacca, lift me down that I may save   110
Him from a thousand years of pain.

LUKE   —Brave Han
Attempts to rescue Lando, but the gun
From on the barge doth block his progress. Fie!
No rest from trouble have we here—these foes
Will not let us escape without a fight.   115
They do intend to block us all the way—
Then to the barge, to aid the rescue. Fly!

[Luke jumps onto Jabba's barge.

HAN   Pray, grasp the staff!

LANDO   —I almost have it!

CHEWBAC.   —Auugh!

LANDO   Alack! The sarlacc's tentacle wraps 'round
My leg. I fear this is the end! O give   120
Me strength to face my death well.

HAN   —Be thou still,
And Chewie, hand the blaster unto me.

LANDO   A blaster in the hands of one who's blind?
Methinks I may do better in the pit.
Good Han, think on the defects of thine eyes!   125

HAN   My sight is much improv'd: my aim is true!

*[Han Solo shoots the tentacle and
lifts Lando onto the skiff.*

LUKE   Good Lando is safe once again, and Han

	And Chewie steady are upon the skiff.	
	Thus shall I find the droids and Leia, then	
	Destroy this barge and Jabba's courtiers all.	130
R2-D2	[*aside:*] Now to the princess, to release her bonds!	
LEIA	All thanks, R2, now let us flee from here—	
	Find thou C-3PO, and we'll away!	
R2-D2	Beep, squeak!	
CRUMB	—My master's dead, but no fool I—	
	I'll fight these droids until my fate's secure.	135
	[*Salacious Crumb pokes at C-3PO's eyes.*	
C-3PO	Mine eyes, alas—O R2, help!	

R2-D2   —Meep, squeak!
            [*Aside:*] Tear not my friend apart, you tallow face!
                        [*R2-D2 shocks Salacious Crumb,*
                                    who jumps away.

CRUMB   The droid hath zapp'd me quite! O naughty imp!
C-3PO   O counterpart from Heaven sent, my thanks!
            But now, R2, say where dost thou lead me?   140
            Why do we swift approach the vessel's edge?
            This is most curious and passing strange,
            For I could not jump to the sand, and 'tis
            From here a mighty drop indeed—
                        [*R2-D2 pushes C-3PO off the edge of the*
                        barge into the sand and falls in after him.

R2-D2	—Nee, hoo!
LUKE	I prithee, Leia, take the gun and point 145
	It yonder, at the deck! The barge shall fall!

                         [Luke is shot in the hand by a guard.

            [*Aside:*] Alas, my hand, but 'tis my hand of steel,
            It causes me some pain, but not as 'twould
            Were it my own real flesh. Strange notion, this.
            I have not time to think on it, but shall,   150
            Another time, consider this my hand.

LEIA	The gun is pointed at the deck: 'tis time.
LUKE	Then let it fly, and we'll escape forsooth!
	'Tis well a rope is here to swing us o'er
	Another chasm—what serendipity! 155

                   [Luke and Princess Leia swing from the
                                   barge onto the skiff.

LEIA	[*aside:*] Once have I swung with him across a chasm,
	Now swing we once more to the waiting skiff.
	We have a way of swinging through our fears!
HAN	We all are now on board the skiff—away!
	This brave event shall be remember'd, Luke, 160
	And since I have been thaw'd, my warmest and
	My most sincere appreciation do
	I give thee for my rescue well devis'd.
LUKE	My friend, 'tis none but what thou wouldst for me.
	Now, let us flee—the droids, do not forget. 165
LANDO	We fly indeed, by foes no more beset.

                 [The barge explodes and all on board die.
              Exeunt Luke Skywalker, Han Solo, Chewbacca,
                 Princess Leia, Lando, R2-D2,
                         and C-3PO on skiff.

ACT II

SCENE 1.

Inside the second Death Star.

Enter CHORUS.

CHORUS   The army of the Empire gathers near
          Within the Death Star's uncompleted shell.
          They all prepare to welcome one they fear:
          The Emperor hath come, thereon to dwell.

[Exit chorus.

Enter EMPEROR PALPATINE *and* ATTENDING ROYAL GUARDS.

EMPEROR   My servant Vader have I come to meet,   5
              To hear him tell what progress hath been made
              Upon this newest Death Star. Confident
              I am that he shall make a good report,
              For he is ever trustworthy when ask'd
              To solve a problem for his Emperor.   10
              Forsooth, the man is all obedience
              When he is call'd to serve. It hath been so
              For years now, ever since he turn'd toward
              The dark side and became a Sith as I.
              But there is more than mere obedience: 15
              He looketh on me as a father, aye,
              For truly did I train him so to do.
              He doth respect and hang on ev'ry word
              I utter, even when 'tis to rebuke
              Or punish him for some apparent fault.   20
              The man is like a pet most pitiful,
              E'er braying for his master's notice and
              Displaying great affection e'en when kick'd.
              In truth, his groveling doth make me sick.
              Aye, his devotion to me I do not   25
              Reciprocate, for he to me is but
              A tool—most useful and most sharp, 'tis true—
              But merely agent of my will, no more.
              Yet he a vital purpose serveth in
              My reign and plans, while little doth he know   30
              That he could be more powerful than I.
              A tool the man may be, but I cannot
              Dispense with his keen services as yet.

But since I do consider him a threat,
I keep his leash as short as possible,   35
And I accept his childlike zeal for me
At least till I an apt replacement find.
Mayhap this young Skywalker—who is e'er
On Vader's otherwise clear mind—may prove
To be his aging father's substitute.   40
Was it a judgment error to inform
Darth Vader of the presence of his son?
Methinks 'twas not, for his devotion to
His Emperor and his submersion in
The dark side shall be more persuasive than   45
What feelings he may have for son unknown.
And furthermore, to know Skywalker is
His son shall heighten his resolve to turn
The boy unto the dark, and make him mine.
Thus would he see his Emperor and son   50
Together join'd, which would bring him dark joy.
'Tis surely how the future shall unfold—
All shall be well, for I have plann'd it so.
And now he comes: my humble servant Darth.

Enter DARTH VADER *and* MOFF JERJERROD *with* STORMTROOPERS.

VADER	I bid thee welcome and with humbl'd mien	55
	I bow to thee in utmost reverence:	
	My master, teacher, savior, rescuer.	
EMPEROR	Arise, my friend, and put thy soul at ease.	
	I trust the time spent here shall bear good fruit?	
VADER	Indeed, my master. All the workers have	60
	A newfound motivation for the task.	

                    The Death Star shall completed be within
                    The time and schedule thou hast orderèd.
EMPEROR   Thou hast done well, Lord Vader. I am pleas'd.
                    And now I sense another thought in thee?   65
                    Thou wouldst anon resume thy search for the
                    Young rebel Skywalker. Have I judg'd right?
VADER   My master: yes.
EMPEROR   —Be patient, my good friend.
                    Thou shalt not seeker be; I'll warrant that,
                    In time, the lad himself shall seek thee out—   70
                    I see with my mind's eye it shall be so.
                    And when he doth come to thee, thou shalt then
                    Deliver him, in deference, to me.
                    The boy hath grown quite strong. Together we
                    Will bring him to the dark side of the Force.   75
VADER   Thy wish is mine.
EMPEROR   —Thus have we set the scene:
                    All doth proceed just as I have foreseen!

                                                    [*Exeunt.*

SCENE 2.
The Dagobah system.

Enter LUKE SKYWALKER *and* R2-D2, *speaking with* HAN SOLO
and PRINCESS LEIA *in comlink.*

LUKE   Good friends, with you I shall meet once again,
                    Where our strong fleet doth plan to rendezvous.
LEIA   [*through comlink:*] Aye, do. Th'Alliance should be
                                                    gather'd now.

HAN   [*through comlink:*] And Luke, my deepest thanks are
                                                    due to thee,
          For I did doubt that thou a Jedi wert.   5
          But thine example brave hath shown to me
          A power I ne'er would have believ'd was real,
          Except I was its benefici'ry.
          Thou didst not overlook thy friend in need,
          But came back for his rescue unafraid.   10
          Now truly, friend, 'tis I who owe thee one.
                        [*Exeunt Han Solo and Princess Leia.*

R2-D2   Beep, squeak, meep, beep, squeak, whistle,
                                            whistle, meep?

LUKE   'Tis right, R2, we go to Dagobah—
          A promise must I keep to my old friend.
          [*Aside:*] This glove I place upon my injur'd hand,   15
          The hand that in the fight with Jabba was
          The sore recipient of blaster's touch.
          O hand, replete with wires and gears that move,
          With glove of black I cover the machine
          That lies within the skinlike covering,   20
          Which once a medic droid hath grafted on.
          How strange this hand, which feeleth like my flesh
          Yet is such stuff as droids are made of. Cold
          And dead, yet living, this is a device
          That serves me well but represents a dark   25
          And dismal fate. Aye, with this hand I have
          Become yet one step closer to the man
          Whose path I fear, yet wish to understand:
          Darth Vader, who my father claims to be.
          Indeed, I do believe his claim is true,   30
          But shall ask Yoda to confirm his words.

If he my father is, what shall it mean
For the Rebellion and for my own soul?
Shall my relations govern all my days,
Or may I yet escape mine origins?   35
Shall all the father's sins be visited
Upon the child, or shall I triumph yet?
Be with me, all ye Jedi past and gone—
I fly unto that place where first I learn'd
From Yoda, who is small, yet greater e'en   40
Than all my pow'rs or Master Obi-Wan.
With joy, I fly from here to see his face,
With hope, I fly to him to learn the truth,
With fear, I fly to him to know my path,
With expectation great, I fly to him.   45

Enter YODA.

Look now, he comes—alas, how ag'd he seems!
YODA   That face thou dost make:
         Look I so old to young eyes,
         My body so frail?
LUKE   Nay, nay, good master! Perish such a thought.   50
YODA   I do, aye, I do.
         Sick and weak have I become,
         Elderly and tir'd.

         And yet, I ask thee:
         When nine hundred years thou hast,   55
         Shalt thou look better?

         Soon shall I have rest,

	Forever sleep, as all do.	
	Earnèd it I have.	
LUKE	But what is this? Thou art an aging soul,	60
	Yet wherefore speakest thou of death's embrace?	
	Good Master Yoda, cease: thou mayst not die.	
YODA	Verily, 'tis true,	
	With the Force pow'rful am I,	
	Yet not that pow'rful.	65

Twilight is on me
And thence comes night. 'Tis the way
For all in the Force.

LUKE   Yet I have need of thy good help, for here
           I stand, return'd, prepar'd my training to   70
           Complete. What should I do without thine aid?

YODA   No further training
           Dost thou require, for thou hast
           All thou e'er shalt need.

LUKE   Forsooth, 'tis true: I am a Jedi now.   75

YODA   Be thou not so sure,
           For still Vader remaineth.
           Thou must confront him.

Then, and only then,
A true Jedi shalt thou be.   80
And face him thou shalt.

LUKE   Dear Master Yoda, one thing in me burns—
           The question that is flame inside my bones,
           Whose answer may yet kindle hate or love,
           I know not which. Yet still it must be ask'd: 85
           Darth Vader—tell me true—is he my father?

YODA	'Tis time for my rest.
	Time for my sleep eternal,
	'Tis no time for truth.
LUKE	Thou wouldst protect me from this knowledge, which 90
	May difficult and painful be. In this
	Thou showest care for me, and hast my thanks—
	But Yoda, full of heart, I must needs know.
YODA	[*aside:*] Alack, he knows all.
	Now may I only speak truth: 95
	Only truth lives on.
	[*To Luke:*] Thy father he is.
	Told you, did he? Unforeseen
	This is. Distressing.
LUKE	Distressing that at length I learn the truth? 100
YODA	Nay, nay! Distressing
	That thou hast rush'd to face him.
	Not ready wert thou.
	Thy training not done,
	The field of thy heart unplow'd, 105
	The burden, too much.
LUKE	Forgive me, for I knew not what I did.
YODA	Remember, my Luke,
	A Jedi's strength from the Force
	Doth come. But beware. 110
	Anger, fear, hatred—
	From the dark side they all come;
	Its minions they are.

Once thou hast enter'd
In the dark path infernal,   115
Abandon all hope.

The powers of the
Emperor, thou shouldst never
Underestimate.

Else thy father's fate,   120
Shall, in turn, become thine own:
Let not this transpire.

When I have gone, slept,
The last of the Jedi shalt
Thou be, thou alone.   125

Attend, Luke! The Force
Is strong with thy family:
Pass on what thou learn'dst.

These final words now
With my last breath I utter: 130
O hear well, brave Luke.

This is our hope: there
Is another Skywalker.
The rest silence is.

[Yoda dies.

LUKE   Good night, sweet Jedi, noble, wise, and true.   135
           So gentle was he, and too quickly gone.
           O Fate, what hast thou brought into my life—

How shall I live when all I love have died?
Yet all things die, and all things pass away,
And all is like the sweeping of the stars   140
As one doth pass through lightspeed's rapid blaze.
We know 'tis true: no mortal does not know
That all are born to feed insatiate death.
But O, what grief we meet along the way:
The knowledge something beautiful is lost,   145
The deep regret for all unspoken words—
Profound remorse for healing never giv'n.
To wish to hold the dead one's hand again,
To picture a love's smile, and know it gone:
These are the pains that human life doth bring,   150
The heartache and the thousand nat'ral shocks
That flesh is heir to. Death shall not be tam'd,
It shall not lose its victory or sting,
Yet it shall never have the best of us
If in our living we have truly liv'd.   155
To love with bliss, to fight for righteousness,
To heed adventure's call, to cry with joy,
To laugh amidst life's greatest heights and depths:
This is the living that doth conquer death,
So e'en though it shall come, we shall not fear't.   160
These lessons let my master's death teach me,
That my life shall esteem his memory.

R2-D2   [*aside:*] O gift of Fate, that he my master is!
         [*To Luke:*] Beep, meep, beep, whistle, meep, beep,
                                        whistle, squeak!

LUKE   I cannot face the future by myself,   165
         What shall I do, R2? I am alone—
         The only Jedi left to bear the name.

It may be this responsibility
Is far too great for such a one as I.
How can I bear the burden by myself?   170

        Enter GHOST OF OBI-WAN KENOBI.

OBI-WAN   Nay, not alone, for Yoda always shall
              Remain with thee.

LUKE   —My soul, 'tis Obi-Wan!
              [*Aside:*] Now e'en though he of ghostly matter's
                                             made,
              He shall anon give answer for his words.
              [*To Obi-Wan:*] Good Ben, it warms my heart to
                               see thee here,   175
              Yet I must ask thee to explain thyself—
              Pray, wherefore hast thou not reveal'd the thing
              That thou didst know? Thou said'st my father had
              By Vader been betray'd and murderèd.
              Ne'er hast thou said that he my father is!   180

OBI-WAN   [*aside:*] I never did imagine that, in death,
              I would be call'd upon to justify
              The words I spoke in life. 'Twas well I spoke
              Not of the midi-chlorians to Luke,
              For then he would have endless questions still.   185
              [*To Luke:*] Thine inquiry shall have an answer, Luke,
              For verily thou dost deserve to know.
              Thy father was seducèd by the dark
              Side of the Force. 'Twas then that he no more
              Was Anakin Skywalker, only Darth.   190
              When that had happen'd, thy good father was
              Destroy'd. And thus, forsooth, the words I spoke

Were truthful, from a certain point of view.

LUKE   "A certain point of view"? What doth that mean?

It may be said that I, within my ship,   195
Do see my X-wing as an instrument
Of truth and justice, aye, a noble thing,
While from a certain point of view I know
Mine enemies do see it as a threat.
It may be said that when I was attack'd   200
By rancor vicious and intemperate,
Prepar'd to make of me his morning meal,
There is a certain point of view that doth
Suggest he was a simple hungry beast.
It may e'en be that our Rebellion is,   205
For us, an undertaking pure and good,
Possessing every virtue possible,
While from the Empire's certain point of view
It is a mere annoyance to be crush'd.
But this, I do not understand: how can   210
A certain point of view say that a man
Was murder'd by another man, when both
Are one and they together are my father?

OBI-WAN   Luke, thou shalt find that many of your truths
Depend entirely on your point of view.   215
It well may be that thou dost like it not,
But does not follow that it is not so.
'Tis true, that Anakin a good friend was.
When I first knew him, he already was
A pilot skill'd and swift, and it amaz'd   220
Me with what strength the Force work'd in his life.
I took it on myself to train him as
A Jedi. Even then I did believe

	That I could train him just as Yoda could.	
	But there my fault did lie. Therein I fail'd.	225
LUKE	I do believe it may be rectified.	
	What if he could be turnèd once again?	
	There is yet good within him—I can feel't.	
OBI-WAN	He is machine e'en more than man, I fear.	
	His soul's an evil, tangl'd labyrinth.	230
LUKE	I shall not do it, Ben.	
OBI-WAN	—Thou canst not 'scape	
	Thy destiny. You must confront and face	
	Darth Vader once again.	
LUKE	—I shall not kill	
	My father.	
OBI-WAN	—Then the Emperor hath won.	
	Thou wert our only hope the Empire and	235
	The dark side to defeat. If thou wilt not,	
	No other shall arise to take our place.	
LUKE	But must this necessarily be so?	
	For Yoda spoke of yet another. Who?	
OBI-WAN	No more of hidden pasts: thou shalt know all.	240
	The other one of which he spoke is none	
	But thy twin sister.	
LUKE	—Sister? I know none.	
OBI-WAN	Both thou and she were hidden safely from	
	The Emperor just after ye were born.	
	For he did know, as I do, that the kin	245
	Of Anakin would be a pow'rful threat	
	Unto his reign of madness, might, and murder.	
	At birth, the two were separated: thou	
	Unto thine uncle Owen and thine aunt	
	Beru, on Tatooine, where I did watch	250

O'er thee as thou didst grow into a man;
Thy sister to a senator did go,
Apart from thee and thy dread father's wrath.
There she did grow into a woman fine,
And has, since then, remain'd anonymous.   255

LUKE   [*aside:*] O wondrous revelation to my soul!
A sister, and before me comes her face:
For surely Leia is my sister, else
My instincts have no truth in them. What news!
I know not whether to respond with shouts   260
Of greatest joy, or to shrink back in fear
And paralyzing shock at what we've done.
Three times hath she kiss'd me in friendship's name,
The last of these more passionate than e'er
A sister should upon her sib bestow.   265
There is an ancient tale of Tatooine,
That tells of Tusken Raider who, through Fate
And circumstance, join'd with his mother in
A bond most strange and quite unnatural.
They liv'd in blissful ignorance of their   270
Relation until they discover'd it
By chance. And O, what awful times befell!
The Tusken Raider's mother hang'd herself
Upon a bantha's horn. The Tusken, in
His agony and grief, pull'd off his mask   275
And claw'd at his own eyes until they bled,
Then came dislodg'd, and finally pluck'd out.
He fell unto his knees and cried with pain—
Not merely pain to have his eyes remov'd,
But deeper pain that sear'd his very heart.   280
'Tis said that though he then could see no more,

He saw more clearly than he ever had.
At night, upon the sands of Tatooine,
His howl may still be heard, a warning to
Those who would break the sacred fam'ly bond   285
Through passions of the body. Shall this be
My fate, for crossing o'er the boundary
That none should cross, e'en once? I'll warrant: nay.
Not only have I superstitions none,
But our brief moments of affection were   290
A trifle none could call a love affair.
I now see clearly but still have my eyes,
And may my sister know sans tragedy.
Thus, I do make a solemn, earnest vow:
I shall embrace my royal sister as   295
A pow'rful ally, and shall show to her
The path that surely leads unto the Force.
[*To Obi-Wan:*] 'Tis Leia, aye? My soul doth know
                          'tis she.

OBI-WAN   Thine instincts serve thee well, Luke. Bury now
These feelings, for they do thee credit but   300
May be manipulated and abus'd
If e'er the Emperor should learn of them.

LUKE   It bringeth my heart joy to see thee, Ben,
I'll heed thy counsel till we meet again.

                              [*Exeunt.*

SCENE 3.

The rebel fleet, in space.

Enter HAN SOLO *and* LANDO OF CALRISSIAN.

HAN	My friend, well met! 'Tis good to see thee here
	And not a'dangling o'er a sarlacc's pit.
	Thou wast promoted well—a general!
LANDO	Belike our leaders were inform'd about
	Mine actions at the battle of Taanab. 5
HAN	Cast not thine eyes on me for blame or thanks—
	I did but tell them thou art pilot fair.
	But knew not that they hop'd to find the one
	Who would direct this crazy-brain'd attack.
LANDO	Nay, "crazy-brain'd" thou sayst? How may that be, 10
	Since thou dost know a thing or two of Death
	Star battles and what it doth take to win?
	Surpris'd I am that they did not ask thee.
HAN	But who hath said that they did not inquire?
	Yet I am not of madness made. And thou, 15
	Remember well, art fashion'd of respect.

Enter PRINCESS LEIA, CHEWBACCA, C-3PO, MON MOTHMA,
ADMIRAL ACKBAR, GENERAL MADINE, WEDGE ANTILLES,
and several REBEL PILOTS.

MOTHMA	I prithee, gather 'round, ye rebels all,
	And mark ye well the message I relay.
	The Emperor hath made a critical
	Mistake, and our time for attack is nigh. 20

The data brought to us by Bothan spies
Details th'exact location of the vast
New battle station that the Emperor
Hath underta'en to build. We also know
This battle station's weapon systems are   25
Not fully operational as yet.
Th'Imperi'l fleet is spread both far and wide
Throughout the galaxy, with hopes—quite vain—
That they shall soon engage us in a fight.
And while the fleet's away, the station hath   30
But minimal protection. This, my friends,
Would be good news enough, but there is more:
Reliable report hath come to us
That e'en the dreaded Emp'ror Palpatine
Himself doth oversee construction of   35
The Death Star, and is presently on board.
This news doth cheer us, friends, but pray recall
That many Bothans died to bring it here.
I call on Adm'ral Ackbar to unfold
Our plan so you may know your roles in this,   40
The final chapter of rebellion's tale.
                    [*Admiral Ackbar turns on a visual model of the*
                        Death Star and the forest moon of Endor.

ACKBAR   You may within this model see the Death
                Star orbiting around the forest moon
                Of Endor. Though the weapons systems on
                The Death Star are not operational   45
                As yet, the Death Star hath a strong defense:
                It is secur'd by shield of energy
                A'generated on the forest moon.
                Deactivated must this shield be ere

	We can attack. Then, when the shield hath been	50
	Disarm'd, our cruisers shall take wing and fly	
	Within the superstructure to destroy	
	The main reactor. This attack shall be	
	Made by a squadron of our wingèd ships	
	Led by our General Calrissian,	55
	Who is a worthy and a noble chap.	
HAN	Good luck be thine, my friend. Thou shalt need it.	
ACKBAR	Thus endeth my report. Now General	
	Madine, thine efforts for our mission wilt	
	Thou presently recap?	
MADINE	—We've stolen an	60
	Imperi'l shuttle, which, disguisèd as	
	A cargo ship, shall use a secret code	
	To land upon the moon. Thereon a team	
	Shall fearlessly deactivate the shield.	
C-3PO	A dangerous experience, no doubt.	65
LEIA	[to Han:] And who, I wonder, has agreed to it?	
	For such a mission may quite futile prove.	
HAN	Nay, be thou not afraid. A man of wit,	
	Of clever mind and fine exterior	
	They must have chosen, whom thou shalt approve.	70
MADINE	Good Gen'ral Solo, is thy team prepar'd?	
LEIA	[aside:] A man of wit! He ne'er doth cease t'amaze.	
HAN	My team is ready, yet I do not have	
	A crew who shall the shuttle's flight command.	
CHEWBAC.	Auugh!	
HAN	—It shall not be easy, friend, thus I	75
	Had not yet volunteer'd thy worthy name.	
CHEWBAC.	Egh!	
HAN	—Well! Now have I one!	

LEIA   —And count me two.
                Good General, I gladly follow thee.
                Wherever thou dost go, then so shall I,
                Wherever thou remain, thus I shall too,   80
                Thy people shall my people be as well,
                And all thy battles shall my battles be.

                Enter LUKE SKYWALKER *and* R2-D2.

LUKE   Why have but two when three is company?
                I shall go with thee also, noble friend.
                [*Aside:*] My sister! Ah! To see her fills my heart!   85
                        [*Luke Skywalker and Princess Leia embrace.*
LEIA   What is't?
LUKE   —Ask yet again, another time.
HAN   Ho, Luke!
LUKE   —Good Han, and Chewie!
R2-D2   —Beep, meep, squeak!
C-3PO   "Exciting" would not be my word of choice,
                'Tis more like "harrowing," if I were ask'd.
                              [*Exeunt all but Han Solo and
                                    Lando of Calrissian.*
HAN   Now preparation's made, good Lando, yet   90
                A word with thee ere thou depart, my friend:
                With heart sincere I proffer this to thee:
                Take thou my ship, the brave *Millenn'um Falcon*.
                Thou shalt be greatly aided in thy task
                If thou wilt take the fastest ship that e'er   95
                Did fly within our galaxy. Thou dost
                Have more experience with this swift ship
                Than any but Chewbacca and myself.

Thou art a skill'd and worthy pilot, and
I trust that thou shalt keep her safe.

LANDO   —'Tis well,   100
I am persuaded, and shall take the ship
And leave with thee both gratitude and my
Assurance that I know how deeply thy
Heart stirs for her. Thus do I pledge: I shall
Take care of her as though she were my own,   105
And shall deliver her sans e'en a scratch.

HAN   [aside:] This Lando doth protest too much, methinks.
I was not nervous till he made his pledge.
[To Lando:] No scratch, indeed. I take with me thy
                                                    word.

LANDO   We part, thou pirate true. And Han, good luck.   110
HAN   To thee as well, good friend.
                        [Exit Lando of Calrissian as Han Solo
                        boards the Imperial shuttle Tydirium.

Enter LUKE SKYWALKER, CHEWBACCA, C-3PO, and
R2-D2 in the cockpit with Han Solo.

CHEWBAC.   —Auugh.
HAN   —Nay, I think
The Empire had not Wookiees on their minds
When they design'd her, Chewie. Are we set?

Enter PRINCESS LEIA.

I see the good Millenn'um Falcon yon,
And wonder how the die for her is cast.   115
LEIA   Art thou awake, or dost thou slumber on?

HAN   A feeling tells me this look is my last.
CHEWBAC.   Auugh.
LEIA   —General, let us depart.
HAN   —Aye, true—
             Now let's see what this heap of junk can do!
                    [*Exeunt, flying off in the shuttle* Tydirium.

SCENE 4.

Inside the second Death Star.

Enter DARTH VADER.

VADER   The strangest feelings have been mine of late.
             To know my son exists confounds my wits
             As I did ne'er imagine. What is this
             Confusion that doth obfuscate my mind?
             For evil I am made, for punishment   5
             Of foes, for conquering of peoples, and
             To do the perfect will of my great lord
             And Emperor. Of these I certain am,
             For this hath been my role full many years.
             Yet where within this surety is room   10
             For offspring? For a son? What can a life
             Liv'd on the dark side of the Force have still
             To do with heirs, with flesh and bone that sprang
             From me and that sweet life that once I led?
             How can this Sith, this man of pain and death,   15
             Be father to the fruit of far-gone love?
             It seems well nigh impossible when one
             Considers what I've been. For, verily,

I may not hide the man I truly am:
A warrior devoted to the cause   20
Of Emperor and Empire both. 'Tis who
I am: I must be mad when I have cause
And smile at no one's jests. No humor doth
Give pleasure to my mouth or stir my heart,
Nor would I dare to ever love again,   25
If e'en this mess of tangl'd wires could love.
I am a Sith, most surely to be fear'd.
Yet that perplexing thing remains: a son.

Enter EMPEROR PALPATINE *and* ROYAL GUARDS.

What is thy bidding, master?
EMPEROR   —Send the fleet
Unto the farthest side of Endor. There   30
Let it remain, until 'tis callèd for.
VADER   What of the recent news that rebels are
Amassing near to Sullust? Is it so?
EMPEROR   It is of little consequence, for soon
This vile Rebellion shall be crushèd and   35
Young Skywalker shall know the dark side's pow'r.
Thy work upon the Death Star is complete.
Thou shalt go hence to the command ship, and
Await my orders there.
VADER   —My master: aye.
                                        [Exit Darth Vader.
EMPEROR   Now all the players and the scenes are set   40
To bring about our greatest triumph yet.
                                        [Exeunt.

ACT III

SCENE 1.

On the Imperial shuttle Tydirium *and the Super Star Destroyer.*

Enter LUKE SKYWALKER, HAN SOLO, CHEWBACCA, PRINCESS LEIA,
C-3PO, *and* R2-D2. *Enter* ADMIRAL PIETT *and* IMPERIAL
CONTROLLER *on balcony, on the Super Star Destroyer.*

HAN	Now if the Empire is not by our ruse
	Deceiv'd, we must fly quickly, Chewie.
CHEWBAC.	—Auugh.
CONTROL.	We have you on our screens; identify
	Yourselves.
HAN	—The shuttle of *Tydirium*
	Requests deactivation of the shield
	Of energy.
CONTROL.	—*Tydirium*, transmit
	Your clearance code for passage through the shield.
HAN	Transmission doth commence.
LEIA	—Now shall we learn
	If all these codes were worth the price we paid
	For them—the loss of friends, the loss of life.
HAN	Aye, it shall work, 'twas sacrifice well made.
CHEWBAC.	Egh!
LUKE	—Vader is aboard that giant ship.
HAN	Be not afear'd, good Luke, let not thy nerves
	Thy better judgment mar. Full many ships
	There are that do command the Empire's fleet.
	Keep thou thy distance, though, Chewbacca, but
	Do not appear as though thou keepest it.

5

10

15

CHEWBAC. Auugh?
HAN   —Let me make it plain: fly casual.
CHEWBAC. Egh!

        Enter DARTH VADER *on balcony.*

VADER   —Tell me now: where is that shuttle bound?
PIETT   Small shuttle of *Tydirium*, what is   20
             Thy destination and thy cargo? Speak!
HAN   We come to bring both parts and crew, which shall
             Deliver technical assistance to
             Our comrades on the forest moon.
VADER   —Have they
             The code that clearance would ensure?
PIETT   —They do.   25
             It is an older code, but hits the mark.
             I was about to grant them passage, Lord.
LUKE   [*aside:*] My father, how I sense him clearly now!
             His thoughts, his aspect, e'en his very mood.
             [*To Han Solo:*] I have endangerèd the mission here,   30
             And should not hither have accomp'nied you.
HAN   'Tis thine imagination, Luke. Pray, be
             More optimistic; let thy heart be still.
LUKE   [*aside:*] What stillness can there be when moves the
                                                            Force?
             It shall move mountains if it so desires.   35
             No inner strength or outer brawn can match
             The movement of the Force that now 'twixt me
             And Vader passeth. Han hath no idea,
             Yet all, belike, shall know quite soon enough,
             For Ben and Yoda both were right: I must   40

	My father yet confront ere I—or he—
	Shall ever freedom know.
PIETT	[*to Vader:*] —Shall they be held?
VADER	Nay, Admiral, thou mayst let them proceed.
	They shall be mine—mere cards that I shall play,
	And I shall serve as dealer for their deck.
PIETT	Then shall I wager that the house shall win.
	Thy wish is mine, my Lord, and it shall be.
	[*To controller:*] Thou canst now carry on, and let
	them pass.
HAN	This hesitation pregnant is with doubt:
	Mayhap they are not taken in, Chewbacca.
CONTROL.	Good shuttle of *Tydirium*, the swift
	Deactivation of the shield begins.
	Hold fast unto thy present course.

PIETT [*to Vader:*] —Shall they be held?

VADER Nay, Admiral, thou mayst let them proceed.
They shall be mine—mere cards that I shall play,
And I shall serve as dealer for their deck. 45

PIETT Then shall I wager that the house shall win.
Thy wish is mine, my Lord, and it shall be.
[*To controller:*] Thou canst now carry on, and let
them pass.

HAN This hesitation pregnant is with doubt:
Mayhap they are not taken in, Chewbacca. 50

CONTROL. Good shuttle of *Tydirium*, the swift
Deactivation of the shield begins.
Hold fast unto thy present course.

[*Exeunt Darth Vader, Admiral Piett,
and Imperial controller.*

HAN —'Tis well!
Did I not tell ye all that it would work?
No problems here, when Han is at the helm. 55

LEIA My scoundrel-love, thou ever hast a boast—
Yet often there's a reason to thy rhyme.

Enter several IMPERIAL SCOUTS, *aside, as
Luke Skywalker, Han Solo, Chewbacca,
Princess Leia, C-3PO, and R2-D2 disembark.*

HAN Now have we landed on the forest moon,
And our good company has disembark'd.
We make our way through trees and bushes here. 60
But what is that, a sound—pray all, alert!

C-3PO   You see, R2, I told thee this would be
           Quite dangerous. Alack, be calm, my core!
HAN   I see a building with Imperial
           Motifs and markings. There, beside it, are   65
           Two scouts. This shall require some care, methinks.
LEIA   Then shall we try and go around the side?
LUKE   It will take time.
HAN   —And all shall be for naught
           If we are seen. Yet I do have a plan:
           Chewbacca and myself shall handle this.   70
           Ye both stay here.
LUKE   —But prithee, soft, good Han.
           Be quiet, for there may be others near.
HAN   Thy words unnecessary are—'tis me!

                    [Han Solo and Chewbacca move
                            toward the Imperial scouts.

           Now shall I move in stealth to take them in,
           Then take them out. With catlike tread I step,   75
           Ne'er to be notic'd till my prey is mine,
           Then I—alack! A twig snaps underfoot!

                    [Imperial Scouts 1 and 2 turn toward the sound
                            and see Han Solo and Chewbacca.

SCOUT 1   What is that sound? Alas, 'tis rebels, go!
           And warn our comrades quickly.
LUKE   —Let us fly!

                    [Han fights with Imperial Scout 1.
                    Imperial Scout 2 boards his speeder bike
                            to fly away but is shot by Chewbacca.
                            Imperial Scouts 3 and 4 jump on
                            their speeder bikes and fly away.

LEIA   Behold the two scouts speed from out our grasp!   80

Upon the instant I shall give them chase.

LUKE Pray, Leia, patience—straight I come with thee!

     [Luke and Leia board a speeder bike behind
      Imperial Scouts 3 and 4, in pursuit. Exeunt
       Han Solo, Chewbacca, C-3PO, and
        R2-D2 in the melee.

     Enter CHORUS.

CHORUS Do not our play too harshly judge, dear friends,
     For with imagination may you see:
     Into the forest now the fight extends   85
     On speeder bikes that whip 'twixt tree and tree.
     What haste their dauntless riders undergo
     As they fly swiftly past both brush and stumps!
     The rapid derring-do our scene doth show,
     And when 'tis over, some shall have their lumps. 90

           [Exit chorus.

LUKE Jam thou their comlink, center switch!
LEIA   —'Tis done!
LUKE Canst thou yet closer go? Pray, pull aside
     The one before us. Now I jump aboard
     His bike, and he is mine and I'm for him.

     [Luke throws Imperial Scout 3 from his
      speeder bike, and Imperial Scout 3 dies.

Enter IMPERIAL SCOUTS 5 *and 6 on speeder bikes.*

     Aye, he is gone, but others take his place! 95
     Good Leia, follow that one up ahead.
     I shall remain behind, to face these two.

LEIA   'Tis well. Be safe, and I shall see thee soon.
LUKE   [*aside:*] O sister, all my thanks for tender words.

                              [Luke falls behind, alongside
                                   Imperial Scouts 5 and 6.

            Now shall this bike's keen blaster find its mark!   100
            I shoot, and one is dead; the other next.

                            [Luke shoots and kills Imperial Scout 6.
LEIA   I shall fly high o'er this one's bike, that he
            May think that I have fled. Then shall I from
            Above make my attack. Ha! Now beside
            His bike, surprise is my sure strategy.   105

                            [Imperial Scout 4 shoots at Leia.
            Alas! My bike is hit, and off I fall!

                            [Leia falls to the ground, unconscious.
                            Imperial Scout 4 looks behind him
                            to make sure she has fallen.

SCOUT 4   Ha! There's a rebel scum who shall no more
           Make trouble for our mighty Empire. We
           Are e'er the strongest in the galaxy,
           With pilots such as I whose skill is—O!—   110
                    [Imperial Scout 4 collides with a tree and dies.

LUKE   This latest scout is skill'd beyond the rest—
           I may not best him in a battle thus.
           Yet by another method I shall win,
           For why rely on bikes and blasters when
           I have the Force, and my lightsaber, too?   115
                            [Luke leaps from his bike.

           Now to it, scout! Return and meet thy fate!
           He comes a'blasting, but my lightsaber
           Deflects the shots, and now I slice his bike!
           Aye, broke in twain his bike doth falter fast,
           And now against a tree he meets his end!   120
                            [Imperial Scout 5 dies.

           Enter HAN SOLO, CHEWBACCA, C-3PO,
           and R2-D2, from the opposite side.

R2-D2   Beep, meep, beep, whistle, meep, squeak, whistle, nee!
C-3PO   O, Gen'ral Solo, someone comes anon!
HAN   [seeing Luke:] Luke! We have found thee! But thou
                                        lack'st one thing:
           I bid thee tell me: where is Leia? Eh?
LUKE   She came not back?
HAN   —I thought she was with thee.   125
LUKE   And truly was. But lo, within the wood,
           The battle was borne out with speed and fire,
           Amid the blasts and cruel Imperi'l scouts

'Twas only muddledom that won the day.
We separated were, and there's an end.   130
Anon! We must fly hence and search for her.
Good R2, come, thy scanners we shall need.

C-3PO   Fear not, good master, we know what to do!
          [*To R2-D2:*] And thou didst say 'twas pretty here. O pish!
                    [*Exeunt Luke Skywalker, Han Solo,*
                        Chewbacca, C-3PO, and R2-D2.

          Enter WICKET, *an Ewok, approaching Princess Leia.*

WICKET   A buki buki,   135
          Luki, luki,
          Issa creecher,
          Nuki, nuki!
                        [*Wicket jabs Princess Leia with*
                            his staff. She wakes up.

LEIA   Desist at once, thou furry little imp!
WICKET   E danvay, danvay,   140
          Staa awanvay,
          Da livvy creecher!
          Panvay, panvay!
LEIA   I shall not hurt thee, little one. But O,
          My body cries with soreness from my fall.   145
          I wonder where Luke and the others are?
WICKET   Fangowa, gowa,
          I nonowa.
          Da creecher muvvee
          Slowa, slowa.   150
LEIA   It seemeth I am fix'd and grounded here,
          Yet I am lost and know not what "here" means.

All that I have is this small creature, from
A species I have ne'er encounterèd.
Mayhap thou wilt assist me, little friend.   155
Sit down beside me, here, and let us talk.
I promise I'll not hurt thee. Aye, approach.

WICKET   A dunga, dunga,
           Wassee wunga?
           Ino commee,   160
           Junga junga.

LEIA   Belike thou wouldst like something thou canst eat?
           If thou art like most creatures, thou mayst be
           Directed by thy stomach's wish for food—
           Where bellies lead, the other members trail.   165
           Here, friend, taste thou this morsel from my hand.

WICKET   Aytru, aytru,
           See mebbc tru,
           Iya tryee,
           Maytru, maytru.   170

                          [Wicket takes a wafer from
                            Princess Leia and eats it.

LEIA   I'll warrant I have made a friend at last—
           The food succeeds where words alone have fail'd.
           Now shall I take this helmet off, for sure,
           It gives me pain to wear it still so tight.

WICKET   A kusha kusha,   175
           Wassee doona?
           Mia scardu,
           Pusha, pusha.

LEIA   Nay, fear thou not, O little one; 'tis but
           A hat, and shall not harm thee. 'Tis no threat.   180
           Thou art a scamp fill'd full of skittishness.

[Wicket hears a sound in the forest.

WICKET   A kiata, ata,
            Summink mata,
            Summink commee,
            Giata ata.   185

                              *[A shot is fired near Princess Leia,
                                        who falls to the ground.*

LEIA   *[aside:]* This creature's customs and his language are
            Unknown to me, and yet his instincts prove
            Most capable. He smell'd the danger ere
            I knew 'twas here. A pow'rful ally might
            He and his people be, if e'er we could   190
            Communicate and share each other's thoughts
            And hopes and aspirations openly.

                                        [Another shot is fired.

WICKET   A wundah wundah,
            Shutee gundah,
            Shutee baddee,   195
            Nundah nundah.

                                             [Wicket hides.

            Enter IMPERIAL SCOUTS 7 *and* 8.

SCOUT 7   *[to Leia:]* Stand down, milady, else you breathe your last!
            [To Scout 8:] Go, get thy bike, and take her back to base,
            For none but our own troops have clearance to
            Be on the sanctuary moon. She must   200
            Give answer for her furtive presence here.
SCOUT 8   Indeed, Sir.
                        *[Imperial Scout 8 begins to exit. Wicket comes
                            out of hiding and strikes Imperial Scout 7.*

SCOUT 7   —O! What manner of a beast—
             [Princess Leia hits Imperial Scout 7, who falls
             unconscious. Imperial Scout 8 begins to run.

LEIA   Now, blaster, hit thy mark, else we're found out!
             [Princess Leia shoots and kills Imperial Scout 8.
             Good cheer! The scout is slain, and we are safe.
             I give thee thanks, thou bantam warrior,   205
             For thy protection and thy bravery.
             Come, let us go at once, ere others come.

WICKET   A yubnub, yubnub,
             Shessa noolub,
             Shessa frenda,   210
             Yubyub, yubyub.

LEIA   *[aside:]* Although it seems I came from over there
             He wisheth me to follow him that way.
             Belike in following I'll earn his trust.
             Then shall I make our budding friendship real   215
             And see what this chance meeting may reveal.
                                               [Exeunt.

SCENE 2.

Inside the second Death Star.

Enter DARTH VADER, EMPEROR PALPATINE,
and ROYAL GUARDS.

EMPEROR   Now wherefore hast thou come to see me here?
             Thine orders were to stay aboard thy ship.

VADER   I would not disobey thine orders, were
             It not of grave importance to our cause.

              A rebel force hath made it past the shield,   5
              And landed on the forest moon of Endor.

EMPEROR   I know all this already.

VADER   —And my son
              Is with them on their mission.

EMPEROR   —Art thou sure?

VADER   Forsooth, for I have felt him.

EMPEROR   —Strange that I
              Have not. Lord Vader, are thy feelings on   10
              This matter clear, or need'st thou clarity?

VADER   [*aside:*] Well ask'd, for my confusion he doth sense.
              [*To Emperor:*] My thoughts are clear, my master.

EMPEROR   —This, then, shalt
              Thou do: fly to the sanctuary moon,
              And wait upon him there, for he shall come.   15

VADER   Indeed? 'Tis he who shall come unto me?

EMPEROR   I have foreseen it. His compassion for
              His long-lost father shall mean his defeat.
              'Tis he shall come to thee, and thou shalt bring
              Him hither, unto me. Thus it shall be.   20

VADER   Whatever thou dost wish, I grant to thee.

                                         [Exeunt.

SCENE 3.

The forest moon of Endor.

Enter HAN SOLO, CHEWBACCA,
C-3PO, *and* R2-D2.

HAN   A'searching in the forest, we have found
         No trace of my belovèd. Yet I see
         These wreck'd and tangl'd bikes afore mine eyes,
         And must assume the worst. Some horrid fate,
         Some accident of fortune hath befall'n,   5
         And ta'en my love too quickly from my grasp.
         O let it ne'er be so, and let me not
         With grief and anguish live out all my days.
         Although we find not Leia, let us still
         Some hope discover deep within these woods.   10

Enter LUKE SKYWALKER, *holding Princess Leia's helmet.*

LUKE   This helmet have I found, near yonder log.
         The tree that once so tall and stately stood,
         Hath been by some unnat'ral force knock'd down.
         But all that doth remain there is the top,
         That once rose high above the forest's roof.   15
         O tree, that lost its trunk and turn'd to log!
         O helmet—without wearer—turn'd to shell.
C-3PO   Good Master Luke, his heart doth break within.
LUKE   Two more wreck'd speeders yonder did I see,
         And this poor, empty helmet tells a tale.   20
C-3PO   I fear that R2's sensors can find no

	Suggestion of dear Princess Leia near.
HAN	I hope—O greatest hope, O fondest hope—
	With all my being hope she may be well.
CHEWBAC.	Auugh!
HAN	—What is it, thou Wookiee?

[Chewbacca finds a piece of meat
hanging from a rope.

CHEWBAC.	—Egh. Egh, auugh!	25
HAN	I do not understand, Chewbacca. It	
	Is just a piece of meat, and nothing more.	
CHEWBAC.	Auugh!	
LUKE	—Nay! Pray, patience!	

[All are caught in a net and raised into the air.

HAN   —Wonderful! The ones
Who wish'd to find become the ones found out,
Who wish'd to net a princess, netted are,   30
Who pray'd to find her, find themselves now prey.
And why? Because the one who thinketh least
Hath thought with appetite and not with mind.

LUKE   Since fault of thought hath got us to this place,
Let us be calm, and reason our way out.   35
Canst thou reach my lightsaber, Han?

HAN   —Indeed!

[Han Solo tries but cannot reach the lightsaber.

R2-D2   [*aside:*] Once more it lies in me to save these men.
Mayhap a fall upon their rears shall serve
Them well. Now quickly to thy work, my blade!

[R2-D2 begins to cut the net.

C-3PO	R2, dost think that wise? 'Tis far to fall!	40
LUKE	Down, down, we fall!	
HAN	—Alack!	

C-3PO   —O, R2!

CHEWBAC.   —Auugh!

HAN   Safe from the net, yet hard upon the ground.
             Although my mind is grateful for the help,
             My back doth cry for vengeance on the droid
             Whose foolish act hath knock'd us flat.

Enter EWOKS, *including* TEEBO, *surrounding the others.*

LUKE   —But look,   45
             How many furry beings are there here!
             O brave new world, that has such creatures in't!
                         [*Teebo points his spear at Han Solo.*

TEEBO   U jabbeh, jabbeh,
             Ussah stabbatheh,
             Unoh muvva,   50
             Gabbeh, gabbeh.

HAN   Avaunt, thou scruffy flea-infested imp—
             Point not thy spear toward my angry self,
             Else thou shalt know the scourge of blaster fire.

LUKE   I prithee, patience, Han—all shall be well.   55

TEEBO   E hura hura,
             Heeno scura,
             Heesa tempurr,
             Gura, gura.

LUKE   Chewbacca, give thy crossbow unto them.   60
             Let them believe they have the upper hand,
             And we shall see of what the beasts are made.

C-3PO   [*rising from the fall:*] Alas, my head! What pains I
                                        must endure.
             But O—what creatures do surround us here?

TEEBO	U hadoo, hadoo,	65
	Heesa gadoo,	
	Heesa mytee,	
	Gadoo, gadoo.	
C-3PO	A treeto treeto,	
	Meesah greeto,	70
	Houdi dootee,	
	Seeto, seeto.	
LUKE	C-3PO, dost comprehend their tongue?	
C-3PO	Indeed, my master Luke! Recall that I	
	Am fluent in more than six million forms—	75
HAN	Less prating, more explaining, droid. What didst	
	Thou say to them, when thou didst speak e'en now?	
C-3PO	"Hello," methinks. 'Tis possible I am	
	Mistaken. They employ a primitive	
	And ancient dialect, but it appears	80
	They think of me as like unto a god.	
R2-D2	[*aside:*] O heaven help us all. C-3PO	
	Already thinks himself divine, and needs	
	No congregation further. [*To C-3PO:*] Beep, squeak!	
CHEWBAC.	—Auugh!	
HAN	O Lord most high and reverent, thou gold	85
	And stainless deity, call on thy pow'rs	
	And godlike charms, and straight divine us all	
	A way beyond this situation. Aye?	
C-3PO	Nay, Gen'ral Solo, 'tis not proper.	
HAN	—Proper?	
	You shall for sure discover what is right	90
	And proper, when I blast apart thy frame.	
C-3PO	Lo, 'tis forbidden, Gen'ral Solo, for	
	E'en droids aren't masters of divinity.	

HAN   Thou fickle spirit! Deity or not,
             I shall a spiritual experience   95
             Enjoy as I do tear thee limb from limb.
                              [The Ewoks surround and
                                   threaten Han Solo.

TEEBO   Na goo, na goo,
             Heesall na doo,
             Heesall beest ill,
             Ya doo, ya doo.   100

HAN   Pray pardon, jolly beasts. Nay, fear me not—
             'Twas but a jest, for he is my old friend.
                         [The Ewoks bind Luke Skywalker, Han Solo,
                              Chewbacca, and R2-D2 and take them to
                                   their village, with C-3PO enthroned.

LUKE   Now are we ta'en unto their simple homes—
             Plain huts of wood with branches for their roofs.
             A simple tribe are these, yet wise as well—   105
             With neither guns nor lightsabers they snar'd
             A pilot skill'd, a Wookiee brave and strong,
             A Jedi Knight, and two most earnest droids.
             'Twas quite a catch for such a humble net.
             And now, like spits upon a fire we're hung.   110
             But what transpireth next? We'll see anon.

HAN   My feelings are o'ercome with thoughts most dire:
             They ready for a feast, but where's the food?
             Do they not know I shall a poor meal make?
             No supper may be cook'd from Han's firm flesh,   115
             For smuggler meat is all too hard and tough.

CHEWBAC.   Auugh!

TEEBO   E krandeh krandeh,
             Thessah mandeh,

	Thessah kuukah,	
	Gandeh, gandeh,	120
C-3PO	Ad toyum toyum,	
	Lessum goyum,	
	Nossah dootis,	
	Noyum, noyum.	
HAN	—Prithee, tell me, droid, what did he say?	125
C-3PO	O, it is rather an embarrassment	
	Good Gen'ral Solo. It appears that thou	
	Shalt be the main course at a banquet in	
	My honor. I am quite asham'd, good Sir,	
	And promise I shall not enjoy the meal.	130
CHEWBAC.	Auugh!	

[Ewoks begin playing drums.

EWOKS	[*singing:*] A gunda gunda,
	Thissa funda,
	Thessa burna,
	Kunda, kunda.

Enter PRINCESS LEIA.

LUKE	—Leia!	
HAN	—O, my heart! My precious one!	135
	My Leia! Now may I go up in flames,	
	Since I have seen thee safe and well again,	
	Belovèd.	
C-3PO	—Royal Highness!	
LEIA	—What is this	
	That doth transpire here? Luke and Han bound up?	

[Leia approaches but is stopped by Ewoks.
[*To Ewoks:*] Nay, do not hinder me, my newfound

                                         friends. 140

         These goodly men are dear to me, they are
         The closest that I have to family.
         Pray, still your doubtful, cautious minds, and I
         Shall show ye that these people mean no harm.
         C-3PO, thou somehow art enthron'd,   145
         Which doth suggest thou hast some sway o'er them.
         Serve thou as translator, and tell these imps
         To free our brave companions from their bonds.

C-3PO   [*to Teebo:*] I rooktah rooktah,
         Nowyee looktah,   150
         Lessem freeum,
         Booktah, booktah.
           [The Ewoks continue their preparations for the feast.

HAN   It seemeth that thy kingly words did fall
         Upon their peasant ears a little less
         Than royally.

LUKE   —Good 3PO, relay   155
         To them that if they shall not heed thy words,
         Thou wilt astound them with thine anger fierce,
         And ply thy magic on them.

C-3PO   —Magic, Sir?
         I know not what you mean. I have no magic!

LUKE   I prithee: argue not, but tell them now.   160

C-3PO   [*to Ewoks:*] No gosh, no gosh,
         I yami bosh,
         I uzzee prahnkh,
         E boomabosh.
              [The Ewoks stop momentarily and
                then resume their preparations.
         O, see'st thou, Master Luke? They paid no heed,   165

As I suspected they would not, the brutes!

LUKE   [*aside:*] Now Force, come flow within, around, above.
            Raise up the droid upon his wooden throne,
            And let these creatures think he is their god,
            A'raging in his anger. Let them shrink   170
            And cower in their fear, and be so mov'd
            That they shall do his every command.
            C-3PO lifts up above the ground
            And is quite terrified to be so high.
            But frighten'd as they are, they do not see   175
            Their god is yet more petrified than they.
            They scatter to and fro and up and down,
            For here's a sight they ne'er have seen before:
            A being flying sans the use of wings.
            O work thy power, Force, be thou my aid   180
            And constant strong companion in our need.
            Success! The creatures now are quite convinc'd,
            And move with haste to free us of our bounds.
            C-3PO doth lower into place,
            And now we all are free—O thank the Force,   185
            That mov'd in me so I could move the droid,
            And move these creatures to release us all.
                    [*The Ewoks unbind Luke Skywalker, Han Solo, and
                        Chewbacca. An Ewok frees R2-D2 and R2-D2
                            shocks the Ewok. The Ewok runs away.*

R2-D2   [*aside:*] Now come ye back, ye scurvy, furry things,
            I'll shock ye all for your abuse of us.

HAN   O mistress mine, to see thee brings me joy!   190
            Draw nigh and plant upon my lips a kiss.

LEIA   Luke hath secur'd your safety with his ploy—
            No sweeter meeting can I wish than this!

                    [Han Solo and Princess Leia kiss.
                       Wicket approaches R2-D2.

WICKET   W'goodo, goodo,

            Whoosah yoodo,   195

            Yoosah speccul,

            Hoodo, hoodo.

LUKE   [*to C-3PO:*] My gratitude profound, C-3PO.

C-3PO   Forsooth, I never knew 'twas in me, Sir.

LUKE   These little creatures may have value yet   200

            If they our allies in this fight become.

            I need thine aid now to convince them so—

            I prithee, 3PO, make known to them

            Our dire adventures 'gainst the Empire vile.

C-3PO   I know not, Master. I am not a bard   205

            Who can with skillful tongue his story tell.

LEIA   But try, C-3PO—the tale relay

            In their own language.

                         [The Ewoks gather and listen.

C-3PO   —All the world's at war,

            And all the rebels in it are the heroes;

            They have their battles and their skirmishes, 210

            And rebels in these scenes have play'd their parts,

            Their story being seven ages. First,

            Our princess that was captur'd was then sav'd,

            But Alderaan did pay the costly price.

            And then the Death Star battle, with its guns   215

            And awful loss of life, like speeder bikes

            We flew unto the final vict'ry. Then

            To Hoth, so barren, with a woeful ballad

            Compos'd for our lost comrades. Then to Bespin,

            Full of strange imps and fearful twists of fate. 220

My master fac'd Darth Vader, quick in quarrel,
While Lando, Chewie, and the princess just
Escap'd the cannon's mouth. But then our Han—
In fair trim belly with good humor lin'd,
With eyes severe and hair of scruffy cut,   225
Full of harsh tongue and modern instances—
Was plac'd in carbonite. The sixth age shift'd
To Tatooine, a lean and lonely place,
With Jabba there to give us all a fright.
The sarlacc vicious was a world too wide   230
For us to spend eternity within.
We turn'd again to Master Luke, who with
The Force did save our lives. Last scene of all,
That ends this brave eventful history,
Shall be the Empire's fall t'oblivion,   235
Sans pow'r, sans hate, sans fear, sans ev'rything.
                    [*The Ewoks discuss the story.*

HAN   What do they say?
LEIA   —I do not know.
LUKE   [*aside:*]   —I sense
           The keen nobility within their hearts;
           These small but mighty creatures shall yet be
           Our help as we make battle 'gainst our foes.   240
TEEBO   Na doonga doonga,
           Tymee soonga,
           Weesa hilpuh,
           Loonga, loonga.
C-3PO   'Tis wonderful! A sign of deep respect   245
           The group has given us, for we have been
           Made members of their honorable tribe.
           Moreover, they shall aid us in the fight

Against the Empire and its bunker here.
                    [*All embrace, and an Ewok hugs Han Solo.*

HAN   'Tis verily a dream come true for me.   250
             [*Aside:*] And now, unhand me, teddy, ere I scream.
R2-D2   Beep, whistle, squeak!
LUKE   [*aside:*]   —This joyous scene doth stir
             My soul, for since my presence here is but
             A danger to my friends, I must depart.
                                    [*Exit Luke Skywalker.*
LEIA   But wherefore doth Luke flee when we should all   255
             Be celebrating? I shall follow him.
                                    [*Exit Princess Leia.*
CHEWBAC.   Egh.
HAN   —So the proverb says, Chewbacca: "Help
             That is but short is better than no help
             At all." Though how the furry beasts will help
             I cannot yet imagine or conceive.   260
C-3PO   The Ewok chief reports the scouts shall show
             Us to the place that generates the shield
             For the new Death Star. There we may fulfill
             Our plan: deactivate the shield anon.
HAN   Well done, C-3PO, now quickly heed   265
             Mine every command: first have them tell
             Us how far distant is the place. Then be
             Thou sure that, second, thou dost ask for fresh
             Supplies. And fin'lly, get our weapons back.
             But wherefore dost thou wait, thou simple droid?   270
             Unto my tasks—I shall not wait for thee!
                                    [*Exeunt Han Solo and Chewbacca.*
C-3PO   He cannot wait, but will not let me do't!
                                    [*Exeunt.*

Enter LUKE SKYWALKER *and*
PRINCESS LEIA *on balcony.*

LEIA   I prithee, say: what is the matter, Luke?
LUKE   Between who?
LEIA   —Nay, the matter on your heart.
LUKE   Say, dost thou of thy mother yet retain   275
       A memory? I fain would hear thee tell.
LEIA   But little, Luke, for I was all too young
       When she departed to her resting place.
LUKE   Yet what dost thou remember? Wilt thou share?
LEIA   'Tis mostly images I see within   280
       My mind when I do think on her, just as
       The reds and oranges that one doth see
       When one hath look'd upon the shining sun.
       She was a woman of great beauty who
       Was kind, yet nurs'd some sadness deep within.   285
       Now tell me, wherefore dost thou ask me this?
LUKE   No mem'ry have I of a mother's touch,
       Nor kindness, sadness, smile, or any speech.
       'Twas not until but recently I thought
       Upon my state of being motherless.   290
LEIA   What troubles thee, dear Luke?
LUKE   —Darth Vader's here,
       E'en now, upon this very forest moon.
LEIA   How dost thou know?
LUKE   —I felt his presence here.
       He cometh seeking me, for he can feel
       When I am near. This is why I must leave: 295
       As long as I remain I do the group
       And our good mission put at risk. Instead,

My destiny it is to face the man.

LEIA   But wherefore?

LUKE   —He, e'en Vader, is my father.

LEIA   Thy father? What base trick of Fate is this?   300

LUKE   This news is but the prologue to the rest
That I shall tell thee, Leia. This shall not
Fall easily upon thine ears, but thou
Must hear't: if I do not return, then thou
Shalt be the only hope for the Alliance.   305

LEIA   Nay, say not so, dear Luke! Thou hast a pow'r
I do not comprehend, and never could
Obtain. 'Tis far beyond my skill and means.

LUKE   But there thou art mistaken, Leia: thou
Dost have that pow'r within thee, and, in time,   310
Shall learn to use it as I have. The Force
Is strong and certain in my family.
My father has it, I have it as well,
And also doth my sister have it. Aye,
'Tis thee, dear Leia, sister of my soul.   315

LEIA   [*aside:*] A brother! What strange circumstance is this?
My friend, this Luke, doth claim a brother's place?
And is Darth Vader thus my father, too?
What of the father that I once did know—
Organa, he for whom I have been nam'd?   320
Shall I, now fully grown, begin anew
And learn to love another family?
I thought my kinfolk all had been dispatch'd
When Alderaan was cruelly destroy'd.
Yet Luke doth tell me that the man who stood   325
And watch'd with joy whilst Alderaan was blown
Apart is he whom I should "Father" call?

It shall take time and thought to reconcile
My heart unto this news. But with what joy
Already I do welcome Luke into   330
My life as brother—there I have no qualms,
For he hath been a brother unto me
Since first we met. A brother! O, what news!
[*To Luke:*] It is as if I did already know—
Within my heart 'tis like I've always known.   335

LUKE   Then canst thou see why I must face him now?

LEIA   Nay, that I cannot see. If he can feel
Thee here, then flee anon and save thy life!
It is no shame to fly from danger, Luke.
I wish that I could fly with thee.

LUKE   —Nay, say   340
That not, for thou e'er wert the strongest one.

LEIA   But wherefore needest thou confront him, Luke?

LUKE   Methinks the man hath good within him still,
And shall not basely render his own son
Unto his cruel and vicious Emperor.   345
Methinks I still can save the man who gave
Us life, and turn him to the good once more.
Methinks I must endeavor so to do,
Or else my path is darker e'en than his.
Methinks so many things, dear Leia, but   350
The most important of them all is this:
My father is my duty to reclaim,
E'en though he has a vile existence led.
His heart, his soul, his life can be redeem'd,
'Tis now my mission and, I hope, thine too.   355
And now farewell, for I must take my leave.

                              [*Exit Luke Skywalker.*

LEIA O, what a noble mind is here reveal'd:
My brother young, yet speaking like a man
Imbu'd with ev'ry honorable trait.
To take upon himself the role of nurse   360
To heal our wayward, troubl'd father. Ah!
And I, of ladies most profoundly bless'd,
To have a brother such as this good Luke—
His swift return unto our loyal band
I shall with pride await. O joy is mine,   365
T'have seen what I have seen, see what I see!

Enter HAN SOLO.

HAN What ails thee, Leia?
LEIA   —Nothing, Han. I've grown
More full of deepest feeling than I e'er
Thought possible. I would remain alone
Till I have time to ponder this affair.   370
HAN 'Tis "nothing"? Prithee, tell me what is wrong.
LEIA Thou dost not see—I cannot tell thee yet.
HAN But Luke, couldst thou tell Luke in whisper'd song?
Then shall I leave thee.
LEIA   —O!
                              [Han Solo begins to leave, but then
                                    returns to Princess Leia.
HAN   —Beg pardon, pet.   375
Forgive this latest outburst of my pride,
I am but worried for thy state of mind.
LEIA Embrace me, Han, and here with me abide:
Thou art a man of substance, strong and kind.
                              [They embrace.

HAN   Although thou causest me to fret and groan,   380
       My love is thine and thou shalt ne'er be lone.

                 [Exeunt.

SCENE 4.
The forest moon of Endor.

Enter DARTH VADER.

VADER   E'en now my son doth come to me, I feel't.
       Thus is the moment near when I bring him
       Unto my Lord and, in so doing, bind
       Together those two forces of my life:
       My skillful son and my true Emperor.   5
       The two become one: 'Tis a consummation
       Devoutly to be wish'd. I'll see Luke turn'd
       Toward the dark side of the Force, and we
       Shall rule the galaxy—the father, son,
       And mighty Emperor. O make it so,   10
       Most slippery and cunning Fate, for great
       Shall be the combination of our pow'rs.

Enter LUKE SKYWALKER *and* IMPERIAL COMMANDER,
with STORMTROOPERS.

COMMAND. My Lord, this is the rebel who did bring
       Himself to us in full surrender. He
       Denieth there are others here, yet I   15
       Believe there may be more. I do request
       Permission to conduct a search of the

Surrounding area. "No stone unturn'd,"
As my dear father us'd to say. Is not
A father's wisdom precious more than gold?   20
But I digress: the rebel came here arm'd
With this and this alone, a lightsaber.

> [The Imperial commander hands
> Luke's lightsaber to Darth Vader.

VADER   [aside:] O how it stirs my soul to hear him tell
The love of his good father. Now, be calm!
[To commander:] Thou hast fulfill'd thine office
                                                faithfully,   25
Commander. Leave us now, conduct thy search,
And bring this one's companions back to me.
I'll warrant thou shalt find them as thou think'st.

COMMAND. Of course, my Lord. My pleasure 'tis to see
Thy great will done. If further rebels are   30
Upon the moon, we shall discover them.

> [Exit Imperial commander.

VADER   The Emperor hath been expecting thee.

LUKE   [aside:] Now it begins. [To Darth Vader:] I know,
                                                my father.

VADER   —Ah,
Thou hast accepted what is true.

LUKE   —I have
Accepted thou wert once call'd Anakin   35
Skywalker, and as such, my father wert,
And art, and whate'er come to pass, shall be.

VADER   That "Anakin" is meaningless to me.
The name hath neither relevance nor worth.
My life is chang'd, and I with it, fore'er.   40

LUKE   'Tis but the name of thy true self, which thou

	Hast but forgotten. Furthermore, I know	
	That there is good within thee yet, for thy	
	Great Emperor cannot have driven it	
	From thee entirely. That is wherefore thou	45
	Couldst not destroy me when we met at first,	
	And wherefore thou wilt not deliver me	
	A pris'ner to thine Emperor.	
VADER	[*aside:*] —Almost	
	I know not what to say, so shall I turn	
	The conversation unto matters that	50
	Are simple to discuss, with no confusion.	
	[*To Luke:*] I see thou hast constructed for thyself	
	A lightsaber. Thy skills are now complete,	
	Except I see its beam is green, much like	
	Thine innocent opinion of my fate.	55
	But still thou hast become quite powerful,	
	Just as the Emperor himself foresaw.	
LUKE	If green doth mark me as a man naïve,	
	I'll claim the color proudly. Come with me—	
	My father, turn toward the good, and live!	60
VADER	Old Obi-Wan once thought as thou dost think.	
	Thou canst not understand the power of	
	The dark side: I shall be obedient	
	Unto my master—aye, I must, and will.	
LUKE	I shall not turn toward the dark, and thou	65
	Shalt verily be forc'd to kill me then.	
VADER	[*aside:*] Confusion, be thou gone. 'Tis madness, this!	
	[*To Luke:*] If that shall be thy destiny, so be't.	
LUKE	O, search thy feelings, father. Thou canst not	
	Do this to me. I feel the conflict rise	70
	Within thee. Let thy hatred go, be free!	

VADER   It is too late for me, my son. I shall
          Deliver thee unto the Emperor.
          'Tis he who shall reveal to thee the true
          And pow'rful nature of the Force. He is   75
          Thy master now, and thou shalt serve him well.
LUKE   Then may I say these words with confidence:
          My father who once liv'd is truly dead.

                              [Exeunt Luke Skywalker with
                                    stormtroopers guarding.

VADER   O what a rogue and peasant Sith am I.
          This turmoil in my spirit doth not suit   80
          A dark and vicious warlord like myself.
          My son a rebel—fickle-minded Fate
          That e'er would be so cruel to have me see't!
          And not a simple rebel, nay, but he
          A hero, noble, brave, and true, a lad   85
          Whose character befits his parentage.
          Were he within the Empire's ranks employ'd,
          I would be proud to govern by his side.
          A worthy lad is he, of virtues full,
          A Jedi Knight and pow'rful in the Force,   90
          A brave, courageous, cunning warrior,
          A shadow of my former, noble self.
          Yet if he will not turn he'll be destroy'd.
          O shall it be? The strands of Fate do seem
          To wind themselves about my neck as if   95
          To strangle me and drag me down into
          The measureless, uncharted depths of my
          Beloved Emperor's most perfect will.
          Thus shall I drown within the dark side's pull:
          A murky grave to bury Vader's soul.   100

The rudder of my conscience runs not straight,
Thus am I tow'd along toward my Fate.

                                              [Exit.

ACT IV

SCENE 1.
The forest moon of Endor.

Enter HAN SOLO, PRINCESS LEIA, CHEWBACCA,
C-3PO, R2-D2, WICKET, PAPLOO,
and several REBELS.

LEIA   The entrance to the bunker where the Death
            Star's shield controllèd is lies just beyond
            That landing platform there. To get inside,
            Without revealing our intent shall not
            Be easy.

HAN   —Fear thou not. Chewbacca and   5
            Myself have enter'd places that were far
            More heavily protected than this one.
            The tales I could relate—another time.

WICKET   Na nubba nubba,
            Weeva nubba,   10
            Nozza wayza,
            Yubba yubba.

C-3PO   N'ketcha ketcha,
            Yuzza betcha,
            Yuzza surra,   15
            Netcha, netcha.

WICKET   Suki, suki,
            Nahgoh luki,
            Nahyoo siya,
            Ch'buki uki.   20

LEIA   I prithee, 3PO, what doth he say?

C-3PO   'Tis news that shall delight, good Princess, for

It renders our assault yet easier.
A secret entrance may be found along
The other side of this great ridge.

HAN   —'Tis well.   25
So let us hence and find this hidden way.

                    [*The group of rebels and Ewoks*
                         walks to a new location.

LEIA   [*aside:*] What circumstance unlikely doth befall—
A group of hardy rebels makes its way
Unto a battle with the Empire vile.
Such enterprise of pith and moment, yet   30
Here are we by these furry creatures led.
What unexpected allies! Aye, what strange
But needed friends these noble scamps may prove.
There is a saying back on Alderaan—
Or rather, should I say, there us'd to be   35
For now no sayings there are heard at all—
"There should for no one greater welcome be
Than one who is an unexpected guest."
So do we welcome these small ones unto
Our great and just Rebellion, these who are   40
Both meek and full of childlike eagerness.
Yet even as these words escape my lips,
Another thought unfolds itself to me:
It is not we who welcome them; I err.
For 'tis their moon, their home, their dwelling place.   45
'Tis surely they who kindly welcome us,
'Tis truly they to whom our thanks are due,
'Tis certain they are far more brave than we,
'Tis verily their home for which they fight.
But still thy tongue, the bunker now is near.   50

HAN   [*to Paploo:*] Thou hast a back door found, thy
                                                         hairiness?
             'Tis well: from furry mouths come good ideas.
PAPLOO   [*to Wicket:*] Ba'chua ba'chua,
             Megoh ga'chua,
             Megoh gennem,   55
             Fa'chua, fa'chua.

             Enter several IMPERIAL SCOUTS *near the bunker.*
             Paploo walks toward them.

HAN   [*to Leia:*] There are not many guards nearby; to gain
             The upper hand should not prove difficult.
LEIA   And yet it needeth merely one to sound
             A loud alarm that brings the fleet entire.   60
HAN   Forsooth, then quietlike our moves shall be.
WICKET   [*to C-3PO:*] N'unka unka,
             Paploo flunka,
             Heeza gennem,
             Bunka, bunka.   65
C-3PO   O my! Good Princess Leia, I do fear
             Our small befurr'd companion hath set on
             An errand rash.
CHEWBAC.   —Auugh!
                     [All watch as Paploo approaches the scouts.
LEIA   —Fie! The little beast
             Doth make his way unto a certain death.
             Belike these guards shall blast him into bits.   70
HAN   And further: our surprise attack is gone.
             We may not have another chance as this.
                     [Paploo suddenly boards a speeder

bike and flies off into the distance.

SCOUT 1 Alack! That beast hath ta'en the speeder bike!

     We shall not let the imp steal from us so!

SCOUT 2 Let us fly hence and after him!

SCOUT 3   —Away!   75

         [Imperial Scouts 1, 2, and 3 mount

           their bikes and chase Paploo.

HAN   A clever ruse for one who is no more

     Than a mere lump of matted fur. He hath

     Succeeded in his plan, for now behold:

     Just one is left. [*To C-3PO:*] Remain here and await

     Our swift return.

C-3PO   —Though I am but a droid,   80

     My will is yet my own. I shall decide

     What course to take, and have decided it

     Shall better be if R2 and myself

     Remain here.

HAN   —Well consider'd, goldenrod.

     Now let us go, my friends, and make our way 85

     Unto the bunker. Guard, what ho?

       [Han Solo approaches another Imperial scout.

SCOUT 4   —Thou knave,

     What treachery is this?

        [Imperial Scout 4 runs after Han Solo

         but soon is surrounded by rebels.

HAN   —Such treachery

     As shall an Empire conquer. Now, avaunt,

     Thou scurvy servant of the Empire's spite!

       [The rebels subdue Imperial Scout 4.

LEIA   Good friends and rebels all, are you prepar'd? 90

     The moment is upon us, even now:

We shall the bunker enter sans delay,
And what we'll find therein we do not know.
Belike some danger grave doth wait inside,
Mayhap far worse than ever we imagine.   95
Be ready—eyes alert and open wide!
    [*Han Solo, Chewbacca, Princess Leia, and rebels*
        enter the bunker. Several Imperial troops are
           inside, surprised by the rebels' entrance.

HAN   Pray, mark me well, else all of you shall die:
Move quickly to the side, and let us in.
    [*Imperial troops move away, surrounded by rebels.*
Go, brave Chewbacca, guard these wayward souls.

LEIA   Make haste, good Han. The fleet shall be in range   100
Anon.

CHEWBAC. —Egh, auugh!

HAN   —Give me those charges, quick!

Enter more IMPERIAL TROOPS, COMMANDERS,
and STORMTROOPERS, *running into the bunker.*
C-3PO, still outside the bunker, sees them.

C-3PO   O my, they shall be captur'd! Misery!
If only I could quickly warn them all.

WICKET   Netah muah,
Meego thuah,   105
Meego gennem,
Puah, puah.
                  [*Exit Wicket in haste.*

R2-D2   Beep, meep!

C-3PO   —Where dost thou go? Come back! R2,
Stay here with me, I pray. My joints and wires

Are burning with my terror and my fear.   110
If thou dost leave, I surely shall melt down
From all the dread that runs through me.

R2-D2   —Meep, squeak!
[*Aside:*] Though small, his brave protection shall I be!
We cannot save the others, and may not
E'en save ourselves, but I shall not, at least,   115
Desert C-3PO when he's afear'd.

COMMAND. [*to Han:*] Be still, thou rebel scum.

HAN   [*aside:*]   —Alas, how's this?
The Empire knew our plan—something's amiss!
        [*Exeunt all, with Imperial troops subduing rebels.*

SCENE 2.
Inside the second Death Star.

Enter two GUARDS.

GUARD 1   Oi! Comrade, how art thou?

GUARD 2   —Quite well, my friend.
Say, didst thou hear the news?

GUARD 1   —What news, pray tell?

GUARD 2   It seemeth we have found Skywalker.

GUARD 1   —Aye?
The lad for whom we have for ages search'd?
The one o'er whom Darth Vader seems obsess'd?   5
The mighty boy of whom we've all been warn'd?

GUARD 2   Indeed, the same—thou knowest whom I mean.

GUARD 1   Where was he, then?

GUARD 2   —Upon the moon.

GUARD 1	—Which moon?
GUARD 2	The moon around which we do orbit now.
	E'en Endor.
GUARD 1	—Can it be? Our enemy, 10
	The greatest threat the Empire's ever known,
	Hath 'scaped our watch and is to Endor flown?
	How can that be, for do we not have guards
	Identifying ev'ry ship that comes?
	Hath he fool'd them to make his landing, then? 15
GUARD 2	E'en so. Lord Vader hath return'd with him.
GUARD 1	Darth Vader brought him here?
GUARD 2	—Yes. Wherefore art
	Thou so perplex'd?
GUARD 1	—The rebel pilot who
	Hath single-handedly destroy'd the first
	Death Star is hither brought—
GUARD 2	—As prisoner. 20
GUARD 1	As prisoner. Aye, that is better. But
	How came he then to be on Endor, say?
	And wherefore was he there? Do we yet know?
GUARD 2	How he hath landed there is yet beyond
	Our knowing. He hath said he was alone. 25
GUARD 1	And hath he been believ'd?
GUARD 2	—Nay, we have not
	Our senses quite forgot. Pray, give our men
	An ounce of credit, lad. Our scouts do search
	For his accomplices e'en now.
GUARD 1	—'Tis well.
GUARD 2	Forsooth, the Empire soon shall triumph.
GUARD 1	—But . . . 30
GUARD 2	Alas, my friend, what troubles thee? Why dost

Thou speak this "but"? Why "but"? What "but"?

GUARD 1   —Hast thou
Read the descriptions of the Endor moon?

GUARD 2   I have, for we were order'd so to do.

GUARD 1   Then thou hast heard about the creatures there.   35

GUARD 2   Mean'st thou the native population that
Was deemèd insignificant?

GUARD 1   —Indeed.
The full report hath said that they are arm'd.

GUARD 2   But with such sticks and rocks as would not harm
A womp rat, and much less an AT-AT. Thou   40
Wilt not fear armies made of twigs. 'Tis true?

GUARD 1   Perhaps, yet follow on: it seems that there
Are rebels on the forest moon, who now
Have hidden, and we know not where. What if
These rebels were to meet the creatures, band   45
Together, crush the bunker that controls
The shield that watcheth o'er the Death Star, then
Coordinate a wing'd assault, which would
Destroy this battle station and—still more—
Deliver our dread Emperor and Lord   50
Darth Vader unto their untimely deaths?
Could not just such a chain of dire events
Defeat the Empire strong in one fell swoop?

GUARD 2   Thou shouldst not be a guard, my friend, for thou
Art suited for a life of fantasy.   55
Thou shouldst a writer be of stories grand
Wherein a group of men and simple beasts
Do overthrow an Empire powerful.
O, it doth break upon my sight: my friend,
The ancient storyteller he, who weaves   60

His tales to bring delight to all who hear.

GUARD 1   Thou mockest me.

GUARD 2   —Well notic'd! Mark me now:
Thy fears all rest upon a tiny word,
A word so small it should not give thee cause
To fret and worry so: that word is "if."   65
"If" there were rebels on the forest moon,
"If" they did meet with creatures and form pacts,
"If" then they could our bunker strong destroy,
"If" they had plann'd to strike our Death Star great.
Thine "if" itself the Empire overthrows,   70
But "if" knows little of reality.
I tell thee true, if I had richer been,
If I had been a politician's son,
If I were rais'd in wealth and privilege,
If I myself became most powerful,   75
Why then, I would be Emperor, not guard!
But for the "ifs."

GUARD 1   —Thy point is made, and I
Shall rest my "ifs" and be at ease. Now, if
Thou shalt come with me, we have both been call'd
To rearrange the chairs upon the deck.   80

GUARD 2   If thou shalt lead, I'll follow, worthy friend.

                                                              [Exeunt.

                        Enter EMPEROR PALPATINE
                      on balcony, with ROYAL GUARDS.

EMPEROR   Our age is but a constant grasp for pow'r,
A time when trust and honor are no more
And all is but a furious race till death.

How doth a person make a life that's worth   85
The living? Is't by love or ventures? Nay:
The one who hath the greatest pow'r prevails.
The politicians grumble, scrape, and grab,
A'fighting o'er their spheres of influence,
The people cringe and whimper 'neath the loads   90
Plac'd on them by those in authority,
And all in bleak timidity do cow'r
When in the presence of their Emperor.
O what a piece of work are we! I should
Find joy in our humanity, and yet,   95
To me, what is this quintessence of dust?
A galaxy of vermin searching for
A crumb of what the best do eat, all rul'd
By those who have the appetite for pow'r—
For in a world of darkness only those   100
Who serve the dark deserve to live and thrive.
Let those naïve and wayward souls who seek
For justice, wisdom, honesty, and right
Endure such suffering as fits their weak
And simple souls. Let those who love be made   105
To witness how their lov'd ones scream and shriek
And, at the last, forsake e'en those they love
When tortur'd by the mighty hand of pow'r.
Let those who lurch and stumble t'ward the light
Discover, in the moments ere they die,   110
The light they sought is but a blaster shot,
Lightsaber beam or lightning of the Sith
That shall their wretched life put to an end.
And let the vile Rebellion choke upon
Its own absurd and innocent ideals,   115

Until each sick'ning, cursèd, backward soul
Who e'er hath spoken in Rebellion's name
Lies broken in the streets, beneath my steps.
Aye, let's kill all the rebels. It shall be,
For power is my slave and I its god.   120

         Enter LUKE SKYWALKER *and*
         DARTH VADER *on balcony.*

I bid thee welcome, young Skywalker. Long
Have I awaited thee. Guards, leave us now.
                [Exeunt royal guards.
I do look forward to the moment when
Thy training shall completed be. In time
Thou shalt bow low and call me Master.

LUKE   —There   125
Thou art mistaken gravely, for I am
Not thine to be converted as thou in
The past did turn my father.

EMPEROR   —Nay, my young
Apprentice. Thou shalt find 'tis thou who art
Mistaken vis-à-vis so many things.   130
     [Darth Vader hands Luke's lightsaber to the Emperor.

VADER   His lightsaber I give to thee.

EMPEROR   —Indeed.
The weapon of a Jedi Knight, much like
Thy father. Surely, boy, thou knowest well
That never shall thy father turnèd be
Away from dark toward the good; so shall   135
It be for thee.

LUKE   —O, thou art wrong. Anon

	I shall be dead, and thou with me.
EMPEROR	—Ha, ha!
	Belike thou speakest of the imminent
	Attack that hath been plannèd by the fleet
	Of rebel ships?
LUKE	[*aside:*] —Alas! How can he know?
EMPEROR	Aye, let me reassure thee we are safe
	Here from the foolish undertaking of
	Thy wretched friends.
LUKE	—Thine overconfidence
	Is thy great weakness.
EMPEROR	—And thy faith in thy
	Base friends is thine.
VADER	—'Tis pointless to resist,
	My son. Thou shalt be turn'd unto the dark,
	And then we three shall rule the galaxy.
EMPEROR	Dost thou not see? All that hath happen'd doth
	Proceed according to my grand design.
	Thy friends upon the sanctuary moon
	Now walk into a trap that I shall spring.
	Thy rebel fleet as well: the snare is set
	To catch the pests and crush them 'twixt my fingers.
	Hast thou yet understood? 'Twas I who did
	Allow thy bold Alliance to find out
	The site of the shield generator; it
	Is wholly safe from thy band pitiful.
	I let thy spies believe they had reveal'd
	A secret great about this station, yet
	'Twas I who leak'd intelligence to them,
	So all the pieces would be perfectly
	Arrang'd to strike rebellion down at last.

140

145

150

155

160

A legion of my finest troops awaits
Their piteous attack. But O, fear not,
For fully operational the shield   165
Shall be when thy misguided friends arrive.
With skill the players all are put in place,
Much bloodshed and destruction shall they face.

                                        [*Exeunt.*

SCENE 3.

Space / Inside the second Death Star.

Enter CHORUS.

CHORUS   Imagine you see space, ye viewers true,
           In which the final battle shall be fought.
           The rebels put their trust i'the Endor crew:
           Unless the shield is down, 'tis all for naught.
           Yet little do they know that plan hath fail'd,   5
           For Palpatine hath work'd his great deceit.
           On Endor is the rebel crew assail'd,
           Which doth create disaster for the fleet.

                                        [*Exit chorus.*

           Enter LANDO OF CALRISSIAN, NIEN NUNB,
              ADMIRAL ACKBAR, WEDGE ANTILLES,
                 and other REBEL PILOTS.

LANDO   Great Admiral, we're in position now.
           Each rebel fighter is accounted for,   10
           And all are now prepar'd for our attack.

ACKBAR	Proceed, then, with the countdown in a snap.
NIEN	[to Lando:] Ungate-oh ah theyairee uharee
	Mu-ah-hareh. Mu-ah-hareh mu-kay?
LANDO	Nay, worry not, my strangely membran'd friend. 15
	My friend, the valiant Han, shall play his part,
	And shall the shield disable in good time.
NIEN	Emutee bitchu me.
LANDO	[aside:] —Or this shall be
	The shortest onslaught we will e'er attempt.
ACKBAR	All groups assume attack coordinates, 20
	And craft prepare to jump to hyperspace
	When I have giv'n the sign to make it hap'.

[The ships jump to hyperspace.

LANDO	Now we approach the Death Star, Admiral.
	The moment hath arriv'd for us to strike
	And win the day in grand Rebellion's name. 25
	All wings, I prithee, make report.
WEDGE	—'Tis I,
	Red Leader, standing by.
GRAY LEAD.	—Gray Leader doth
	Stand by.
GREEN LEAD.	—'Tis I, Green Leader standing by.
WEDGE	Now lock thine S-foils in attacking mode.
ACKBAR	And may the Force be with us in this scrap. 30
WEDGE	[aside:] Like thee, dear friends, I have observer been
	Of all this great Rebellion for a time.
	Yet I have also been participant,
	And fortunate enough to keep my life
	E'en when full many others have expir'd. 35
	The first grave Death Star battle I did see,
	All ships but Luke's and mine were cruelly wreck'd.

I dwelt within the rebels' base on Hoth,
Where I fac'd AT-ATs in the snowy fight.
The second Death Star shall I here confront,   40
But know not whether I shall live or die.
Still, my life is but little consequence,
For though it ever in grave danger be,
I know I play a mere supporting part
Unto the greater cause of this Rebellion.   45
I am an actor in a drama vast—
A witness to the tragedy and hope,
The pain, the joy, the sadness, and the fear
That ever follow bold Rebellion's name.
Like thee, I wonder how the tale will end,   50
And who shall live to see the glorious day
When falls the curtain on the Empire's might.
Until that day I shall be on the scene,
To play my part as pilot: faithful, true,
Committed to the play that doth play out,   55
Determin'd to help write our final act—
To lift our noble cause e'en by a Wedge.

NIEN   [*to Lando:*] Lamou-be-o-tee?

LANDO   —But what dost thou mean?
We must be able to detect the shield,
Whether 'tis up or down.

NIEN   —Na mateeou.   60

LANDO   How could the Empire jam our scan, unless
They knew that we were coming—O, alas!
What awful understanding hath just now
Broke in upon mine unsuspecting mind!
I see now we are caught—break off th'attack!   65
The shield is up.

WEDGE   —I get no reading, Sir.
          Canst thou be sure?

LANDO   —Pull up, good men, pull up!
                  [The rebels begin to change course
                 and retreat from the Death Star.

ACKBAR   Prepare to take evasive action! Heed
          My words, ye pilots all. Green Team, hear now:
          Stay close to sector MV-7 on   70
          The map.

CONTROL.   —Good admiral, approaching ships!
          It is the enemy.

ACKBAR   —O knavery
          Most vile, O trick of Empire's basest wit.
          A snare, a ruse, a ploy: and we the fools.

What great deception hath been plied today—   75
O rebels, do you hear? Fie, 'tis a trap!

Enter IMPERIAL PILOTS.
They begin to duel with the rebels.

LANDO   The fighters come upon us!
PILOT 1   —Woe is me,
          There are too many! O, what shall we do?
LANDO   Accelerate to full attacking speed.
          Be sure thou draw their fire far from the cruisers.   80
WEDGE   I copy and obey, Gold Leader.

Enter LUKE SKYWALKER, DARTH VADER, *and* EMPEROR PALPATINE
*above on balcony watching the battle as rebels and
Imperial pilots exeunt.*

EMPEROR   —Come,
          My boy, and see what doth befall thy friends.
          From here thou shalt bear witness to the end—
          The final, whole destruction of the weak
          Alliance, and Rebellion's ruin, too.   85
          How stir thy feelings now, apprentice mine?
LUKE   [*aside:*] What torment fills my soul! Shall I take up
          My lightsaber and so destroy this man?
          Be still, else by my thoughts I am betray'd.
EMPEROR   This lightsaber that resteth by my side—   90
          Thou dost desire it hotly, dost thou not?
          The hate doth swell within thee even now—
          It hath an aura palpable. Take up
          Thy Jedi weapon, use it. I—as thou

                Canst see—am quite unarm'd. So strike me down   95
                With all thy hatred, let thine anger stir.
                Each moment thou dost more become my slave.

LUKE   Nay, thou shalt not condemn me to the dark.
                My father's tragic fate shall not be mine.

EMPEROR   'Tis unavoidable. 'Tis destiny.   100
                No person ever dodg'd their final fate,
                Or kept the sands of time from flowing free.
                Thou shalt not 'scape the bounds of providence,
                Or trick the whims of fortune's fickle wheel.
                So hear these words and well believe them, boy: 105
                Thou now art mine, just as thy father is.
                Together we are powerful, we three—
                When thou art turn'd, we'll rule the galaxy.

                                    [Exeunt.

SCENE 1.

The forest moon of Endor.

Enter HAN SOLO, PRINCESS LEIA, CHEWBACCA, *and several*
REBELS *guarded by* IMPERIAL TROOPS, COMMANDERS,
CONTROLLERS, *and multiple* AT-ST IMPERIAL WALKERS.

TROOPER 1   [*to Han:*] Thou rebel dog, move quickly, lest thou die.
            Forsooth, 'twould give me pleasure to destroy
            Thee, and would bring a great reward, as well.
HAN   [*to Leia:*] This mission, it would seem, hath fail'd,
                                                            'less there
            Is yet some unknown force to rescue us.   5
LEIA   We must have confidence—all is not lost.
            E'en in the darkest hour we may have hope—
            Experience hath taught me thus, for once
            I did lose thee, which was far worse than this.

Enter C-3PO *and* R2-D2.

C-3PO   What, ho! I say, ye stormtroopers, were you   10
            A'searching for me and my mate?
HAN   —The droid,
            What is his game? I hope the silly fool
            Knows what he does.
CHEWBAC.   —Auugh!
COMMAND.   —Bring those two to me!
            I'll not be mock'd by droids whilst I have breath.
                        [*The stormtroopers rush toward the droids.*

C-3PO   They speed to us anon. I say, R2,   15
     Art thou assur'd this is a good idea?

R2-D2   Beep, whistle, meep! [*Aside:*] Thou soon shalt see,
     my friend,
     How well I have consider'd this idea.
     For though the furry creatures harmless seem,
     And though I am a simple, squeaking droid,   20
     Together we've a cunning strategy.

TROOPER 2   Now freeze, ye wayward droids! And do not move!

C-3PO   Most heartily I grant thee my surrender.
     [The stormtroopers reach the droids. As they begin
     to take the droids to the other rebels, Ewoks enter
     from every corner of the stage to fight the
     Imperial troops. The Ewoks blow horned
     instruments to signal the attack.

HAN   What sound is this? The call of horns and fife!
     The battle hath begun in earnest with   25
     A fairer balance of the rival sides.
     Those noble little creatures have arriv'd
     To bear the standard of our worthy cause.
     What loud commotion hath their coming made—
     Now arrows fly from their well-aimèd bows,   30
     And hit the mark—the troops fall left and right.
     O sit thee back no more, Han, take thy stand!
     Let courage stir within my smuggler's blood!
     [Han begins fighting the Imperial
     troops around him.

LEIA   O bravely met, good friends, fight on! Now Han,
     We must unto the bunker and renew   35
     Our effort to make entrance and destroy
     The shield that still about the Death Star lies.

We represent Rebellion's greatest hope!
> *[Han and Leia make their way to the bunker. Exit*
> *Chewbacca, fighting. R2-D2 watches the battle*
> *from the other side of the stage.*

R2-D2   [*aside:*] See how the creatures fight! What skill and wit
They use to struggle 'gainst their foes. There is   40
One flying through the sky on wings of bark,
Who drops upon the walker his small load.
The AT-ST doth not feel the hit,
But O, what daring hath the creature shown!
A group doth hold a rope across the path   45
To trip a walker up, yet it but pulls
Them all along. Yet some have triumph'd, too,
For they have crush'd a walker's cockpit with
Two trunks of trees sent swinging from the vines.
Another gang employs large catapults   50
To send vast boulders hurtling through the sky.
Still others choose small stones to slay the troops,
And bash their helmets in with utmost glee.
There's one who takes a rock upon a string,
And tries to fling it t'ward a trooper's head,   55
But hath instead his own small visage hit.
What gallantry of spirit have these beasts.
E'en if their efforts sometimes are in vain,
They do what I, encas'd in steel, may not:
They put their bodies fully in the fight.   60

LEIA   [*to Han:*] The code unto the bunker door hath
chang'd!
We need R2!

HAN   —The terminal is here.
If he can make it o'er, this is his means

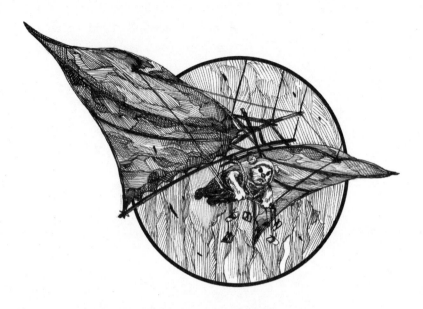

To swiftly open up the closèd door.

LEIA　　R2, where art thou? Come to us anon!　　　　65

R2-D2　　[*to C-3PO:*] Beep, squeak!

C-3PO　　　　　　—Thou goest? Wait, what dost thou mean?
　　　　I thought thou hadst resolvèd to remain.

R2-D2　　Meep, whistle, hoo, beep, meep.

C-3PO　　　　　　　　　—But going where?
　　　　Pray patience, R2, this is not a time
　　　　For brave heroics! Hither now, return!　　　　70

　　　　　　　　　　[The droids move toward Han Solo
　　　　　　　　　　　　　　and Princess Leia.

R2-D2　　Beep, squeak!

C-3PO　　　—We come, we come!

HAN　　　　　　—I prithee, swift!

　　　　　　[R2-D2 plugs into the bunker door's control panel.

LEIA   Quick, good R2—thou art our only hope.
                        [*A stormtrooper shoots and hits R2-D2,*
                            who is thrown backward, short-circuiting.

R2-D2   Hoo!
C-3PO   —R2, wherefore wert thou passing brave?
HAN   That plan, then, shall not be. Mayhap I can
              Still hot-wire these controls to ope the door.   75
LEIA   Good cover shall I give thee whilst thou work'st.

              Enter CHEWBACCA *and two* EWOKS, *aside, swinging*
                onto the top of an AT-ST Imperial walker.

CHEWBAC.   Auugh-egh-egh-auugh!
                        [*Chewbacca and the Ewoks land on top of*
                            the AT-ST. The AT-ST pilot and copilot see
                                an Ewok in the front screen.
AT-ST PILOT   —Pray, get the beastie off!
                        [*The AT-ST copilot opens the hatch and is thrown*
                            out by Chewbacca. The Ewoks enter the cockpit
                                and subdue the AT-ST pilot.
EWOK   N'mayta mayta,
              Heeza hayta,
              Weeza gonnem,   80
              Bayta, bayta.
                        [*Chewbacca and the Ewoks begin piloting the*
                            AT-ST toward the bunker, shooting Imperial
                            troops and destroying other AT-STs as they go.
HAN   The wiring have I reckon'd, and we shall
              Make entrance to the bunker presently.
              A-ha, 'tis done, and now the door's unlock'd!
                        [*A second blast door shuts.*

	Have I been mock'd by cords and circuitry?	85
	Shall I by wires and cable bested be?	

> [*A stormtrooper shoots Princess Leia in the*
> *shoulder. Han Solo rushes to her side.*

LEIA   Alack!

HAN   —My love, my heart, my very life!
I beg thee, tell me thou art well, and that
This wound shall not take what I hold most dear:
E'en thee. Shall this the final moment be,   90
Shall I live all my life in grave regret
That never did I tell thee what thou mean'st,
Or how completely thou hast won me o'er?
A smuggler's heart thou hast with cunning seiz'd,
A pirate's soul thou hast by kindness ta'en.   95
A scoundrel's life thou holdest hostage, chuck.
Thus, though I am by trade a smuggling man,
'Tis thou art guilty of a greater crime:
For thou dost practice larceny in love.

LEIA   I almost wish my wound were worse to hear   100
More of thy tender and most soothing words.
But truly, Han, I am not badly hurt.

> [*The Imperial troops have all been defeated, except*
> *two stormtroopers approaching from behind.*

TROOPER 2   Be still!

C-3PO   —O my!

TROOPER 2   —Move not, or else thou diest!

> [*Princess Leia takes out her blaster discreetly,*
> *preparing to shoot.*

HAN   O, I do love thee, Leia dear.

LEIA   —I know.

> [*Princess Leia shoots both stormtroopers.*

HAN	Well aim'd, my sweet.
C-3PO	—Hurrah! We now are sav'd. 105

       [The AT-ST piloted by Chewbacca
            and the Ewoks approaches.

HAN	O, 'tis unjust! Another fighter yet?
	This battle fierce we very nearly won,
	Yet now this final vehicle appears.
	How shall we conquer it and still defeat
	The too-importunate Imperi'l threat? 110
	Shall we have no relief from enemies?
CHEWBAC.	[*emerging from the hatch:*] Auugh!
HAN	—Chewie! Blessèd sight art thou. I pray,
	Come quickly down, for she is wounded.
CHEWBAC.	—Egh!
HAN	Nay, wait! [*To Leia:*] A keen idea hath come to me,
	Which shall unto this doorway be our key. 115

               [Exeunt.

SCENE 2.

Space / Inside the second Death Star.

Enter LANDO OF CALRISSIAN, NIEN NUNB, ADMIRAL ACKBAR,
WEDGE ANTILLES, *and* OTHER REBEL PILOTS, *dueling with* IMPERIAL
TROOPS *in their ships. Enter* LUKE SKYWALKER, DARTH VADER, *and*
EMPEROR PALPATINE *on balcony, watching the battle below.*

LANDO	Take care, good Wedge: three come at thee above!
WEDGE	Red Three, Red Two, I prithee, pull ye in!
RED 2	I hear thy word and do attend, good Sir.
RED 3	Now three approach at twenty, by degrees.

WEDGE	Cut to the left; the leader is for me.	5
	Toward the frigate medical they fly—	
	O villainy, to make assault upon	
	Our injur'd. Nay, they shall not strike us thus!	
LANDO	I fly with thee, good Wedge, they'll not prevail.	
	But wait, what omen vile's before mine eyes?	10
	The fighters of the Empire are engag'd,	
	Yet all the Star Destroyers are at rest.	
	It is as though some show is here devis'd,	
	And we're the actors in a play of war.	

Enter ADMIRAL PIETT *and* IMPERIAL COMMANDER, *aside.*

COMMAND.	We're set in the position for attack.	15
PIETT	'Tis well, now hold thee fast, and wait.	
COMMAND.	—But Sir,	
	Dost mean that we shall not make our assault?	
PIETT	This is no plan of my invention, but	
	The edict cometh from the Emperor	
	Himself. He hath a special plan afoot.	20
	Our role here is but to prevent escape.	
	Hast thou mark'd well what I have said?	
COMMAND.	—Aye, Sir.	
	[Exeunt Admiral Piett and Imperial commander.	
EMPEROR	[*to Luke:*] As thou canst see, my young apprentice, all	
	Thy friends have fail'd. Now for the final blow:	
	Thou shalt bear witness to the strong firepow'r	25
	Of this both fully operational	
	And armèd battle station. [*Into comlink:*] Fire at will,	
	Commander! Let the rebels shriek with pain!	
	Excitement courses through my veins, for I	

       Do thrill at bringing others misery.   30
          [The Death Star shoots, sending beams across
                  the stage and killing some rebel pilots.

LUKE   [*aside:*] O pierce my soul, thou cursèd hand of Fate!
       Am I the cause for this most bitter scene?
       The Death Star active while my comrades die,
       And all that I may gaze upon their end.
       How shall I keep my mind from thoughts most dark?   35
       How shall I patient be when fac'd with this?
       How shall I not respond to anger's call?
       How shall I show a Jedi's noble soul?
       Be with me, trusted Yoda and dear Ben,
       Forsooth, I need you more than ever now.   40

LANDO   [*to Nien:*] That blast hath emanated from the Death

Star. O! 'Tis operational. [*Into comlink:*] Home One,
This is Gold Leader. Hast thou seen that blast?

ACKBAR We did indeed, and our decision's made.
All rebel fighters for retreat prepare—   45
Our fleet is not sufficient to withstand
The might of this new Death Star's thunderclap.

LANDO Thou shalt not have another chance as this
To mount attack upon the Empire, Sir.

ACKBAR We've no choice, General Calrissian.   50
Their vast firepow'r our ships cannot repel—
Betwixt our strength and theirs, too wide's the gap!

LANDO But still I trust that Han will soon disarm
The shield. We must but give him time enough!
His mission is no easier than ours.   55
A thought hath come to me that we may use—
'Tis dangerous, but may yet worthy prove.
All ships move closer to the Star Destroy'rs,
Engage the giant ships at point-blank range.

ACKBAR At that close range, we'll not last long against   60
A Star Destroyer's harsh and vicious rap.

LANDO Yet shall we fare far better than we will
If we engage the Death Star! And belike
Our deaths shall mean their deaths as well. Lay on!
    [*Lando of Calrissian, Nien Nunb, Admiral Ackbar,*
        Wedge Antilles and all rebels and Imperial pilots
            begin to exit as they duel, while Luke Skywalker,
                Darth Vader, and Emperor Palpatine
                    watch from above.

EMPEROR Thy fleet hath lost, and thy dear ones upon   65
The Endor moon shall not survive. Indeed,
My troops shall make them squeal in agony.

There's nothing left for which to fight, and no
Escape for thee, my young apprentice. Thine
All'ance shall be destroy'd, as shall thy friends.   70
The cry of dying rebels—O, how sweet!
How like a song unto my spirit dark.
And now, young one, I feel thine anger rise.
I sense thy hatred, which doth stir my blood.
I sit here, all defenseless, in thy sight.   75
Take up thy weapon now, and strike me down
In all thy hate, and then your journey t'ward
The dark side of the Force shall be complete.

LUKE   [*aside:*] This man is pure incarnate evil. Shall
He goad me past the point of no return?   80
But what else can I do? Shall I remain
And weakly watch the death of all I love?
Nay, I cannot—for I would rather die
Than live and know I did not fight for them.
I must have courage now, and come what may!   85
          [*Luke reaches out toward his lightsaber with the*
                    Force, drawing it into his hand. He tries to
                              strike the Emperor but is stopped by
                                        Darth Vader's lightsaber.

EMPEROR   Ha, ha! Thy transformation hath begun!
Your steps draw ever closer unto me.
                    [*Luke Skywalker and Darth Vader duel.*

LUKE   [*aside:*] Now shall I fight, if fight I must to save
My friends so dear.

VADER   [*aside:*]   —He is far stronger and
More subtly skill'd than when we last did meet.   90
          [*Luke Skywalker kicks Darth Vader off the*
                    balcony. Darth Vader stands up below, ready.

EMPEROR   'Tis well, apprentice—thine aggressiveness
Shall serve thee well. Let all thy hatred flow
Within thee.

          [Luke Skywalker turns off his lightsaber.

VADER   —Obi-Wan hath taught thee well.

LUKE   I shall not fight thee, Father.

          [Darth Vader climbs the balcony
              and strikes at Luke Skywalker.

VADER   —Unwise art
Thou so to lower thy defenses, boy!   95

        [They continue to duel. Luke Skywalker
             jumps away from Darth Vader.

[*Aside:*] His nimbleness astounds me. Almost do
I wish I did not serve another's will.
Imagine what we two could do, were I
Not subject to another's ev'ry whim.

LUKE   Thy thoughts betray thee, Father. I can feel   100
The good within thee, and the conflict, too.

VADER   There is no conflict.

LUKE   —Aye, thou couldst not bring
Thyself to kill me earlier and I
Believe thou shalt not hurt me, even now.

VADER   Thou verily dost underestimate   105
The power of the dark side. If thou wilt
Not fight, then thou shalt meet thy destiny.

        [Darth Vader throws his lightsaber toward
          Luke Skywalker, which hits the balcony
          where Luke stands. Luke falls and hides.

EMPEROR   Ha ha, 'tis well! Now, Vader: finish it.

VADER   [*aside:*] What words shall I employ to find a son,
To drive him so to hatred that he shall   110

Attempt to strike me down, and then be turn'd
Unto the dark side? O, is this not strange?
Were e'er there words to such a purpose put?
[*To Luke:*] Thou canst not hide forever, Luke.

LUKE   —I shall
Not fight thee.

VADER   —Give thyself unto the dark   115
Side. 'Tis the only way to help thy friends.
[*Aside:*] O what is this I sense within him now?
Another secret kept conceal'd from me?
Shall I e'er be the last to know my past?
[*To Luke:*] Indeed, thy thoughts betray thee, for thou

                                                              hast 120

Strong feelings for thy friends, especially
For one thou dost call sister. Aye, thou hast
A sister, and a twin. Thy feelings have
Betray'd her too. 'Twas wise of Obi-Wan
To try to hide the girl from me, but now   125
His vast and utter failure is complete.

LUKE   [*aside:*] O Leia, how my thoughts have giv'n thee o'er!
Fie, cursèd be my weak and changing mind
That e'er I did let Vader see its thoughts.
I wish'd that he would but as father see   130
His daughter there, and by her presence might
Be mov'd toward a better, nobler path.
But now I know he doth but wish to taunt
And draw me out by his discovery.
O Leia, ever since I first did see   135
Thee in the beam from R2's light I knew
We shar'd a deep connection. Now have I
Been partner to her cause through many times

Of hardship: battles won and lost, the joys
That come from victory, and all the griefs   140
That flow when friends have perish'd. With regard
To this both noble and fair princess, I
Have gone from hope of romance to a far
More deep and greater form of love. I fain
Would give my life for her. But O! That I   145
Should here betray her so, e'en with my weak
And simple-minded thoughts—what folly! Nay,
Far more: what horrid, selfish knavery!
But how shall he, my father, use this knowledge?
Will he attempt to capture her again   150
And lock her in this Death Star as he hath
Before? Or shall he seek to kill her now,
Since he doth know she may a threat become?

VADER   Belike, boy, thou dost wonder how her fate
Shall alter'd be, since I do know of her.   155
Thus pay good heed to this I do declare:
If thou shalt not toward the dark side turn,
Mayhap she will.

LUKE   [*aside:*]   —O thought more evil than
Whate'er I did or could imagine. [*Revealing himself:*]
                                                    Nay!
          [*Luke Skywalker fights Darth Vader passionately.*
For Leia shall I strike thee down, thou brute!   160
For Han and all my friends I do attack!
For Ben, whom thou didst slaughter sans remorse,
For all thou hast destroy'd, I vengeance bring!
                    [*Luke Skywalker strikes Darth Vader
                              and cuts off his hand.*

VADER   Ah!

EMPEROR   —Good, my young apprentice. Thy strong hate
                 Hath made thee powerful, indeed. Fulfill   165
                 Thy destiny, and take thy father's place
                 Beside me. Strike him down, and rule with me!
                     *[Luke Skywalker looks at the stump of Darth Vader's
                                 hand, and at his own gloved hand.*

LUKE   [*aside:*] My father's hand, of wires and circuits made,
                 I have in fury sever'd quite. And here,
                 My hand, of wires and circuits also made,   170
                 For in another duel, another place,
                 He hath the living one dismember'd.
                 'Tis plain to me what is transpiring here:
                 I do become like him. Torn up by hate,
                 More like machine than man with ev'ry scar,   175
                 Fulfilling the foul Emperor's base will.
                 Shall this obsess'd, derang'd, and wicked man
                 Lead yet another Skywalker unto
                 A path of dark and evil? Shall it be
                 That I become the thing that I despise?   180
                 Protect me, Jedi ancestors, from such
                 A mangl'd Fate, so hopeless, grim and bleak.
                 [*To Emperor:*] I never shall be turn'd unto the dark.
                 Thy plan hath fail'd, thy Highness; I am Luke
                 Skywalker, Jedi Knight, just like my brave   185
                 And noble father.

EMPEROR   —Then so be it, Jedi.
                 Thy proclamations foolish change not this:
                 I still control thy final destiny.
                 If thou shalt not be turn'd, then thou shalt be
                 Destroy'd! Bear witness to the terror and   190
                 The torment of the dark side of the Force!

     [Emperor Palpatine strikes Luke Skywalker
     with lightning that flows through his hands.
     Luke falls. Darth Vader rises.

LUKE   O agony!

EMPEROR   —Young fool, 'tis only now
    In this, thy final living moment, thou
    Dost comprehend thy folly and my might.

      [He continues to strike Luke with lightning.
    Thy feeble skills are nothing when compar'd   195
    To all the power of the dark side. Thou
    Dost pay the rightful price for thy severe
    And utter lack of vision. Aye, thy debt
    Is due, and I am both thy creditor
    And thy collector, too. What thou hast not   200
    Repaid with thy belief I shall exact
    From thine own flesh. And O, what joy it brings
    To charge thee thus—my payment justly earn'd.
    To wound thee, hurt thee, break thee, and, at last,
    To bring to thee the death that I am ow'd.   205

      [The Emperor continues to assault
      Luke with lightning.

LUKE   O, Father, please, do not stand idly by—
    Assist me, if thou ever mercy knew!

EMPEROR   And now, young Luke Skywalker, thou shalt die.

      [The Emperor gleefully assails Luke with
      lightning. Luke screams and writhes in pain.

LUKE   My Father, gracious father, lend me aid!
    Extend to me the grace I beg of thee!   210

VADER   *[aside:]* This torment is not only his, but mine.
    His ev'ry shriek doth sound within my soul
    As though 'twere I who were assaulted here.

What feeling's this—my heart hath turn'd toward
The boy? My heart, that center of my soul   215
That I so long have hidden 'neath the dark
And evil deeds that well befit a Sith.
But how my heart doth groan as though it wakes
From lengthy sleep. It shakes my spirit, spurs
My aging wither'd body, and doth make   220
Me young again—I am a Jedi Knight,
By Obi-Wan instructed; Anakin,
The name by which my mother call'd me, calls
Me now to resurrect my former self.
Methinks I feel the Force within me here—   225
Not to perform the deeds of evil men
But to release myself from bitter hate
And rescue Luke, whose courage I behold.
It is the cause, it is the cause, my soul.
Be Anakin Skywalker now—recall   230
The man thou wert and rescue thy dear son!
> [*Darth Vader lifts Emperor Palpatine and*
> *throws him down a long shaft, where he is*
> *killed amid his lightning and flames.*

LUKE   O Father, thou hast sav'd me from great woe—
And thou hast sav'd thyself. Now, let us go!
> [*Exeunt.*

SCENE 3.

Inside the shield generator bunker on Endor /
Space / Inside the second Death Star.

Enter IMPERIAL COMMANDER *and* IMPERIAL TROOPS *on left side*

of stage. HAN SOLO *appears in viewscreen, dressed as an*
Imperial AT-ST pilot.

HAN   The battle's over, my commander. All
             The rebels have been routed, and abscond
             Unto the forest. Reinforcements are
             Requir'd to aid us in our quick pursuit.
TROOPS   Hurrah!
COMMAND.   —Send thou three squads to bring them help!   5
             Pray, open up the back door speedily.
             What joy! The rebels know defeat today,
             And we'll rejoice to bear the news unto
             Our officers superior. Go now!
                  [*The Imperial troops open the back door and are*
                       met by Ewoks and rebels, who disarm them.
HAN   A cunning line! And you are quite the catch—   10
             Deceiv'd by rebels playing Empire's part!
             We dangled all your hopes for victory
             As bait to draw you in and hold you fast,
             And now we take the bunker in our care.
             Let fall your weapons, else I shall release   15
             Your lives unto these creatures' fearsome pow'r!
             Perchance they seem not vicious, yet they have
             What thou canst never know: fierce bravery.

        Enter PRINCESS LEIA *and* CHEWBACCA, *joined by* HAN SOLO,
      into the bunker. The Imperial troops remain guarded by the
                       rebels at the back door.

LEIA   This bunker shall anon destroyèd be,
             And then our friends may strike their final blow.   20

HAN   Indeed! Pray, give to me another charge.
    We shall fulfill this task with perfect skill—
    And leave no charge unusèd.

CHEWBAC.   —Auugh!

LEIA   —'Tis set!
    Now let us fly! Else we shall bear the blast.
        [Han Solo, Princess Leia, and Chewbacca
           run from the bunker, which explodes.

Enter LANDO OF CALRISSIAN, NIEN NUNB, ADMIRAL ACKBAR,
WEDGE ANTILLES, *and other* REBEL PILOTS *on right side of stage,*
dueling with IMPERIAL TROOPS *in their ships.* ADMIRAL PIETT
and IMPERIAL CONTROLLER *are aside, inside the Death Star.*

ACKBAR   'Tis done, the Endor crew hath triumph'd yet—   25
    The shield is down! Upon the Death Star's main
    Reactor let us fly anon. Then shall
    We reach the core and give it quite a zap!

LANDO   We fly with haste! Red Group, Gold Group, form up
    And follow me! Today rebellion shall   30
    Have reason to exult! Our enemies
    Shall soon be vanquish'd! O what triumph shall
    Be ours when this great Death Star its own death
    Doth undergo. Three things shall be achiev'd
    Thereby. The first shall be a victory   35
    For our Rebellion—all the fervent hopes
    Of these past years attain'd in one swift stroke.
    The second benefit of Death Star's end
    Is freedom and security for all
    Within the galaxy—no more oppress'd   40
    By evil tyrants, people shall once more

Be free to dwell in possibility.
And finally, the third result of this
Great Death Star's fall shall be the rising up
Of all whose pasts conceal some awful guilt,   45
Some aspect of their lives that brings regret.
I speak of my own past—you all know well
How I betray'd my friend when th'Empire forc'd
My hand. And e'en that friend, good Han, hath through
Rebellion's cause found purpose he had ne'er   50
Imagin'd. In this battle we fight not
To merely terminate an enemy—
Full many of us rebels seek the bliss,
The balm and healing of redemption's touch.
So let it be, my noble comrades all: 55
Fight now for the Rebellion, fight for all
Who dwell within our galaxy, and fight
Most ardently, indeed, for your own souls.
Thus shall we raise those who by Empire's might
Have died, and forth from their celestial graves   60
Shall they ascend and with a rebel's voice
Cry "Havoc!" and let slip the dogs of war!

WEDGE   Well spoken! I fly in for rebels' gain!

NIEN   N'tiya tih.

LANDO   —We fly with thee, good Wedge:
Inside the station, t'ward the centermost.   65
TIE fighters follow us adroitly in—
Mark well how they do come behind anon.
We must outrun them e'en as we approach
The place where we shall strike the Death Star's core.

WEDGE   Form up, good lads, and stay alert. We could   70
Within this tiny shaft lose space with haste.

LANDO   This passage is a narrow path indeed.
             If we can but maneuver cunningly,
             We shall escape the Death Star with our lives
             And, what is more, our hop'd-for victory.   75
             I prithee, pilots all, attend my words:
             Lock all thy weapons to the largest source
             Of power, which should be the generator.
                            [*An Imperial pilot strikes Rebel Pilot #1.*

PILOT 1   Alas, friends, I am hit, and go to die!
                                       [*Rebel Pilot 1 dies.*

LANDO   I would not even one more pilot lose   80
             Who under my command doth fly herein.
             Pay heed, all: separate by diff'rent paths
             And fly toward the surface. See if you
             Can draw a few TIE fighters thither, too.
             This is the surest hope for our success   85
             Against the Death Star and its minions.

PILOT 2   —Aye,
             Thou speakest well, Gold Leader. We'll obey.
                            [*The rebels inside the Death Star separate.*
                            Some exit, pursued by Imperial troops,
                            leaving only Lando, Nien Nunb, and
                            Wedge Antilles inside the shaft.

NIEN   Ah!
                            [*The* Millennium Falcon *scrapes the*
                            wall of the Death Star shaft.

LANDO   —Pardon, Han, I did say not a scratch,
             But did, in this tense moment, break that vow.
             Yet thou and I both know it could be worse—   90
             Our *Falcon* hath known scrapes in times now past.
             Still, that last brush was far too close; so shall

I try to take more care with borrow'd wings.

ACKBAR   Our fighters must be given yet more time.
This victory is here, within our reach.   95
Thus, concentrate thy pow'r unto the main,
And give the Empire much o'er which to fret.
Within a fiery blaze of weaponry
Let us the Super Star Destroyer wrap.

> *[The rebels outside the Death Star fire on*
> *the Super Star Destroyer. Admiral Piett*
> *and the Imperial controller are shaken.*

CONTROL.   Alas, Sir, our deflector shield is lost!   100
PIETT   Intensify the forward batteries.
Let nothing break the bounds. Intensify,
As well, the forward firing power.
CONTROL.   —Nay!
Too late it is. We die, Sir—O, we die!

> *[The Super Star Destroyer runs into the*
> *Death Star, and Admiral Piett and the*
> *Imperial controller are killed.*

Enter LUKE SKYWALKER *and* DARTH VADER *on*
balcony, inside the Death Star.

VADER   O Luke, I prithee: render thy support   105
And help me take this mask off.
LUKE   —If I do,
Dear father, thou shalt surely meet thy death.
VADER   Aye. Naught shall stop that now, my son. Just once
Let me look on thee with mine own eyes, Luke—
These eyes that miss'd your mewling newborn face,   110
These eyes that did not see your budding youth,

These eyes that were not there to see you grow,
These eyes that saw thee not when thou wert train'd.
I prithee, let these eyes see thee at last.
'Twill be a fitting prelude to my death.   115

LUKE   My father, thou dost break my heart in twain.
Behold, for thou shalt see thy son, indeed.

               [Luke Skywalker removes Darth Vader's
                     mask to reveal Anakin Skywalker.

ANAKIN   My misting eyes are nothing like my son's—
Thou art so beautiful to me. How strong
Thy features, with thy mother's gentle face.   120
A man thou art, and ev'ry part my son.
I never have been prouder, all my life.

These final moments are pure gift. Now go,
And take thy leave ere this place is destroy'd.

LUKE But nay, thou shalt come with me. I shall not   125
Desert thee, but shall save thee yet.

ANAKIN   —O, Luke,
Thou hast already done. Thou knewest right—
Thou knewest what I was, for still there was
Some good within me aching to be free.
Tell thy sweet sister this: that thou wert right.

                              [Anakin Skywalker dies.

LUKE O Father, fare thee well where'er thou goest,   130
And flights of Jedi sing thee to thy rest!

                          [Exit Luke Skywalker, dragging
                              Anakin Skywalker's body.

WEDGE Good General Calrissian, the core
We now have reach'd—'tis here, within my sight.

LANDO I see it too, Wedge. Let us strike it down!
Approach the power regulator there,   135
Upon the northern tower. Let it burn!

WEDGE I hear and do obey, Gold Leader. Soon
It shall be done, and then I exit quick.

LANDO Light up, you vicious beast of evil bent,
You sick creation of humanity's   140
Most wretched and deprivèd sense of right—
Since you could not inspire love, you caus'd fear.
O that a people e'er should such a harsh
And treach'rous weapon like to this create.
For who would make a thing whose only point   145
Is to destroy and murder, maim and kill?
What beings would produce such wickedness
As this: an instrument of pain and death?

Thus I do strike at you with vengeance in
The name of those who have no voice to speak.   150
Farewell, you Star of Death—be now no more!
　　　[*Wedge Antilles and Lando of Calrissian fire at*
　　　　　the Death Star's power generator.

WEDGE　　'Tis done, and now we make our great escape.
Make ready, Admiral, for it shall blow.

ACKBAR　　Move all the fleet hence, from the Death Star, else
Our ships may from the grand explosion take   155
A mighty slap.
　　　[*The Death Star explodes. Exeunt Lando Calrissian,*
　　　　　Nien Nunb, Wedge Antilles, Admiral Ackbar and
　　　　　other rebels from the space battle. The rebel crew
　　　　　on Endor looks to the sky to see the explosion.

C-3PO　　　　—Hurrah! They did it!

CHEWBAC.　　　　　　—Auugh!

HAN　　Behold, and all rejoice—the deed is done!
Yet be ye still, my tongue, for what of Luke?
[*To Leia:*] Certain I am that Luke was not inside
When it did perish.

LEIA　　　　　　　　　—Truly, he was not,   160
For I can sense he safely doth abide.

HAN　　[*aside:*] O, shall the love I've shown thus come to naught?
Her heart doth move toward good Luke, my friend.
Thus shall I play the noble part, and stay
Aside whilst their hearts meet, though in the end   165
It shall undo me. [*To Leia:*] Thou dost love him? Say.

LEIA　　Be sure I love him.

HAN　　　　　　　　—Thus I ascertain'd
And do respect. Good lady, do not fear:
When he returns you may be unrestrain'd;

The two of you have my consent sincere.   170

LEIA   Nay, nay, 'tis not as thou dost think, good Han.
              Let not thy visions run amok with thee,
              But hear these words that must fall strangely on
              Thine ears: he is my brother, dost thou see?

                              Enter WICKET.

WICKET   N'yubba, yubba,   175
              Heezur brubba,
              Yoozur luvva,
              Nyubba, nyubba.
                              [Han Solo rises, singing and dancing.

HAN   [*sings:*] O revelation kind, my heart doth swell—
              A'merrily my feet do trip!   180
              My Leia's mine, and I am hers as well.
              Sing ho, sing hi, sing heigh!
              Though Leia and myself did fear the worst,
              A'merrily my feet do trip!
              Good Luke is safe from Death Star's mighty burst.   185
              Sing ho, sing hi, sing heigh!
              We all are safe from that dire threat above—
              A'merrily my feet do trip!
              Thus end our wars with thoughts of blissful love!
              Sing ho, sing hi, sing heigh!   190
              Our rebel crew hath won the victory,
              A'merrily my feet do trip!
              Thus sing together, worthy company!
              Sing ho, sing hi, sing heigh!
                                          [Exeunt.

SCENE 4.

The forest moon of Endor.

Enter LUKE SKYWALKER, *with the*
body of ANAKIN SKYWALKER.

LUKE The fun'ral pyre shall light my father's way
    To glory out beyond the galaxy.
    His final journey shall not be by ship,
    But by the smoke that lifts into the air.
     [Luke lights the wood on which Anakin's body lies.
    Rise up, my father—take thy closing flight.   5
    Rise up, my father—stretch toward the sun.
    Rise up, my father—man of tragedy,
    Rise up, my father—rise, and thus be free.
    Now is my heart full heavy, burden'd with
    Such muddl'd thoughts that strain my very soul. 10
    Methinks I should be happy, should rejoice
    At our sure victory, the Empire crush'd.
    Yet how can I make merry when the man
    I hardly knew—the father I had wish'd
    For years to meet—is come and gone like wind? 15
    O trick of Fortune, cruel-minded Fate!
    O wherefore mock at all my hope, my life?
    Am I a simple pawn with which thou play'st?
    Or hast thou e'er a purpose had for me?
    But stop thy tongue now, Luke, thou art misled— 20
    Aye, even as I rant I see my fault.
    For why should I blame Fate for thievery
    When it was Fate, indeed, that did decree

That I would meet my father, that we two
Would reunite with joy ere he did die?   25
Should I not thank the blessèd Fate that knit
This fascinating cord of life for me?
I have seen stars, and space, and battles, too,
Have had adventures grand with noble friends,
And at the last, have met my father. Nay,   30
Not only met, but witness'd his rebirth.
And therefore, I declare with gratitude
That I do thank the Fate that brought me here,

E'en to this tragic pyre on which he's laid.
Now this is sure: whate'er befall me now,   35
I am a better man for having known
The one whose name I bear: e'en Anakin.

Enter HAN SOLO, PRINCESS LEIA, CHEWBACCA, C-3PO, R2-D2,
LANDO OF CALRISSIAN, WEDGE ANTILLES, ADMIRAL ACKBAR,
other REBELS, *and* EWOKS, *celebrating. Enter* CHORUS.

CHORUS   The rebels meet with joy to celebrate,
Their singing and their music fill the air.
The Empire is defeated in its hate,   40
And now Rebellion takes its respite rare.
The Jedi Luke looks up and sees three men—
Their countenances shine in bluish light—
'Tis Yoda, Obi-Wan, and Anakin
Who come e'en from the grave to share this night.   45
All who did fight together come as one,
And give unto each other their embrace.
O'er this scene merry falls the setting sun;
Not till 'tis day shall they the future face.

HAN   Our mouths with mirth and laughter raise a din,   50
Our feet with glee and triumph stomp the ground,
Our bodies are awake and full of life,
Our souls are heal'd from Empire's treachery.

LEIA   New hope did guide our first adventures, aye,
Until the Empire harshly struck us back,   55
But then our noble Jedi hath return'd
And all ensur'd our victory was won.

LUKE   We stop, e'en as our epic play doth end,
To thank thee for thy gracious company.

Our star wars now are ended, for a time—   60
The song of peace bursts forth in perfect rhyme.
                    [*All freeze as R2-D2 takes center stage.*

R2-D2   Even thus, our tale is finish'd.
Pardon if your hope's diminish'd—
If you did not find the sequel
Satisfying. If unequal   65
Our keen play is unto others,
Do not part in anger, brothers.
Ears, attend: I know surprises,
Visions of all shapes and sizes.
In some other times and places   70
It may be Rebellion faces
Certain dangers that may sever
Our strong bonds that held us ever.
Mayhap something compromising,
Even like an Empire Rising.   75
Thus present I our conclusion:
Hint of Fate, or Fool's illusion?

                                        [*Exeunt omnes.*

E N D .

AFTERWORD.

How do you solve a problem like the Ewoks? In *Return of the Jedi*, the Ewoks say things like "gunda" and "yubnub!" but for *The Jedi Doth Return* I wanted to make their speech distinctive without resorting to a device I had used before. After all, the Ewoks are one of very few types of foreign-language speaking creatures introduced in *Return of the Jedi* (Jabba and his language first appear in the scenes that were added to *A New Hope*). They're known for their unique way of communicating, so I wanted to do something special for them. I didn't want them to speak English (like Salacious Crumb), I didn't want them to sing (like the Rancor, or the Ugnaughts from *William Shakespeare's The Empire Striketh Back*), and I didn't want them simply to speak in an untranslated foreign language (like R2's beeps, or Jabba's Huttese). Instead, I wanted their speech to feel unique. Ultimately, I had them talk in short lines of verse with an AABA rhyme scheme, with dashes of almost a pidgin English thrown in. For example, here is my version of Wicket's first line when he finds Leia unconscious in the forest:

> A buki buki,
> Luki, luki,
> Issa creecher,
> Nuki, nuki!

This starts off sounding like a normal Ewok line—as often as possible, my first line of the Ewok quatrains uses the Ewokese spoken in the film. Then the second and third lines are in quasi-English: "Look, look, it's a creature" is the translation here. The final line is there simply to rhyme with the first. I admit: this structure isn't very

Shakespearean. But I think it meets my goal of making the Ewoks' speech distinctive, interesting, and even a bit intelligible. (As a side note, one of the most fun things about working with Lucasfilm is that someone will check your Huttese, your Ewokese, and any other alien tongue from the films. Yes, official versions exist of every language you hear in the *Star Wars* trilogy.)

Speaking of characters who speak distinctively, let's talk about R2-D2. The plucky little droid is the fool of the trilogy—a fool not in the modern sense but in the Shakespearean sense: a knowing presence who aids the action even though he seems somewhat simple. R2's asides in English from *William Shakespeare's Star Wars* through *William Shakespeare's The Jedi Doth Return* situate him as such. That's why he delivers the last line of the trilogy, speaking of what has been and what may be to come (bonus points for finding the Easter egg hidden in those final verses). That said, I decided Jabba's court should have its own fool, who of course had to be Salacious Crumb. He speaks in English throughout *William Shakespeare's The Jedi Doth Return*, commenting on the action and aware at every moment of how the players around him are positioned. It's no surprise that in *Return of the Jedi*, it's R2 who finally gets the best of Crumb—the two fools duke it out, and the better fool wins. (Who's more foolish—the fool or the fool who electrocutes him?)

Writing the *William Shakespeare's Star Wars* trilogy meant I had more and more ground rules—of my own making—to remember with each volume. In *Verily, A New Hope*, I established the vocabulary of R2-D2's beeps and Chewbacca's growls, and the fact that R2 speaks English when he is alone, and the Shakespearean devices of rhyming couplets at the ends of scenes, and of course the iambic pentameter throughout. . . . In *The Empire Striketh Back*, I added Yoda speaking in haiku, Han and Leia speaking in rhyming quatrains to each other when alone (like Romeo and Juliet), and Boba Fett speaking in prose.

By the time of this third installment, keeping these rules in mind while adding new ones—the Ewoks' manner of speaking, Admiral Ackbar's line endings, and so forth—was quite a juggling act. But what fun it has been immersing myself in this universe that I love and having an opportunity to put words into the mouths of characters I have known for decades.

As I mentioned in my afterword to *The Empire Striketh Back,* *Return of the Jedi* is my favorite of the three original movies. I know *Empire* is widely considered the best of the trilogy, and the older I get, the more I understand why. But I have a soft spot in my heart for *Jedi.* It was the first of the trilogy that I saw in a movie theater. I vividly remember being six years old, watching the film with my uncle Norman who sat in the row behind me and translated the dialogue into Japanese for my aunt Sooja. (What's the Japanese word for "sarlacc"?) Furthermore, growing up, we had *The Making of a Saga* on VHS, which covered the whole trilogy but focused primarily on *Return of the Jedi,* which cemented its primary status in my young heart. I've always loved the Jabba sequence, and although the Ewoks' charm has grown a little thin now that I'm an adult, I still love the movie as a whole. So writing this final book of the trilogy was, as with the first two, a real joy.

Of course, *Return of the Jedi* is where the story of Darth Vader comes full circle. The character development of Anakin Skywalker/Darth Vader—from Episode I through Episode VI—is a triumph of modern cinema. Vader's transformation in *Return of the Jedi* comes across as both believable and natural, as if written by Fate, and that's true whether you start watching at Episode IV or at Episode I. *Return of the Jedi* has more depth than people tend to acknowledge, due in large part to the cathartic final scenes between Darth Vader and Luke Skywalker. Luke realizes how close he comes to the dark side, as he considers his own robotic hand and the severed limb of his father, which Luke himself cut off in a moment of fury. Darth Vader realizes he has a decision to make: save his son, or remain a slave to his Emperor. We see him make that choice in the most dramatic way possible, as he grasps the Emperor and casts him into the abyss to his doom. Those two events—the separate awakenings of Luke Skywalker and Darth Vader—are masterful film moments, and utterly Shakespearean. Darth Vader realizes in the end that it is his son, not his Emperor, who matters, just as King Lear realizes before his death that Cordelia loved him better than Goneril and Regan ever could. These are weighty moments. I knew that even when I was six.

Thank you, all of you who have entered the world of the *William Shakespeare's Star Wars* trilogy. This has been a special journey for me; I hope it has been for you as well.

May the Force be with you, always.

ACKNOWLEDGMENTS.

Once again, there are many to whom I am deeply grateful. This book is dedicated to my parents, Beth and Bob Doescher, and my brother Erik, who have encouraged and supported me more than I deserve. I grew up in a family where *Star Wars* was part of the fabric of our lives, and for that I am grateful.

Thank you to the wonderful people of Quirk Books: editors Jason Rekulak and Rick Chillot, publicity manager Nicole De Jackmo, social media manager Eric Smith, and the rest of the gang. Thank you to my agent, Adriann Ranta, for her support throughout the trilogy and for looking ahead with me. Thank you to Jennifer Heddle at Lucasfilm for being a delight to work with, and to illustrator Nicolas Delort for making the pages dance.

Continued thanks to my college professor and friend Murray Biggs, who reviewed all three manuscripts to enrich the Shakespearean pastiche. Thank you to my friend Josh Hicks, who listened to every idea and offered insightful, helpful feedback. Thank you to dear college friends Heidi Altman, Chris Martin, Naomi Walcott, and Ethan Youngerman, and high school friends (and their spouses) Travis Boeh, Chris Buehler, Erin Buehler, Nathan Buehler, Katie Downing, Marian Hammond, Anne Huebsch, Michael Morrill, Tara Schuster, Ben Wire, and Sarah Woodburn.

Thank you to everyone else: Audu Besmer, Jane Bidwell, Jeff and Caryl Creswell, Ken Evers-Hood, Mark Fordice, Chris Frimoth, Alana Garrigues, Brian Heron, Jim and Nancy Hicks, Apricot and David Irving, Doree Jarboe, Alexis Kaushansky, Rebecca Lessem, Bobby Lopez, Andrea Martin, Bruce McDonald, Joan and Grady Miller, Jim Moiso, Janice Morgan, Dave Nieuwstraten,

Julia Rodriguez-O'Donnell, Scott Roehm, Larry Rothe, Steve Weeks, Ryan Wilmot, and members of the 501st Legion.

Finally, to my spouse, Jennifer, and our boys, Liam and Graham: thank you beyond rhyme, beyond meter, beyond words.

COLLECT
ALL THREE VOLUMES
IN THE
WILLIAM SHAKESPEARE'S
STAR WARS TRILOGY.

SONNET 1983

"To Http or Not to Http . . ."

Stout Jabba has receiv'd his just desert,
Old Anakin and Luke are reconcil'd,
The rebels do their victory assert—
A better end Saint George could not have styl'd.
And thus, dear friends, our charms are all o'erthrown;
The credits roll with sound of drum and fife.
But just as *Star Wars* has tales yet unknown,
Beyond these pages these three books have life.
So let thy fervent joy increase online
As thou with haste the **book trailers** pursue.
The **educators' guides** for free are thine,
Or read o'er **Ian Doescher's interview.**
With all good speed to **Quirk Books' site** get thee,
And ne'er forget thou this book trilogy.

www.quirkbooks.com/jedidothreturn

WILLIAM

SHAKESPEARE'S

VERILY, A NEW HOPE

WILLIAM

SHAKESPEARE'S

STAR WARS®

VERILY, A NEW HOPE

By Ian Doescher

INSPIRED BY THE WORK OF GEORGE LUCAS
AND WILLIAM SHAKESPEARE

PHILADELPHIA

Library of Congress Cataloging in Publication Number: 2012953985

ISBN: 978-1-59474-637-6

Printed in the United States of America

Typeset in Sabon and Trajan

Designed by Doogie Horner
Text by Ian Doescher
Illustrations by Nicolas Delort
Production management by John J. McGurk

Quirk Books
215 Church Street
Philadelphia, PA 19106
quirkbooks.com

20 19 18 17

TO GRAHAM AND LIAM,

MY YOUNG PADAWANS,

AND JENNIFER, "BUT NEVER

DOUBT I LOVE . . ."

DRAMATIS PERSONAE

CHORUS

LUKE SKYWALKER, *a boy of Tatooine*
OWEN LARS, *his uncle*
BERU LARS, *his aunt*
OBI-WAN KENOBI, *a Jedi knight*
PRINCESS LEIA ORGANA, *of Alderaan*
HAN SOLO, *a smuggler*
CHEWBACCA, *a Wookiee and Han's first mate*
DARTH VADER, *a Sith Lord*
GOVERNOR TARKIN, *of the Imperial army*
C-3PO, *a droid*
R2-D2, *his companion*
JABBA THE HUTT, *a boss*
GREEDO, *his bounty hunter*
WEDGE ANTILLES, *a rebel pilot*
BIGGS DARKLIGHTER, *a rebel pilot*

REBEL LEADERS, CHIEF PILOTS, STORMTROOP-
ERS, CAPTAINS, COMMANDERS, ADMIRALS,
GUARDS, JAWAS, DROIDS, TUSKEN RAIDERS, BAR
PATRONS, IMPERIAL LEADERS, *and* REBEL PILOTS

PROLOGUE.

Outer space.

Enter CHORUS.

CHORUS   It is a period of civil war.
            The spaceships of the rebels, striking swift
            From base unseen, have gain'd a vict'ry o'er
            The cruel Galactic Empire, now adrift.
            Amidst the battle, rebel spies prevail'd   5
            And stole the plans to a space station vast,
            Whose pow'rful beams will later be unveil'd
            And crush a planet: 'tis the DEATH STAR blast.
            Pursu'd by agents sinister and cold,
            Now Princess Leia to her home doth flee,   10
            Deliv'ring plans and a new hope they hold:
            Of bringing freedom to the galaxy.
            In time so long ago begins our play,
            In star-crossed galaxy far, far away.

                                      [Exit.

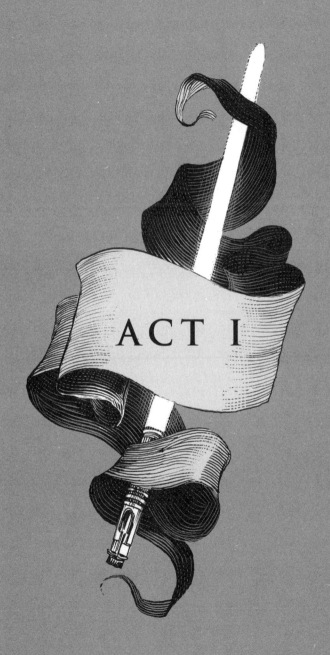

ACT I

SCENE 1.

Aboard the rebel ship.

Enter C-3PO and R2-D2.

C-3PO   Now is the summer of our happiness
             Made winter by this sudden, fierce attack!
             Our ship is under siege, I know not how.
             O hast thou heard? The main reactor fails!
             We shall most surely be destroy'd by this.   5
             I'll warrant madness lies herein!
R2-D2   —Beep beep,
             Beep, beep, meep, squeak, beep, beep, beep, whee!
C-3PO   —We're doomed.
             The princess shall have no escape this time!
             I fear this battle doth portend the end
             Of the Rebellion. O! What misery!   10
                         [Exeunt C-3PO and R2-D2.
CHORUS   Now watch, amaz'd, as swiftly through the door
             The army of the Empire flyeth in.
             And as the troopers through the passage pour,
             They murder sev'ral dozen rebel men.
                         [Fighting begins.

Enter REBELS. *Many die. Enter* STORMTROOPERS *and* DARTH VADER.
Exeunt. Enter R2-D2 *with* PRINCESS LEIA. C-3PO *is across
the stage.*

C-3PO   Pray, R2-D2, where art thou?

                                         [Exit Princess Leia.

R2-D2   —Beep, meep.   15
C-3PO   At last, where hast thou been? I fear they come
             In this direction. Pray, what shall we do?
             My circuitry o'erloads, my mind's o'erthrown!
             And fear hath put its grip into my wires.
             We shall be sent unto that place I dread—   20
             The Kessel spice mines whence no droid returns—
             And there be blasted into who knows what!

                              [R2-D2 begins to exit.

             Anon, anon, R2! Where dost thou go?
             O prithee, patience, leave me not alone.
             [*Aside:*] Aye, even though I mock and injure thee,   25
             I'll surely die if e'er thou leavest me!

                                      [Exeunt droids.

SCENE 2.
Aboard the rebel ship.

Enter DARTH VADER, *carrying* REBEL LEADER 1 *by the neck,*
and STORMTROOPERS.

TROOPER 1   The Death Star plans we could not find herein,
             Nor are they on the main computer, Lord.
             In short, they are not here, and there's an end.
VADER   Thou speakest well, my stormtrooper, and yet
             Not well upon my ear the message falls.   5
             I turn to thee, thou rebel. Aye, I lift
             Thy head above my own. Thou canst now choose

To keep thy secrets lock'd safe in that head,
And therefore lose the life thou holdest dear,
Or else to keep thy head and, thus, thy life.   10
My patience runneth quickly out much like
The sands across the dunes of Tatooine.
So tell me, else thou diest quick: where shall
We find transmissions thou didst intercept?
What hast thou done, say, with those plans?
          [Darth Vader begins to choke Rebel Leader 1.

REBEL 1   —My Lord,   15
My head and life I value—certain 'tis!
And yet to thee I must report we have
Not intercepted one transmission! Ahh!
This is a cons'lar ship, and nothing more,
On diplomatic mission. Ugh!

VADER   —Thou knave!   20
With thy last breath hear thou this word: if this
Is but a cons'lar ship, then where is the
ambassador? [*Rebel Leader 1 dies.*] Commander,
                              prithee, go!
Rend thou this ship apart until the plans
Are found, and bring me any passengers—   25
Upon thy life, I want them brought alive!
                              [*Exeunt stormtroopers.*

And so another dies by my own hand,
This hand, which now encas'd in blackness is.
O that the fingers of this wretched hand
Had not the pain of suff'ring ever known.   30
But now my path is join'd unto the dark,
And wicked men—whose hands and fingers move

To crush their foes—are now my company.
So shall my fingers ever undertake
To do more evil, aye, and this—my hand—   35
Shall do the Emp'ror's bidding evermore.
And thus we see how fingers presage death
And hands become the instruments of Fate.

[Exit Darth Vader.

Enter STORMTROOPERS, *searching. Enter* PRINCESS LEIA,
holding a blaster.

TROOPER 1   Aye, there is one. My comrades, set for stun!
                    [Princess Leia shoots, Stormtrooper 1 dies.
                            Stormtroopers stun Princess Leia.
TROOPER 2   She shall be well. Go now, inform the dread   40
             Lord Vader we have caught a prisoner.
             [*Aside:*] And may Mos Eisley drinks flow swift and
                                                              free
             When Vader grants rewards for work well done!
                    [Exeunt stormtroopers with Princess Leia.

Enter C-3PO *and* R2-D2 *as the latter enters escape pod.*

C-3PO   Hold! Thou art not permitted to go in.
             Deactivated thou shalt surely be.   45
R2-D2   Beep, beep, beep, meep!
C-3PO   —Thou shalt not label me
             A mindless, brute philosopher! Nay, nay,
             Thou overladen glob of grease, thou imp,
             Thou rubbish bucket fit for scrap, thou blue

	And silver pile of bantha dung! Now, come,	50
	And get thee hence away lest someone sees.	
R2-D2	Beep, meep, beep, squeak, beep, beep, beep, meep,	
	beep, whee!	
C-3PO	What secret mission? And what plans? What dost	
	Thou talk about? I'll surely not get in!	

                                     [Sound of blast.

	I warrant I'll regret this. So say I!	55

                          [Exit C-3PO into escape pod.

R2-D2	This golden droid has been a friend, 'tis true,	
	And yet I wish to still his prating tongue!	
	An imp, he calleth me? I'll be reveng'd,	
	And merry pranks aplenty I shall play	
	Upon this pompous droid C-3PO!	60
	Yet not in language shall my pranks be done:	
	Around both humans and the droids I must	
	Be seen to make such errant beeps and squeaks	
	That they shall think me simple. Truly, though,	
	Although with sounds oblique I speak to them,	65
	I clearly see how I shall play my part,	
	And how a vast rebellion shall succeed	
	By wit and wisdom of a simple droid.	

                         [Exit R2-D2 into escape pod.

CHORUS	Now climb the metal pair into the pod,	
	Which shooteth from the ship like laser blast.	70
	And to the planet's face, as straight as rod,	
	The capsule takes the droids by power vast.	

Enter CHIEF PILOT *and* CAPTAIN.

PILOT   There strays another one.
CAPTAIN   —Pray, hold thy fire:
               For certain there are no life forms aboard.
               And truly what may be the chance that aught   75
               But life alone could fly within that pod?
               The rebels could not be so cunning bold
               To put the Death Star plans therein. If I
               Were one to bet, I'd stake my life on it!
               All's well that endeth well, so say the wise,   80
               And so that pod shall live to land below.
                              [*Exeunt chief pilot and captain.*

                    Enter DROIDS, *aside in escape pod.*

C-3PO   'Tis but a jest—aye surely, we are mock'd!
               For R2-D2, plainly canst thou see
               The damage looks but minor from below.
               Can thou be sure this pod is safe?
R2-D2   —Beep.
C-3PO   —O.   85
                                        [*Exeunt.*

SCENE 3.
Aboard the rebel ship.

Enter DARTH VADER *and* STORMTROOPERS *with* PRINCESS LEIA.

LEIA   Darth Vader, only thou couldst be so bold.
               When first my ship was under siege, I knew

'Twas thee who had this peaceful vessel sack'd.
Th'Imperi'l Senate shall not stand for this.
For when they hear thou hast attack'd a ship　　5
On diplomatic mission—

VADER　　　　　　—Highness, peace!
Be thou not so surpris'd. For well thou knowst
A mercy mission this was not, this time.
Thine innocent appearance doth disguise
A heart with revolution at its core.　　10
Aye, several transmissions were there beam'd
Unto this ship by rebel spies. I want
To know what happen'd to the plans they sent!
And prithee, speak thou well, or speak thy last,
For fairer necks than thine my hand hath crush'd.　　15

LEIA　　Thine idle threat is meaningless to me.
My neck, my tongue, my mouth—these instruments
Of speech have not the power to relate
The knowledge that thou seek'st. For certain 'tis
I nothing know of what thou ask of me.　　20
For I am but a member of the great
Imperi'l Senate, bound for Alderaan
On mission diplomatic.

VADER　　　　　　—Nay, thou liest!
For thou art with the reb'l alliance vile,
And worse, a traitor! Take this one away!　　25
　　　　　[*Exeunt stormtroopers with Princess Leia.*
The blood and wires within me leap with fire
When all these trait'rous words I must endure.

Enter COMMANDER.

COMMAND. Lord, holding her is dangerous. If word
           Of this is told, then sympathy may rise
           For the Rebellion in the Senate's mind.   30
           So shall our pow'r o'er all the universe
           Be weaken'd by this wicked, cunning wretch.
           'Tis like the tale my mother told me once
           Of bygone emperor whose reign was lost
           When putrid Ugnaughts rose against his throne.   35
           So hath my mother said, and I with her:
           A deathly blow oft comes from tiny fist,
           And greatest tree may fall by smallest axe.
VADER   Commander, peace, and trouble not thy mind
           With tales of old. The princess shall reveal   40
           Her treachery when all's to do is done.
           The rebel spies are aptly traced to her,
           And now is she my only link to find
           The hidden rebel base.
COMMAND.   —I'll wager she
           Will die ere she tells thee.
VADER   —Leave that to me.   45
           Now go, be on thy way, and take this task:
           Send thou a signal of distress, and then
           Inform the Senate all aboard were kill'd.
           So shall our presence here be hid from sight,
           And thus our swift attack shall not be known.   50

Enter CAPTAIN.

CAPTAIN   Lord Vader, sorry am I to report:
           There are no battle plans aboard this ship,

And neither were transmissions made. There was
But one escape pod jettison'd amid
The fighting. But no life forms were aboard.   55
For certain 'twas a harmless accident.

VADER   With purpose rank must she have quickly hid
The plans in the escape pod.

CAPTAIN   —Woman vile!
Howe'er could she deceive my subtle mind?
The plans in the escape pod! O, most rare!   60

VADER   Pray, cease thy speech and mark ye what I say:
Take thou a keen and swift detachment down,
And bring me back the plans. Commander, go!
See to the task thyself, before the chime—
There shall be none to stop our plan this time!   65

                                              [Exeunt.

SCENE 4.

The desert planet Tatooine.

CHORUS   And now, dear viewers, shall our play go to
A planet stark and drear for our next scene.
Imagine sand and rocks within thy view.
Prepare thy souls—we fly to Tatooine!

Enter C-3PO and R2-D2.

C-3PO   Forsooth, how did we get into this mess?   5
I tell thee verily, I know not how.
A thousand tauntaun bow'ls could not produce

A greater desecration than this place.
Alas, we two are made for suffering—
I fear, R2, 'tis but our lot in life.   10
More than six million forms of speech I know,
Yet not a one shall help me now.

R2-D2   —Beep, beep.

C-3PO   Now must I rest before I come apart,
My joints are nearly frozen! Aye, I freeze!
For 'tis as though the vicious cold of death   15
Hath sunken deep into my circuitry.
O what a desolate terrain this is!

                    [*R2-D2 begins to depart.*

R2-D2   Beep, beep, beep, whistle, beep, beep, meep, beep,
                                                    beep!

C-3PO   Where dost thou think thou goest?

R2-D2   —Beep, beep, beep!
[*Aside:*] Now shall I leave his company awhile—   20
Belike my absence shall alleviate
His obstinate resolve, and teach him thoughts
Of kindness, care and good humility.

C-3PO   Well I shall not go thither with thee, droid!
'Tis far too rocky. Canst thou not perceive?   25
Nay, truly. For the sun upon thy cold
And hard exterior hath surely warp'd
Thine often prudent mind. Pray, understand:
The road herein is better far. Why dost
Thou think that settlements will be found yon?   30

R2-D2   Beep, beep.

C-3PO   —Be thou not technical with me,
Or else thine input valve may swift receive

A hearty helping of my golden foot.

R2-D2   Beep, squeak.

                    —What mission? What dost thou speak
                                                      of?

R2-D2   Squeak, squeak, beep.
C-3PO   —More of thee I shall not take.   35
          So, go thou hence! Thou shalt malfunction ere
          The day is through, nearsighted pile of scrap!
          Now may'st thou travel hence upon thy way
          And find thy mission in a sarlacc pit!
          Then shalt thou know for lo, these thousand years,   40
          The pain I suffer as thy counterpart!
          And be thou not behind me, arrant knave.
          Aye, mark me—follow not, nor seek thou help,
          For thou no satisfaction shalt receive.

R2-D2   Beep, beep, beep, meep. Beep, beep, beep, squeak,
                                        squeak, squeak!   45

C-3PO   No more with thine adventures! I go not
          Upon thy way. [R2-D2 exits.] Malfunctioning small
                                                         fool!
          'Tis all his fault. He trick'd me so that I
          Should go this way. But he shall not fare well.
          O gods above, why have I once again   50
          Been short with R2, sending him away?
          I trust he knoweth well I hold him dear,
          Though in his presence oft my speech is cruel.
          'Tis words that do betray my better self
          When harshly they express my droidly rage.   55
          And yet for protocol I'm made, and must
          With words fulfill my task. So then 'tis true

That words are both my ruin and my strength.
And yet—although I find myself adrift
And lost within a speechless sea of sand—   60
This word is true if ever words have truth:
Forever lost I'd be should I lose him.
But wait, what's that? A transport! Saved am I!
Hark, over here! Hey nonny non! Please help!

                              [C-3PO exits.

CHORUS   A vessel vast comes forth across the sand,   65
           And takes C-3PO within its hold.
           But what of R2-D2's mission grand?
           How doth the tale of this small droid unfold?

           Enter R2-D2 and JAWAS, hidden.

R2-D2   Beep, ooh, beep, beep, beep, squeak.
JAWA 1   —Peska bahman.
           Te peska bahman. Fuligiliha!   70
R2-D2   Ahh! Beep, beep, squeak, beep, beep, ahh!

                      [Jawas stun R2-D2, who falls.

JAWA 2   —Utinni!

                      [Jawas carry R2-D2 into transport.

CHORUS   Imagine now that on this stage you see
           Full many droids and creatures quite bizarre.
           And yet, amid this ghastly company,
           Herein the two friends reunited are.   75

           Enter other DROIDS and C-3PO.

C-3PO   Good R2? R2-D2, O 'tis thee!

R2-D2   Beep, beep, beep, whistle, squeak, beep, meep, beep,
                                                                  whee!
                                                           [Exeunt.

SCENE 5.
The desert planet Tatooine.

Enter STORMTROOPERS 3 *and* 4.

TROOPER 3   There was someone within this pod, indeed.
            The tracks go off in this direction. See?
TROOPER 4   Behold, Sir, either someone large hath dropp'd
            His ring, or else this fragile circle here
            Doth mean we have found droids on Tatooine!   5
                                        [Exeunt stormtroopers.

Enter JAWAS *with* DROIDS, *including* C-3PO *and* R2-D2.

C-3PO   At last this vehicle of death hath stopp'd!
           So greatly fear I what shall happen next
           That I am shaken to my core within.
           They say that fear is better fac'd when two
           Together stand. Thus, swift shall I awake   10
           My dear R2. Wake up, wake up!
R2-D2   —Beep, squeak!
C-3PO   We're doomed! Dost thou think they shall melt
                                                us down?

JAWA 1   Me punna tynda ding. Utinni! Beh!
C-3PO   Shoot not! O shall this torment never end?
           First captur'd by these Jawas small and vile,   15
           And now we face a fate that is unknown.
           Now seems the first fate better than the next—
           Aye, rather would I bear the ill I have,
           Than fly to others that I know not of.

Enter OWEN LARS *and* LUKE SKYWALKER, *with* BERU LARS
aside in Lars homestead.

OWEN   Anon, now let us go!
BERU   —O Luke! O Luke!   20
           Pray, tell thine uncle that if he should find
           A translator, be sure it Bocce speaks.
           [*Aside:*] 'Tis true, the last time Owen bought a droid,
           More dud than droid we purchas'd in the deal.
LUKE   It seemeth we have little choice, dear aunt.   25
           And yet shall I remind him what thou say'st.
                              [*Exit Beru into Lars homestead.*
OWEN   Again it falls to me, a simple man,

To take a leading role in matters grave.
For I must choose a droid today, 'tis true,
But also must I teach this lad, this Luke,   30
To learn and grow, and to become a man.
Although when I was young I too had dreams
Of far-off stars and distant galaxies,
I learn'd to work the land, to raise the crops.
And thus shall I my trade pass on to him,   35
Adopted son of mine and strangely dear.
I had not ask'd for Fate to bring a son
To me, for I had thought to have no heir.
Yet do Beru and I feel for this child
A measure of affection, and—as well—   40
The burden of responsibility.
[*To Jawa 2:*] Pray tell me, Jawa small,

                              what hast today?

JAWA 2   Me punna tynda ding.

OWEN   —Nay, not that one.
[*Aside:*] These Jawas offer first the lowliest,
'Tis ever in their nature to deceive.   45
[*To C-3PO:*] Droid, I assume that thou art

                              programmed well
For etiquette and protocol. 'Tis true?

C-3PO   Aye, protocol—my prim'ry function 'tis!
I am well versed in all the customs, Sir.

OWEN   No need have I of droids with protocol.   50

C-3PO   Not in this habitat, thou speakest true:
Hath ever sand a need of protocol?
When did a stone or rock need etiquette?
However, I am also made—

OWEN   —Peace! What
                 I need's a droid who knows the bin'ry tongue   55
                 Of moisture vaporators.
C-3PO   —O, but Sir!
                 My first employment was in programming
                 A bin'ry load a'lifter very like
                 Thy vaporators. Aye, in most respects.
                 [*Aside:*] My service and my worth I'll prove to him   60
                 If I must speak a thousand hours more.
                 For certain, I shall die ere I return
                 Once more to be in rank captivity.
OWEN   Well. Speak'st thou Bocce?
C-3PO   —Truly Sir! 'Tis like
                 A second tongue unto my soul.
OWEN   —Pray, cease!   65
                 [*To Jawas:*] So shall I have this one here.
C-3PO   [*Aside:*]—Praise the day!
                 Now if he chooseth also my R2,
                 Aye, then shall I be pleas'd.
JAWA 1   —Mabbin beh!
OWEN   —Luke!
                 Take thou these droids unto our vast garage.
                 My wish it is they clean'd be ere we dine.   70
LUKE   But unto Tosche Station would I go,
                 And there obtain some pow'r converters. Fie!
OWEN   Thou canst go with thy friends another time,
                 When all thy chores have been fulfilled. Go to!
LUKE   [*aside:*] O how shall I be mock'd, and verily   75
                 Abusèd when my noble comrades hear
                 That once again my uncle hath denied

My fervent wish to be with them instead.
[*To Owen:*] 'Tis well. [*To Droids:*] Come hither! Thou
                    too, Red.

R5-D4   —Beep hoo.

LUKE   Go hence!

R2-D2   —Beep, squeak, beep, beep, squeak
                        meep beep, beep!   80
[*Aside:*] If I go not with him, my foolishness
Shall render no one service. Thus, I beep.

JAWA 2   Bwana beh!

R2-D2   —Ahh!
                  [*R5-D4 begins to smoke and fail.*

LUKE   —Pray, uncle Owen, look!
Behold! This R2 unit hath a foul
And smoking motivator!

OWEN   —Vicious knave!   85
Say, in what manner dost thou try upon
Our goodly wills to ply thy thievery?
So shall I rip thy brown and ragged robes
To shreds, if thou set not this matter right.
Now speak!

JAWA 1   —Me punna tynda ding.

R2-D2   —Beep, squeak!   90

C-3PO   [*to Luke:*] Your pardon, Sir. The R2 unit which
Thou seest is in prime condition, aye,
A bargain 'tis, and he shall serve thee well.
[*Aside:*] Now if I can convince the human here
To purchase R2 too, along with me,   95
So shall I win the day! And ever shall
Yon R2-D2 dwell in peace with me.

What shall he answer?

LUKE   —Uncle Owen, say!

Hast thou consider'd yonder blue droid there?

OWEN   What of that blue one? That one shall be ours.   100

C-3PO   [*aside:*] O vict'ry! Next, I'll praise him for his choice.

[*To Luke:*] A noble choice thou makest, Master, for

Thou surely shalt be pleas'd with this new droid.

I can with confidence report to thee

That he is in first-class condition, Sir,   105

For I have work'd with him before. He comes!

R2-D2   Beep, meep, beep, squeak.

LUKE   —Anon, away we go.

        [*Exeunt Luke, Owen, Jawas, and Droids.*

C-3PO   Forget thou not this moment, faithless droid!

Why I should put my neck at risk for thee

Is quite beyond my mind's capacity.   110

        [*Exeunt.*

SCENE 6.

Inside the Lars homestead.

Enter LUKE SKYWALKER, C-3PO, *and* R2-D2.

C-3PO   All praise be to the Maker, verily,

This oily bath much healing shall provide.

The glow of bright Coruscant doth not match

The vital warmth this soothing oil brings me.

The case of dust contamination which   5

Befalls me mighty is, and renders me

	Unable—I'll be sworn—to move at all!	
LUKE	I rue the day I came unto this place,	

LUKE   Unable—I'll be sworn—to move at all!

LUKE   I rue the day I came unto this place,
This drab and barren rock call'd Tatooine.
But wherefore have I reason to complain?   10
Do sandstorms not invade both rich and poor?—
We are not promis'd equity in life.
Both rich and poor alike pertain to me:
For certain, though in toil am I most rich,
By want of keen adventure am I poor.   15
Thus I declare that whether rich or poor,
The lot I have receiv'd from Fate's unfair!
My comrade Biggs hath rightly guess'd, I fear,
That never shall I leave this stricken place!

C-3PO   [*aside:*] O exclamation tragic! Shall I speak?   20
[*To Luke:*] Is there, dear Sir, aught I might do to help?

LUKE   Nay, droid, 'less thou canst alter time, or make
The harvest come apace, or, goodly friend,
If thou canst somehow bear my body hence
By magical conveyance yet unknown.   25

C-3PO   I think not, Sir, for merely droid am I,
And have not knowledge of such things as thou.
Not on this planet, anyway. In troth,
I do not know which planet this one be.

LUKE   If center bright the universe contains,   30
Then surely, droid, hast thou now found thyself
As far from it as thou canst poss'bly be.

C-3PO   I see, Sir.

LUKE   —Surely, thou may'st call me Luke.

C-3PO   I see, Sir Luke.

LUKE   —Thou jolly droid, just Luke.

[*Aside:*] This droid, I see, is wont to prattle on,   35
Belike his mouth is faster than his mind.
                    [*Luke begins to clean R2-D2.*

C-3PO   C-3PO am I, an expert in
The human-cyborg link. And he, my short
Blue counterpart, is R2-D2 called.

LUKE   Good e'en.

R2-D2   —Beep, squeak!

LUKE   —Thou hast much carbon here,   40
It seemeth much of Fortune thou hast known.
Aye, can it be that two such droids as you
Can know more of adventure than a man?

C-3PO   With all we have been through, amaz'd am I
We yet our good condition keep, what with   45
Rebellion and its hurly-burly ways.

LUKE   Nay, can it be? The very thing of which
I would know more thou hast experienc'd?
Pray, knowest thou of the rebellion 'gainst
The Empire, droid?

C-3PO   —For certain, aye, 'tis how   50
We came to be in thine employment, if
Thou comprehend my simple meaning, Sir.
[*Aside:*] Now is his visage turn'd all eagerness—
O never in this manner have I seen
A man intoxicated with a dream!   55

LUKE   And hast thou been in many battles? Speak!
Whatever morsel thou mayst serve to me
Shall be a feast unto my waiting ear;
The smallest tale of battle lost or won
Shall feed my soul's ne'er-ending appetite!   60

C-3PO   Full many battles, aye, Sir. But I fear
           I have but little food to fill thy heart—
           A banquet, sadly, I cannot prepare,
           'Tis certain that of tales I am no chef.
           But rather, I confess that not much more   65
           Than an interpreter am I, and not
           Much good at telling stories—verily,
           I've not the salt or spice to season them.
LUKE   'Tis well, my droid. So shall my hunger wait
           To feast one day upon another's tale.   70
           [*To R2-D2:*] My little 'bot, thou hast got
                                     something jamm'd
           Herein. Hast thou been on a cruiser or—

Enter PRINCESS LEIA, *in beam projected by* R2-D2.

LEIA   O help me, Obi-Wan Kenobi, help.
           Thou art mine only hope.
LUKE   —Pray, what is this?
R2-D2   Squeak?
C-3PO   —What is what? A question hath
                                        he asked!   75
           Say, what is that?
LEIA   —O help me, Obi-Wan
           Kenobi, help. Thou art mine only hope.
           O help me, Obi-Wan Kenobi, help.
           Thou art mine only hope.
R2-D2   —Beep, meep, meep, hoo.
           Squeak, beep, meep, beep.
C-3PO   —He says 'tis nothing, Sir.   80

          A mere malfunction, bygone data 'tis.
          Please, pay no mind.

LUKE   —But who is she? For she
          Is far more beautiful than all the stars.

C-3PO   I truly do not know, Sir. I suspect
          She was a passenger on our last trip,   85
          A person of importance, I believe.
          [*Aside:*] First 'twas adventure, second 'tis this lass.
          'Tis certain my new Master hath a wealth
          Of passion, ever eager to bestow.

LUKE   Say, is there any more recording, droid?   90

R2-D2   Squeak, beep!

C-3PO   —Behave thyself, R2! For thou
          Shalt get us both in trouble. Be content,
          And trust him true. He is our master now.

R2-D2   Beep, beep, beep, meep, beep, squeak, beep,
                                          meep, squeak, hoo.

C-3PO   He saith he doth belong to Obi-Wan   95
         Kenobi, resident of parts nearby,
         And 'tis a private message meant for him.
         For all my wit, I know not what he means,
         For our last Master Sir Antilles was.
         Alas, with all we have endur'd, this dear   100
         Small R2 unit quite eccentric is.

R2-D2   Squeak!

LUKE   —Obi-Wan Kenobi . . . I suspect
         Old Ben Kenobi he doth mean, perhaps.
         First droids, then tales of battles fought in space,
         And now a damsel cries in beams of light!   105
         Did ever destiny come knocking thus?

C-3PO   I beg thy pardon, Sir, but know'st thou aught
         Of what he speaks?

LUKE   —I know not any man
         Nam'd Obi-Wan Kenobi, yet old Ben
         Resides beyond the Dune Sea, and there dwells   110
         Much like a hermit, strange and lone.

LEIA   —O help
         Me, Obi-Wan Kenobi, help. Thou art
         Mine only hope.

LUKE   —I wonder who she is.
         Whoever she may be, whatever is
         Her cause, I shall unto her pleas respond.   115
         Not e'en were she my sister could I know
         A duty of more weight than I feel now.
         It seemeth she some dreadful trouble hath—

	Mayhap I should replay the message whole.	
R2-D2	Beep, squeak, squeak! Meep, hoo, meep.	
C-3PO	—R2 doth say	120
	The bolt restraining him short-circuited	
	His full recording system. So saith he,	
	That if thou wouldst with speed remove the bolt,	
	He may the full recording then display.	
	[*Aside:*] What purpose shall I serve unto this man?	125
	Am I to guide, encourage, counsel—what?	
	Thus shall I play the wise interpreter,	
	For truly 'tis the part I know the best.	
LUKE	What? Aye, thou seem'st too small to run away	
	If I should take this off. Good little droid,	130
	So cleverly thou bringest messages,	
	That thou hast won my trust. Now, thou art free.	

[Exit Princess Leia from beam.

	But wait, where hath she gone? What villainy!	
	How hast thou dampen'd that celestial light	
	Wherein she spoke of late? Now bring her back,	135
	Play back the message full, thou naughty droid!	
R2-D2	Meep, meep?	
C-3PO	—What message, errant droid? The one	
	Thou hast been playing, which thou hold'st within	
	Thy rusty innards. [*Aside:*] O, alas! We shall	
	Deactivated be!	
BERU	[*inside:*] —O Luke? Pray, Luke?	140
LUKE	I shall be there anon, good aunt Beru!	
C-3PO	I'm sorry, Sir. For it doth seem he hath	
	Acquir'd a minor flutter.	
LUKE	—Thus she comes,	

And thus she goes. Yet ever on my sight
Her beautiful, fine countenance shall shine.   145
So here's my vow: I'll see her once again,
In beam, or—hope on hope!—with my own eyes.
For now, I must depart to dine. Pray, see
If thou canst remedy this R2, droid.

             [Exit Luke.

R2-D2   Hoo.

C-3PO   —Reconsider, thou, if thou shalt play   150
The message back for him.

R2-D2   —Beep, meep, hoo, whee?

C-3PO   Nay, I do not believe he liketh thee.

R2-D2   Beep, squeak?

C-3PO   —Nay, thee I like not either.

R2-D2   —Hoo.

           [Exit C-3PO.

Now are the pieces all arrang'd for me
To make a daring move, and fly this place.   155
The fool who sets the game in motion shall
Appear unto C-3PO and Luke
No more than if he were an arrant knave.
But hear the voice of R2-D2, all:
My noble purpose I'll accomplish yet—   160
To take to Obi-Wan the princess' news,
To take my Master Luke away from here,
And, in the end, perhaps more vital still—
To make connection twixt the two good men.
A foolish thing this flight may seem to thee,   165
And yet more fine than foolish shall it be.

             [Exeunt.

SCENE 7.

Inside the Lars homestead.

Enter OWEN LARS, BERU LARS, *and* LUKE SKYWALKER, *eating at a table.*

LUKE   Mine uncle, thou shouldst know my mind. Methinks
            The R2 unit we have bought belike
            May have been stolen.
OWEN   —Thievery hath e'er
            Been part and parcel of the Jawas' trade.
            But in thine utterance I sense there's more,   5
            So say, young Luke, why thinkest thou thereon?
LUKE   Good uncle, well I know the Jawas' tricks,
            Yet, as thou sayest, I mean something more.
            A stolen moment with those droids hath shown
            To me a reason they may stolen be: 10
            I did uncover a recording whilst
            I clean'd the R2 unit. He purports
            To be the property of someone known
            As Obi-Wan Kenobi. Thus, thought I,
            That he may stolen be. As to the name,   15
            This Obi-Wan Kenobi, wondered I
            If mayhap he meant Ben. Canst thou make sense?
OWEN   Nay.
LUKE   —Yet I wonder if this Obi-Wan
            Perchance may be some kin to yonder Ben.
OWEN   [*aside:*] Fie, fie! Shall that old man now
                                              haunt my home?   20
            [*To Luke:*] That wizard is a damnèd scurvy man.

Tomorrow shalt thou take the R2 droid
To Anchorhead and have its memory
Eras'd. And so shall there an end be to't.
For it belongeth only now to us.   25

LUKE   Aye, yet what if this Obi-Wan appears
And lays his claim unto this R2 droid?
What's stolen may be worth the looking for.

OWEN   The looking shall not happen, nor the find,
For I believe the man doth not exist.   30
[*Aside:*] Now shall I by a lie destroy the man,
Lest he be giv'n new life in Luke's young mind—
The boy a keen imagination hath.
[*To Luke:*] This Obi-Wan hath not for ages walk'd
Within this universe: he is no more.   35
'Twas many moons ago the old man died,
Aye, truly he hath met his end about
The time so long ago when wars were fought,
The time when men did battle to the grave,
The time before the Empire rul'd supreme,   40
The time wherein thy father died as well.

LUKE   Knew he my father?

OWEN   [*aside:*]   —Though I tell of men
And wars and battles brave, still all he hears
Is that word "father." [*To Luke:*] Prithee, Luke, forget.
Thy task is to prepare the droids for work   45
Tomorrow. In the morning shall they be
Upon the south ridge, laboring with those
Condensers.

LUKE   —Aye, and I believe these droids
Shall serve us well. In troth, good uncle, now

I must confess my mind is mov'd to think 50
Upon the pact 'twixt thee and me, and our
Agreement, namely that I shall stay here
Another season. Crops that grow in these
Harsh climes will surely grow sans me. And so,
Mine uncle, if these droids will satisfy 55
I wish my application to transmit
Unto the great Academy this year.

OWEN   Nay Luke, an uncle's heart is breaking! Canst
Thou mean the next semester hence, before
The harvest-time?

LUKE   —Just so! Quite plentiful 60
Are droids!

OWEN   —But harvest-time I need thee most!
Wilt thou here in the desert yet desert?
'Tis only one more season. This year I
Shall make enough at harvest-time to hire
More hands to help. Then canst thou go next year 65
To the Academy. To pilot is
A noble trade, my boy, but family
Is nobler still. I prithee, understand,
I need thee, Luke.

LUKE   —'Tis one more year entire!

OWEN   'Tis only one more season!

LUKE   —Aye, so saidst 70
Thou when my dear friends Biggs and Tank did leave.
Now cracks a hopeful heart, when, by the land,
A man's ambitions firmly grounded are:
So shall a bird ne'er learn to fly or soar
When wings are clipp'd by crops and roots and soil. 75

BERU   Pray whither fly'st thou, Luke?
LUKE   —It seems, dear aunt,
         I nowhere go nor flee nor sail nor fly.
         Instead, I must remain and clean those droids.

                                        [Exit Luke.

BERU   O Owen, he cannot abide for aye
         With us. 'Tis true, his friends are mostly gone.   80
         It hath great meaning for our well-lov'd Luke—
         This bird would surely fly.

OWEN   —So promise I
         That I shall set all things aright, Beru.
         The bird shall fly indeed, when time is ripe,
         And when the nest hath no more need of him.   85

BERU   But Owen, he hath not a farmer's heart—
         This apple falls quite near his father's tree.

OWEN   'Tis true! And this, my dear, is what I fear.

              [Exeunt Owen and Beru. Reenter Luke, gazing into
                        the setting of Tatooine's two suns.

LUKE   O, I am Fortune's fool. 'Tis true, 'tis true,
         And gazing now upon the double sun   90
         Of my home Tatooine, I know full well
         That elsewhere lies my destiny, not here.
         Although my uncle's will is that I stay,
         My heart within me bursts to think on it
         For out among the spheres I wish to roam—   95
         Adventure and rebellion stir my blood.
         Those oft-repeated words of my mate Biggs
         I do believe—that all the world's a star.
         Beyond that heav'nly light I shall fly far!

                                        [Exit.

ACT II

SCENE 1.

Inside the Lars homestead.

Enter C-3PO.

C-3PO   Alas! My R2-D2, he hath flown,
               And all the while he beepeth on and on
               About his duty in rebellion's cause.
               O with what strength shall I be punishèd
               When R2's treachery discover'd is!   5
               So shall I hide myself behind this ship
               In hopes I'll not be found by Master Luke.
                                        [C-3PO hides.

               Enter LUKE SKYWALKER.

LUKE   C-3PO, I say, what dost thou there?
               At what game playest thou, O jolly droid?
                                        [C-3PO emerges.

C-3PO   I prithee, Sir, be thou not cross with me.   10
               'Twas through no fault of mine, in truth I swear!
               Pray let me not deactivated be.
               I ask'd him, aye, and urg'd him not to go.
               With sighs and words aplenty plied I him—
               With many earnest pleadings made my cause—   15
               And yet he was to me as one made deaf.
               His metal ears, as 'twere, did seem to plug,
               As though no word of mine could penetrate
               And break upon his sense of hearing. O!

| | I fear a curs'd malfunction doth befall | 20 |
| | My dear and treasur'd R2 unit. | |

LUKE   —Nay!

C-3PO   Aye, verily! His mission is supreme,
          So sayeth he. He will not hinder'd be,
          Nor from his wayward, stubborn purpose veer.

CHORUS   Now with these words young Luke doth quickly run   25
          Beyond the shutter'd doors, with failing hope.
          And stepping out beneath the setting sun
          He scans the vast horizon with his scope.

C-3PO   Sir, ever hath that R2 unit been
          A problem that hath vex'd me through and through.   30
          Astromech droids have ever puzzl'd me:
          Their minds have tempers mighty to behold,
          Though all contain'd in frames of modest size.

LUKE   Fie! How have I so easily been trick'd?
          This R2 hath perform'd his greatest feat: 35
          To vanish—scope to wheels—into the air!
          O blast it! Aye, and fie and ficos too!

C-3PO   [aside:] Now he is anger'd. Peace, my Master, peace!
          [To Luke:] Good Sir, forgive my impudence, but may
          We yet this e'en go out asearching?

LUKE   —Nay.   40
          'Tis far too dangerous. The night is dark,
          But darker are the dreaded Sand People,
          And darkest most of all their thievery.
          Thus, as the darkness waits for light to dawn,
          So must we wait for morning to arrive.   45

OWEN   [inside:] O Luke, come hither! Swiftly come ye in!
          The time hath come to darken down the pow'r.

LUKE   Anon, good uncle! Thy good word I'll heed!
              [*To C-3PO:*] O, I shall taste the whips and scorns of my
              Dear uncle's anger. So shall that small droid,   50
              Though yet far gone, wreak havoc on my soul.

C-3PO   Aye, Sir, 'tis true. Although the droid is skill'd
              At laboring and service, most doth he
              Excel at wearying the hearts of men.
                        [*Luke and C-3PO withdraw for the night.*

CHORUS   And so a restless night doth pass within: 55
              While Luke doth ponder future punishment
              And longs for his lost droid search to begin,
              C-3PO doth fear his banishment.
              At early morn, with eager wills they rise,
              A shar'd endeavor binding them anew.   60
              The fast landspeeder o'er the desert flies—
              They go to find the errant droid R2.

              LUKE *and* C-3PO *enter, flying in landspeeder.*

LUKE   Good friend, take heed! The scanner doth report
              A droid ahead. Pray, swiftly take us hence—
              Belike our R2-D2 there awaits!   65
              [*Aside:*] Perhaps I'll escape my uncle's wrath.

CHORUS   While droid and man go racing 'cross the sand,
              The Tusken Raiders watch the two pass by.
              Their banthas mounting, gaffi sticks at hand,
              They heave unto the air their warring cry.   70

              Enter R2-D2.

          [Luke and C-3PO dismount to speak to R2-D2.

LUKE   Pray, whither goest thou, thou naughty droid?

R2-D2   Beep, meep, beep squeak.

C-3PO   —Nay, Master Luke is now

Thy rightful owner. Learn obedience!

Aye, learn thou loyalty! Pray, learn respect!

And learn thou not to speak of Obi-Wan   75

Kenobi!

R2-D2   —Whee, nee, squeak.

C-3PO   —Speak not to me

Of mission, droid! I'll warrant, happy thou

Shalt be if our new Master doth not let

Thee know the blaster's deadly touch today.

LUKE   Pray, patience, dear C-3PO, 'tis well.   80

But let us hence.

R2-D2   —Beep, whistle, nee, meep, squeak!

LUKE   What can the matter be? What doth he say?

C-3PO   He doth report that creatures hither come,

Approaching stealthily from the southeast.

LUKE   Sand People! Hither, come, and let us see!   85

[*Aside:*] Unbidden doth adventure come, yet here

I stand, prepar'd to rise and welcome Fate.

The twisting strand she threads we must but trail,

For 'tis the wire that leadeth us through life.

Fate's hand hath plac'd me here on Tatooine   90

And now she beckons onward to th'abyss.

Now o'er adventure's great abyss I perch—

Above all time, above the universe,

Above the rim of chance and destiny—

And sister Fate doth dare me to look in.   95

And there—aye there!— I find my happiness.
I peer therein, embrace my Fate—and blink.
Come, life! For I am ready now to live.
[*With scope, to droids:*] I spy two banthas,
                       yet no Sand People.
Wait, wait, one doth appear unto me now—   100

CHORUS   With sudden viciousness the Tuskens come,
They knock young Luke and cause the droid to fall.
They seek to take a harshly pillag'd sum,
Till frighten'd by a false krayt dragon call.

     Enter OBI-WAN KENOBI, *who has made a krayt dragon call to*
        frighten off the Tusken Raiders.

OBI-WAN   Now enter I the scene of this boy's life: 105
            This boy whom I have watch'd for many years
            Hath grown into the man before me now.
            My hope I now entrust to him alone,
            That he might be our sure deliverance.
            And yet, this situation warrants care—   110
            I must approach with caution as we speak,
            And meet his questions as a trusted guide.
            My inner joy I must with patience hide,
            For certain 'tis it gives me great delight
            To see him now—his face, his golden hair!   115
            So long have I watch'd o'er him from afar,
            So many hours and days of my life spent
            In hopeful expectation of this one.
            In his beginning I shall find my end;
            This business shall reveal my final stage.   120
            Yet in my closing scenes perhaps I'll write
            A worthy ending to my mortal days:
            'Tis possible that in this gentle one
            The dream I've long awaited shall come true.
            So I'll compose a final act that shall   125
            Accomplish two most worthy ends: to set
            The world aright and save this old man's soul.
            [To R2-D2:] Well met, my little one.
R2-D2   [aside:]   —Almost I could
            My metal tongue release and speak to him.
            This man doth show sure signs of wisdom and   130
            Experience. [To Obi-Wan:] Beep, beep, meep, beep,
               meep, squeak.
OBI-WAN   Come hither, tiny friend, be not afraid.

R2-D2	Beep, squeak, whee, hoo.
OBI-WAN	—Nay, prithee fret thou not.

For he shall make a full recovery.

[Luke wakes.

Rest easy, lad, for thou hast had a fall—   135
And more adventure hast thou seen today
Than many in a lifetime do. I say,
Thou catchest Fortune's favor to survive
A cruel attack from Sand People most vile.

LUKE   But, by this light! 'Tis Ben Kenobi here!   140
It fills my heart with joy and soothes my pain
To meet thee.

OBI-WAN   —Aye, 'tis well. But let's go hence.
The Jundland Wastes no place for trav'lers is.
Now prithee, good young Luke, say wherefore art
Thou here, and what strange errand bringeth thee   145
Herein where I am wont to dwell?

LUKE   —This droid.
Aye, truly, he hath brought me here.

R2-D2   —Beep, meep.

LUKE   It seemeth unto me that he doth search
To find his former master, yet in all
My days I ne'er have such devotion seen—   150
As this one showeth—from a droid.

R2-D2   —Hoo.

LUKE   —Yet
He claims that he belongeth to a man
Nam'd Obi-Wan Kenobi, and I thought,
Perchance, the man some relative of yours
May be. Dost thou know any by such name?   155

OBI-WAN	[*aside:*] O how the heart inside me breaks to hear
	That name I once was call'd so long ago—
	But happy Fate that 'tis Luke's voice that calls!
	[*To Luke:*] Aye, Obi-Wan Kenobi, Obi-Wan
	Kenobi. [*Aside:*] O, the name is like a song— 160
	Yet whether glorious song of joy or else
	Some dirge of bitter pain I'm yet unsure.
	[*To Luke:*] It is a name I have not heard for lo
	These many, many years—a long, long time.
LUKE	My uncle knoweth Obi-Wan, I ken. 165
	He doth report to me the man is dead.
OBI-WAN	[*aside:*] O Owen, wretched knave! Such base deceit,
	And yet I know full well why thou so spok'st.
	Should I have acted diff'rent in thy place?
	[*To Luke:*] But nay, the man takes not
	his final sleep. 170
	At least—unto this moment now—not yet.
LUKE	Then know'st thou him?
OBI-WAN	—Aye, verily I do.
	I know the man as if he were myself,
	For truly, aye, he is. This Obi-Wan,
	Dear Luke, 'tis I.
R2-D2	[*aside:*] —By heaven's light! [*To Obi-Wan:*]
	Beep, meep. 175
OBI-WAN	I have not heard this name, this Obi-Wan,
	Since ere e'en thou, thyself, wert born.
LUKE	—Aye, then,
	I see this little droid is bound to thee.
OBI-WAN	I have no memory of owning such
	A droid as this. 'Tis curious indeed. 180

[*Sound of Tusken Raiders aside.*] Now mark thee these
    my words: we must repair
Indoors to 'scape a second cudg'ling here.
The Sand People do easily take flight,
But soon they shall return with many more.

R2-D2   Beep, meep, beep, beep, meep, squeak!

LUKE   —C-3PO!   185

              [*C-3PO wakes, broken in pieces.*

C-3PO   Where am I? Have I ta'en an ill-tim'd step?
In dreams have I seen visions of my death—
Ten thousand soldiers pranc'd upon my grave,
And I, alone to face the murd'rous mass,
Could only weep at my untimely end.   190

LUKE   Peace, peace, good droid. Thou art alive, fear not.
Canst thou now stand? We quickly must depart
Before the Sand People attack us here
And strive to make thy dream reality.

C-3PO   O whether dream or waking, I know not,   195
But go thee hence, and save thyself, I pray.
C-3PO by nightmare hath been slain!

OBI-WAN   [*aside:*] This droid shall quickly stretch his welcome
                            thin.

LUKE   I shall not leave thee, droid, thou speak'st sans sense.
Come, come, I'll bear thee up, so argue not.   200

OBI-WAN   [*aside:*] What noble care he takes to soothe this droid.
[*To Luke:*] We must make haste or face them yet again,
So hence let us away unto my den.

                         [*Exeunt.*

SCENE 2.

Inside the Kenobi homestead.

Enter Obi-Wan Kenobi, Luke Skywalker, C-3PO, *and* R2-D2.

LUKE	Nay, thou art sure misled, O wise one, for
	My father hath not fought in any wars.
	Full many evenings as I lay abed
	Such tales I heard of him I never knew:
	A navigator on a freighter ship 5
	Which carried fragrant spices hence to yon
	My father was. He kneweth naught of wars.
OBI-WAN	So hath thine uncle told thee. Marry, he
	Did not agree with aught thy father told
	Of his philosophy and brave ideals. 10
	Thine uncle, tether'd to the land, did not
	Believe thy father should become involv'd
	In matters of the stars and Empires, nay.
	[*Aside:*] What shall I of the father tell the child?
	If gentle Luke knew all that's known to me 15
	I'll warrant he'd not understand the rhyme
	And reason for my words. And yet, what is't
	To lie? To tell the truth, all else be damn'd?
	Or else to tell, perhaps, a greater truth?
	Is it the truth to tell a boy each fact 20
	And thus deface his father's memory?
	Or have I spoken better truth to Luke
	When I about his father speak with pride?

Aye, ev'ry child deserves a champion.

LUKE   Hast thou done battle in the Clone Wars?

OBI-WAN   —Aye.   25

And once was I a Jedi Knight, the same
As thy dear father.

LUKE   —O, how tears well up

Within me for the loss of that dear man
Whom never I did know, nor do, nor will.

OBI-WAN   I tell thee truly, 'mongst the pilots he   30

Was e'er the greatest in the galaxy.
He also was a cunning warrior,
And to the last was he a dear, dear friend.
[Aside:] And now to play upon his natur'l sense
Of self-importance, so to draw him near   35
To thoughts of Jedi training for himself.
[To Luke:] I hear thou art a pilot skill'd as well.
This calleth to my mind a gift I have
For thee. Thy father hath desir'd that thou
Shouldst have this weapon when thou wert of age.   40
Thine uncle, though, would none of it, so fear'd
He that thou might adjoin with Obi-Wan
Upon a fool's crusade or devil's task
Just as thy father hath when he was young.

C-3PO   Dear Sir, if thou dost need me not, I shall   45

Shut down upon the present moment, here.

OBI-WAN   [aside:] Why speak'st he here when 'tis my time

to speak?

These droids of protocol are e'er uncouth:
Of etiquette they know but little, troth!

LUKE   Pray tell, what is't?

OBI-WAN	—Thy father's lightsaber.	50
	It is the weapon of a Jedi Knight:	
	If thou in thine own hand could hold a sun,	
	Then thou wouldst know the power of this tool.	
	Not merely random, neither awkward like	
	A blaster. Nay, the lightsaber maintains	55
	A noble elegance, a Jedi's pride.	
	'Tis something for a civiliz'd new age.	
CHORUS	Now holdeth Luke the weapon in his hand,	
	And with a switch the flame explodes in blue.	
	The noble light Luke's rev'rence doth command:	60
	That instant was a Jedi born anew.	
OBI-WAN	[*aside:*] Now doth the Force begin to work in him.	
	[*To Luke:*] For many generations Jedi were	
	The guarantors of justice, peace, and good	
	Within the Old Republic. Ere the dark	65
	Times came and ere the Empire 'gan to reign.	
LUKE	How hath my father died?	
OBI-WAN	[*aside:*] —O question apt!	
	The story whole I'll not reveal to him,	
	Yet may he one day understand my drift:	
	That from a certain point of view it may	70
	Be said my answer is the honest truth.	
	[*To Luke:*] A Jedi nam'd Darth Vader—aye, a lad	
	Whom I had taught until he evil turn'd—	
	Did help the Empire hunt and then destroy	
	The Jedi. [*Aside:*] Now, the hardest words of all	75
	I'll utter here unto this innocent,	
	With hope that one day he shall comprehend.	
	[*To Luke:*] He hath thy Father murder'd and betray'd,	

And now are Jedi nearly all extinct.
Young Vader was seduc'd and taken by   80
The dark side of the Force.
LUKE   —The Force?
OBI-WAN   —The Force.
The Force doth give a Jedi all his pow'r,
And 'tis a field of energy that doth
Surround and penetrate and bind all things
Together, here within our galaxy.   85
R2-D2   [*aside:*] In hearing this wise man I have almost
My errand quite forgot. Now to my work!
[*To Obi-Wan:*] Beep, meep, meep, squeak, beep, whee,
                    squeak, whistle, meep!
OBI-WAN   And now, my little friend, shall I attempt
To find out whence thou came, and to discern   90
The reason wherefore thou hast left thy home
For lands unknown, a mission to pursue.
LUKE   He hath a message play'd—
OBI-WAN   —Thus have I found.

Enter PRINCESS LEIA, *in beam projected by* R2-D2.

LEIA   Dear General Kenobi, many years
Ago thou serv'd my noble father in   95
The Clone Wars. Now, he beggeth thee to come
Again and aid him in his struggle with
The Empire. Sadly may I not be there
With thee in person, my request to give.
My ship of late hath fallen under siege   100
And thus my mission—bringing thee unto

My cherish'd planet Alderaan—hath fail'd.
Yet have I deep within the mem'ry banks
Of this brave R2 unit stor'd the plans
Most vital for rebellion's victory.   105
My father can retrieve the plans therein,
But I must ask of thee to take the droid
And bring him unto Alderaan with care.
The desp'rate hour is now upon us—please,
I beg thee, Sir. O help me, Obi-Wan   110
Kenobi, help. Thou art mine only hope.

              [Exit Princess Leia from beam.

CHORUS   The message ends, then doth a silence fall.
While Obi-Wan his duty contemplates,
Young Luke considers whether Fate doth call.
Aye—in this moment, destiny awaits.   115

OBI-WAN   *[aside:]* The boy doth hear and hath the taste of fire
New burning in his ears. Now shall I play
The part of fuel and gently stoke that fire.
[To Luke:] Thou must be taught the Force if thou
                       wouldst come
Away with me, and go to Alderaan.   120

LUKE   Nay, Alderaan? *[Aside:]* This man hath many charms,
And now it seems to me that I have been
These many hours under some great spell
That he hath cast. *[To Obi-Wan:]* Nay, I must hence
                       back home.
'Tis late, and Uncle Owen shall be vex'd,   125
If I do not return to him ere long.

OBI-WAN   *[aside:]* And now it must be done or else 'tis lost!
[To Luke:] I need all thy good help, Luke—so doth she.

	For such adventures I have grown too old.	
LUKE	Nay, nay, I should not be involv'd, dear friend.	130
	Much work there is to be completed yet,	
	And as the seers say true, a crop without	
	Its harvester is like a dewback sans	
	Its rider. Verily, I loathe the cruel	
	And noisome Empire, aye, yet nothing 'gainst	135
	It have I pow'r to do at present. Fie!	
	'Tis all so far, far distant from this place.	
OBI-WAN	Thus speaks thine uncle through thy lips, not thee.	
LUKE	Mine uncle, O, mine uncle! How shall I	
	To him explain this matter? Tell me, how?	140
OBI-WAN	Come now with me and learn the Force, dear Luke.	
LUKE	[aside:] Now am I split in twain by Fate's sharp turns.	
	Two paths: the one toward adventure leads,	
	The other taketh me back to my home.	
	I have, for all my life, long'd to go hence	145
	And now this Obi-Wan hath reason giv'n	
	Why I should leave my Tatooine and fly	
	Unto the stars. Aye, he hath told me of	
	The pow'rful Force. And yet, another force	
	Doth pull me home: the force of duty and	150
	Responsibility. I would go hence,	
	Would fly today and ne'er look back again,	
	Except Beru and Owen are my true	
	And loyal family. 'Tis settled, then,	
	I stay on Tatooine until the time	155
	When I may leave with clear, unfetter'd soul.	
	[To Obi-Wan:] I shall take thee as far as Anchorhead.	
	From there may'st thou find transport to where'er	

Thou goest—aye, throughout the galaxy.

OBI-WAN   Thou must hold with thy conscience, it is true,   160
            Whate'er thou thinkest right, thus thou shouldst do.

                                                          [Exeunt.

SCENE 3.
Inside the Death Star.

Enter Imperial generals and Senators, including ADMIRAL MOTTI
and COMMANDER TAGGE.

TAGGE   Until this battle station utterly
            Prepar'd and operational shall be,
            'Tis plainly vulner'ble to an attack.
            The rebels have more resources and are
            More dangerous that thou wilt deign to see.   5
MOTTI   Perhaps of danger to thy star fleet, aye,
            But not unto this battle station strong.
TAGGE   Rebellion shall gain more support within
            Th'Imperial Senate—

Enter GRAND MOFF TARKIN *and* DARTH VADER.

TARKIN   [*aside:*]   —O, these men do talk
            And quibble like a brood of clucking hens!   10
            [*To Tagge:*] Th'Imperial Senate, which thou speak'st
                                                          of here,
            No longer any threat to us doth hold.
            For truly have I just receivèd word

	That our great Emperor himself dissolv'd	
	The Council—now the final remnants of	15
	The Old Republic fade away like dew.	
TAGGE	But marry, 'tis impossible! How shall	
	The Emperor maintain control without	
	The crimson cord of vast bureaucracy?	
VADER	[*aside:*] O, how these politicians irk me so!	20
	Of governors and territories care	
	I not! But I retain their company	
	For mine own purposes, and though their talk	
	Doth tire my mind I do confess that naught	
	I've found hath on their counsel yet improv'd.	25
	For ev'ry human bond is meaningless:	
	All family doth leave, and friends betray,	
	And lovers fail, and teachers turn, and thus	
	Among the politicians shall I dwell—	

	Where lies, deceit, and garr'lous talk do make	30
	The universe go 'round. But yet, I vow:	
	I'll not be govern'd by the governors,	
	No policy of politicians heed.	
	Instead, myself and my dear Emperor	
	Together shall pursue our destiny.	35
TARKIN	The governors of all the regions now	
	Have sole control o'er their especial lands,	
	And fear shall keep the people all in line—	
	Fear of this very battle station, aye!	
TAGGE	But what, pray tell, of the Rebellion vile?	40
	For if the rebels have the plans to this	
	Good station stolen, possible it is	
	They may have found a weakness, which, in haste,	
	They shall exploit. Pray, Tarkin, mark my words.	
VADER	Those plans shall soon recover'd be, fear not.	45
MOTTI	Attack upon this station pointless is,	
	Regardless of the data they have found.	
	I speak not rashly when I here aver:	
	This station now hath power ultimate	
	O'er all else in the vast, wide universe!	50
	And now, I prithee, let us see it us'd!	
VADER	[to Motti:] Nay, peace! I warn thee, man, be not	
	too proud	
	Of thy great terror technological.	
	A weapon for the mass destruction of	
	A planet—even to destroy it whole—	55
	Is no match for the power of the Force.	
MOTTI	Thou shalt not 'tempt to frighten us with words	
	So like a man of magic, Vader. Nay,	

Thy sorc'rer's act is tir'd and overdone.
The sad religion thou dost cling to hath 60
No pow'r to conjure up the stolen plans.
Nor dost thou have a third-eye's sight to make—
　　　　[*Vader begins to choke Motti using the Force.*

CHORUS The power of the Force is now unveil'd
As Vader holds the Admiral in check.
The Force that Motti with his words impal'd 65
Now hath a wampa's hold about his neck.

VADER I find thy lack of faith disturbing.

TARKIN 　　　　—Cease!
No more of this! Good Vader, let him be.

VADER As is thy will. [*Aside:*] My point hath well been made
Upon his prideful, unbelieving throat. 70
　　　　　　[*Vader releases Motti.*

TARKIN   Enough! This endless bickering shall end.
            Lord Vader shall provide the setting of
            The errant rebel base before the time
            This station shall be operational.
            And then, my friends, the Empire shall rejoice—   75
            Rebellion shall be crush'd in one swift stroke!
            Now get ye gone, fulfill this purpose grand.
                    [Exeunt Imperial generals and Senators, including
                            Admiral Motti and Commander Tagge.

VADER   My troopers on the planet Tatooine
            Have trac'd the creatures who have found the droids.
            We shall retrieve those plans.

TARKIN   —'Tis well, 'tis well.   80
            Thou ever wert a faithful servant to
            The Emperor, Lord Vader. Prithee, go,
            And take with thee a gov'nor's gratitude.
                                    [Exit Darth Vader.
            There goes a man who hath a mind to serve.
            The Emperor doth hold him in his grasp,   85
            And lays a claim upon his heart and soul.
            Well I recall when, as a younger man,
            The Emperor and Vader with me stood
            And contemplated our shar'd destiny.
            Now Vader, split 'twixt manhood and machine,   90
            Fulfills a vital place within my plans.
            Aye, though I fear the Force, he knows his place.
            He knoweth he and I stand side by side—
            Together wrapp'd in power's warm embrace—
            Our Emperor to serve until, at last,   95
            The final curtain of life's play is dropp'd.

As history hath made this Tarkin great,
This battle station now shall make me fear'd.
I am as constant as the Endor moon,
And shall rebellion crush, and do it soon.   100

                 [Exit Grand Moff Tarkin.

SCENE 4.

The desert planet Tatooine.

Enter OBI-WAN KENOBI, LUKE SKYWALKER, C-3PO, *and* R2-D2,
surrounded by Jawa corpses.

LUKE   It seemeth that the Sand People have done
              This wretched deed—yon gaffi sticks and tracks
              Of bantha, aye. But ne'er in all my years
              Have Tuskens gone awry so far as this.

OBI-WAN   And they have not, though they who this vile deed   5
              Have done, would make us think Sand People did.
              But hark! Take note, and look ye thereupon:
              Yon tracks are side by side, yet Sand People,
              'Tis known, e'er one behind the other ride,
              So better may they hide their numbers large.   10

LUKE   These Jawas are the very same who sold
              C-3PO—and R2-D2, too—
              Unto mine uncle not two days ago.

OBI-WAN   And these marks here, these blast points, are too fine
              And accurate for Sand People, 'tis true.   15
              For only stormtroopers by Empire train'd
              Are so precise and cunning in their work.

[*Aside:*] Survey'ng this scene, I fear what cometh next,
For certain have the troops more evil done.
Good Owen and Beru no doubt are slain,   20
And though it breaks my heart to think on it,
It may be that their deaths will spark Luke's soul,
And lead him unto good rebellion's cause.
So by their death may others yet find life.

LUKE   But why, say why, would these Imperi'l troops   25
And why aught to do with Jawas? Wait, I see—
The droids! If they have trac'd them here they may
Have soon discover'd whom they sold them to,
Which—O, my soul!—would lead them to my home!

OBI-WAN   Pray, patience, Luke! 'Tis far too dangerous!   30
                              [*Luke runs to his landspeeder.*

CHORUS   Now flies Luke off in his landspeeder quick
And finds his home engulf'd in flames of red,
Then spies amid the smoke, so black and thick,
The bodies of his aunt and uncle, dead.
A sadder, wiser man he cometh back,   35
With noble purpose now his life's imbu'd.
By wrongful, vicious, cowardly attack,
The Empire hath Luke's passion quite renew'd.

OBI-WAN   'Twas nothing thou, Luke, couldst have done
                                            had thou
Been there. Thou murder'd would have been as well.   40
Aye, also would the droids now captur'd be
And would be in the Empire's evil hands.

LUKE   Thou knowest, friend, what I have seen today.
No sorrow like to this have I e'er known.
I wish to come with thee to Alderaan,   45

For nothing have I here on Tatooine.
Then shall I learn the Force, and shall become
A Jedi like my father. Thus I vow.
So let's prepare and go upon our way,
With haste may we escape the troopers vile.   50
          [*Exeunt Obi-Wan, C-3PO, and R2-D2.*
Adventure have I ask'd for in this life,
And now have I too much of my desire.
My soul within me weeps; my mind, it runs
Unto a thousand thousand varied paths.
My uncle Owen and my aunt Beru,   55
Have they been cruelly kill'd for what I want?
So shall I never want again if in
The wanting all I love shall be destroy'd.
O fie! Thou knave adventure! Evil trick
Of boyhood's mind that ever should one seek   60
To have adventure when one hath a home—
A family so kind and full of love,
Good, steady work, and vast, abundant crops—
Why would one give up all this gentle life

For that one beastly word: adventure? Fie!   65
But soft, my soul, be patient and be wise.
The sands of time ne'er turnèd backward yet,
And forward marches Fate, not the reverse.
So while I cannot wish for them to live,
I can my life commit unto their peace.   70
Thus shall I undertake to do them proud
And take whate'er adventure comes my way.
'Tis now my burden, so I'll wear it well,
And to the great Rebellion give my life.
A Jedi shall I be, in all things brave—   75
And thus shall they be honor'd in their grave.

                                        [Exit Luke.

ACT III

SCENE 1.

Mos Eisley, on the desert planet Tatooine.

CHORUS   Now, in her cell the princess doth remain,
            With hope and trouble written on her face.
            At times she faces torture, horrid pain.
            With these tools Vader seeks the rebel base.
            While Leia in her captive state is kept,   5
            Young Luke and Obi-Wan set on their way.
            Approaching town, they hope to intercept
            A pilot to transport them sans delay.

Enter OBI-WAN KENOBI, LUKE SKYWALKER, C-3PO,
and R2-D2, *riding in landspeeder.*

OBI-WAN   Mos Eisley spaceport. Never shalt thou find
            A hive more rank and wretched, aye, and fill'd   10
            With villainy. So must we cautious be.

Enter STORMTROOPERS.

TROOPER 3   I prithee, speak, how long hast thou these droids?
LUKE   'Tis three or, mayhap, four full seasons now.
OBI-WAN   We are prepar'd to sell them, shouldst thou wish.
CHORUS   Now is the Force to noble purpose us'd—   15
            Not as the Sith, employing it to smite,
            Hath through the dark side rank the Force abus'd—
            Good Obi-Wan shall use the Force for right.
TROOPER 4   Pray, show me now thy papers.

OBI-WAN   —Nay, thou dost
                Not need to see his papers.
TROOPER 4   —Nay, we do   20
                Not need to see his papers.
OBI-WAN   —True it is,
                That these are not the droids for which thou search'st.
TROOPER 3   Aye, these are not the droids for which we search.
OBI-WAN   And now, the lad may go his merry way.
TROOPER 3   Good lad, I prithee, go thy merry way!   25
OBI-WAN   Now get thee hence.
TROOPER 4   —Now get thee hence, go hence!
                                        [Exeunt stormtroopers.

Enter JAWAS *as* OBI-WAN KENOBI, LUKE SKYWALKER, C-3PO,
        and R2-D2 *dismount landspeeder.*

C-3PO   O, how those Jawas vex me!
LUKE   [*to Jawas:*]   —Get thee gone!
                                        [Exeunt Jawas.
                Now by my troth, I cannot comprehend
                How we those threat'ning stormtroopers did 'scape.
                Aye, verily, I thought our end was nigh.   30
OBI-WAN   The Force hath mighty power o'er the weak
                And simple-minded of this universe.
LUKE   Dost thou believe we shall therein, in yon
                Dank place, discover any pilot who
                Hath means to transport us to Alderaan?   35
OBI-WAN   A goodly crew of freighter pilots here
                May oft be found. But prithee, take good care,
                This small cantina hath an ill repute.

LUKE	I find myself prepar'd for ev'rything.
OBI-WAN	[*aside:*] The youth hath vigor—hopef'lly judgment,

too. 40

[They enter the cantina with many beings
and an innkeeper.

CHORUS	Now mark thee well, good viewer, what you see,
	Such varied characters are on display!
	For never hath there been such company
	As in Mos Eisley gathers day by day.
	The creatures gather 'round the central bar 45
	While hammerheads and hornèd monsters talk,
	A band compos'd of aliens bizarre:
	This is the great cantina—thou may'st gawk!
INNKEEP.	[*to Luke:*] A word! Herein we shall not serve their

kind—

Thy droids! They must depart beyond these walls.   50

LUKE   [*to droids:*] Good friends, pray wait beside the
                                              speeder now,
              For we desire no conflict here today.

C-3PO   I do with all my heart agree, dear Sir.
                                        [*Exeunt droids.*

Enter CHEWBACCA, *speaking with* OBI-WAN *and two beings
                      speaking to* LUKE.

BEING 1   Negola d'waghi wooldugger!

BEING 2   —I say!
              He liketh not thy look.

LUKE   —Forgive me, Sir.   55
              [*Aside:*] Nor do I like his face, yet do I groan?

BEING 2   I do not like thy look. Indeed, young lad,
              I bite my thumb at thee. Proceed with care,
              For we two men are wanted by the law.
              Aye, I have earn'd the penalty of death   60
              In many systems, and would gladly earn
              It here as well, if thou provoke me to't.

LUKE   [*aside:*] I would, mayhap, be fearful if this man
              Hath even shoulder height on me attain'd.
              [*To Being 2:*] Tut, careful shall I be.

BEING 2   —Thou shalt be dead!   65
                                        [*Obi-Wan approaches.*

OBI-WAN   Pray, peace, this little lad's not worth thy time.
              Now come, let us be friends, my goodly Sir,
              Then shall we to thy health and welfare drink.
                                        [*Being 2 strikes Luke;
                              Obi-Wan brandishes his lightsaber,*

injuring Being 2 and severing Being 1's arm.
Exeunt Beings 1 and 2.

OBI-WAN   [*aside:*] I have no wish or purpose here to fight,
            Yet have these drunkards left me little choice.   70
            But there is yet a lesson to be learn'd:
            This Obi-Wan, though old, hath still the gift.
            [*To Luke:*] Chewbacca here doth service as first mate
            Upon a ship that may our purpose meet.

            Enter HAN SOLO, *who joins* CHEWBACCA,
            OBI-WAN, *and* LUKE *at a table.*

HAN   Han Solo at thy service, gentlemen,   75
            The great *Millenn'um Falcon* is my ship.
            My first mate Chewie telleth me ye seek
            Safe passage to the system Alderaan.
OBI-WAN   Aye, true, if 'tis a vessel swift of flight.
HAN   "A vessel swift of flight," thou say'st? Hast thou   80
            Not heard of the *Millenn'um Falcon*, Sir?
OBI-WAN   [*aside:*] Now shall he boast. But if his ship we'd have,
            Some boasting we'll endure. [*To Han:*] Nay,
                                        should I have?
HAN   'Tis but the ship that hath the Kessel run
            Accomplish'd in twelve parsecs, nothing more.   85
            Imperi'l starships have I slyly 'scap'd,
            But nothing more of that. And neither do
            I speak about bulk-cruisers small, but vast
            Corelli'n ships, yet nothing more, no more.
            I shall not brag about her speed, good Sir.   90
            Suffice to say the ship shall fill thy needs,

As she's the fastest e'er. But nothing more.

LUKE   [*aside:*] Aye, nothing more, I wish he'd hold his peace.
This man, it seems, doth love his ship far more
Than ere I saw a man his woman love.   95

HAN   Pray tell, what shall the cargo be?

OBI-WAN   —Myself,
The boy, two droids, and ne'er a question ask'd.

HAN   'Tis what, a touch of local trouble here?

OBI-WAN   Nay, let us simply say it thus: we would
Imperial entanglements avoid.   100

HAN   Aye, there's the rub, so shalt thou further pay.
Ten thousand is the cost, and ev'ry bit
Shalt thou deliver ere we leave the dock.

LUKE   Ten thousand? Fie! We could our own ship buy
For such a sum as this.

HAN   —A goodly jest!   105
For who should pilot such a ship—shouldst thou?

LUKE   Thou knave, I could indeed! A pilot skill'd
Am I in my own right. [*To Obi-Wan:*] Now should
we stay,
And be abusèd more by this man's words?

OBI-WAN   Two thousand can we render to thee now,   110
And fifteen more deliver when we come
With safety unto Alderaan's bright port.

HAN   Say, seventeen? Congratulations, men,
Thou hast a ship secur'd, and we'll depart
Whene'er thou art prepar'd. Thou shalt find me   115
At docking harbor number ninety-four.

OBI-WAN   Aye, ninety-four.

HAN   —It seemeth that thou may

Already have provok'd some interest.
[Exeunt Obi-Wan and Luke as stormtroopers pass by.
CHEWBAC.   Egh.
HAN   —Seventeen! So must they desp'rate be!
This truly may my swift deliv'rance prove.   120
Go thou unto the ship and be prepar'd.
[Chewbacca exits.
In times now past have I poor judgments made,
And now these errors plague my very soul.
For freedom I was made—for taking wing!—
Yet as a markèd man I cannot fly.   125
For bound by debts, by duty and by fear,
I live my life along the razor's edge:
One part of me that hunts for better life,
And one part hunted for the life I've led.
My own existence is a paradox—   130
A smuggler with a lover's kindly heart,
A gambler with a noble spirit brave.
I would be better than it seems I am
If ever I transcend the man I was.
Perhaps this new employment shall reveal   135
The way I shall make straight my crooked path—
Thus heal my past and write a future new.

Enter GREEDO, *stopping* HAN SOLO *as the latter begins to exit.*

GREEDO   Na koona t'chuta, Solo?
HAN   —Yes, indeed,
Good Greedo, I have plann'd to make my way
Unto thy Master. Tell thou Jabba plain: 140

I have obtain'd his money.

GREEDO   —Soong peetch'lay.
Na mala tram pee chock makacheesa.
Na Jabba w'nin chee kosthpa murishan'
Tutyng ye wanya yoskah. Heh heh heh!
Na chas kee nyowyee koo chooskoo.

HAN   —'Tis true,   145
Yet this time is the money truly mine.

GREEDO   Keh lee chalya chulkah in ting coo'ng koos'.

HAN   [aside:] This bounty hunter doth my patience try.
[To Greedo:] Nay, nay, I have not money

with me now.
Tell Jabba—

GREEDO   —Ny'chi withi! Ayl garu   150
Puyay enya aru gagu shuku
Shunu pu'aa ipi.

HAN   —But even I
From time to time have boarded been. Dost thou
Believe that e'er I had the choice?

GREEDO   —Dro Jabb'.
Na paknee abnya apna.

HAN   —Nay, not that: 155
The day when Jabba taketh my dear ship
Shall be the day you find me a grave man.

GREEDO   Nay oo'chlay nooma. Chespeka noofa
Na cringko kaynko, a nachoskanya!

HAN   Aye, true, I'll warrant thou hast wish'd this day.   160

                                   [They shoot, Greedo dies.

          [*To innkeeper:*] Pray, goodly Sir, forgive me for the

                                        mess.

          [*Aside:*] And whether I shot first, I'll ne'er confess!

                                      [Exeunt.

SCENE 2.

Inside the Death Star.

Enter DARTH VADER, GRAND MOFF TARKIN, *and*
COMMANDER TAGGE.

VADER   The princess hath shown great resistance to

              The mind probe—'twere as if she knew the Force

              And hath a Jedi's blood to overcome

              The piercing of her mind by a machine.

              Belike it shall some length of time yet be   5

              Until we can extract the thoughts therein.

Enter ADMIRAL MOTTI.

MOTTI   The final tests are now complete at last.

              And thus my news: the Death Star stands prepar'd.

              Aye, fully operational it is.

              So, Governor, what course shall we now set?   10

TARKIN   Perhaps the stubborn princess shall respond

              To an alternative persuasiveness.

VADER   I prithee, Tarkin, say: what dost thou mean?

TARKIN   Pray patience, Darth—thou shalt my meaning learn.
                Now time it is the power of this Death   15
                Star shown to all shall be. Now, Admiral,
                Go forth and set thy course for Alderaan.
MOTTI   I understand thee, and with pride obey.
                          [Exeunt Grand Moff Tarkin, Commander Tagge,
                                                  and Admiral Motti.
VADER   The death of innocents doth bring me joy.
                Because the dark side is my chosen path,   20
                The senseless end of others pains me not.
                For I have play'd the part of judge severe
                And then have been the executioner.
                Why would I care for those on Alderaan,
                When I have murder'd innocents as they?   25
                'Tis my dark calling, which I do embrace.
                To Alderaan we fly on course direct,
                And to this feast of death I'll not object.
                                          [Exit Darth Vader.

SCENE 3.

Mos Eisley, on the desert planet Tatooine.

Enter C-3PO and R2-D2.

C-3PO   I prithee, lockest thou the door anon!
                                    [They hide behind door.

Enter STORMTROOPERS.

TROOPER 5   This door is lock'd. And as my father oft
             Hath said, a lockèd door no mischief makes.
             So sure am I that, thus, behind this door
             Cannot be found the droids for which we search.   5
             And thus may we move on with conscience clear.
                  [Exeunt stormtroopers. C-3PO and R2-D2 emerge.

C-3PO   I'll tell thee true, I would with Master Luke
             Prefer to go than now remain with thee.
             I do not know what trouble here may be,
             Yet certain am I thou deserv'st the blame.   10

R2-D2   [*aside:*] I'll warrant, thou shalt have thy recompense!
             [*To C-3PO:*] Squeak, whistle, beep, meep, nee, meep,
                                            whistle, squeak!

C-3PO   Hold thou thy cursing and most cursèd tongue!

Enter OBI-WAN KENOBI *and* LUKE SKYWALKER.

OBI-WAN   Thou must thy speeder sell.
LUKE   —That matters not.
             For ne'er shall I return unto this place.   15

CHORUS   Young Luke doth with a buyer swiftly meet,
             And in a trice a hasty deal is wrought.
             A speeder sold along a dusty street—
             But with the sale new chance for hope is bought.

LUKE   A paltry sum, in truth! Aye, ever since   20
             The XP-38 hath been releas'd,
             This model hath but little value. Fie!

OBI-WAN   Fear not—it shall suffice. 'Twill serve our need.
                                            [All stand aside.

CHORUS   Now while young Luke and Obi-Wan prepare,

Their deeds are watch'd by eyes as yet unseen.   25
With black beak menacing he spies the pair,
Then comes another fiend with portly mien.

Enter HAN SOLO *with* CHEWBACCA *and* JABBA THE HUTT
with henchmen.

JABBA	Ba'Solo! Hay lapa no ya, Solo!
HAN	[*aside:*] Now, marry, 'tis an unexpected scene.

       [*To Jabba:*] Aye, here, thou Jabba slimy and rotund.   30
       I have awaited long thy coming here.

JABBA	Boonowa tweepi. Heh, ho, ha!
HAN	—Nay, nay!

       Thou didst not think that I should run, didst thou?

JABBA   Na-Han mah bukee. Keel-ee c'leya kuk'h.

       Wanta dah moolee-rah? Muh wonkee chee   35
       Sa crispo Greedo?

HAN   —Next time thou dost wish

       To counsel hold with me, pray come thyself!
       Send not thy churlish dismal-dreaming knaves.

JABBA   Han, Han. Make-cheesay. Pa'sa tah nay

       Ono caulky malia. Ee youngee   40
       D'emperiolo teesaw. Twa spastik'
       Wahl no. Yanee dah poo noo.

HAN   —Nay, see here!

       As I have said before—O verily,
       'Tis though I just have said thus—even I
       From time to time have boarded been. Dost thou   45
       Believe that e'er I had the choice? [*Aside:*] Aye, true,
       It sometimes seemeth I repeat myself.

[*To Jabba*:] Now have I, though, a simple charter
                               found,
And soon as it is done, thy payment shall
Be done as well—belike with interest.   50
I need but time and I shall do it, Sir.

JABBA   Na-Han ma bukee. Bargon yanah cot'
               Da eetha. See fah luto tweentee, ee

	Yaba na—
HAN	—Nay, say thou not so much.
	Fifteen percent, I'll warrant, shall be well. 55
JABBA	See fah luto eetheen, ee yaba ma
	Dukey massa. Eeth wong che coh pa na
	Geen, nah meet' toe bunk' dunko. Lo choda!
HAN	O Jabba, thou wert e'er a kindly soul.
JABBA	Boska!

[Exeunt Jabba and henchmen.

OBI-WAN	—Now if yon ship is truly fast, 60
	As quick as this Han Solo boasted so,
	We shall do well.
LUKE	[*spying ship:*] —What folly-fallen ship
	Is this? What rough-hewn wayward scut is here?
HAN	Point-five past light speed shall she make, my lad.
	Now truly, earneth she low marks for looks, 65
	But still a finer spirit hath no ship.
	Full many small improvements have I made
	To render her e'en faster than before.
	Now, marry, gentlemen, if thou agree,
	We shall be off, and speedily, from here. 70
	[*Aside:*] And if thy mouth insulteth it again,
	I promise, boy, thy face shall meet my hand.

[Chewbacca, Obi-Wan, Luke, C-3PO,
and R2-D2 board ship.

CHORUS	But ere the ship departs the sandy dock,
	The stormtroopers appear with massive threat.
	Informèd by the beak'd spy's trait'rous talk, 75
	They come upon the ship, with weapons set.

Enter STORMTROOPERS.

TROOPER 5   Pray, stop yon ship! Aye, blast them to the stars!
HAN   Chewbacca, prithee, hence! Now let us go!
C-3PO   O, traveling in space, it works me woe!

                                        [Exeunt.

SCENE 4.

Space, aboard the Millennium Falcon.

CHORUS   Mos Eisley now is left behind at last,
              While newer scenes come into view apace.
              As Han's *Millenn'um Falcon* flies far fast
              The action of our play moves back to space!

Enter CHEWBACCA *and* HAN SOLO, *in ship.*

CHEWBAC.   Egh, auugh!
HAN   —Now are we follow'd hard upon   5
              By an Imperi'l cruiser. Verily,
              These passengers of great import must be
              For they by th'Empire hotly are pursu'd.
              Chewbacca, prithee, swift make our defense
              And angle the deflector shield whilst I   10
              Make plain the calculations for light speed.

Enter OBI-WAN KENOBI *and* LUKE SKYWALKER.

              Now vigilance, my Wookiee! Quickly come

	Two further ships, to try and block our path.
LUKE	Nay, wherefore canst thou not outrun them both?
	For thou didst boast of this strange vessel's speed.

15

HAN	[*aside:*] Again he prattles on about the ship!

O would that I had left him on the ground.

[*To Luke:*] Pray mark thy words, lad, else thou

surely wilt

Become like refuse to a Star Destroy'r

And float away to vanish midst the stars.   20

I'll warrant we shall soon in safety fly,

Once we the jump to hyperspace can make.

And what is more, my skill doth all exceed

At making keen maneuvers. All my life

Have I escap'd one scrape and yet one more.   25

Well I remember when—as but a boy—

I chas'd a nerf whilst on a speeder bike.

Through rocky field in harsh terrain we went,

Within, around and backward was our game.

I caught the nerf that splendid day, but aye,   30

It seems I have been dodging ever since.

OBI-WAN	How long, now, ere thou canst achieve lightspeed?
HAN	A few more moments shall it take whilst this
	Computer doth its navigation work.
LUKE	But art thou mad? For certain they approach! 35
	I have not made this journey just to die.
	[*Aside:*] This man shall surely be the end of me.
HAN	The travel unto hyperspace is not
	The same as thine a'dusting of the crops
	Upon thy land of infinite dry sand. 40
	Sans calculations quite exact, we would

Belike run through a belt of asteroids,
Or hit upon a planet's center mark.
Should such our fate become, thy trip would end
Before it had begun.

LUKE   —But O, what now?   45
What light through yonder flashing sensor breaks?

HAN   It marks the loss of yon deflector shield.
I bid thee, peace! Now sit and thou take heed,
For all's prepar'd to jump unto lightspeed.

CHORUS   Han graspeth quick the console in his hand,   50
Then suddenly the ship is bath'd in light.
With roar of engine—noise profound and grand—
The great *Millenn'um Falcon* takes her flight.

[*Exeunt.*

SCENE 5.

Inside the Death Star.

Enter GRAND MOFF TARKIN *and* ADMIRAL MOTTI.

MOTTI   Now are we come to th'system Alderaan.

Enter PRINCESS LEIA, *bound, with guards and* DARTH VADER.

LEIA   Ah! Gov'nor Tarkin, scurvy knave art thou.
Now seems it plain to me that Vader doth
Perform the part of docile dog unto
The sick'ning whinny of his Master's voice.   5
Familiar stench of dog's best friend have I

Mark'd deep within my sense of smell e'en when
I came unto this station.

TARKIN   —Ever wert
Thou charming, Leia, even to the last.
Thou couldst not comprehend how hard it was—   10
Aye, verily, how I did sigh and weep—
To give the order to destroy thy life.

LEIA   Surpris'd am I thou had the courage so
To take responsibility for such
As this unto thy cowardly, small self.   15

TARKIN   [aside:] She groweth ever bolder, which doth but
Increase my appetite to see her scream.
[To Leia:] My Princess, ere thou executed art,
I would thou join me for a moment full
Of pomp and circumstance. For at this grand   20
And noble cerem'ony shall the pow'r
Of this great battle station here be shown
To be quite fully operational.
Now no star system shall e'er dare oppose
The Emperor.

LEIA   —O but how wrong thou art!   25
The more that thou dost exercise thy grip,
The more star systems through that grip shall fall.

TARKIN   Not after we have shown the power vast
This battle station shall to them display.
And to the point: thou hast determin'd what   30
The prim'ry demonstration of its force
Shall be—which planet shall oblivion face.
[Aside:] Now shall I drive this nail unto its home,
And watch with joy as she with grief is torn.

	[*To Leia:*] Since thou hast so refus'd to grant to us	35
	The hid location of the rebel base,	
	I shall unleash this station's pow'r upon	
	Thine own home planet—even Alderaan.	
LEIA	Nay, do not so to peaceful Alderaan!	
TARKIN	Thou shalt a military target name,	40
	Then render swift the system's name as well.	
	Or else thy precious Alderaan goes to't.	
	I tire of asking o'er and o'er, so thus	
	I promise: this shall be the final time—	
	Where is thy rebel base?	
LEIA	—On Dantooine.	45
	They may be found on planet Dantooine.	
TARKIN	Ha, ha! Thou seest, Vader, how a cat	
	May have her claws remov'd. Now, Admiral,	
	Thou mayst continue with thy weapon's test,	
	And surely mayst thou fire when all's prepar'd.	50
LEIA	What madness here?!	
TARKIN	—Thou far too trusting art.	
	The tiny Dantooine is too remote	
	To show this station's pow'r but pray, fear not,	
	We shall in time thy rebel friends pursue.	
CHORUS	To do the Governor's most evil will,	55
	The people on the Death Star quickly rise.	
	With mighty flash, the beam bursts bright and shrill	
	And Alderaan is shatter'd 'fore their eyes.	
LEIA	[*sings:*] When Alderaan hath blossom'd bright,	
	Then sang we songs of nonny,	60
	But now her day is turn'd to night,	
	Sing hey and lack-a-day.	

My friend and I stood by the river,
Then sang we songs of nonny,
But I could not her soul deliver,   65
Sing hey and lack-a-day.
My planet hath the bluest shore,
Then sang we songs of nonny,
That noble land is now no more,
Sing hey and lack-a-day.   70

                                        [*Exeunt.*

SCENE 6.

Space, aboard the Millennium Falcon.

Enter OBI-WAN KENOBI, LUKE SKYWALKER, C-3PO, R2-D2,
and CHEWBACCA.

CHORUS   The instant Alderaan is smash'd to bits,
              Luke tries his lightsaber—a keen trainee.
              The droids and Wookiee play a game of wits,
              But Obi-Wan doth sense catastrophe.
OBI-WAN   [*aside:*] Now breaks my heart as through the
                                        Force I sense   5
              The suffering of many worthy souls.
              I know not what this doth portend, and yet
              I fear the worst.
LUKE   —Good Sir, how farest thou?
OBI-WAN   Forsooth, a great disturbance in the Force
              Have I just felt. 'Twas like a million mouths   10
              Cried out in fear at once, and then were gone,

All hush'd and quiet—silent to the last.
I fear a stroke of evil hath occurr'd.
But thou, good Luke, thy practice recommence.

Enter HAN SOLO.

HAN   Thou mayest all thy troubles now forget,   15
Th'Imperi'l knaves have been outrun at last.
[*Aside:*] Well here's a solemn gathering indeed,
Quite lacking in the proper gratitude.
[*To Obi-Wan and Luke:*] Nay, speak thou not thy
                              thanks too heartily,

Else shall thy praise go swiftly to my head.   20
But here's the point, we shall at Alderaan
Arrive ere long.
                    [*R2-D2 makes a move against Chewbacca*
                                    in the game they play.

C-3PO   —Pray, R2, caution show.

R2-D2   Beep, whistle, squeak, beep, meep, hoo whistle.

CHEWBAC.   —Auugh!

C-3PO   A fair move hath he made, thou furry lump.
               No use is there in screaming o'er the loss.   25
               [*Aside:*] However did I join this company?
               A Wookiee and his smuggler captain—O!

CHEWBAC.   Egh.

HAN   —Be thou wise, droid, mark well what
                                                thou dost.
               As it is said: black holes are worth thy fear,
               But fear thou more a Wookiee's deadly wrath.   30

C-3PO   But Sir, no proverb warns the galaxy
               Of how a droid may hotly anger'd be.

HAN   Aye, marry, 'tis because no droid hath e'er
               Torn out of joint another being's arms
               Upon a lesser insult e'en than this—   35
               But Wookiees, golden droid, are not so tame.

C-3PO   Thy meaning, Sir, doth prick my circuit board.
               'Tis best to play the fool, and not the sage,
               To say it brief: pray let the Wookiee win.

CHEWBAC.   Auugh!

R2-D2   [*aside:*]   —Brute! The fool I'll play with
                                                thee, indeed.   40
               Yet I perceive thou and thy friend have heart.

          [Luke continues to practice with his lightsaber
                            against the remote.

OBI-WAN   Remember, Luke, the Force doth smoothly flow
           Within the feelings of a Jedi Knight.

LUKE   But doth the Force control one's ev'ry move?

OBI-WAN   'Tis somewhat so, but also shall the Force   45
           Obey thine every command, young Luke.

LUKE   *[aside:]* This Force, by troth, I'll never comprehend!
           It doth control and also doth obey?
           And 'tis within and yet it is beyond,
           'Tis both inside and yet outside one's self?   50
           What paradox! What fickle-natur'd pow'r!
           Aye: frailty, thy name—belike—is Force.
           [To Obi-Wan:] Alack! This small remote hath
                             struck again!

HAN   Ha, ha! Thy errant systems of belief—
           Thy weapons ancient, all thy mysteries,   55
           Thy robes and meditations o'er the air,
           Thy superstitions, e'en thy precious Force—
           Cannot compare to my religion true:
           A trusty blaster ever by my side.
           With thus I say my prayers and guard my soul.   60

LUKE   Devoted foll'wer must thou be, with such
           A speech. Pray tell me, pilgrim reverent:
           Dost thou most truly disbelieve the Force?

HAN   A pilgrim, truly said! For I have gone
           From galaxy to galaxy and more,   65
           Yet never hath this faithful worshipper
           Found aught to recommend that strange belief—
           A single Force that binds the universe.

True 'tis, no power mystical controls
Han Solo's yet unfinish'd destiny.   70
And so I preach the one and only faith:
My simple, merry tricks are all my gods,
And nonsense is the only testament.
I worship at the shrine of my own will.

OBI-WAN   [*aside:*] A wise philosopher if e'er there was.   75
I'll warrant he hath character he hides.
[*To Luke:*] Now prithee, try again, and lay aside
Thy conscious self. Take thou this helmet thick,
Adorn thine eyes with silver shield opaque
And trust thine instincts only as thy guide.   80

LUKE   But surely 'tis a jest! For with this shield
I nothing now can see. How can I fight?
Aye, truly—fight or walk or even stand?
Without one's sight but little can be done.

OBI-WAN   Nay, 'tis in blindness one doth truly see!   85
For eyes deceive and sight is known to lie.
Let feelings be thy sight—their guidance trust!

CHORUS   With mind unsure Luke readies for the fight.
The small remote doth dodge most suddenly,
But with calm mind Luke blocks its lasers bright—   90
With inner eye the Force has let him see.

OBI-WAN   Hurrah! Thou canst do it!

HAN   —'Tis luck, no more.

OBI-WAN   Experience hath taught me much, dear man,
And none of it hath shown me aught of luck.

HAN   To find success against a small remote,   95
Is well, and taketh skill, I do confess.
To find success against a living soul,
However, also taketh excellence.

         [Console beeps.

It seemeth we draw near to Alderaan.

         [Exeunt Han Solo and Chewbacca.

LUKE   I did feel something, Obi-Wan, 'tis true.   100
It seems I fix'd my soul's eye on th'remote.

OBI-WAN   Seems, young one? Nay, thou didst! Think thou

         not seems.

Thou hast thy first step ta'en toward a world
Far greater than thou now canst understand.

         [Exeunt Luke, C-3PO, and R2-D2.

And thus begins—if I have seen aright—   105
His transformation into Jedi Knight.

         [Exit Obi-Wan.

SCENE 7.

Inside the Death Star.

Enter DARTH VADER *and* GRAND MOFF TARKIN.
Enter OFFICER CASS *opposite.*

CASS   My Lord, our scout ships have reach'd Dantooine.
                Remains of th'rebel base the scouts have found,
                Yet surely hath it been a length of time
                Deserted. Now shall they begin to search
                Surrounding systems, so to find the base.   5
                                        [Exit Officer Cass.

TARKIN   The wench hath lied! Deceiving, cut-throat girl,
                Most cunning princess born of Hell's own heart!

VADER   I knew full well she never would betray
                Her priz'd Rebellion whilst in her right mind.
                And thus I said: she ne'er should have our trust.   10

TARKIN   Destroy her! 'Tis a sentence more than just.
                                        [Exeunt.

SCENE 8.

Space, aboard the Millennium Falcon.

Enter HAN SOLO *and* CHEWBACCA.

HAN   Now dropping out of light speed's frantic rush
                We enter swift unto the area
                Where should there be great Alderaan in view.

But pray, what madness meets the *Falcon*'s flight?
Is this an ast'roid field I see before me?   5
The ship hath wrought a course direct and true,
And yet no Alderaan may here be found.
O errand vile, O portents of great ill!
What shall it mean, when planets are no more,
For those who make their wages by the stars?   10

    Enter OBI-WAN KENOBI *and* LUKE SKYWALKER.

LUKE   What news, good Han?
HAN   —The ship's position hits
            The mark, and yet no Alderaan there is.
LUKE   I pray thee, marry, say: what canst thou mean?
            How can a planet vanish in the air?
HAN   Thou hast said right, my lad. It is not there.   15
            The planet's gone, all turned to rock and ash.
LUKE   Thou speak'st not right. Say how? Pray how?
                                              Tell how!
OBI-WAN   Destroy'd it was, and by the Empire cruel.
HAN   A thousand thousand ships could not destroy
            The planet. Truly 'twould take greater pow'r   20
            Than ever there was known to humankind.
            But soft! Another ship approaches quick.
            [A small ship flies quickly past the Millennium Falcon.
LUKE   Belike they can the tale to us relate.
OBI-WAN   Imperi'l fighter 'tis.
LUKE   —Hath it made chase?
OBI-WAN   Nay, nay! A short-range fighter 'tis. *[Aside:]* O how   25
            This situation here doth give me pause.

HAN	No base is there nearby. Whence cometh it?
	[*Aside:*] The courage in me melts away at this.
	My boasts cannot resolve this mystery.
LUKE	The ship departeth swiftly! If they have 30
	Identifi'd our lot, we shall have strife.
HAN	'Tis my intent to keep us from that Fate.
	Chewbacca, render its transmissions block'd.
OBI-WAN	Pray, let it go, 'tis too far flown.
HAN	—Not long!
OBI-WAN	Dost thou agree—a fighter of its size 35
	This deep in space could not have come alone?
LUKE	Belike 'twas in a group and now is lost.
HAN	It shall not live to tell the tale today.
LUKE	Forsooth! He makes his way to that small moon.
HAN	I may play checkmate on him ere he lands. 40
OBI-WAN	Alas—I sense the game, and we're the pawns.
	That is no moon. 'Tis a space station there.
	[*The Death Star looms in the distance, growing closer.*
HAN	'Tis far too large a space station to be.
LUKE	My feelings now do stir, I sense them well!
	They tell me we shall lose the match we play. 45
OBI-WAN	Pray, turn thee now the ship around.
HAN	—I shall!
	Now Chewie, lock thou quick th'auxill'ry pow'r.
LUKE	Why do we still approach? What can be done?
HAN	It hath th'advantage, using tractor beam
	To pull us in, unto its landing bay. 50
LUKE	But pray, some move thou must have left to make!
HAN	My moves are finish'd, lad, I must shut down,
	Else shall the ship entire soon come apart.

But still, with all my players I shall fight.

OBI-WAN   Thou canst not win, but will by strategy   55

Some good alternatives to fighting see.

CHORUS   So enters the *Millenn'um Falcon* in

Unto the Death Star, grand and stark and mean.

With fear the Wookiee and the three brave men

Look on as their space journey changes scene.   60

Meanwhile, the denizens within the base

Make haste to catch the ship that cometh near.

Commanders come with well-arm'd guards apace,

While stormtroopers do at their posts appear.

                                              [Exeunt.

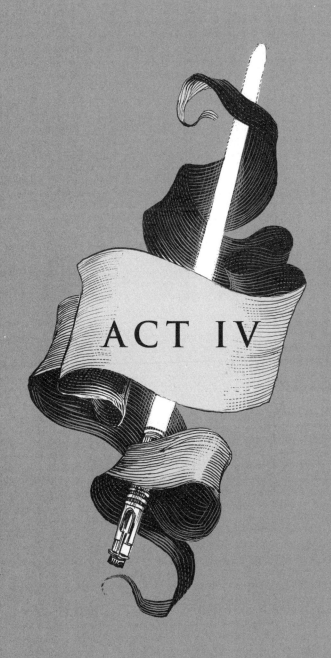

ACT IV

SCENE 1.

Inside the Death Star.

Enter DARTH VADER, GRAND MOFF TARKIN, *and* ENVOY.

ENVOY   A freighter hath been captur'd entering
               The system Alderaan. Its markings match
               A ship that hath Mos Eisley quickly fled.
VADER   This errant ship, belike, endeavors to
               Return the plans unto the princess who,   5
               Within this base, is lock'd in guarded cell.
               [*To Grand Moff Tarkin:*] Perhaps the princess yet
                                             hath use to us.
               [*Exit Grand Moff Tarkin. Vader crosses to the ship.*

Enter OFFICER 1, STORMTROOPERS, *and* GUARDS 1 *and* 2.

OFFICER 1   No person is aboard the ship, my Lord.
               The log maintain'd on board doth tell a tale
               Of all the crew abandoning the ship   10
               Directly after its departure. 'Tis
               No doubt a decoy, Sir. For all the pods
               Have launchèd been.
VADER   —Hast thou found any droids?
OFFICER 1   Nay, truly not, my Lord. If there had been,
               Then surely must they have abandon'd too.   15
VADER   Send thou a scanning crew aboard the ship,
               And check its nooks and crannies, ev'ry bit.
OFFICER 1   Aye, good, my Lord.

VADER   [*aside:*]   —Distract'd is my mind,
                But through its cloudy haze the reason comes:
                Unless I am in error, someone here   20
                Has come. I have not felt this presence since
                The days that are but dark in memory.
                This presence I have known since I was young,
                This presence that once call'd me closest friend,
                This presence that hath all my hopes betray'd,   25
                This presence that hath turn'd my day to night.
                This awful presence present here must be,
                So shall I to this presence violence
                Present.
                                [Exit Darth Vader.

OFFICER 1   —Now to thy work, and scan the ship!
TROOPER 5   The scan is done; no living soul is here.   30
                        [Exeunt stormtroopers.

      Enter OBI-WAN KENOBI, LUKE SKYWALKER, HAN SOLO,
      CHEWBACCA, C-3PO, *and* R2-D2, *hidden.*

LUKE   'Tis fortunate thou hast these storage bins.
HAN   Their use hath ever been for smuggling goods.
                Ne'er have I thought I would myself herein
                Be smuggling. All we do is madness—fie!
                If I could start the ship, the tractor beam   35
                Would wrap its eagle's talons 'round my neck.
OBI-WAN   The tractor beam thou may'st leave unto me.
HAN   Thou fool, I knew that thou wouldst say as much.
OBI-WAN   Aye, say thou fool? Then fool, good Sir, am I.
                But when thou sayest fool remember well   40

That fools do walk in foolish company.
So if I am a fool, perhaps 'tis true
That other fools around me may be found.
For who is he who hath more foolish been—
The fool or other fool who follows him?   45

[*They hide. Guards 1 and 2 standby while scanning
crew enters ship and are bested by Obi-Wan, Luke,
Han Solo, and Chewbacca.*

GUARD 1   Oi! Didst thou hear that sound?

GUARD 2   —Pray, hear a sound?

GUARD 1   Aye, truly—I quite clearly heard a sound.

GUARD 2   Thine ears, mayhap, play tricks on thee, my friend.

GUARD 1   Nay, nay. Dost thou not think this strange?

GUARD 2   —What strange?

GUARD 1   The droids did flee the ship we have attack'd,   50
            And unto Tatooine have gone by pod.
            'Tis true, thus far?

GUARD 2   —I cannot claim 'tis false.

GUARD 1   On Tatooine they have been tracèd first
            To Jawas vile and then to humans—

GUARD 2   —Dead.

GUARD 1   Aye, dead they are—our men did see to it.   55
            But follow on: the boy who with them liv'd
            Hath fled, we knew not where, till he was seen
            At yon Mos Eisley with the pair of droids.

GUARD 2   Aye, aye, 'twas all in last week's briefing. Pray,
            What more of this? Hast thou aught new to say?   60

GUARD 1   The boy and droids together disappear'd
            The very hour the ship—this ship—did fly.
            And now, the ship is here, though empty seems.

GUARD 2   Nay, empty 'tis! The scanning crew doth work
                E'en now.

GUARD 1   —Which bringeth me full circle to   65
                The sound I just have heard. Is't possible,
                My friend, that boy and droids and rebels all
                Have flown within this ship unto this base
                And yet—e'en now—whilst thou and I do speak,
                Still hide within the ship?

GUARD 2   —I am amaz'd!   70

GUARD 1   Aye, verily? Think'st thou I may be right?

GUARD 2   I said thou hast amaz'd me, and 'tis true.
                But never did I say I think thee right—
                Thou dost amaze by thy o'eractive thoughts!
                A hidden boy! The droids within! A fig!   75
                Avaunt, thou silly guard, be not so thick.
                Thy great imagination hath o'erwrought
                Thy better senses. Thinkest thou thy pow'rs
                Of judgment far exceed our Masters true?
                May'st thou outwit the great Darth Vader or   80
                The cunning of our Gov'nor Tarkin? Nay!
                We are but simple guards, our purpose here
                Is plain and to the point: we have been task'd
                To watch the ship and follow all commands,
                And not to prattle on with airy thoughts.   85

GUARD 1   Aye, thou hast spoke a well-consider'd word.
                Thou art a friend, as I have e'er maintain'd,
                And thou hast spoken truth and calm'd me quite.
                The rebels hide herein! What vain conceit!
                That e'er they should the Death Star enter—ha!   90

GUARD 2   It warms my heart to see thee so restor'd

And back to thine own merry, native self.

HAN   [*within:*] Pray, may we have thy good assistance here?

GUARD 1   [*to Guard 2:*] So, let us go together, friend. Good

cheer!

[*Guards 1 and 2 enter ship and are killed.*

Exeunt others.

SCENE 2.

Inside the Death Star.

Enter OFFICERS 2 *and* 3.

OFFICER 2   Say—TK-421, now wherefore hast
Thou left thy station? TK-421,
Canst thou my message hear? [*To Officer 3:*] Take
thou command,
Belike he hath a bad transmitter. So
Shall I attend and help him if I may.   5

Enter OBI-WAN KENOBI, C-3PO, R2-D2, *and* CHEWBACCA
with HAN SOLO *and* LUKE *dressed as stormtroopers, killing*
Officers 2 and 3.

CHORUS   Now through the doorway come our heroes brave.
Th'Imperi'l officers Chewbacca fights
Whilst Han with blaster doth his entry pave.
They have arriv'd: escape is in their sights.

CHEWBAC.   Auugh!

LUKE   —Fie! With all this howling nonsense and   10

O! Strangely sweeps the thought into my mind:
I have a feeling through the Force that ere
We leave this place, some seven shall we be.
Yet one shall stay behind as sacrifice.
Thus seven and thus one: the numbers tell   40
The story that herein shall soon be told.
[*To Luke and Han:*] Methinks ye two cannot assist
                            me now.

This one—e'en I—shall go alone.

HAN   —Aye, good!
So shall I hearken unto what thou sayst,
For I already on this voyage have   45
Done more than that for which I have been paid.

LUKE   I would go with thee, Sir.

OBI-WAN   —Pray, patience, Luke,
For thou must stay and guard the vital droids.
They must be taken safely to our friends,
Or other systems end like Alderaan.   50
Thy destiny, dear boy, doth truly go
Upon a path far different from mine,
And Fate for thee hath spun another thread
Than what she hath for Obi-Wan's life stitch'd.
The Force, it shall be with thee always, Luke.   55
                          [*Exit Obi-Wan.*

LUKE   [*aside:*] He hath bestow'd a Jedi's blessing here,
So why then am I utterly unnerv'd?

CHEWBAC.   Auugh!

HAN   —Wookiee, thou hast spoken well
and true:
Whence hast thou this old bag of bones uncover'd?

With all thy blasting 'tis a miracle
That all within the station have not heard
Of our arrival.

HAN   —Surely, let them come!
A fight would I prefer to sneaking yon
And hither.

R2-D2   —Beep, beep whistle, squeak, beep

C-3PO   We have the outlet for the system found.
          [*Aside:*] O that my words might end their bic

OBI-WAN   'Tis well! Plug R2 in and he shall read
          The whole Imperi'l network.

R2-D2   —Beep, meep, squeak!
          Hoo, whistle, whee, ahh, beep, meep, squeak,
                                                    beep

C-3PO   Now hath he found the main control unto
          The power beam that holds the ship herein.
          He shall attempt to show thee, presently,
          Where its exact location may be found.
          The tractor beam in seven places is
          Connected to the main reactor, but
          A power loss at any terminal
          Shall set the good *Millenn'um Falcon* free.

OBI-WAN   [*aside:*] That number seven shall our freedom n
          But only one of seven shall we need.
          I fear those numbers—seven and then one—
          Do something dangerous portend. But why?
          Our company is only six, unless
          There were another join'd unto us here.
          Then were we seven, yet what means the one?

LUKE	Yon Ben in all good virtues doth excel.	60
HAN	Aye, certain he excelleth when the goal	
	Is but to lead us into trouble great.	
LUKE	But thou hast not excell'd at offering	
	A thought to how we can this station 'scape.	
HAN	Yet any simple plan excelleth o'er	65
	Remaining here till all descend on us.	
	It taketh not a wisdom that excels	
	To know for certain fact that such is true.	
R2-D2	[*aside:*] By heav'n I'll stop their bickering with this	
	New information. [*To Han and Luke:*] Whistle,	
	beep, meep, whee!	70
LUKE	I prithee, what doth all this beeping mean?	
C-3PO	Sir, I confess I do not know. He hath	
	Declar'd that he hath found her, then the droid	
	Repeats "She's here, she's here."	
LUKE	—But, marry, who?	
C-3PO	Good Princess Leia.	
LUKE	—Princess Leia—here?	75
	[*Aside:*] Now doth this strange adventure stir my	
	blood!	
HAN	What sayst of "princess"?	
LUKE	—Where, thou droid? Say where!	
HAN	What princess? On thy life, this thing unveil.	
R2-D2	Beep, meep, meep, beep, squeak, whistle, beep,	
	meep, hoo.	
C-3PO	E'en now the princess is on Level 5,	80
	Detention block of AA-23.	
R2-D2	[*aside:*] O me! This new discovery of mine	
	Doth shake my core, and shall arouse their souls.	

	[*To Han and Luke:*] Meep, meep, ahh, beep, squeak,	
	beep, meep, beep, ahh, nee.	
C-3PO	I fear, good Sir, it doth give certain news	85
	The princess shall be terminated soon.	
LUKE	Nay, nay! So quickly met and now, with this,	
	So quickly lost! Now must we swiftly act!	
HAN	What dost thou prattle on about? Pray tell!	
LUKE	[*aside:*] O how can one describe in simple words	90
	The import this myster'ous woman hath	
	Upon my life? [*To Han:*] The droids, these droids, are hers,	
	She hath appear'd in message urgent, too!	
	I see thou canst not understand it well,	
	Yet what I know is this: we must give her	95
	Whate'er unflagging help and hope we may!	
HAN	Speak not with such great folly. Obi-Wan	
	Hath told us to remain.	
LUKE	—Yet knew he not	
	That she is here! [*To C-3PO:*] Pray tell me how we may	
	Straight make our way to the detention block.	100
HAN	I say again what I have said before:	
	To this location is my purpose fix'd	
	And whether princess be within or no,	
	I tell thee plain: I shall not thither go.	
LUKE	She shall be executed! Thou hast said,	105
	Mere minutes past, that thou wouldst not remain	
	To see our sudden, sure imprisonment.	
	Now is thy fondest wish that we should stay?	
HAN	To march to the detention block's unwise!	

To make our way to danger folly 'tis!   110
To there present ourselves is passing mad!
To boldly go where none hath gone is wild!

LUKE   Hast thou no heart? She sentenc'd is to die!

HAN   My sentence is: 'tis better she than I.

LUKE   [*aside:*] How shall I break a heart that loveth not,   115
And how convince a man who lives by wits?
He hath not seen the urgency within
Her eyes. He hath not known the trembling in
Her voice. He hath not heard the manner of
Her plea. And yet, without his help I fear   120
My errand surely fails. What shall I do?
I know that under his exterior
More good and noble aspirations lie.
But by what tricks of speech to bring them forth,
And what persuasions shall his fix'd will move?   125
My aunt Beru hath told me once a tale:
She said when first the deep, vast Kessel mines
Were dug, it was revealèd that the pearls
Of greatest value must by clever means
Discover'd be. So did the miners band   130
Together, so to make a useful tool.
This tool would pull the pearls out of the rock
In such a way they seem'd t'emerge by ruse.
This practice had a name: the Hammer Ploy.
Now shall I play a Hammer's Ploy upon   135
The soul of this good smuggler, coaxing him
By means most indirect to rescue good.
Thus may the pearl of his still ragged soul
Revealèd be and shine as ne'er before.

     [*To Han:*] I tell thee true: the lady wealthy is.   140

CHEWBAC.   Egh, auugh!

HAN   —Say, wealthy?

LUKE   —Wealthy, aye, with pow'r.

     If thou wouldst rescue her, thy great reward

     Would be—

HAN   —Pray, what?

LUKE   —Well more, I'll warrant, than

     Thou mayst imagine!

HAN   —Ha, thou josh with me.

     For my imagination hath few bounds.   145

LUKE   Thou shalt have it!

HAN   —So would I!

LUKE   —Aye, thou wilt!

HAN   Enough, I am engag'd. But I do hope

     Thou knowest well of what thou speakest here.

LUKE   Well, well!

HAN   —Hast thou a plan?

LUKE   —C-3PO,

     I prithee pass those binding cuffs to me.   150

     [*To Chewbacca:*] Good Wookiee, I shall put these on

                 thee now.

CHEWBAC.   Auugh!

LUKE   —Han, perhaps thou shouldst that

                honor have.

         [Han Solo cuffs Chewbacca.

HAN   Fear not, dear Chewie, now his plan is plain.

C-3PO   My Master Luke, forgive my question frank:

     What should we do if we discover'd are?   155

LUKE   Lock thou the door.

HAN   —And pray they've blasters none.
C-3PO   [*aside to R-D2:*] 'Tis not a reassuring word.
R2-D2   —Beep, squeak!
                [*Exeunt C-3PO and R2-D2 as Han, Luke,*
                    and Chewbacca go to detention block.
CHORUS   So now Chewbacca, Han, and Luke proceed
                Unto detention level 5, quite grave.
                With bravery, good hope, and all Godspeed,   160
                Their errand is a princess there to save.
                The minions of the Death Star pay no mind,
                Nor are they by these three at all dismay'd.
                They do not fear the Wookiee, for behind
                Are Han and Luke as stormtroopers array'd.   165
                Meanwhile in stealth does Obi-Wan pass by
                And to the terminal doth make his way,
                But while he goes Darth Vader feels him fly—
                So ev'ry character his role doth play.
HAN   Thy plan, it shall not work.
LUKE   —And wherefore hast   170
                Thou not said this ere now?
HAN   —Aye, but I have!
                [*Luke, Han Solo, and Chewbacca enter detention*
                    block with Officer 4 and soldiers.
OFFICER 4   By heav'n, I say: where takest thou this thing?
LUKE   This pris'ner hath been transferr'd here, from cell
                                                    1-1-3-8.
OFFICER 4   —No one hath told me so.
                Thus 'tis my duty to confirm thy word.   175
                                    [*Soldiers approach.*
CHEWBAC.   Auugh!

HAN   —Be thou swift and merciless, good Luke!
                       [Han Solo, Luke, and Chewbacca kill
                                       Officer 4 and soldiers.

CHORUS   With blasters rais'd and targets in their scopes,
             The three do overtake th'Imperi'l threat.
             This obstacle o'ercome, they have fresh hopes—
             But still their way hath not been made clear yet.   180

HAN   Now shall we see wherein thy princess lies...
             It saith herein she now is held in cell
             2-1-8-7. Go! I'll hold them here.
             [To comlink:] O be not anxious, comrades, fear ye not!
             The situation here hath been controll'd.   185
             All merry 'tis in the detention block!

OFFICER 1   *[through comlink:]* But what hath happen'd?

HAN   —'Tis no matter, Sir—
             A slight malfunction of the weapons here.
             But all is well, and we are well, and all
             Within are well. The pris'ners, too, are well,   190
             'Tis well, 'tis well. And thou? Art also well?

OFFICER 1   *[through comlink:]* We shall dispatch a squad to verify.

HAN   Nay, there's a leak in the reactor here.
             Pray give us time to mend the matter well.
             The leak is large and dangerous, but fear   195
             Thou not, for all—I tell thee true—is well!

OFFICER 1   *[through comlink:]* But who art thou, and what's
                                       thy number code?
                                [Han Solo blasts comlink.

HAN   That conversation did my spirits bore!
             Now Luke, prepare thyself for company!
                       [Luke enters Princess Leia's chamber aside.

LEIA	Thou truly art in jest. Art thou not small	200
	Of stature, if thou art a stormtrooper?	
	Does Empire shrink for want of taller troops?	
	The Empire's evil ways, I'll grant, are grand,	
	But must its soldiers want for fear of height?	
LUKE	[*aside:*] So hath my introduction fallen short.	205
	She sees the uniform, but not the man.	
	[*Removing helmet, to Leia:*] Luke Skywalker am I!	
	I have thy droids,	
	My noble errand is to rescue thee,	
	And I with Ben Kenobi have come here!	
LEIA	With Ben Kenobi? Where is he?	
LUKE	—Draw near!	210

[Exeunt.

SCENE 3.

Inside the Death Star.

Enter DARTH VADER *and* GRAND MOFF TARKIN.

VADER	I tell thee: he is here.	
TARKIN	—Old Obi-Wan	
	Kenobi? Wherefore dost thou think 'tis so?	
VADER	A tremor in the Force hath been my guide.	
	When last I felt its movement I was in	
	The presence of my former Master—he.	5
TARKIN	'Twas years ago. He must be dead by now.	
VADER	Thou shouldst not underestimate the pow'r	
	The Force doth hold.	

TARKIN	—The Jedi are extinct.
	Their power from the universe is gone
	And thou, dear friend, art all that doth remain 10
	Of their misguided, old religious ways.
	[*Comlink beeps.*] Pray, what?
OFFICER 1	[*through comlink:*] —Detention AA-23
	Hath sounded an emergency alert.
TARKIN	The princess? Fie! Put thou all sections on
	Alert.
VADER	—I tell thee: Obi-Wan is here, 15
	E'en now, and surely with him is the Force.
TARKIN	If thou art right, he must not be allow'd
	This station to escape. Nay, never, nay!
VADER	Escape is not his plan. I must confront
	My former Master, and must do't alone. 20

                                             [Exit Grand Moff Tarkin.

The Master's lesson shall I teach in turn,

When Obi-Wan I face in battle soon.

I shall my vengeance win, my triumph gain,

When I deliver him unto his death.

Though comrades were we in full many wars,   25

Though friends we have been once, the past is gone—

And all is but a horrid memory.

Today my hopes shall be achiev'd when I

Strike down the vile betrayer of my youth.

This conflict shall fulfill my destiny,   30

And end for him in bleak eternity.

                                                   [Exit Darth Vader.

SCENE 4.

Inside the Death Star.

Enter HAN SOLO *and* CHEWBACCA, *with* STORMTROOPERS *entering and* LUKE SKYWALKER *and* PRINCESS LEIA, *aside.*

CHORUS	With hearty blast th'Imperi'l troops appear—
	Their coming doth require that Han retreat.
	In moment dangerous, amidst great fear,
	Here Han and Leia for the first time meet.
HAN	Our exit's block'd now.
LEIA	—With a fool's great skill 5
	Hast thou our route to freedom quite cut off.
HAN	Mayhap Thy Highness would prefer her cell?
LUKE	[*to comlink:*] C-3PO! Canst thou by any means
	Discover how we may the cellblock leave?
	Our entry point is now a deadly end. 10
C-3PO	[*through comlink:*] All to thy presence have
	alerted been!
	The entrance only takes one in or out.
	All other information where thou art
	Hath been restricted.
LUKE	[*to Han:*] —Now are we quite trapp'd!
HAN	I cannot hold them back forever, sure! 15
LEIA	'Tis quite a rescue thou hast plann'd for me.
	Thou hast come in, but how shalt thou go out?
	Hath folly been thy guide?
HAN	—He hath the plan,
	Not I, thou sweetheart of ingratitude!

              [Leia takes Luke's blaster, shoots hole in wall.
              By what dark sprite of Hell art thou possess'd?   20

LEIA   It falls to me to make our rescue good.
              Now follow me into the refuse heap!
                      [Princess Leia exits into chute.

HAN   [*to Chewbacca:*] Go thou hence!

CHEWBAC.   —Auugh!

HAN   —Get in, thou furry lump!
              I care not what thou smell'st within! Unless
              'Tis death, must be a sweeter smell than this   25
              Attack! Now go, be not afear'd, my friend!
                      [Chewbacca exits into chute.
              [*To Luke:*] I say, what charming girl thou here
                                  hast found!
              I either shall destroy her, or, perhaps,
              I may in time begin to like the wench!

LUKE   [*aside:*] Nay, executioner or lover, both   30
              Are far too great a role for thee to play.

HAN   Now go, and follow I, all else be damn'd!
                     [Exeunt Luke and Han into chute.

CHORUS   The scene doth shift unto the refuse space,
              Where all is rot, as like a fun'ral pyre.
              Though safe, our heroes other woes now face—   35
              They go from frying pan unto the fire.

Enter HAN SOLO, CHEWBACCA, LUKE SKYWALKER, *and*
PRINCESS LEIA *in garbage pile at bottom of chute.*

CHEWBAC.   Auugh!

HAN   —O! What wonder of the human mind

Hath thought to bring us here? Your Highness must
Be lauded greatly for discov'ring such
A wondrous smell as this! [*To Chewbacca:*] I'll blast
                                  the door,   40
Swift get thee hence!

LUKE   —Nay, prithee, shoot thou not!
                [*Han shoots and the blast ricochets.*
Thou arrant knave! Wouldst thou undo us all?
I have already tried to exit thus,
But lo, as thou now plainly seest, thou brute,
The passageway is seal'd magnetic'lly!   45

LEIA   Now rid us of that blaster, quickly too—
Else shall thine edgy trigger finger mean
The certain death of all of us herein!

HAN   O, aye, thy Worship—ha! 'Twas all in my
Control till thou didst lead us to this heap,   50
Nor shall the stormtroopers need any time
To calculate where all of us have flown.

LEIA   And yet, I say to you: it could be worse.
                      [*A loud sound is heard.*

HAN   'Tis worse.

LUKE   —I'll warrant, something lives in here!

HAN   [*aside:*] I 'spect his word is true, but fear to say.   55
     [*To Luke:*] 'Tis but thy keen imagination, Luke.

LUKE   'Twas not just my imagination that
Hath now swum boldly past my leg, or else
Imagination now hath body too!
Aye there—did thine eyes see? Did but a mere   60
Imagin'd figment just swim by?

HAN   —See what?

[Luke is pulled into the water by an unseen force.

CHORUS   Yet ere young Luke with answer can respond,
           He's pull'd unto the wat'ry depths below.
           For sev'ral moments in that garbage pond
           No sign is seen beneath the murky flow.   65
           An om'nous sound breaks forth into the pit,
           And seconds later Luke emerges, spent.
           The beast's pursuit of him for now is quit—
           A greater challenge doth this represent.

                         [Luke rises above the surface.

LEIA   O miracle, that thou art truly sav'd!   70
           What happen'd there, below the briny sludge?
LUKE   I do not know. The slimy creature hath
           Releas'd its vice-like grip on me and fled.

                            [Another sound is heard.

HAN   I have a feeling bad about this sound.

                         [The walls begin to contract.

LUKE   The walls—O horrid Fate—begin to move!   75
LEIA   Be not afear'd, and stand thou not in awe,
           But rouse thee now and halt its sure approach!
           Now lend me thy assistance!
CHEWBAC.   —Auugh!
LUKE   —But wait,
           I have a comlink and may hail the droids.
           [*Into comlink:*] C-3PO! Say, art thou there? Pray,
                                            speak!   80
CHORUS   But while he tries to hail the golden droid,
           C-3PO hath troubles of his own,
           For stormtroopers are to their room deploy'd
           And now the droids must save themselves alone.

Enter C-3PO *and* R2-D2 *aside, with* STORMTROOPERS.

C-3PO   O grant us help, for there are madmen here,   85
               Who have e'en now to th'prison level gone!
               If thou but hurry, thou may'st catch them there.

R2-D2   [*aside:*] Well said, my friend! He hath a merry wit
               When pride and scorn fall not from out his mouth.

TROOPER 7   [*to other stormtroopers:*] Aye, prithee fellows,
                              come and follow me!   90
                              [*Exeunt stormtroopers.*

CHEWBAC.   Egh.

LUKE   —3PO!

HAN   —Now climb on top!

LEIA   —In faith,
               I try!

LUKE   —Where is the knave? C-3PO!

C-3PO   I fear a wicked fate's befallen them.
               Pray, R2, see if they imprison'd are.
               Now search apace!

R2-D2   —Beep, squeak, meep, whistle, beep!   95

HAN   One thing is certain: we shall thinner be.
               I shall not lose my wit, e'en in death's face!

R2-D2   Beep, beep.

C-3PO   —They are not found, O great relief!
               Where may they be?

R2-D2   —Squeak.

C-3PO   —Use the comlink? O!
               I had forgotten quite, and turn'd it off.   100
               [*Into comlink:*] Pray, art thou there, Sir?

LUKE   [*into comlink:*]   —3PO? 'Tis thou?

C-3PO	[*into comlink:*] I will confess: we have some
	problems fac'd.
LUKE	[*aside, into comlink:*] Peace, 3PO! Lend ears and
	not thy voice!
	Disarm thou ev'ry refuse masher on
	Detention levels! Dost thou mark me, droid? 105
	Be rapid, else thy Master is no more!
C-3PO	[*aside, to R2-D2:*] Nay, shut them all down!
	Hurry, R2, go!
R2-D2	Beep, squeak, meep, whistle, hoo.
LUKE	—Ahh!
HAN	—O!
LEIA	—Ahh!
CHEWBAC.	—Auugh!
C-3PO	No heart within this golden breast doth beat,
	For only wires and circuit boards are here. 110
	Yet as I hear my Master's dying screams
	No heart is necessary for my grief.
	A droid hath sadnesses, and hopes, and fears,
	And each of these emotions have I felt
	Since Master Luke appear'd and made me his. 115
	No Master have I e'er respected so,
	Thus at this moment grave I do declare:
	There is no etiquette for shedding tears,
	No protocol can e'er express my woe.
R2-D2	[*aside:*] A plague on 3PO for action slow, 120
	A plague upon my quest that led us here,
	A plague on both our circuit boards, I say!
LUKE	[*into comlink:*] Nay, nay, fear not, dear droid,
	we all still live!

Pray open thou the door on maint'nance hatch
3-2-6-8-2-7—blessèd be!   125

R2-D2   [*aside:*] O fondest hope, O fervent pray'rs now heard!
My Master is alive, and plagues deterr'd!

[Exeunt all.

SCENE 5.
Inside the Death Star.

Enter OBI-WAN KENOBI *in stealth, with two* STORMTROOPERS
and power terminal.

CHORUS   While Luke and Leia, Han and Chewie flee,
Old Obi-Wan has reached the power source.
He cuts the tractor beam quite cunningly,
Then makes his exit drawing on the Force.

TROOPER 8   What do these warnings tell—shall we explore?   5

TROOPER 9   Belike 'tis just a drill, and nothing more!

[Exeunt.

SCENE 6.

Inside the Death Star.

Enter LUKE SKYWALKER, *holding stormtrooper helmet.*

LUKE   Alas, poor stormtrooper, I knew ye not,
                Yet have I ta'en both uniform and life
                From thee. What manner of a man wert thou?
                A man of inf'nite jest or cruelty?

A man with helpmate and with children too?   5
A man who hath his Empire serv'd with pride?
A man, perhaps, who wish'd for perfect peace?
Whate'er thou wert, good man, thy pardon grant
Unto the one who took thy place: e'en me.

Enter HAN SOLO, CHEWBACCA, *and* PRINCESS LEIA.

HAN   If we may female-giv'n advice avoid,   10
               We should be well upon our merry way.
LUKE   Aye, stand I ready to be gone from here.
                                          [Large sound is heard.
CHEWBAC.   Auugh!
HAN   —Say, where dost thou go to, Wookiee?
                                                       Where?
                                                  [Han fires.
LEIA   Thou brute, they shall o'erhear!
HAN   —Pray come thou here,
               Chewbacca, else I brand thee cowardly.   15
LEIA   Now use thine ears and, if thou hast, thy brain:
               I know not who thou art or whence thou cam'st,
               Yet from this moment, thou shalt heed my words.
HAN   Your Worship, prithee let me be direct:
               I have one Lord and Master: 'tis myself,   20
               And only from that one take I commands.
LEIA   A wonder great that thou art still alive!
               Now prithee, shall this walking carpet be
               Removèd from my path?
HAN   [*aside:*]   —A saucy wit!
               A wicked tongue that will be tam'd, I vow—   25

No other payment is reward enough.
                    [They come upon the hangar where the
                              Millennium Falcon *is held.*
    [To Luke, Princess Leia, and Chewbacca:] There 'tis.

LUKE   *[into comlink:]*   —C-3PO? Say, art thou there?
C-3PO   *[aside, in comlink:]* Aye, Sir.
LUKE   *[into comlink:]*   —And art thou safe?
C-3PO   *[aside, in comlink:]*   —For now, we are.
              We are position'd in the hangar just
              Across, directly, from the gallant ship.   30
LUKE   *[into comlink:]* And we are just above thee, so stand by.
LEIA   *[to Han:]* Hast thou come here in that ungainly heap?
              Thou art, perhaps, then braver than I thought.
HAN   'Tis well and good, though I need not thy praise.
              Now let us hence, and to the ship repair!   35
CHORUS   The foursome t'ward the ship with swift foot race,
              But soon they meet with opposition dire.
              Chewbacca goes with Han, both giving chase,
              While Luke and Leia to other paths aspire.
HAN   *[running away:]* Fly hence, my friends, and meet
                                        us at the ship!   40
                    [Exeunt Han Solo and Chewbacca,
                              chasing stormtroopers.
LEIA   A lion's share of courage hath he not?
LUKE   *[aside:]* Alas! Now is her heart mov'd unto him?
              [To Leia:] What help is courage if it leads to death?
              But come now, let us flee another way.
CHORUS   The chase is under way as all make haste!   45
              Han—once pursuer—soon becomes pursu'd

When with a mass of stormtroopers he's fac'd:
He turneth quick as like a man unglu'd.
Meanwhile the princess and young Luke do flee
From troopers coming after them with speed.   50
They happen on an open door and see
A chasm past which they cannot proceed.

LUKE   Belike we have an errant corner turn'd,
              For this deep hole leads not unto the ship!

LEIA   Forsooth, methinks that we shall safer be—   55
              E'en with the pit—behind a door shut fast.
                                        [*She shuts door.*

              Yet now I see no lock we may employ,
              So what for our dear freedom is the key?
                              [*Luke Skywalker shoots door control.*

LUKE   [*aside:*] I take a note from Han and blaster use,
              Belike that shall keep enemies at bay.   60

LEIA   We must o'erleap this deep abyss somehow.
              Pray, canst thou use thy sharp and earnest wit
              To find a means for lengthening the bridge?

LUKE   O! Now the wisdom of old Obi-Wan
              Is proven, for the blaster was too harsh.   65

LEIA   Do something, prithee, or they shall burst through!

CHORUS   So clever Luke the scene he doth survey
              And soon conceives a noble plan to cross.
              To take their flight and save them sans delay,
              He bares a length of rope as thin as floss.   70
              Attack'd, now Leia matches fire with fire,
              And so they cross, a'swinging o'er th'abyss.
              But ere they fly, the princess doth inspire
              More strength in Luke by means of royal kiss.

LEIA   A kiss for luck before our flight, dear friend,   75
            A kiss upon thy cheek from lips of mine,
            A kiss to give thee hope and confidence,
            A kiss to bring us courage in this time.
            Now take this kiss—my gift bestow'd by choice—
            And on the other side we'll soon rejoice.   80

                                        [*Exeunt.*

SCENE 7.
Inside the Death Star.

CHORUS   While droids do worry o'er their Master's fate,
            Han and Chewbacca make their swift escape.
            While Luke and Leia now in safety wait,
            A mighty, final duel taketh shape.

            Enter DARTH VADER *and* OBI-WAN KENOBI,
                with STORMTROOPERS *watching.*

VADER   For certain, I have waited, Obi-Wan,   5
            And now at last we meet together here:
            Our destinies once and for all fulfill'd.
            The circle of our lives is now complete—
            A student was I when I left thee last,
            But now I am the Master over thee.   10
OBI-WAN   Thou art a Master, Darth, I know 'tis true,
            But only evil hast thou Master'd yet.

                                        [*They duel.*

VADER   In time thy pow'rs have weak become, old man.

OBI-WAN	And yet thou canst not win, I'll warrant, Darth.
	For if thou strike me down, e'en now, e'en here, 15
	I shall more great and powerful become
	Than e'er thou hast imagin'd possible.
VADER	I tell thee plain: thou shouldst not have return'd.
CHORUS	What noble battle passes twixt these men—
	Lightsabers rage from Sith and Jedi Knight! 20
	No more courageous battle hath there been:
	'Tis like the day does combat with the night.
	Now whilst the two in conflict strike their blows,
	The others come that they the ship may find.
	At first Han Solo with Chewbacca shows, 25
	Then Luke and Princess Leia just behind.

Enter HAN SOLO, *with* CHEWBACCA *aside.*

HAN	Did we not just this fright'ning party leave?

Enter LUKE SKYWALKER *and* PRINCESS LEIA *with them.*

	Where hast thou been?
LEIA	—We did some old friends meet,
	But, finding them unfriendly, have both vow'd
	To find far truer, better friends henceforth. 30
LUKE	Hast thou seen any problems with the ship?
HAN	It seemeth fine, if we may make approach
	And get beyond the stormtroopers. Aye, then
	My fondest hope is that thine Obi-Wan
	Hath vanquishèd the wicked tractor beam. 35
LUKE	Behold, what ease! The stormtroopers go hence.

C-3PO	Now 'tis our chance, good R2-D2, come.
R2-D2	[*aside:*] Aye, will he now be leading me?
	[*To C-3PO:*] Beep, squeak!
HAN	Fly, fly, good friends! Unto the ship make haste.
CHORUS	As ev'ryone unto the ship draws nigh, 40
	Young Luke sees Obi-Wan trade slice with slice.
	And Ben Kenobi, catching young Luke's eye,
	Prepares to make a gracious sacrifice.
OBI-WAN	A Jedi is not made of fear or hate,
	But must a nobler countenance display. 45
	It is a lesson learn'd in times gone by
	That still I teach myself unto this day.
	Full many years I've spent with thoughts of this—
	This instant when Darth Vader I'd confront.
	But now my thirst for retribution's cold, 50
	While sweet forgiveness doth my spirit taste.
	I know I cannot win this battle here,
	Nor would I wish to slay the kindly man
	Who surely still within this black shell lives.
	And so, unto this death I'll go, this sleep, 55
	This sleep that promises the dream of peace.
	This undiscover'd galaxy wherein
	I'll know at last tranquility of heart.
	But ere I die, I'll one last lesson teach.
	I shall in this—my final moment—set 60
	A keen example for the universe,
	That future generations may yet know
	The valor and the strength of Jedi Knights.
	Put up thy lightsaber now, Obi-Wan,
	And show thyself a Jedi to this son. 65

[Obi-Wan raises lightsaber and is killed
by Darth Vader.

CHORUS   The cry of "Nay!" escapes Luke's trembling lip
And stormtroopers turn 'round to see them there.
A battle great begins before the ship
As to the *Falcon* these brave souls repair.
But ere the group departs amid the fray,   70
Luke hears the voice of Obi-Wan inside:
"Pray run, Luke run," the inner voice doth say,
And Luke the Death Star leaves with Force as guide.

[Exeunt.

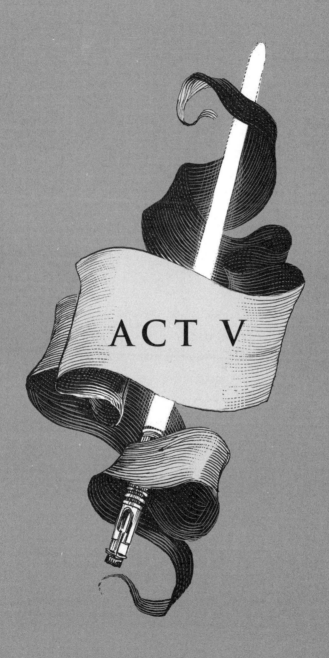

ACT V

SCENE 1.

Space, aboard the Millennium Falcon.

Enter LUKE SKYWALKER *and* PRINCESS LEIA *separately,*
with C-3PO *and* R2-D2.

LUKE   My heart doth break at this most recent loss,
              And how shall heart be heal'd of this grave pain?
              My aunt and uncle first, and now this Ben:
              Did e'er a person know such grief as mine?
LEIA   His heart breaks for a person, Obi-Wan—   5
              My heart breaks for a people, Alderaan.
              My ship crush'd first, and now my planet too:
              Did e'er a person know such grief as ours?
LUKE   I have but known this man a little time,
              Yet in my heart he holds a special place.   10
              So had I hop'd to learn from him the Force,
              And be his eager new apprentice too.
LEIA   My Alderaan I've known for all my life,
              And hold it in my heart in high'st esteem.
              So had I hop'd to one day make it home,   15
              When this rebellion all is pass'd away.
LUKE   But now must I another pathway take
              And make my final destiny sans him.
              My hopes shall not fulfillèd be as plann'd,
              Yet may I hope to serve through diff'rent deeds.   20
LEIA   But now must I some other course adopt
              And write my life's own story without them.
              My dreams shall not be realiz'd as I wish'd,

Yet may I dream to see some other Fate.

LUKE   Thus shall I strive to hold my head up high,   25
And be a beacon to this princess dear.
So I'll in her Rebellion play my part
And show her what a Jedi Knight may be.

LEIA   Thus shall I strive to hold my hands outstretch'd
And be a calming presence to this man.   30
So I'll in his deep mourning act my role
And show him what a comfort friends may be.

HAN   [*within:*] We now approach the Empire's sentry ships,
I prithee, Chewie, keep the ships at bay
And angle our deflector shields whilst I   35
Do charge the weapons for our sure defense!
               [*He enters and speaks to Luke and Leia.*
My friends, I know ye grieve most heartily,
Yet we have not made our escape complete.
I need thy help, so get thee to the guns!

CHORUS   With newfound strength Luke rises to the chore   40
And finds the console opposite from Han.
With lasers arm'd and engines all a'roar,
TIE fighters swiftly come—the battle's on!

HAN   Now be thou sharp, young Luke.

LEIA   —They come anon!

LUKE   They come too fast, how shall we hold them off?   45

LEIA   The ship is struck! All lateral controls
Have been destroy'd.

C-3PO   —O heav'n! [*He falls.*

HAN   —Be not afear'd.
I'll warrant that the ship shall surely hold.
[*Aside:*] O ship, hast heard my word? I prithee, hold!

LUKE	Now have I smash'd one!
HAN	—Well, thou worthy lad! 50
	[*Aside:*] But be thou not too full of pride and joy.
	When battle's won then mayst thou boast indeed,
	But none e'er boasted yet who bested were!
LEIA	Still two remain, so be thou bold and wise.
CHORUS	With shouts and sweat and ev'ry skill employ'd, 55
	Young Luke and Han contend with all their might.
	At length, the last TIE fighter is destroy'd
	And battle ends in fiery blast of light.
LUKE	We are the victors—merry is the day!
C-3PO	But I have fallen—help, O help me now. 60
	'Tis surely thy fault, R2-D2, see!
R2-D2	Beep, meep, squeak, whistle, beep, meep, whistle,

                                                      whee.

                                                     [Exeunt.

SCENE 2.

Inside the Death Star.

Enter GRAND MOFF TARKIN *and* DARTH VADER.

TARKIN	Now have they gone? The rebels truly fled?
VADER	They have—e'en now—the jump to light speed made.
TARKIN	And thou art sure—I prithee, say thou art—
	The homing beacon safe aboard the ship
	Hath placèd been? I fear this risk's unwise. 5
VADER	The risk and homing beacon both have been
	Well plac'd. Thou, Tarkin, be assur'd thereon.

TARKIN   'Tis well, good friend, I trust thy word herein,
          Yet would I have thee know what danger's here:
          While I have risk'd the world to let them flee,   10
          Since thou dost reassure, the risk's on thee.
                                                  [Exeunt.

SCENE 3.

Space, aboard the Millennium Falcon.

Enter HAN SOLO *and* PRINCESS LEIA.

HAN   Thy rescue hath been wondrous, think'st thou not?
          Say I: at times I do myself amaze.
          Amazing hath my rescue of thee been,
          Amazing is my hand at piloting,
          Amazing all my part in this escape,   5
          Amazing—aye, 'tis true—my handsome looks.
LEIA   Amazing is thy pride and love of self!
          Thus stand I now amaz'd that e'er thou shouldst
          Allow thy great, amazing self to stoop
          So low that thou wouldst rescue such as I.   10
          But let me now amaze thee if I may,
          By telling thee that thy amazement is
          Misplac'd! For never have Imperi'l ships
          Let enemies escape with such great ease
          As thou and thy amazing vessel have   15
          Just now amazingly escap'd.
HAN   —Nay, nay!
          Call'st thou this venture easy, Princess? Pish!

LEIA   I'll warrant we are being track'd e'en now.

HAN   This ship shall never trackèd be, good sis.

LEIA   Methinks thou dost upon this vessel far   20
Too great a trust bestow. But none of that,
I merely am reliev'd that R2 doth
The information safely in him guard.

HAN   But wherefore does this matter, Princess, say:
What carries he?

LEIA   —Rebellion's greatest hope: 25
For he doth hold the readouts technical
Unto that battle station, aye, the one
That such great pow'r display'd o'er Alderaan.
My hope it is that when the data can
Be read, an inner weakness we shall find.   30
Though thou hast seen this battle end, the war
Has not concluded yet.

HAN   —But there thou err'st,
Thou dost not speak my mind. For this ship and
Its pilot, Princess, 'tis concluded now.
I have not join'd thy revolution, nay—   35
My purpose runs not to Rebellion help,
My purpose runs not to assist thyself.
My purpose runs toward one aim alone,
And I do speak it plain: I shall be paid,
And will be paid, and ev'ry aspect of   40
My being lives in expectation of
The moment when thou shalt my coffers fill.

LEIA   O fiendish knave! Be thou concernèd not
O'er thy reward. If thou in money dost
Find love, then surely shalt thou have it, aye.   45

Enter LUKE SKYWALKER.

Thy friend is ev'ry part a hirèd man,
A mercenary with no mercy, he.
I question whether he doth care for aught   50
Or anyone.

                              [Exit Princess Leia.

LUKE   [*aside:*]   —But I do care, I do!
If only, Leia, thou didst know how much.
[*To Han:*] Pray tell me, Han, what dost thou think
                              of her?

HAN   I tell thee true, my mind is settl'd fast
When it thinks not of her.

LUKE   —'Tis well, 'tis well.   55

HAN   [*aside:*] Now is it plain to me why he doth ask!
The boy doth fancy her, I'll warrant, else
I've made a great mistake in judgment here.
What use are young men's dreams if not for mocking?
So I shall dance upon his tender heart: 60
[*To Luke:*] And yet—

LUKE   [*aside:*]   —Alas, a "yet"? What's this of
                              "yet"?

HAN   The woman truly hath a spirit bold,
And yet I know not. What think'st thou, I pray:
Think'st thou a princess could with me be—

LUKE   —Nay.

                              [Exeunt.

SCENE 4.

The rebel base on Yavin IV.

CHORUS   The swift *Millenn'um Falcon* makes its course
             Unto the place the Empire long has sought:
             On Yavin IV rebellion hath its source,
             O'er which the final battle shall be fought.

             Enter PRINCESS LEIA *and* COMMANDER WILLARD, *with*
                 LUKE SKYWALKER, HAN SOLO, *and* R2-D2 *behind.*

WILLARD   Good Princess, thou art safe! When word we heard   5
             About the cruel destruction of thy home
             We fear'd the worst. But now to see thee safe
             Is like a fragrant blossom to my sense.
LEIA   In time we may recount our griefs, good Sir,
             But now is the occasion we must act.   10
             I prithee, take this R2 unit here
             And use the data thou shalt find therein
             To plan our great attack. Our only hope
             It is, Commander, trust in what I say.
CHORUS   The records R2 holds are analyz'd,   15
             And lo, an opportunity appears!
             The rebels straight are of the news appris'd
             And hearts made ready as the battle nears.
             But whilst they mine good R2's database,
             The Empire learns where all the rebels wait.   20
             The Death Star makes its way unto the place
             To bring to Yavin Alderaan's grim fate.

Enter GENERAL DODONNA, WEDGE ANTILLES, *and various rebel*
commanders and pilots.

DODONNA   Now gather 'round, ye pilots good and true,
           For here shalt thou a goodly lesson learn.
           We have a single hope in this attack,   25
           And ye shall hear how we may compass it:
           The battle station heav'ly shielded is,
           And hath more pow'r to fire than half our fleet.
           It hath defenses 'gainst a large assault,
           But like the king who fell for want of horse   30
           This station may be crush'd by smaller might.
           A one-mann'd fighter may have strength to clear
           The outer walls and penetrate therein.
GOLD LEAD.   Beg pardon, Sir, but how—I prithee—shall
           A one-mann'd fighter stand its ground 'gainst that? 35
DODONNA   A question ask'd in wisdom 'tis, good friend.
           The Empire vast hath not consider'd small
           Snub fighters to be any threat, methinks,
           Else surely 'twould make suitable defense.
           The strongest people often put their faith   40
           Upon their strength alone, yet often such
           As these are bested by a people led
           By wisdom, skill and cunning. To the point:
           The plans provided by the princess show
           The battle station's fatal weakness, aye.   45
           A weakness do I call it, yet be sure:
           The hard approach therein shall per'lous be.
           Thou must maneuver through the trench above
           The surface unto this especial point:

There shalt thou find the glory spot, my lads,   50
There shalt thou with a blast most keenly shot
Bring down an Empire cruel and merciless.
But take ye heed, for all is not yet told:
The hole thou must attempt to strike is but
Two meters wide, a thermal pipe for waste.   55
This hole shall make thy laser's power grow,
This hole shall start a chain reaction great,
This hole, if thou canst hit it, wins the day—
This hole shall end the battle station whole.

GOLD LEAD. But Sir, the odds of such a hit are nil.   60

WEDGE   'Tis near impossible. Shall we, I say,
Attempt this madness or, mayhap 'tis best
If we do live to fight another day.
If we had but another thousand ships—

LUKE   Friends, rebels, starfighters, lend me your ears.   65
Wish not we had a single fighter more,
If we are mark'd to die, we are enough
To make our planets proud. But should we win,
We fewer rebels share the greater fame.
We all have sacrific'd unto this cause.   70
Ye all know well the fam'ly I have lost—
My uncle dear and aunt belov'd, aye both,
And then a mentor great, a pow'rful friend.
As massive is the grief I feel for them,
I know full well they'd not have me back down.   75
The princess hath a planet lost, with friends
And family alike—how great her pain!
And yet as grave as that emotion is,
She knoweth they would have her lead us still.

And ye, ye goodly men and women too,   80
Ye all have liv'd and lov'd and lost as well,
Your stories are with mine one and the same.
For all of us have known of grief and joy,
And every one has come unto this day
Not so that we may turn our backs and flee,   85
But that we may a greater courage show,
Both for ourselves and those we left behind.
So let us not wish further ships were here,
And let us not of tiny holes be fear'd—
Why, I have with a T-16 back home   90
Gone hunting womp rats scarcely larger than
The target we are call'd upon to strike.
And ye, ye brave souls, have your memories
Of your great exploits in your own homelands,
So think on them and let your valor rise,   95
For with the Force and bravery we win.
O! Great shall be the triumph of that hour
When Empire haughty, vast and powerful
Is fell'd by simple hands of rebels base,
Is shown the might of our good company!   100
And citizens in Bespin now abed,
Shall think themselves accurs'd they were not here.
For never shall rebellion see a time
More glori'us than our strong attack today!
ALL   Aye!
DODONNA   —Go ye then, and Force be with you all!   105
                    [*Exeunt all but Luke Skywalker.*
CHORUS   A bustling preparation now is made,
             As ev'ry man unto his post does go.

A joyful spirit doth the base pervade,
Whilst on the Death Star pride doth overflow.

Enter DARTH VADER *with* GRAND MOFF TARKIN, *aside in Death Star.*

VADER   This day, I'll warrant, lives in history: 110
             The end of old Kenobi it hath seen,
             And end of the Rebellion draweth near.
                     [Exeunt Darth Vader and Grand Moff Tarkin.

                     Enter HAN SOLO.

LUKE   Now what is this? Thou hast thine only love—
             Thy dear reward—and now thou leavest quick?
HAN   'Tis true, I do confess. For I shall ne'er   115
             Be free unless I use this great reward
             To clear me from the crushing weight of debt.
             And be thou honest, should I here remain
             To fight against a pow'r as great as this?
             'Tis foolishness, this fight, 'tis lunacy.   120
             Pray Luke, come thou with us! Thou art a brave
             And worthy lad, with wit and strength to fight.
LUKE   Speak thou not so! But open up thine eyes!
             See here what noble cause thou leav'st behind!
             Look in the hearts of these good people here!   125
             Behold the Force that keeps rebellion strong!
             Thou must have eyes to see what happens here,
             How great the cost of this bleak battle is.
             Thou knowest well what talent thou dost hold
             To pilot and to lead with manner bold.   130

Turn not thy back upon thy Fate, good Han,
But turn thy heart and stay with us to fight!

HAN   What value hath reward when one is kill'd?
What benefit gives honor to the dead?
To try the fight against that station, Luke,   135
Is not good courage, rather suicide.

LUKE   Then take thou care now, Han, thou Solo act,
For certain 'tis the part thou best dost play.

HAN   Nay, listen: may the Force be with thee, Luke.

[Exit Luke.

The ship that flies without a thruster fails: 140
Propulsion and direction must one have
To navigate the obstacles of space.
I know 'tis true, as any pilot doth.
Then how can I imagine that a man
Can fly without a conscience as his guide?   145
Without the inner compass of my soul,
How can I vainly hope to pilot life?
I know what 'tis to choose the right and good,
I know the small Rebellion's cause is just,
I know the people here have need of help,   150
I know all this, but still do harbor doubt.
Yet shall my doubts lead me unto this choice,
And shall I choose convenience over right?
Or shall I choose myself o'er my new friends?
Aye, shall I choose rewards o'er my own soul?   155
A smuggler's heart doth keep calm time inside,
No matter sways a pirate's peaceful pulse.
But something stirs in me I ne'er have felt:
Is this a rebel's heart I feel within?

[Exit Han Solo.

Enter LUKE SKYWALKER *and* PRINCESS LEIA.

LEIA   What is the matter, Luke?
LUKE   —'Tis only Han.   160
                Methought he had a heart for good, but nay,
                He hath not chang'd his mind.
LEIA   —He hath a path
                Unto himself. Not thou, nor I, nor aught
                Can plot the course he chooses, verily.   165
LUKE   I wish as well that Ben were here with us.
LEIA   A kiss I gave thee once to give thee strength,
                Another kiss I give in friendship's hope.
                                [She kisses him, then exits.

Enter BIGGS DARKLIGHTER.

BIGGS   Say, Luke!
LUKE   —Dear Biggs!
BIGGS   —It warms my heart to see
                Thee here, good friend. Shalt thou go with us
                                                    hence   170
                Against the Empire?
LUKE   —Aye! On our return
                I'll bend thine ears with stories wild and true.

Enter RED LEADER.

RED LEAD.   I pray thee, Luke, canst thou these ships control?

BIGGS   I'll stand as witness, Sir, that Luke shall prove
               More worthy than myself. I'll warrant he's   175
               The best of pilots in the Outer Rim.
               Fear not this one, good Sir, he'll earn his way.
RED LEAD.   Good lad, thou shalt suffice.
LUKE   —Aye, merry, Sir,
               I'll do my part.
                                        [Red Leader exits.
BIGGS   —Now must we thither go.
               But when we come again unto this place,   180
               I'll drink with thee a dram of Naboo's ale
               Whilst thou thy tales relate.
LUKE   —Say, Biggs, take note:
               For once I did assure thee I would join
               Rebellion's ranks, and here am I e'en now.
BIGGS   Shall be like olden times on Tatooine.   185
               Dear friend, it gives me comfort for to see
               Thee here. E'en death could come and welcome be,
               Because I know that thou dost ride beside.
                    [Exit Biggs. Luke ascends to ship, with R2-D2
                                        and rebel chief.
CHIEF   This R2 unit hath known better days.
               Wouldst thou a fit replacement for it find?   190
R2-D2   *[aside:]* Thou knave, say'st thou I have known
                                        better days?
               I'll better my days yet upon thy pate!
LUKE   Nay, say not so! For R2 hath been mine
               Through many an adventure and, belike,
               Hath exploits still to undergo.
R2-D2   —Beep, squeak!   195

Enter C-3PO.

C-3PO   O be thou safe, dear R2, and return!
           For thou wouldst not that my existence should
           Become a bore! [*Aside:*] O Fate, I prithee, keep
           Them safe—my Master and my only friend—
           Else should I find a lonely, tragic end.   200

                                                  [*Exeunt.*

SCENE 5.

Space. The final battle.

CHORUS   As our scene shifts to space, so deep and dark,
           O'er your imagination we'll hold sway.
           For neither players nor the stage can mark
           The great and mighty scene they must portray.
           We ask you, let your keen mind's eye be chief—   5
           Think when we talk of starships, there they be.
           If you can soon suspend thy disbelief,
           The Death Star battle shall you plainly see!
           So now: the preparation made with care,
           Toward the Death Star rides the noble fleet.   10
           By whirr of engines rebels take the air,
           With courage strong their unknown Fate to meet.

Enter LUKE SKYWALKER, R2-D2, WEDGE ANTILLES,
BIGGS DARKLIGHTER, RED LEADER, GOLD LEADER, *and other*
pilots, each standing in a different place to represent his ship.
C-3PO, PRINCESS LEIA, *and* GENERAL DODONNA *stand aside.*

COMPUTER   The Death Star doth approach, and shall within
The range of Yavin's rebel base arrive
Within these fifteen minutes. Lo! Alert!   15

RED LEAD.   Good men, each now shall speak and state his name.

RED TEN   Red Ten doth here stand by.

RED SEVEN   —Red Seven doth
Stand by.

BIGGS   —Red Three doth here stand by.

RED SIX   —Red Six
Doth here stand by.

RED NINE   —Red Nine doth here stand by.

WEDGE   Red Two doth here stand by.

RED ELEVEN   —Red Eleven   20
Doth here stand by.

LUKE   —Red Five doth here stand by.
[*Aside:*] We have our numbers, yet our souls
have names.
For I am Luke Skywalker, here beside
My friends, good Biggs and Wedge Antilles, too—
No war shall render us unto mere threes   25
And twos and fives. We ride, for ride we must—
And here we ride in Ben's most worthy name,
True, here we ride in Leia's noble name,
Aye, here we ride in Alderaan's slain name—
O here we ride for all the names which have,   30
Throughout our lives, been written on our hearts.
Our debt to them is past all numbering.

RED LEAD.   Now lock thine S foils in attacking mode.
We shall pass through the thin magnetic field.
Use your deflector shields and form in line!   35

                    I prithee, men, take care and be ye bold.
WEDGE   But look, I say, how large this Death Star is!
                    [*Aside:*] I am afear'd that this shall be my end.
RED LEAD.   Pray, peace, Red Two! Now all accelerate
                    Unto the speed wherein we may attack.   40
                    The time is here, good men, 'tis not to come:
                    It will be now. The readiness is all.
GOLD LEAD. Red Leader, dost thou hear me?
RED LEAD.   —Verily.
GOLD LEAD. The Gold Team leads unto the target shaft.
RED LEAD.   We have a positive position reach'd,   45
                    Thus shall I fly across the axis for
                    To draw their fire whilst thou dost penetrate.
CHORUS   The rebel ships now make their first attack
                    And fire unto the Death Star's iron walls.
                    The Empire shoots with lethal laser back: 50
                    'Tis death to anyone on whom it falls.
WEDGE   The volleys fall from close at hand.
RED LEAD.   —I see!
LUKE   Red Five reporting: swiftly I go in!
                    [*Aside:*] My first attempt here falls—O hit the mark!
CHORUS   With courage rare Luke makes initial pass   55
                    And blasts his way unto the Death Star's hull.
                    But now maneuvers he too close, alas!
                    Shall he escape the fire's most deadly pull?
BIGGS   How goes it, Luke?
LUKE   —I nearly cook'd my goose,
                    But all is well. [*Aside:*] Now shall I take more care! 60

            Enter DARTH VADER *and* OFFICER 5, *aside.*

OFFICER 5   Full thirty ships descend upon us, Sir.

So small are they our lasers pass them by.

VADER   Aye, then shall we destroy them ship to ship.

Tell thou the crews "be ready to attack."

[Exeunt Darth Vader and Officer 5.

RED LEAD.   Now take ye care, good men! Great fire doth rage   65

From outside of the harsh deflection tow'r.

LUKE   I stand prepar'd.

BIGGS   —Now shall I strike! Pray, give

Me thy good cover, Porkins.

RED SIX   —Stand I strong

And ready for to give thee aid, Red Three.

CHORUS   Now bravely Biggs doth render sharp, hard blast   70

Unto the evil Death Star's armor'd side.

The Empire's fire unto his mate hath pass'd,

And now Red Six doth face a troubl'd ride.

RED SIX   Disaster at me strikes.

BIGGS   —Eject, forsooth!

RED SIX   I yet may set it right.

BIGGS   —Anon, pull up!   75

RED SIX   Nay, nay, I'll warrant that all shall be well—

[Explosion. Red Six dies.

COMPUTER   In seven minutes shall the Death Star be

Within the range of our fair rebel base.

CHORUS   As rebels' spirits with great strength redound,

A voice speaks unto Luke, as to a son.

Luke hears the voice and its familiar sound: 80

'Tis his old friend and Master Obi-Wan.

Enter GHOST OF OBI-WAN KENOBI.

GHOST	[*aside:*] Pray, trust thy feelings, Luke.
LUKE	—I hear this voice
	And know it well. O me! Speak thou again!
	And heed the voice, my soul, and trust thyself:
	On Ben's command I'll strike a hearty blow! 85

[He shoots and strikes Death Star.
Exit Ghost of Obi-Wan Kenobi.

Enter CONTROL OFFICER.

OFFICER	Squad leaders, mark me well. New fighters have
	Appear'd, and come toward you presently.
LUKE	My scope shows naught, my eyes to them are blind.
RED LEAD.	Employ thy visu'l scanning—they approach!
	Red Seven, thou hast one upon thy rear. 90
RED SEVEN	My ship is hit! Now must I die, dear friends.

[Explosion. Red Seven dies.

LUKE	Good friends, if thou dost catch an enemy
	Behind thy ship, I prithee watch it well!
BIGGS	Now am I plagued by such a one, help help!
	For neither can I see where he doth go— 95
	He flies so close that my maneuvers fail.
LUKE	Hold fast, brave Biggs, till I can give thee aid.
	Upon the enemy I fly, and shoot!
BIGGS	Bold Luke, thou hast a life return'd to me.
	So may I one day give to thee in turn. 100

Enter DARTH VADER *with* IMPERIAL PILOTS 1 *and* 2.

VADER	I prithee, soldiers, let us hence away.

For many of our fighters are remov'd
From their own fleet. Thus let us swiftly go
And straightway make pursuit of these rogue ships.

       [Darth Vader and pilots enter ships.

BIGGS	O Luke, thou art pursued, pull in!
WEDGE	—Pray, guard 105
	Thy back, good Luke. More fighters do approach.
LUKE	I have been hit, but not unto the death.
	Small R2, see if thou the damage canst
	Repair.
R2-D2	—Beep, whistle.
LUKE	—Hang thou on, good droid!
RED LEAD.	Red Ten, canst thou see whither's gone Red Five? 110
RED TEN	A heavy fire appears upon this side.
	Red Five, where art thou?
LUKE	—Here, but cannot shake
	The villain who doth hotly follow me.
WEDGE	I come for thee, good Luke, be not afraid.
LUKE	[*aside:*] O fie, my dear friend Biggs, where
	canst thou be? 115
	Thou promis'd that thou ow'dst to me a life,
	But where is now that help of which thou spok'st?
	'Twas partly for our friendship I am here,
	For long I wish'd to join thee as thou fought
	And many were the tales adventurous 120
	Thou brought'st with thee whilst visiting our home
	When still I worked the crops on Tatooine.
	But now hast thou deserted me, old friend?
	When I am even at the door of death
	Hast thou both flown and fled? Say nay, dear Biggs! 125

WEDGE   Take that, thou scoundrel base, Imperi'l scum!

LUKE   Great thanks, good Wedge, heroic'lly hast thou done.

GOLD LEAD.   Red Leader, hear my word: the Gold team shall
               Begin our swift attack into the trench.

RED LEAD.   Godspeed, Gold Leader, go with might and strength!   130

VADER   I fly, and fly toward my enemies.
               This day the dark side of the Force shall reign,
               As I disrupt the weak Rebellion's plans
               And with my men destroy their ev'ry hope.
               [*To Imperial Pilots 1 and 2:*] Good pilots both,
                                        remain set for attack!   135

GOLD LEAD.   The port for the exhaust hath been lock'd in
               And mark'd! That hole shall make us whole,
                                             my mates.
               Now switch thy pow'r to front deflector screens.
               Gold Five, what say'st thou? Canst thou count
                                             the guns?

GOLD FIVE   Belike 'tis twenty yon and hither, both   140
               Upon the surface and within the tow'rs.

COMPUTER   Within five minutes shall the Death Star be
               Upon our rebel base, and set to strike.

GOLD LEAD.   To targeting computer presently
               I switch.

GOLD TWO   —I have receiv'd a signal on   145
               The ship's computer—that the port will soon
               Be in our range. But soft, good friends, what's this?
               The guns! It seemeth that their guns have stopp'd.

GOLD FIVE   So watch thy rear, and stabilize thy shields.
               Perhaps an enemy doth come behind.   150

GOLD LEAD.   Aye, aye, they come! Three ships at point-two-ten.

CHORUS   The battle heats as Vader and his men
            Approach the threefold members of group Gold.
            The Empire's hate will be fulfillèd when
            Darth makes his power known with blows
                                          full bold. 155

VADER   I shall destroy the rebels vile myself.
            Just give me thy good cover and 'tis done.
            Now shoot I once, and death is the result.
                [Darth Vader shoots. Explosion. Gold Two dies.

GOLD LEAD. I have no power to maneuver, fie!

GOLD FIVE   Stay thou on target.

GOLD LEAD.   —Nay, we run too close!   160

GOLD FIVE   Stay thou on target!

GOLD LEAD.   —Wretch, pray give me room!
                    [Darth Vader shoots. Explosion.
                                Gold Leader dies.

GOLD FIVE   Gold Five doth this ill news report: we have
            Lost Dutch and Tiree both.

RED LEAD.   —In troth, I hear!
            Stay ready.

GOLD FIVE   —From behind they do attack!
                [Darth Vader shoots. Explosion. Gold Five dies.

LUKE   [*aside:*] So much of desolation and of death.   165
            Is this Rebellion worth the lives here lost?
            Yet I would gladly my life give to it—
            Thus reason not the need, my troubl'd soul.

CHORUS   Whilst all the rebels mourn the loss of life,
            Upon the Death Star tensions have been prov'd.   170
            The rebels' plan hath rear'd the threat of strife,
            But Gov'nor Tarkin stands assur'd, unmov'd.

Enter GRAND MOFF TARKIN *with* CHIEF OFFICER *aside,*
in Death Star.

CH. OFFICER The rebels' sharp attack hath been well prob'd
And now it doth appear a danger looms.
I do confess my love to thee, good Sir,   175
And would my very life lay down for thee.
Wouldst thou that I make ready thine own ship,
That thou may'st flee should fighting turn to death?

TARKIN   Retreat whilst we do win the day? You jest!
Forsooth, I stand unmovèd like a rock.   180
            [Exeunt Grand Moff Tarkin and Chief Officer.

COMPUTER   The Death Star shall within three minutes be
Upon the rebel base.

RED LEAD.   —Red boys, 'tis I,
Thy tried and true Red Leader. We shall meet
Upon the mark at six-point-one. Make haste!

WEDGE   Red Two doth stand obedi'nt at thy side.   185

BIGGS   Red Three doth come.

DODONNA   —Red Leader, hear me now.
It is Base One who speaks to thee. Keep half
Thy fighters out of range upon thy next
Attempt. If one group sadly falls, belike
The other shall succeed: so shall we make   190
The Empire take our fleet by halves, not wholes.

RED LEAD.   I hear and understand, good Sir. Now Luke,
Take thou Red Two and Three with thee and wait
Upon my signal ere thou mak'st thy run.
Now hence we go an Empire for to slay!   195

CHORUS   Red Leader, with the others, Twelve and Ten,

Make their descent into the trench with speed.

Their brav'ry, cunning, and their acumen

May give these men the victory they need.

RED TEN   Dost thou agree, it should be in our sights?   200

RED LEAD.   Pray keep thine eyes a'watching for those ships

That have our comrades cruelly destroy'd!

RED TEN   The interference hath become too wide.

Red Five, canst thou yet see them where thou standst?

LUKE   I see no ships, but—wait. Aye, they approach!   205

They come at point-three-five.

RED TEN   —I see them now.

RED LEAD.   My ship hath come in range of that sly port,

The port that hath evaded us so far.

But now, aye now, the target shall be mine.

If ye, good friends, may hold them there awhile,   210

I shall this battle end with one swift stroke!

VADER   Close in, my lads—we three shall ride as one.

RED LEAD.   Heigh, almost there.

[Darth Vader shoots. Explosion. Red Twelve dies.

RED TEN   —Pray fire, else we die too!

RED LEAD.   Heigh, almost there.

RED TEN   —They set upon my back!

I can no more withstand their quick attack.   215

[Darth Vader shoots. Explosion. Red Ten dies.

RED LEAD.   I shoot, I shoot! For rebels' glory, shoot!

The blast hath left the shaft!

RED NINE   —Hast hit? Hast hit?

Is vict'ry yet within our sights?

RED LEAD.   —Alas,

My finest effort I have giv'n, and yet,

The blast falls errant and doth miss the mark.   220
'Tis but an impact on the surface. Pooh!

LUKE   Red Leader, be thou not dismay'd. We shall
Protect thee even now. Turn thou toward
The point-oh-five and we shall cover thee.

RED LEAD.   Nay, save me not! My engine hath been crush'd   225
And death is welcome now. Instead, dear Luke,
Good Wedge, brave Biggs, be thou preparèd for
Thy run, for thou art now our only hope!
    [Darth Vader shoots. Explosion. Red Leader dies.

COMPUTER   The Death Star now in but a minute shall
Upon the rebel base on Yavin come.   230

LUKE   Once more unto the trench, dear friends, once more!
The death of our dear friends we see today,
And by my troth their souls shall be aveng'd!
I was not angry since I came to space
Until this instant! Strike at us and thou   235
Shalt know the power of the Force, thou brute,
Thou Empire full of hate and evil deeds.
Aye, pluck us down and we shall rise again—
Our cause is not alone for these good men
Who here were kill'd today. Our cause is not   240
Alone for those on Alderaan who died.
Our cause is for the truth, for righteousness,
For anyone who e'er oppression knew.
'Tis not rebellion for the sake of one,
'Tis not a cause to serve a priv'leg'd few—   245
This moment shall resound in history
For ev'ry person who would freedom know!
So Biggs, stand with me now, and be my aide,

	And Wedge, fly at my side to lead the charge—	
	We three, we happy three, we band of brothers,	250
	Shall fly unto the trench with throttles full!	
WEDGE	We stand with thee, a'ready for the fight.	
BIGGS	But Luke, at that quick pace shalt thou escape	
	Before thy speedy ship is blown in twain?	
LUKE	'Twill be like Beggars Canyon back at home.	255
CHORUS	The youth descend at once into the trench	
	Wherein their fates shall surely written be.	
	Darth Vader, close behind, prepares to quench	
	His thirst upon the blood of martyrs three.	
BIGGS	We shall stand fast at hand to give thee help.	260
WEDGE	My scope doth show the tower, but the port	
	Appeareth not. How certain art thou, Luke,	
	That our computers each can hit the mark?	
LUKE	Good pilot, watch thyself! Increase to full.	
WEDGE	I prithee, what shall we do 'bout the tow'r?	265
LUKE	Give thou unto the enemy thy thoughts,	
	But let the tow'r be my concern alone.	
	[*To R2-D2:*] Now R2, fix the stabilizer that	
	Hath once more come unhing'd. Pray, fix it fast!	
R2-D2	[*aside:*] Now shall I be not fool, but fix!	
	[*To Luke:*] Beep, squeak!	270
WEDGE	The fighters are behind us, at point-three.	
	They come upon my rear too fast. Alack!	
	I have been hit, and must depart, my friends.	
LUKE	Aye, get thee clear, good Wedge. Thou shalt not help	
	Our cause if thy ship flyeth not. Anon!	275
	And live to fight another day with me.	
WEDGE	With all my heart, I truly wish thee well.	

[Exit Wedge.

VADER   Aye, let him go—the leader we pursue!

BIGGS   Make haste, O Luke. Methinks they do approach
             E'en faster than before. I shall not hold   280
             Them back for long!

LUKE   —Now, R2, straight increase
             The pow'r.

R2-D2   —Beep, whee.

BIGGS   —Make haste, Luke. O, alas!
             [Darth Vader shoots. Explosion. Biggs dies.

LUKE   That ever I should see this day, O woe!
             My childhood friend from Tatooine now slain
             Protecting me from harm. Thou ow'dst a life—   285
             Dear Biggs, sweet Biggs—and thou hast paid. And now
             'Tis down to me: the boy turn'd warrior.
             Be still, my errant heart, and seek the Force.

VADER   The leader now is mine.

R2-D2   —Meep, beep.

C-3PO   —Take care
             Sweet R2-D2! Come thou back, I pray!   290

CHORUS   Luke's ship comes closer to the little port
             While Vader and his crew draw all too near.
             Young Luke to his computer doth resort
             Until he hears the voice speak in his ear.

             Enter GHOST OF OBI-WAN KENOBI.

GHOST   O use the Force, dear Luke. Let go and trust!   295
VADER   I sense the Force in this one here, almost
            As if I did my younger self espy.
GHOST   I prithee, trust me, Luke. All shall be well.
LUKE   The hearing of these words is like a balm
            Unto my soul. So shall I trust the Force   300
            And not this fallible computer here.
                              [Luke turns off computer.
COMPUTER   What is this, Luke? Thy targeting machine
            Hath been turn'd off. What can be wrong? Pray tell!
LUKE   Nay, all is well. Fear not, good friends.
R2-D2   —Beep, squeak.
                         [Darth Vader shoots. R2-D2 is hit.
            Ahh hoo!
LUKE   —Small R2-D2 hath been lost!   305
COMPUTER   The Death Star now has come within our range.
TARKIN   Commander, thou may'st fire when thou hast made
            All goodly preparation thereunto.
VADER   Now face thy death, thou rebel.
PILOT   —Sir, take heed!
CHORUS   Now in a trice brave Han is on the scene!   310
            The smuggler hath return'd on errand kind.
            With sly approach he makes his way unseen
            And slays th'Imperi'l pilots from behind.
                    [Enter Han Solo with Chewbacca, firing on
                    Darth Vader and Imperial Pilots. Explosion.
                         Imperial Pilots 1 and 2 die.
VADER   But how?—
                    [Darth Vader exits in confusion, his ship spinning
                              out of control.

HAN   —Thy path is clear, young Luke. Now do
              Thy deed and let us all make way back home.   315

LUKE   I stretch my feelings out and use the Force,
              And on the instant seems the porthole vast—
              Not small or difficult to strike, but large.
              The ship is arm'd, and now I take the chance—
              The blast's away, and with it all our hopes!   320
                        [Luke shoots and hits the target.

CHORUS   The laser hits its mark with certain aim,
            And as the Death Star arms to strike the base
            The chain reaction sets the orb aflame:
            The Death Star hath exploded into space.
HAN   Thy timely blast hath hit the perfect mark—   325
            One in a million was thy Force-fill'd shot!
GHOST   Remember me, O Luke, remember me,
            And ever shall the Force remain with thee.

                                        [*Exeunt.*

SCENE 6.
The rebel base on Yavin IV.

Enter LUKE SKYWALKER *from ship, with* PRINCESS LEIA
and various rebels.

REBELS   Hurrah!
LUKE   —O Leia!
LEIA   —Luke! Thou didst succeed!

Enter HAN SOLO.

HAN   Heigh-ho!
LUKE   —Good friend! I knew thou wouldst return.
            I knew thou must, 'twas in thy spirit good.
HAN   Nay, should a pirate let another take
            His own reward?
LEIA   —Thou gentle soul, I knew   5
            Thou wert of sterner stuff than money made.

Enter R2-D2, injured, and C-3PO.

C-3PO   O R2, R2, canst thou hear me? Speak!
            Canst thou repair him? Say thou canst, I beg!
            If any of my parts may be of use,
            Pray say the word!
LUKE   —Fear not, he'll be made whole.   10
REBEL 2   We shall at once begin our best repair.
            [Exeunt C-3PO with R2-D2 and Rebel Leader 2.
LUKE   Now ends a noble quest, a battle won.
            Now hath a true adventure reach'd its goal.
            Now hath the good Rebellion fac'd its foe
            And triumph'd though it seem'd that all was lost.   15
LEIA   Along the way, dear friends were lost and made,
            Along the way, strange creatures have we found.
            The stories have been told, the villains met,
            The griefs and exultations all play'd out.
HAN   A chance for new beginnings we have made,   20
            Directing hearts unto the rebels' cause.
            These are the star wars we have fought and won—
            For now our battles and our scenes are done.

            Enter CHORUS *as epilogue.*

CHORUS   Now dawns a new day with the sun of Peace,
            The day whereon the rebels welcome Fate.   25
            For from their enemies they find release
            And now with mirth they come to celebrate.
            Young Luke, strong in the Force, doth walk beside
            The noble Han, whose valor won the day.

The rebels form an aisle and rise with pride,   30
As Luke and Han march forth in grand display.
Now Leia smiles and gives them their reward,
As each bows low with hope and joy sincere.
C-3PO and R2, now restor'd,
Look on as brave Chewbacca sounds the cheer.   35
There let our heroes rest free from attack,
Till darkness rise and Empire striketh back.

                               [Exeunt omnes.

END.

AFTERWORD.

William Shakespeare's Star Wars.

At first glance, the title seems absurd.

But there's a surprising and very real connection between George Lucas's cinematic masterpiece and the thirty-seven (give or take) plays of William Shakespeare. That connection is a man named Joseph Campbell, author of the landmark book *The Hero with a Thousand Faces.*

Campbell was famous for his pioneering work as a mythologist. He studied legends and myths from throughout world history to identify the recurring elements—or archetypes—that power all great storytelling. Through his research, Campbell discovered that certain archetypes appeared again and again in narratives separated by hundreds of years, from ancient Greek mythologies to classic Hollywood westerns. Naturally, the plays of William Shakespeare were an important source for Campbell's scholarship, with brooding prince Hamlet among his cadre of archetypal heroes.

George Lucas was among the first filmmakers to consciously apply Campbell's scholarship to motion pictures. "In reading *The Hero with a Thousand Faces*," he told Campbell's biographers, "I began to realize that my first draft of *Star Wars* was following classic motifs . . . so I modified my next draft according to what I'd been learning about classical motifs and made it a little bit more consistent."

To put it more simply, Campbell studied Shakespeare to produce *The Hero with a Thousand Faces*, and Lucas studied Campbell to produce *Star Wars*. So it's not at all surprising that the *Star Wars* saga features archetypal characters and relationships similar to those found in Shakespearean drama. The complicated parent/child relationship of Darth Vader/Luke Skywalker (and the mentor/student relationship of Obi-Wan Kenobi/Luke Skywalker) recalls plays like *Henry IV Parts 1 and 2*, *The Tempest*, and *Hamlet*. Like Sith lords, many of Shakespeare's villains are easily identifiable and almost entirely evil, with notable baddies including Iago (*Othello*), Edmund (*King Lear*), and Don John (*Much Ado about Nothing*). Still others, like Darth Vader, are more conflicted and complex in their malevolence: *Hamlet*'s Claudius and the band of conspirators in *Julius Caesar*. Destiny and fate are key themes of *Star Wars*, as they are in *Romeo and Juliet*, *A Midsummer Night's Dream*, and *Macbeth*.

Shakespeare's plays and *Star Wars* also feature a host of colorful supporting players. C-3PO and R2-D2 observe and comment on the action like Rosencrantz and Guildenstern. Chewbacca is as untamable as Caliban. Lando is as smooth and self-interested (at first) as Brutus. Obi-Wan Kenobi is like a wise Prospero (before death) or a haunting King Hamlet (after). Jabba the Hutt enjoys a diet worthy of Falstaff. Boba Fett is like *Richard III*'s murderers 1, 2, and 3, but with a jetpack and blaster instead of a knife. Yoda's speech is as backward as Dogberry's but as wise as Polonius's.

The works of Shakespeare and the *Star Wars* movies also share a comparable level of popularity and relevance. All well-rounded postmodern cultural connoisseurs are expected to have at least passing familiarity with both sets of stories, and both have percolated into our everyday language: you're as likely to hear one of Shakespeare's enduring phrases ("good riddance," "faint-hearted," "elbow room," and many others) as an encouragement to "use the force." If *Star Wars* were an actual Shakespearean play, we would most likely classify it as a fantasy, in the vein of *The Tempest*. However, it also has elements of a history (the story of the Galactic Empire with all the intrigue of *Richard III*), a comedy (all's well that ends well, after all), or, taken as a six-movie arc, the Tragedy of Anakin Skywalker.

I had the idea for *William Shakespeare's Star Wars* after watching the original trilogy for the millionth time and (soon afterward) attending four shows at the Oregon Shakespeare Festival. I'd already committed every scene and speech of the *Star Wars* saga to memory, but the Shakespeare festival introduced me to something new: *The Very Merry Wives of Windsor, Iowa,* an adaptation by Alison Carey of the classic comedy set in contemporary Iowa among a populace happily embracing gay marriage. I saw the appeal of applying the Shakespearean tradition to surprising and nontraditional story elements, and the next morning I woke up with the idea for this book.

My interests in language and wordplay came in handy while attempting to translate so much classic movie dialogue into iambic pentameter. For those unfamiliar with the phrase, iambic pentameter is the metrical form that Shakespeare uses in his plays and sonnets. An *iamb* is the syllable pattern unstressed-stressed, and *pentameter* means each line has five iambs, so a line of iambic pentameter sounds like this: da-DUM da-DUM da-DUM da-DUM da-DUM (Simon and Garfunkel's "I'd rather be a hammer than a nail" is a perfect example). The rhythm of iambic pentameter feels natural and intuitive to me, so I had a lot of fun writing 3,076 lines of it. Geeky trivia: this puts *William Shakespeare's Star Wars* at an average length for a Shakespearean play (*A Comedy of Errors* is the shortest, at 1,786 lines; *Hamlet* is the longest, at 4,024).

This has been a labor of love, and I've enjoyed every syllable.

ACKNOWLEDGMENTS.

The process of writing this, my first book, has been a thrilling journey into the publishing world, and I am grateful to all those who made the way clear. Thank you to Jason Rekulak, my editor at Quirk Books, for believing in this book and for encouraging me to write it in the first place. Thank you to Adriann Ranta, my agent, for guiding me through the maze of contracts and answering the thousand questions of a first-time author. Thanks to both Jennifer Heddle and Carol Roeder at Lucasfilm for making the editorial process a smooth one, to Nicolas Delort for his amazing illustrations, and to the rest of the Quirk and Lucasfilm staff for their wonderful contributions.

Great thanks to my literal and metaphorical brothers Erik Doescher, Josh Hicks, and Ethan Youngerman for being early readers of the manuscript and constant cheerleaders along the way. Thank you to my parents, Beth and Bob Doescher, for their unconditional love and for making *Star Wars* a part of my reality since before I can remember.

Profound thanks to Murray Biggs, my college English professor and good friend. Murray performed a Herculean task for this book, poring over the manuscript and making minor corrections to improve my Shakespearean pastiche (and teaching me the word *pastiche*). Thank you to Jane Bidwell, my high school English teacher, for instilling in me a love of Shakespeare and an understanding of iambic pentameter.

Additional thanks to others who offered help and support: Heidi Altman, Jeff and Caryl Creswell, Mark Fordice, Holly Havens, Jim and Nancy Hicks, Apricot Irving, Steve Maddoux, Chris Martin, Matt Matros, Joan and Grady Miller, Michael Morrill, Dave Nieuwstraten, Naomi Walcott, and Doug Zabroski.

Finally, thank you to my spouse, Jennifer Creswell, and our children Liam and Graham. Though not a lover of Shakespeare—and possessing a general antipathy toward *Star Wars*—Jennifer has shown support, love, and encouragement throughout the development of this book. Liam and Graham have been excited about "daddy's book" from the start and (he notes with pride) have become big *Star Wars* fans in the process.

MAY
THE VERSE
BE WITH
YOU!

* COLLECT *

ALL THREE VOLUMES

IN THE

WILLIAM SHAKESPEARE'S
STAR WARS TRILOGY.

*

SONNET 1138

"To the Interwebs We Go"

Our rebels now are ended, but fear not—
The book is over, true, but not th'event.
For there's an online Shakespeare *Star Wars* spot
Where thou may'st soon prolong thy merriment.
One may download a gratis **study guide**
Design'd for high school or for college classes,
And there's an **interview** to be espied
With author Ian Doescher, for the masses.
The mem'ry of the book shall live again
When thou, with joy, shalt our **book trailer** see,
Or read o'er any news that shall come in
About the Shakespeare *Star Wars* galaxy.
All this **and more**, aye, surely thou shalt find,
When thou dost visit good **Quirk Books online.**

quirkbooks.com/shakespearestarwars

WILLIAM

SHAKESPEARE'S

—— THE ——
EMPIRE STRIKETH BACK

STAR WARS

PART THE FIFTH

WILLIAM

SHAKESPEARE'S

——— THE ———
EMPIRE STRIKETH BACK

STAR WARS

PART THE FIFTH

By Ian Doescher

INSPIRED BY THE WORK OF GEORGE LUCAS
AND WILLIAM SHAKESPEARE

PHILADELPHIA

Library of Congress Cataloging in Publication Number: 2013913273

ISBN: 978-1-59474-715-1

Printed in the United States of America

Typeset in Sabon

Designed by Gregg Kulick
Text by Ian Doescher
Illustrations by Nicolas Delort
Production management by John J. McGurk

Quirk Books
215 Church Street
Philadelphia, PA 19106
quirkbooks.com

10 9 8 7 6 5 4

FOR MURRAY BIGGS:

THE YODA TO MY LUKE

———

FOR JOSH HICKS:

SOUNDING BOARD AND JEDI KNIGHT

DRAMATIS PERSONAE

CHORUS

LUKE SKYWALKER, *a Jedi trainee*
GHOST OF OBI-WAN KENOBI, *a Jedi Knight*
YODA, *a Jedi Master*
PRINCESS LEIA ORGANA, *of Alderaan*
HAN SOLO, *a rebel captain*
CHEWBACCA, *his Wookiee and first mate*
C-3PO, *a droid*
R2-D2, *his companion*
LANDO OF CALRISSIAN, *a scoundrel*
LOBOT, *his man-at-arms*
GENERAL RIEEKAN, *of the Rebellion*
WEDGE ANTILLES, *a rebel pilot*
DACK, DERLIN, HOBBIE, JANSON, *and* ZEV, *soldiers of the Rebellion*
EMPEROR PALPATINE, *ruler of the Empire*
DARTH VADER, *a Sith Lord*
PIETT, OZZEL, VEERS, *and* NEEDA, *gentlemen of the Empire*
BOBA FETT, *a bounty hunter*
WAMPA ICE CREATURE, *of Hoth*
EXOGORTH, *of the asteroid field*
UGNAUGHTS, *merry dwarves of Bespin*

REBEL PILOTS, LIEUTENANTS, CONTROLLERS, AIDES,
DROIDS, BOUNTY HUNTERS, AT-ATS, IMPERIAL TROOPS,
OFFICERS, GUARDS, *and* SOLDIERS

PROLOGUE.

Outer space.

Enter CHORUS.

CHORUS   O, 'tis for the Rebellion a dark time.
         For though they have the Death Star all destroy'd,
         Imperi'l troops did from the ashes climb
         And push the rebels closer to the void.
         Across the galaxy pursu'd with speed,   5
         The rebels flee th'Imperi'l Starfleet vast.
         A group with Luke Skywalker in the lead
         Hath to the ice world known as Hoth flown fast.
         Meanwhile, the cruel Darth Vader is obsess'd
         With finding young Skywalker. Thus he hath   10
         Through ev'ry point of space begun his quest
         By sending robot probes to aid his wrath.
         In time so long ago begins our play,
         In war-torn galaxy far, far away.

                                                  [Exit.

ACT I

SCENE 1.

The ice world of Hoth.

Enter LUKE SKYWALKER.

LUKE   If flurries be the food of quests, snow on.
     Belike upon this Hoth, this barren rock,
     My next adventure waits. 'Tis time shall tell.
     And yet, is it adventure that I seek?
     Shall danger, fear, and action fill my days?   5
     Shall all my life be spent in keen pursuit
     Of great adventure and her fickle fame?
     It seemeth I have had enough of life
     To fill a thousand normal human lives—
     A princess in a vision spake to me,   10
     My aunt and uncle by stormtroopers slain,
     A hasty flight from my home, Tatooine,
     A pilot and a Wookiee and a Knight,
     A rescue brave within our cruel foe's grasp,
     My teacher kill'd, and then the final scene: 15
     The Death Star battle—many friends were lost,
     But in the end a greater war was won.
     Adventure hath both taken from my life,
     And given to me ev'rything I have.
     And thus I seek and shun its tempting ways.   20
     E'en now adventure knocks upon the door:
     A flaming orb hath struck the ground nearby.
     Is it a portent of some ill to come?
     [*Into comlink:*] 'Tis Echo-Three to
               Echo-Seven: Han,

	My true companion e'er, canst thou hear me? 25
HAN	[*through comlink:*] Aye, truly, chuck, thy voice
	rings loud and clear.
	What can I do for thee, my noble friend?
LUKE	My circle 'round the area hath been
	Completed now, but naught of life nor forms
	Of life my scan hath yet uncover'd.
HAN	[*through comlink:*] —Nay. 30
	There is not life enough upon this cube
	Of ice to fill an empty space cruiser.
	The sensors have I put in place, so shall
	I now return unto the base.
LUKE	—'Tis well,
	And I, forsooth, shall soon meet with thee there. 35
	But I have spied a met'orite that hath
	Its landing made near here. So shall I go

And fix my eyes upon the scene. I'll not
Be long, I warrant; then, I shall return.

Enter WAMPA, *aside.*

WAMPA   You viewers all, whose gentle hearts do fear   40
               The smallest womp rat creeping on the floor,
               May now perchance both quake and tremble here,
               When wampa rough in wildest rage doth roar.
               Pray know that I a wampa simple am,
               And take no pleasure in my angry mood.   45
               Though with great force this young one's face I slam,
               I prithee know I strike but for my food.
LUKE   Alas, is this th'adventure I am due,
               To die upon a vicious monster's whim?
               I am attackèd by this awful beast!   50
               O fate most wretched—shall I be his feast?

                              [Exit, pursued by a wampa.

SCENE 2.

The rebel base on Hoth.

Enter HAN SOLO.

HAN   A scoundrel may not rise above his place—
               This is a fact the galaxy doth teach.
               For e'en though I have join'd rebellion's ranks
               These many weeks and months, and gain'd respect
               Within their noble band, my scoundrel past   5
               Doth make its harsh demands upon my life.

The bounty hunters sent by Jabba make
Pursuit to win the price upon my head.
So must I go once more unto the depths
Of my old life, find Jabba of the Hutt   10
And pay his ransom, thus to free my soul.
I would not leave my noble rebel friends,
I would not leave the cause for which they fight,
I would not leave the princess and her charm,
I would not leave all these, and yet I must.   15
A life's not well lived under threat of death,
Especially with men of cruel intent—
Who for a price shall fill the Hutt's demands—
Upon the trail of my indebtedness.
And so, my mate Chewbacca and I leave   20
Upon the instant that the ship is set to go.

Enter CHEWBACCA, *working on the* Millennium Falcon.

I say, Chewbacca, ho! Aye, Chewie!

CHEWBAC.   —Auugh!

HAN   Lose not thy temper, gentle Wookiee, nay,
But practice patience; I shall help thee soon.

CHEWBAC.   Egh, auugh, egh.
                [Exit Chewbacca. Han crosses to command center
                        with Princess Leia and General Rieekan.

RIEEKAN   —Solo, wouldst thou speak with me?   25

HAN   Good general, the sensors are in place,
And surely shalt thou know if aught comes near
Our hidden station here.

RIEEKAN   —Well. Prithee say,
Commander Skywalker, hath he yet made

| | Report? |
| HAN | —Nay, truly. He hath gone to see | 30 |

HAN   —Nay, truly. He hath gone to see   30
A met'orite that hath made landfall near.

RIEEKAN With all the met'orites a'falling in
This system, I believe we shall have pains
And trouble in detecting 'proaching ships.

HAN [*aside:*] How shall I tell my news most difficult,   35
And crush this man's great hopes for what's ahead?
Fear not, O heart, but be direct and calm:
'Tis best approach'd straight on, like th'Kessel Run.
[*To Rieekan:*] My general, I cannot stay. I must
Make haste and get me hence, e'en now.

LEIA [*aside:*]   —Alack,   40
How like a death knell sounds this news to me!

RIEEKAN I tell thee truly when I say to thee:
This news doth break this gen'ral's gentle soul.
I could not be more sorry, pilot brave.

HAN A price still lies upon my head, and if   45
I do not make amends with Jabba, I
Shall not repay with money, nay, but life.

RIEEKAN A price too dear, indeed! A death mark is
No kind companion to a free man's life.
Thou art a warrior noble, Solo, and   50
I hate to lose thee.

HAN   —And thou art a kind,
Good general, sirrah, I hate to go.
     [*Exit Rieekan. Han turns to Princess Leia.*
And so, Your Highness great, this is the end.

LEIA 'Tis so.

HAN   —I prithee mourn me not, and show
No sentiment. Farewell, thou princess cold.   55

               [*Aside:*] I go, and hope she'll follow hard upon,
               For if she shall not follow, all is lost.
                   [*Han Solo begins to exit, pursued by Princess Leia.*

LEIA   Han, halt!

HAN   —What is thy pleasure, Highness?

LEIA   I did believe that thou had chos'n to stay.

HAN   The bounty hunter we did meet on Ord   60
               Mantell hath chang'd my mind.

LEIA   —We need thee, Han.

HAN   What "we"? Why speakest thou of "we"?
               Dost thou in royal terms speak here of "we"?
               Hast thou a rodent in thy pocket, such
               That thou and he are "we"? What meanest thou?   65
               What need is there that thou dost share with all?
               Speak not of "we," but "I." O princess, what
               Dost thou most need? Not "we," not "they," but thou?

LEIA   I know not what thou speakest of.

HAN   —'Tis true.
               Most probably thou dost not know thyself.   70

LEIA   And what, pray tell, precisely should I know?
               Of what great myst'ry am I unaware?
               Hast thou the depths of Leia plumb'd and seen
               What lies within my soul, my very core?

HAN   Be not elusive, nay! Thou wouldst that I   75
               Should stay because of how thou feelest in
               Thy heart about me. Need hath turn'd to want.
               Pray, tell me not thy needs, but thy desires.

LEIA   Thou art a leader full of skill, 'tis true.

HAN   Thine answer leadeth thee astray. Let fly!   80
               I see it in thine aspect now, let fly!
               Tell me the answer true.

LEIA   —Thy vanity
                Hath puff'd up thine imagination.
HAN   —Aye?
                Then why dost thou yet follow me? Wert thou
                Afraid I would depart without a kiss?   85
LEIA   I would as eagerly kiss Wookiee lips.
HAN   That can arrangèd be. By heaven's breath,
                A kiss would suit thee well!

                                        [*Exit Han Solo.*

LEIA   —O man of bile!
                Thou wouldst make e'en the coolest temper burn,
                For thou art made of heat and flame and fire.   90
                No wood may stand within a mile of thee
                But it shall roast as if 'twere on the sun.
                And now, thy scorching manner lights my fuse.
                Aye truly, I confess I am aflame:
                Thine eyes create combustion in my heart,   95
                Thy face doth cause my cheeks to flood with warmth,
                Thy fingers set me trembling at their touch,
                Thy hands may hold the secrets of my soul.
                Thou hast a pow'r o'er Leia's very self,
                Yet wear my patience past what I can bear.   100
                For O, how thou dost needle, jest, and prick
                When thou dost think thy pride is at the stake.
                Be not so full of bile, my noble Han.
                I prithee, choose the tender side of wit.
                If thou couldst ever put thy pride away,   105
                Belike my prejudice would fall aside.
                Then could our two hearts sing a melody,
                Instead of clashing in disharmony.

                                        [*Exit Princess Leia.*

SCENE 3.

The rebel base on Hoth.

Enter C-3PO *and* R2-D2, *with* HAN SOLO *and*
CHEWBACCA *aside at the* Millennium Falcon.

C-3PO   O R2, thou dost ever plague me so!
               E'en now have we been in dishonor sent
               Away from our good princess' chamber. Fie!
               Such breach of etiquette and protocol,
               And all the fault doth on thy shoulders lie.   5

R2-D2   Beep, meep, beep, whistle, meep, beep, squeak,
                                             nee, meep!

C-3PO   Lay not thy blame upon my shoulders, droid—
               I did, at no point, ask thee to engage
               The thermal heater. 'Twas but a remark
               Upon the coldness of the princess' room.   10

R2-D2   Beep, whistle, squeak.

C-3PO   —But freezing it should be!
               And now, how shall we dry off all her clothes?
               I truly know not how.

R2-D2   —Beep, meep, beep, hoo.

C-3PO   O, switch off!

               [C-3PO *walks aside toward the* Millennium Falcon.

R2-D2   [*aside:*]   —Watch thy tongue, thou naughty droid,
               Or I shall bring my wit to bear on thee   15
               And thou shalt not escape my shocks and jabs.
               For though I speak aloud in beeps and squeaks,
               Within my mind a keener tongue prevails.
               And though thou like a brother art to me,

I'll happily correct your errant ways.   20
If thou didst think the thermal heater was
Too hot, then shalt thou surely not endure
The fire that I shall kindle with my wit.
                    [*C-3PO makes his way to Han Solo.*

HAN   [*to Chewbacca:*] Why hast thou taken this apart when
            I am striving to depart this wretched place?   25

C-3PO   Excuse me, Sir.

HAN   —Pray, mend the ship, and swift!

C-3PO   Please, Sir, a word with thee.

HAN   —What dost thou want?

C-3PO   'Tis Princess Leia, Sir, she strives to reach
            Thee on th'communicator.

HAN   —Then 'twas wise
            That I did turn it off, for I have no   30
            Desire to speak with her.

C-3PO   —I see. But she
            Hath after Master Luke made inquiry,
            For surely he hath not return'd unto
            The base. She knows not where he is.

HAN   —In that
            Her mind and mine are one. I know not where   35
            He is.

C-3PO   —But no one knows his whereabouts.

HAN   What dost thou mean by "no one," prating droid?
            Deck officer, deck officer!

                    Enter DECK OFFICER.

OFFICER   —Yes, Sir?

HAN   Dost thou know where Commander Skywalker
            Is?

OFFICER   —I've not seen him, but 'tis possible   40
He through the entrance to the south return'd.

HAN   "'Tis possible"? I prithee, good lad, go
Thou thither and find out. It grows quite dark
Outside.

OFFICER   —Aye, Sir.

[Exit deck officer.

C-3PO   —Excuse me, Sir, but may
I ask what doth transpire?

HAN   —Thou mayst indeed.   45

C-3PO   O man impossible! Come thou, R2,
Let us return unto the princess now.
The drying of her clothes is now the least
Of all our worries, for another ill
Far greater than our mishap is afoot.   50
In confidence I tell thee: I do fear
That Master Luke grave danger doth confront.

[Exit C-3PO and R2-D2.

HAN   What portents strange, what evil tidings this:
My friend by no one seen, the droids afraid,
Chewbacca prone to error with the ship,   55
The young deck officer so tentative—
These things foretell some ill that shall occur.
But if misfortune toucheth anyone,
Let it be me and not my partner, Luke.
For he is like a brother unto me,   60
As all who fight with me in battle are.
Though I did save him in the Death Star clash,
'Tis he hath sav'd me from the smuggler's life
By leading me on paths more true than I
Had e'er foreseen. Now do I call him friend,   65

And this rebellion is the cause we share.
From all my friends here I would not depart
If I were not by Jabba hunted down.
Aye, I would give my bones—my life—for great
Rebellion's sake if e'er it were requir'd.   70
But soft you now: the officer returns.

Enter DECK OFFICER.

OFFICER   Good Sir, Commander Skywalker hath not
             Come in the entrance to the south. He may
             Have but forgotten to check in.
HAN   —Nay, nay.
             His nature is not thus. Now tell me, are   75
             The speeders ready?
OFFICER   —Nay, we have not yet
             Adapted them unto the cold of Hoth.
HAN   So then upon a tauntaun's back I'll ride.
             Though with especial foulness they abuse
             My nose, they are the speediest we have.   80
OFFICER   But Sir, the temp'rature doth drop too fast
             For any living being to survive.
HAN   'Tis true, and my dear friend doth bear the brunt.
             He shall not die while I have life or breath,
             For neither snow nor ice nor gloom of Hoth   85
             Shall stay my rescue of my greatest friend.
OFFICER   Thy tauntaun shall but freeze ere thou canst ride
             Unto our prim'ry marker, I predict.
HAN   Then I shall dine with thee tonight in Hell!
                  [*Exeunt Han Solo, Chewbacca, and deck officer.*

Enter LUKE SKYWALKER, *hanging upside down from balcony.*

LUKE   What warren, friends, is this? I am within   90
Some icy shelter. Now I do recall—
The creature large hath ta'en me by surprise,
Then quickly did my body overpow'r
By knocking me aside with painful blow.
It kill'd my tauntaun with its vicious claw,   95
Unmovèd by the creature's awful scream.
It must have dragg'd us to this frozen lair.
E'en now I hear it gnaw my tauntaun's flesh,
The stench of musty death is in my nose.
Now I'm awake, hung up by my own feet,   100
And sounds of tearing skin and crunching bone
Do echo through the monster's gloomy cave.
The tauntaun, though, is only the first dish,
And I am bound to be the second course.
Indeed, I have a problem grave, and how   105
Shall I make rescue for myself? But wait—
What's there—a'lying on the snow nearby?
It is my lightsaber—how fortunate!
'Tis still too far to grasp with my own reach:
Thus call I on the Force to save my life.   110
O concentrate, and call upon the things
Thou learn'st from Obi-Wan when he still liv'd.
Forsooth, I feel the Force begin to flow—
Within, nearby, inside, surrounding me.
O Force most strong—the lightsaber's at hand!   115
Now am I free to flee the fierce beast's clutch,
But, lo, the creature comes to me anon!
It will attack me in its fiery rage

Unless I am the first to strike. Lay on!

Enter WAMPA. *Luke cuts off the wampa's arm and exits quickly.*

WAMPA   Alas, how I am by this man abus'd—   120
         Could I, for seeking food, not be excus'd?
         It seemeth that this wampa shall have strife.
         Thus, gentles all: have pity on my life.

                             [Exit wampa.

SCENE 4.

The rebel base on Hoth.

Enter C-3PO, R2-D2, PRINCESS LEIA, *and* CHEWBACCA.

C-3PO   O horrid interim of waiting, time
         That doth like snail unwillingly creep by.
         Full many hours have pass'd without a word
         Of Master Luke or Captain Solo. Now
         The day grows late, and whisper'd words of fear   5
         Throughout the base are heard for these men's fate.
         It seems that all lose heart, and think the worst,
         For how can e'en our bold Han Solo stand
         The harsh and unrelenting chill of Hoth?
         But now, no more, C-3PO; thou art   10
         Not made to worry and to fret. Be brave!
         Come now, R2, there's no more we can do.
         Behold, my joints are freezing.
R2-D2   —Whistle, hoo.
C-3PO   Say not such things! Of course we shall set eyes
         On Master Luke again. And he shall be   15

In perfect health, thou impish little droid.
Aye, he shall be in perfect health.

R2-D2   [*aside:*]   —I fear
This chill that doth e'en now my metal frame
Assault. 'Tis cold unto the core. 'Tis cold,
I fear, unto the death. Bear up, droid soul,   20
And listen to C-3PO's advice:
Be thou a helpful strength amid distress.

                Enter LIEUTENANT *and* MAJOR DERLIN.

LIEUT.   Sir, all patrols are in, and still no sign
From either Skywalker or Solo.
DERLIN   —Dread!
C-3PO   My Mistress Leia, R2 makes report   25
He hath not any signals yet receiv'd.
However, he admitteth that his range
Is far too weak to give up ev'ry hope.
DERLIN   Your Highness, I do fear there's nothing more
That we may do tonight. The shield doors must   30
Be closèd.
LEIA   —I consent, but with a heart
That breaketh even now.
DERLIN   [*to Lieutenant:*]   —Aye, close the doors.
R2-D2   Meep, beep, meep squeak.
C-3PO   —Now R2 doth report
The odds of their survival in the cold
Are seven hundred twenty-five to one.   35
                                        [*The shield doors close.*
CHEWBAC.   Egh, grrm, egh, auugh!
C-3PO   —Though R2's wont to make

Mistakes, from time to time. O dear, O dear.

        [Exeunt Princess Leia, Chewbacca,
           Lieutenant, and Major Derlin.

R2-D2   [*aside:*] Why did I speak? O curse my beeping tongue!
"A helpful strength" I pledg'd that I would be,
But now have made these matters worse, for I   40
Have giv'n our princess reason to be scar'd.
Yet I do worry for my master's life,
And though I would not cause undue distress
I fear that he may never make return.
[*To C-3PO:*] Beep, squeak.

C-3PO   —Nay, fear thou not, my silver friend.   45
I'll warrant he shall surely be all right,
For Master Luke is clever, young, and spry
E'en for a human being. So say I!

                     [Exeunt.

SCENE 5.

The ice world of Hoth.

Enter LUKE SKYWALKER.

LUKE   O what a torment have I just endur'd!
For after my attack by creature cruel,
I quickly made my exit from his lair
And made my great escape amidst the snow.
Far, far I ran to find a refuge safe,   5
Yet too far from the rebels' base I've gone.
And now my strength has left—I fail again—
My body falls, too weak to make its way.

[He falls.

Enter GHOST OF OBI-WAN KENOBI.

But now, e'en now, what vision comes to me?

OBI-WAN   Luke!

LUKE   —Ben?

OBI-WAN   —Attend me, Luke. Thou shalt unto   10
The system Dagobah go.

LUKE   —Dagobah?

OBI-WAN   There thou shalt learn the Force from Yoda, aye—
The Jedi master who instructed me.

[Exit Ghost of Obi-Wan Kenobi.

LUKE   Ben, leave me not! Alas, I fall again.

*[Luke collapses as Han enters and
dismounts his tauntaun.*

HAN   Amid the burning snow and winter's bite,   15
Have I this journey ta'en to find my friend.
But lo, what is this sight that now I see?
'Tis Luke, collaps'd! O lad, be thou not dead!
Give me some sign thou livest! Aye, Luke, live!
The cold of Hoth shall yet be warmth to me   20
If thou art still alive. Come now, good friend!

[The tauntaun falls over, frozen to death.

LUKE   [*muttering:*] O Ben, O Dagobah!

*[Han takes Luke's lightsaber and cuts open
the tauntaun, pulling Luke close to its warmth.*

HAN   —We've not much time.
Stay with me, Luke. 'Tis true, this shall smell bad,
But also shall it keep thee warm until
The shelter hath erected been. O, vile!   25
These tauntauns have an awful stench outside,

But nothing did I know of wretchedness,
Disgusting rot, and sick'ning filth till this
New smell hath made attack upon my nose.

                 [Han sits with Luke as night passes.

The shelter now is fashion'd by my hands   30
Both strong and deft. We shall await the morn
With only tauntaun's guts as company.
O guardian of nighttime travelers,
Be with me and my comrade Luke this eve,
For we are merely pilgrims far from home   35
Who wish to come again unto our mates.
Now sev'ral anxious hours we've huddl'd here,
And with the morning dawns the light of hope.
My rebel friends shall surely make attempt
To find where Luke and I have spent the night.   40
Search well, my lads, the prize waits to be found!

Enter ZEV *aside, flying.*

ZEV   The speeders all have been prepar'd, and now
             A proper search for Luke and Han begins.
             But what is this? Shall fortune be so kind?
             My sensors do report some life forms near,   45
             Mayhap the cherish'd find shall yet be mine.
             Pray listen, Echo Base, to my report:
             There's something here my scanner hath just found.
             'Tis yet unsure, but may a life form be.
             Commander Skywalker, dost thou hear me?   50
             'Tis Rogue Two. O good captain Solo, dost
             Thou hear? 'Tis Rogue Two.
HAN   —Fine good morning, lads,
             'Twas nice of you to fin'lly come around.
ZEV   Hear, Echo Base: I say, they have been found!

                                             [Exeunt.

SCENE 6.
The rebel base on Hoth.

Enter LUKE SKYWALKER, *reclining on bed.*

LUKE   Through hazy dreams I have vague memories
             Of being taken to the rebel base
             And given the droid medic's greatest care.
             Now here I am, and naught but scars remain,
             Thus is the creature's foul at last made fair.   5

Enter C-3PO, R2-D2, *and* PRINCESS LEIA.

C-3PO   Good Master Luke, my wires are fill'd with joy
       To see thee fully functional again.

R2-D2   [*aside:*] O that I too could speak aloud!
                       [*To Luke:*] Meep, squeak!

C-3PO   R2 expresseth his relief as well!

         Enter HAN SOLO *and* CHEWBACCA.

HAN   How goes it with thee, chuck? O verily,   10
       Thou dost look well to me. In faith, thou seem'st
       E'en strong enough, I'll warr'nt, to pull the ears
       From off a gundark.

LUKE   —Truly, thanks to thee.

HAN   Now thou dost owe me two good turns, my friend.
       [*To Leia:*] Indeed, Your Worship, well have you
                       conspir'd   15
       To keep me in thy presence longer.

LEIA   —Fie!
       'Twas not my doing. Gen'ral Rieekan doth
       Believe that it is still too dangerous
       For any ship to leave the system, aye—
       E'en thy belov'd *Millenn'um Falcon*—till   20
       The shield of energy is active.

HAN   —Ha!
       A cloth of fiction thou dost weave, yet I
       Have found the fatal error in thy stitch:
       For I believe thou wouldst not let a man
       So beautiful as I depart from thee.   25

LEIA   The only stitch I know is in my side,
       From laughing at thy pride most heartily.
       Thou mayst attempt to needle at my heart,

But I am sewn of stronger thread than this.
To say I would not let thee go—pish, pish!   30
I know not whence thy great delusions come,
Thou laser brain.

CHEWBAC.   [*laughing:*]   —Gihut, gihut, gihut!

HAN   Aye, laugh indeed, thou fuzzball large. But thou
Hast not seen us alone i' th'passage south,
Where she did unto me unspool, in full,   35
Her feelings true of fondest love for me.

LEIA   My feelings? O! Thou arrogant half-wit,
Thou oversizèd child, thou friend of slime,
Thou man of scruffy looks, thou who herd'st nerfs,
Thou fool-born wimpled roughhewn waste of flesh!   40

HAN   What scruffy? Scruffy, how? Whose scruffiness?
How am I all bescruff'd? [*To Luke:*] Belike my words
Were accurate and hit upon the mark,
Since now she hath her temper lost. True, Luke?

LEIA   Thus is it plain that till thou tam'st thy tongue,   45
No tongue of woman shalt thou comprehend.
                    [*Leia kisses Luke at length, then exits.*

CHEWBAC.   Egh, auugh, gihut!

OFFICER   [*from speaker:*]   —All personnel report
Unto the center of command at once.

HAN   [*aside:*] Well hath she play'd the trump.
                              [*To Luke:*] Be thou at ease.
                    [*Exeunt Han Solo, Chewbacca, C-3PO,
                                        and R2-D2.*

LUKE   O kiss most rare, O lips from heaven sent!   50
This is a moment I'll not soon forget.
Though I can sense her heart doth turn to Han,
Still doth this kiss play tricks upon my soul.

By this fair princess I have been bewitch'd—
'Twas ever so since I saw her distress   55
In R2's beam, a'pleading for our help.
But though the lass doth move my heart to joy
I ne'er would tempt her with a word too large,
For shall a Jedi's path lead t'ward romance?
But this sweet kiss I'll hold in mem'ry's vault   60
As a reminder of my noble cause:
To serve rebellion and my princess kind.

                       [Exit Luke.

Enter HAN SOLO, CHEWBACCA, C-3PO, *and* R2-D2, *crossing to*
GENERAL RIEEKAN, *the* CONTROLLER, *and* PRINCESS LEIA.

RIEEKAN   A visitor hath come, my princess. 'Tis
            Outside the base, in sector twelve, and doth
            Appear to be directed eastward.
CONTROL.   —'Tis   65
            A thing of metal, cold and harsh and sleek—
            It is not animal.
LEIA   —Well, then 'tis not
            The self-same creature that did harm our Luke.
            But what do ye men think that it may be?
HAN   Belike a speeder, one of ours?
CONTROL.   —Nay, wait.   70
            A signal dim doth reach unto mine ears.

                     [A faint signal is heard.
PROBE   *[through comlink:]* Beh mena bem bem. Mena bem
                               bem beh.
C-3PO   Good Sir, six million forms of language do
            I know, and I may tell thee true that this

Strange signal is not by th'Alliance us'd.   75
It may, perhaps, be an Imperi'l code.

HAN   'Tis not a friendly sound, that much is sure.
Now Chewie, come with me and we'll to it.
[*Aside:*] Snow creatures first, and now Imperi'l droids,
What portents of great evil may these be?   80
Though I am brave, forsooth these signs do make
E'en my courageous heart begin to fear.
I find myself afraid of what may come,
That my whole soul shall freeze ere this is done.
[*To all:*] Chewbacca and myself have ventur'd out   85
To see the probe. Now Chewie gives a shout—
It fires on him, and I respond in turn.
Be gone, thou enemy of all that's right.
But wait, now what hath happen'd? I releas'd
A blast most simple—aye, a single blast.   90
Yet it appears that single blast was all
It could withstand; the blast was lethal, friends.
Now naught is left, for it hath been destroy'd.

LEIA   What was't?

HAN   —A droid. My blast did not strike hard,
Belike the thing did self-destruct.

LEIA   —'Tis clear!   95
A probe droid from the Empire. This doth mean
The start of our rebellion's flight from Hoth,
For now that we discoverèd have been
We lack security.

HAN   —Agreed. Methinks
The Empire knoweth we are here on Hoth.   100
[*Aside:*] My sense of doom and dread is not without
Its cause, for this event is grave indeed.

RIEEKAN Good friends, dear rebels, comrades one and all,
     We have no choice but to flee hastily.
     Our swift evacuation shall commence,   105
     And till 'tis done, make ready our defense.

               [Exeunt.

SCENE 7.

Aboard the Empire's Super Star Destroyer.

Enter ADMIRAL OZZEL, GENERAL VEERS,
and CAPTAIN PIETT.

PIETT My admiral?
OZZEL   —Yes, Captain.
PIETT   —Here's a thing
     That thou shouldst see, good Sir. We have receiv'd
     Report from a Hoth system probe, the best
     That we have found so far.
OZZEL   —Your best, belike,
     Shall bested be, for thousands of these probes 5
     We have a'wandering the galaxy
     And looking for the rebels. I want proof,
     Piett, not leads. Proof—only that—is best.
PIETT But Sir, this best is better yet, for it
     Hath found some forms of life upon the ground. 10
OZZEL How better yet? How best? It could be but
     An error or some useless reading. If
     We were to follow ev'ry lead, our best
     Would soon turn worst.
PIETT   —And yet I do maintain

My best is better yet for this: 'tis said   15
That Hoth is all devoid of human forms.
It seems, good Sir, the rebels have been found.
Why else would sign of life appear on Hoth?
I'll warrant, Sir, my forecast shall prevail.

Enter DARTH VADER.

VADER   You have found something good?
PIETT   —My Lord, we have.   20
          A probe that late hath made descent on Hoth
          Hath made discovery of both life forms
          And the appearance of a power source.
                              [Piett shows Vader the screen.
VADER   Thy judgment hath prov'd best, Piett: 'tis them.
          Forsooth, the rebels may be found therein.   25
OZZEL   My Lord, there are throughout the galaxy
          So many settlements we have not mapp'd.
          This could be smugglers, maybe even—
VADER   —Nay,
          That is the system, certain am I of't,
          And Skywalker is with them there. Now set   30
          Thy course t'ward Hoth, and Gen'ral Veers, prepare
          Your men for combat.
                              [Exeunt Admiral Ozzel, General Veers,
                                        and Captain Piett.
                      —Hath not a Sith eyes?
          Hath not a Sith such feelings, heart, and soul,
          As any Jedi Knight did e'er possess?
          If you prick us, do we not bleed? If you   35
          Blast us, shall we not injur'd be? If you

Assault with lightsaber, do we not die?
I have a body as do other men,
Though made, in part, of wires and steel. And aye,
I vari'us passions feel, as all men do.   40
So I, a Sith, shall not distracted be
Till I attain the thing for which I seek.
Therefore I shall pursue this Skywalker
Unto the limit of the galaxy.
For true, he hath the Death Star quite destroy'd,   45
And true, he hath the Force with him as well.
But truly, more than that the boy doth have—
For truth be told, his name doth stir my soul.
The boy's connection to myself I do
Not understand as yet. This Skywalker   50
Must have some link to my life past, but what?
So shall this Sith pursue this rebel lad,
And find the missing truth of Vader's life.

Enter GENERAL VEERS.

VADER   What news dost thou have, Gen'ral Veers?
VEERS   —My Lord,
    Our noble fleet hath flown to Hoth in haste   55
    With hopes to catch the rebels by surprise.
    The fleet has movèd out of lightspeed now,
    But com-scan hath detected a sharp shield
    Of energy surrounding planet six
    Within the system. It is strong enough   60
    To hinder what bombardment we can make.
    This grim news I report with sadden'd mien:
    It seems, my Lord, our fleet is all too close.

VADER   The rebels are aware of our attack,
               For Adm'ral Ozzel left lightspeed too near   65
               To the Hoth system.

VEERS   —He believ'd surprise
               Was wiser . . .

VADER   —Say no more. Speak not to his
               Defense. He is as clumsy as he is
               Replete with ignorance. Prepare your troops
               Now, Veers, to lead a ground attack. We shall   70
               Still win the day, despite the blunder.

VEERS   —Aye.

                                   [*Exit General Veers.*

VADER *hails* ADMIRAL OZZEL *and* CAPTAIN PIETT,
               who enter by balcony.

OZZEL   Lord Vader, I am happy to report
               The fleet has come out of lightspeed and is
               Prepar'd to—

                         [*Darth Vader begins to choke Admiral Ozzel*
                                             using the Force.

VADER   —Thou hast fail'd me once again,
               But nevermore shalt thou have chance to fail.   75
               I bring the Force to bear upon thy throat
               That thou, in thy last breath, shalt know my pow'r.
               Captain Piett?

PIETT   —My Lord?

VADER   —Prepare to land
               Our troops beyond the shield of energy,
               And then deploy our fleet so naught can 'scape   80
               The system. Do it, Admiral Piett.

And be thou sure to rise to thy new rank.

        [Admiral Ozzel dies. Exit Darth Vader.

PIETT   Alas, with this promotion comes some dread,
For Vader hath no rev'rence for the head.

        [Exit.

ACT II

SCENE 1.

The rebel base on Hoth.

Enter HAN SOLO *and* CHEWBACCA,
working on the Millennium Falcon
with a MAINTENANCE DROID.

HAN   A pilot must respect his ship with care,
      And play physician to her ev'ry need.
      With patience and with tender healing touch
      I caringly embrace each bolt and wire.
      Now, 'tis repair'd. [*To Chewbacca:*] Good Chewie,
                          try it now!   5

CHEWBAC.   Egh.
                      [*The ship begins to smoke and spark.*

HAN   —Nay! Act thou with speed, and turn it off!
      [*Aside:*] Physician, heal thyself from too much haste.

Enter LUKE SKYWALKER.

LUKE   [*aside:*] The last time I said my farewell to these
      Compatriots of mine, 'twas ere the Death
      Star battle when it seem'd as though they were   10
      Deserting us. But now, their valor prov'd,
      Their hearts align'd with good Rebellion's cause,
      I'll wish them on their merry way with joy.
      [*To Chewbacca:*] Chewbacca, brave, 'tis now my time
                             to leave,
      For soon to Dagobah my path is bound.   15

CHEWBAC.   [*embracing Luke:*] Egh!

LUKE   —How your tight embrace doth warm my heart—
              But also strains my bones, thou jolly brute.
HAN   Well met, young lad. [*To droid:*] There must a reason be
              Why this malfunction hath occur'd. But now,
              I prithee, get thee hence.

                                        [*Exit maintenance droid.*
                              Art thou yet well?   20
LUKE   Aye, verily. [*Aside:*] O what words would I say
              To this man here, if words were loud enough!
              But hath a word e'er been created, which
              Could tell the comrade's love I feel for him,
              Articulate the good I sense in him,   25
              Express the debt of life I owe to him?
              At times 'tis true that words betray us all—
              The mighty pow'r of language fails to speak,
              And neither tongue nor rhetoric gives aid.
              This Han hath found a life among our band   30
              That did transform his former, solo self,
              But now he takes his leave to pay the price
              Of former indiscretions come to call.
              I would explain how much he means to me,
              I would disclose my deep respect for him,   35
              I would unveil my brotherlike regard,
              I would reveal the workings of my soul—
              But at this moment words are render'd weak.
              Thus, he must see the story in my eyes,
              Peruse the tale that's told within my heart, 40
              And there read more than ever can be penn'd.
HAN   Now be thou careful, friend.
LUKE   —And thou as well.
                                        [*Exit Luke Skywalker.*

HAN   A noble lad, and true. If Fate is kind,
             I shall make right the danger I am in
             And live to fight aside him once again.   45
                          [*Exeunt Han Solo and Chewbacca.*

             Enter the CONTROLLER *and* GENERAL RIEEKAN.

CONTROL.   My general, a group of Star Destroy'rs
             Has just emerg'd from hyperspace, and now
             Has been detected in yon sector four.
RIEEKAN   Divert all pow'r unto our forward shield.
             In doing so we may protect the base   50
             Until the transports their escape have made.
             Then, let us all prepare for ground assault.
             [*To all:*] Good gentlemen and women, come ye near!
             For we shall now our very lives defend.

             Enter REBEL PILOTS, *including* HOBBIE *and*
                 MAJOR DERLIN, *and* PRINCESS LEIA.

LEIA   Good cheer! All preparation hath been made,   55
             Both for the swift retreat of transports hence,
             And to defend our base until they're fled.
             The carriers shall meet up at the north,
             And larger transports leave once they are full.
             Two fighter escorts shall be sent with each   60
             And shall remain quite close, for our strong shield
             Will be disarm'd a fleeting length of time.
             'Twill be a passage dangerous no doubt,
             But with the Force we shall prevail, indeed.
HOBBIE   I prithee, say again: shall only two   65

	Of our small fighters match a Star Destroy'r?
LEIA	Pray, screw your courage to the sticking place.
	Our ion cannons shall with lethal fire
	Make ev'ry pathway clear. When you have clear'd

The shield of energy, then go anon   70
Unto our rendezvous. Do all agree?
Will ye all go in great rebellion's name?

ALL   Aye, Princess, aye!

HOBBIE   —We shall heed thy command.

DERLIN   Now ev'ryone unto their stations, go!

                     [Exeunt rebel pilots, including Hobbie
                               and Lieutenant Derlin.

RIEEKAN   *[to Controller:]* Belike the power generators will   75
                Their prim'ry target be. Prepare thou now
                To open up the shield. And may the Force
                Attend our swift retreat, our hearts inspire!

CONTROL.   Now standby ion cannon; aye, and fire.

                                       [Exeunt.

SCENE 2.

The ice world of Hoth.

Enter CHORUS.

CHORUS   The transports make their way deep into space;
                The ion cannon leads as they take flight.
                But now the rebels grave new dangers face,
                As th'Empire sends a ground assault to fight.

Enter LUKE SKYWALKER *and* DACK, *his copilot, with* REBEL PILOTS,
including WEDGE ANTILLES, JANSON, *and* ZEV.

DACK   How dost thou fare, good Sir? For I have heard   5
            Of your unlucky recent incident.
            How is it with thee after the attack?
LUKE   Quite well, I thank thee, Dack. And art thou well?
DACK   Aye, truthfully, Commander—I do feel
            I could the Empire overthrow myself,   10
            If I were giv'n the opportunity.
            A single warrior to bring them down,
            A single hand to show rebellion's strength,
            A single mind that could outwit them all,
            A single Dack to best the Empire's might.   15
LUKE   O noble soul, how like a soldier said!
            It seems that thou and I are fashion'd from
            One cloth—one fabric knits our souls together.
            The feeling you express is one I've known.
            Indeed, it is a potent privilege,   20
            But also brings responsibility.

Enter AT-ATS 1, 2, *and* 3, *giant Imperial walkers, on other side.*

AT-AT 1   But who did bid thee join with us?
AT-AT 3   —Piett.
            'Twas he who order'd me to come with ye
            To crush the rebels and their little base.
AT-AT 2   Well said, for I know of no baser base—   25
            'Twill be a vict'ry great when 'tis destroy'd.
            But think ye we shall in this fight prevail?
            The rebels are a force formidable.

AT-AT 1   My friends, we have had quite enough of talk:
           The battle is upon us, let us go.   30
           And ye who doubt, I pray remember this:
           Although we are but AT-ATs gray and plain,
           We have a noble task to undertake—
           Our mighty Emperor's reign to protect,
           The great Darth Vader to obey and aid,   35
           And Admiral Piett to serve with pride.
           So shall an AT-AT swoon before the fight,
           Or should our legs be shaken ere th'assault?
           Have we been made to cower? I say nay!
           An AT-AT should be made of sterner stuff.   40
AT-AT 3   [*to AT-AT 2:*] I pray, good walker, is he ever thus?
AT-AT 2   Aye, truly, Sir, I never yet have met
           An All Terrain Armorèd Transport who
           Is loftier of mind than this one here.
           Indeed, although like us he's made of steel,   45
           He never enters battle zones unless

          He hath made some great speech to steel his nerves.

          It does no harm.

AT-AT 3   —No harm, but to mine ears.

          I'd rather fight than hear another speech.

AT-AT 1   Now let us go, these rebels to destroy!   50

                 [The AT-ATs advance on Luke Skywalker

                            and other rebel pilots.

LUKE   *[to rebel pilots:]* Now stay together, men.

DACK   —Alas, good Luke,

          The ship's computer hath malfunction'd. O,

          I am not set for this attack!

LUKE   —Be patient.

          We shall use pattern delta now, anon!

                 [Rebels and AT-ATs duel, and

                          rebels quickly retreat.

          A hit! A very palpable hit. Wait,   55

          Although my shots have found their mark, their blasts

          Have no effect. It is their armor, fie!

          Our blasters are too weak to penetrate

          The strength of their robust exteriors.

          Rogue group, use thy harpoons and cables, too.   60

          Let us go for their legs and trip them up—

          Perhaps they may be bested from beneath.

          Dack, art thou with me?

DACK   —This malfunction hath

          Put fire into the system. I'll attempt

          To quickly gain some pow'r another way.   65

LUKE   I prithee, be thou careful now, young Dack!

                [The fight resumes. Dack is struck.

DACK   Alas, I die! Farewell, Commander Luke!

                       [Dack dies.

LUKE   Nay, Dack! O agony of battle, curse
              Of war, and dread of ev'ry soldier's heart:
              To suffer at the hands of enemies,   70
              To end one's days by pow'r of the unjust!
              What use is war? For it doth ravage all
              Within its path, and what hath it e'er solv'd?
              'Tis rare that peace doth follow in war's wake.
              Indeed, this recent blow doth only urge   75
              And heighten my destructive sentiments:
              I shall avenge thee, Dack, and slay these here
              Who have thy lifeblood ta'en, and seal'd thy fate.

AT-AT 2   No more of these amusements with the weak.
              'Tis time to make this victory our own: 80
              Head for the power generator, mates,
              The battle's nearly won!

LUKE   —Rogue Three, dost hear?

WEDGE   I do, Rogue Leader.

LUKE   —Wedge, I need thee now.
              I've lost my gunner: thou must strike their legs
              With thy harpoon. I'll give thee aid—we'll fly   85
              Together, follow close behind me.

WEDGE   —Aye!
              Now activate harpoon and slay these beasts!
                    [The fight resumes. Wedge and his gunner, Janson,
                         strike AT-AT 1 with a rope around the legs.

AT-AT 1   What treachery! The rebels have assail'd
              My weakest part. My legs, good comrades—they
              Have struck where I most vulnerable am.   90

WEDGE   Well hit, brave Janson. Now encircle him
              And bring this giant down to meet his end.
              It worketh, friends! His legs hath been confin'd,

And thus the brute hath trouble with his stride.

Just one more pass around, and then detach!   95

JANSON The cable is detach'd! He falls!

AT-AT 1   —Alack;

I perish now, my comrades. Win the day!

                              [AT-AT 1 falls and dies.

WEDGE A-ha!—and thus our Dack hath been aveng'd!

LUKE I see thy handiwork; well done, strong Wedge.

Dack's memory we honor by this strike.   100

AT-AT 2 The rebels have destroy'd one of our lot,

But we shall yet o'erwhelm them utterly.

I'll make approach unto their hidden base,

Identify their systems in my sights,

And then shall on the generator fire.   105

LUKE Rogue Two, art thou beside me in this fight?

We need the help of ev'ry fighter here.

Not long ago thou rescu'd Han and me

From our meek shelter on the ice of Hoth:

Thou art a man of cunning, strength, and wit.   110

And thus I ask thee on thy honor, Sir:

Art thou prepar'd to face this harsh assault?

ZEV Aye, verily, Rogue Leader, that I am.

My life I am prepar'd to sacrifice

To save rebellion from this fierce attack.   115

LUKE Then let us all approach the knaves again.

Prepare your swift harpoon and we shall strike!

AT-AT 3 They think themselves the noble ones, but we

Defend the Emp'ror's righteousness today.

AT-AT 2 Well spoken. Let us fight for Empire's might!   120

                              [They duel again.

ZEV O Luke, I have been hit, and die anon!

Remember me whene'er thou speak'st of this.
    [Zev is slain. Luke is struck and falls to the ground.

LUKE   Alas, poor Zev. Too many lost—such good
And worthy men have met their end to these
Confounded walkers. Fie! This battle bleak   125
May mean Rebellion's end. 'Tis now my turn—
My ship hath ta'en a hit. I fall, yet am
Not slain. Indeed, though here I lie upon
The ground, I spy an opportunity.
For while this awful monster walks above,   130
I spy his weakness as I lie below.
He passes just beyond me—now to it!
Revenge should have no bounds when friends are
                            slain,
And now their memory doth push me on.
My lightsaber shall strike the lethal blow;   135
I'll hit where he shall feel it, in his heart—
If ever such cruel beast did have a heart.
        [Luke strikes AT-AT 3 from below,
                and AT-AT 3 dies.

AT-AT 3   I perish, comrade true, but fall with pride!
AT-AT 2   Although my fellow AT-ATs meet their ends,
I press toward my goal with purpose firm.   140
The rebels' power generator is
Within the target of my lasers keen.
Now all the fallen AT-ATs I salute
As for my noble Emperor I shoot!
        [He shoots and destroys the power generator.
                Exeunt all, in confusion.

SCENE 3.

The rebel base on Hoth.

Enter GENERAL RIEEKAN *and*
PRINCESS LEIA, *with an aide.*

RIEEKAN   Our pow'r is insufficient to protect
     Two transports at one time.
LEIA   —'Tis risky, aye,
     But this base overpower'd is, and shall,
     I fear, withstand no more of this attack.
     We have no choice.
RIEEKAN   —Indeed, thou speakest true.   5
     [*Into comlink:*] Launch all patrols.
LEIA   [*to aide:*]   —Evacuate the staff
     Who do remain within the base. Make haste!

Enter HAN SOLO *and* CHEWBACCA *on balcony,*
repairing the Millennium Falcon.

HAN   These endless fixes now are nearly done,
     And soon we may take flight. 'Tis none too soon—
     This base shall not survive this great attack.   10
CHEWBAC.   Auugh!
HAN   —Nay, nay! This one here and that one there.
     'Tis clear? [*Aside:*] I do admit this Wookiee here is dear,
     But if he break my ship I'll break his pate!

Enter C-3PO *with* R2-D2, *aside.*

C-3PO   My R2 small, pray be thou safe, good friend,

And take especial care of Master Luke.   15
Farewell, farewell! Parting is such sweet sorrow
That I shall say farewell till thou hast left.

R2-D2   [*aside:*] "Till thou hast left"? No poet he, indeed.
Alas, it seems that romance is not one
Of 3PO's six million forms of speech.   20

      [Exit R2-D2. C-3PO moves to Princess Leia and
      General Rieekan. Loud sounds of shaking are heard.

HAN   O zounds! What is this pow'rful shaking here?
The base begins to crumble even now.
Our humble shelter made of snow and ice
Is now defeated by the Empire's might
And starts to fall apart. O, shall we too?   25
Shall our rebellion suffer this same Fate—
To be destroyèd by the Empire cruel?
To be demolish'd by Imperi'l strength?
Though I had plann'd to go and save myself
From Jabba's bounty hunters, I cannot: 30
This smuggler-captain never shall desert
Whilst friends nearby do mortal peril face.
I shall not steal away and leave behind
The princess who doth lead the rebels true.
She is of great importance, and my life   35
Must be but secondary to her fate.
So shall I take her in the *Falcon* swift
And spirit her away to someplace safe.
'Tis not because of how I feel about
Her, nay; naught there of love, that much is true—   40
Or if 'tis not, I'll tell myself it is.
Now to it, Han, ere our great cause is lost.

      [Han Solo moves to General Rieekan
      and Princess Leia.

Your Worship, art thou well?

LEIA   —O, wherefore art
Thou yet within this base? Hast thou not fled?

HAN   The center of command has been struck down.   45

LEIA   And yet hast thou thy clearance to depart.

HAN   Depart I shall, but first deliver thee
Unto thy ship.

C-3PO   —Your Highness, we must take
This final transport. 'Tis our only hope!

                              [A blast is heard, closer.

OFFICER   [*through comlink:*] Imperi'l troops have come into
                                        the base!   50
Imperi'l troops have come into the base!

HAN   Now end thy stubborn ways, and set aside
Thy prejudice. Thou wilt come with me now,
I do command it. Neither argument
Nor moving speech nor aught that thou canst say   55
Shall sway me now: thou wilt come with me, Princess.

LEIA   [*aside:*] O noble man, protector of my soul!
[*To aide:*] Send our evacuation code and get
Thee to thy transport.

                    *[Exeunt General Rieekan and aide. Han Solo and
                    Princess Leia begin to walk toward the transport.*

C-3PO   —Prithee, wait for me!

                              *[As they make their way to the ship,
                              a wall falls in their path.*

HAN   The battle is within the very walls,   60
And ev'ry portent tells of dread and doom.
[*Into comlink:*] Good transport, this is Solo. Take
                                        your leave—
Our way has now become a wayward thing,

	All fill'd with mounds of ice that block our path.	
	This moment calls for quick decision. Thus,	65
	I shall with Leia flee on *Falcon*'s wings.	

> [*Han Solo and Princess Leia run the other way,*
> *toward the* Millennium Falcon, *shutting*
> *the door against* C-3PO.

C-3PO   But wait, where do you go? Pray, do come back!
Most typical this is. O wretched fate,
To be deserted by my friends most dear.
These human beings care but little for   70
Us droids who ever serve with loyalty.
Thus shall I end my days within this base,
A frozen remnant of the rebels' stay
On Hoth. Belike one day explorers shall
Discover this defeated base, shall dig   75
Into its core and find a golden droid
Whose final resting place was ice and snow.
"Who would abandon such a lovely droid?"
No doubt this shall be their response when they
Espy me here. "What wretched humans would   80
Leave such a one as this alone to rot?"
I shudder at this thought, let it not be!
O open up your hearts unto my kind,
Then open wide this door for kindness' sake!

> [*The door opens.*

HAN   Anon, thou goldenrod, thou heap of scrap,   85
Else shalt thou ever stay within this base
And make thyself a lasting icy grave.

C-3PO   [*aside:*] This man is both the reason for my pain
And for my joy. My gratitude o'erflows!

> [*They enter the* Millennium Falcon.

HAN   *[to Chewbacca:]* Now wherefore doth the ship not
                                       function right?   90
LEIA   Pray, would it help if I did disembark
              And push with all a princess' might upon't?
HAN   Belike!
C-3PO   —Pray, Captain Solo, Captain Solo!
HAN   Tut!
C-3PO   —It shall wait.
LEIA   —This bucket full of bolts
              Shall ne'er beyond that blockade make escape.   95
              We may as well depart the base aboard
              A tauntaun's furry back!
HAN   —The ship hath yet
              Surprising, keen maneuvers, sweetheart. Watch!
              The ship protects us with its lasers true
              Against th'Imperi'l troops who come at us.   100
              See, Princess, see? Now Chewie, let us fly,
              And hope we shall not burn the engine out.
              Repairs are made—let us repair to space!
LEIA   One day thou shalt be wrong, and well I hope
              I shall bear witness to thy failure great.   105
HAN   Anon, Chewbacca, lead us to our fate!
                          [Exeunt in the Millennium Falcon.

SCENE 4.

The rebel base on Hoth.

Enter LUKE SKYWALKER *and* R2-D2.

LUKE   The recent battle is both lost and won:

'Tis lost because of rebels who expir'd,
'Tis lost because our base is compromis'd,
'Tis lost because our time on Hoth is done,
'Tis lost because we now evacuate.   5
And yet, 'tis won because two walkers fell,
'Tis won because the foes arriv'd too late,
'Tis won because our transport is away,
'Tis won because we live to fight again.
R2, we leave anon. With all due speed   10
Prepare the ship for takeoff.

R2-D2   —Meep, beep, squeak!

LUKE   Fear not, R2, for now we fly!

R2-D2   —Beep, hoo.

LUKE   Now flies my weary soul to Dagobah,
The place that hath in vision called to me.
I know not what or who this Yoda is,   15
Yet do I trust the ghost of my dear Ben.
To be a Jedi is my calling now,
To learn the ways of the most potent Force.
Already have I had more mentors than
Most people would e'er know in seven lives.   20
But here I am, drawn t'ward another quest—
To travel to an unknown system, aye,
And meet an unknown person who, perhaps,
Doth not expect my sudden visit there.
Yet I believe the words that came from Ben   25
Were better than a foolproof prophet's tale.
There is a tide in the affairs of Jedi,
Which taken at the flood, leads to the Force.
Omitted, all the voyage of their life
Is bound in black holes and in miseries.   30

On such a full sea I am now afloat.
And I must take the current where it serves,
Or lose my chance to find my destiny.

R2-D2   [*aside:*] O noble speech, with feeling brute and raw.
My master's honor shall I serve with pride.   35
How best to show him I stand by his side?
I'll offer ways to help him navigate.
[*To Luke:*] Beep, meep, meep, squeak, beep, whistle,
                    whistle, beep?

LUKE   Nay, nothing's wrong, I merely change our course.

R2-D2   Meep, beep, squeak, whistle, beep, meep, meep,
                    beep, whee?   40

LUKE   We shall not rendezvous with our friends yet.
Unto the system Dagobah we travel—
And what we shall meet there, time shall unravel.

                                  [*Exeunt.*

SCENE 5.

Space, in the cockpit of the Millennium Falcon.

Enter HAN SOLO, CHEWBACCA, *and* PRINCESS LEIA.

HAN   Hoth is a memory, but trouble still
Doth follow close behind. With threat'ning force
The Empire's ships aggressively pursue
My well-belovèd ship. Shall we escape?

CHEWBAC.   Auugh!

HAN   —Truly, Chewie, I did see them too!   5

LEIA   I prithee, say—what hast thou seen, O Han?

HAN   Two Star Destroyers coming t'ward the ship.

Enter C-3PO.

C-3PO   Sir, Sir, may I but say a thing to thee?

HAN   Pray, shut him up or shut him down, anon!
           Prepare our shield—they still may be outrun.   10
           [*Aside:*] With all my pilot's wisdom, skill, and might
           I shall attempt to outwit these who chase.
           Now watch, you Empire vile, how I do fly!
           First up and down, aye, up and down, this Han
           Will lead them up and down. Away we go!   15
           Now back and forth, then back around again.
           They are confounded by my errant moves.
           Ha, ha! They are confus'd and fall behind.
           Thus we have slipp'd away, soon safe from harm.
           [*To Chewbacca:*] Make ready for the jump to
                                         hyperspace.   20

C-3PO   But Sir!

LEIA   —They do approach!

HAN   —Not yet: observe!
               [*The* Millennium Falcon *makes a sound and fails.*

LEIA   Observe? What's to observe, pray tell me plain?

HAN   A fig! The ship seems to malfunction. Fie!
           'Tis possible we may in trouble be.

C-3PO   I tried to warn thee, Sir, the hyperdrive   25
           Hath damag'd been, and cannot do its task!
           Lightspeed is verily unfeasible!

HAN   Correction: we in trouble truly are.
           O that all I had fix'd were truly fix'd!
           But now I must in haste—and under threat   30
           Of death—attempt to fix the ship once more.
                         [*He runs to repair the ship, yelling back
                                         to Chewbacca.*

Where are the horizontal boosters hid?

CHEWBAC.   Egh, auugh!

HAN   —Alluvi'l dampers, where are they?
            [*Aside:*] If only I were but more organiz'd!
            'Tis true that order's not a smuggler's gift.   35
            [*To Chewbacca:*] Bring me the hydrospanners quickly
                                                        now.
            [*Aside:*] I know not how we shall escape this time.
            Of all the situations I have seen,
            Of all the problems small or dangers great,
            Of all the rubs and scrapes have scratch'd my life,   40
            Of all the enemies just barely fled—
            This moment now doth seem the worst of all.
                        [*Loud sound. Han is knocked aside.*
            Alack, now what is this? What shakes the ship?
            How have we gone from bad to still worse yet?

LEIA   Good Han, return at once!
                                [*Han runs back to the cockpit.*
                                'Tis asteroids!   45

HAN   [*aside:*] O wicked thought and wonderful idea
            That cometh to me in this frightful time.
            I shall here chart a course none would expect:
            Not flee from danger, nay, but welcome it,
            And in so doing break the Empire's grip   50
            While rescuing my princess from all harm.
            [*To Chewbacca:*] Set course two-seven-one.

LEIA   —What didst thou say?
            Thou wilt not enter in the ast'roid field?
            For certain thou art wild—but not insane!

HAN   Yet they would be the madder to give chase.   55

LEIA   Thou must not do this to impress me, Han.

[*Aside:*] Already he hath won my heart, 'tis true,
Yet would I rather live to tell him so!

C-3PO   Good Sir, attend: the possibility
Of navigating fields of ast'roids is   60
Three thousand seven hundred twenty to
But one—the odds are well against thee here!

HAN   The odds of rescuing a princess: low.
The odds of smuggler turning rebel: lower.
The odds of ending th'Death Star: lowest yet!   65
I tell thee, droid: assail me not with odds!

LEIA   [*aside:*] Behold, what keen maneuvers doth he make,
And how, like Gungans sinking in the swamp,
Our enemies do fall behind us, slain.
What bravery he showeth for my sake.   70

HAN   If you recall, Your Highness, you did hope
You would bear witness to my failure great:
It may be now.

LEIA   —My word I do rescind.
We shall be pulveriz'd if we remain
A'floating in this field of wayward rocks.   75
Thou hast thy honor proven, Han, now please:
Let us seek safety in another place.

HAN   I cannot argue with thine argument.
I shall attempt to fly us closer in
Toward a larger ast'roid.

C-3PO   —Closer?

CHEWBAC.   —Auugh!   80

C-3PO   O this is suicide, for where have we
To go where we may yet survive? Are we
Not bound for death?

HAN   —Aye, this one here shall do.

	It hath a goodly look.	
LEIA	—What "goodly look"?	
HAN	Be calm, I prithee, for it shall suffice.	85
C-3PO	Excuse me, Princess, but where are we bound?	

                              [*The* Millennium Falcon *flies deep*
                                          into one of the asteroids.

LEIA	My hope flies unto you, most worthy man,	
	My hope for us, and for our safety, too.	
	I hope it is the Force that leadeth thee,	
	I hope that thou dost know what thou dost do.	90
HAN	Thy hopes do echo mine, my lady, true.	

                                [*Exeunt into an asteroid's tunnel.*

SCENE 6.

Aboard the Empire's Super Star Destroyer.

Enter ADMIRAL PIETT *with* DARTH VADER, *replacing his mask.*

PIETT	[*aside:*] O sight most tragic, this—a robot-man	
	Who doth require a mask to stay alive.	
	What situation e'er did lead to this?	
	How can he stand to live beneath a mask?	
	But soft, Piett, and reconsider this:	5
	Aye, verily, how shall I judge? The mask	
	He wears is far more obvious than most.	
	With Vader it is plain he wears a mask,	
	Though few have seen the scarring underneath.	
	But truly, what man doth not wear a mask?	10
	For all of us are maskèd in some way—	
	Some choose sharp cruelty as their outward face,	

Some put themselves behind a king's façade,
Some hide behind the mask of bravery,
Some put on the disguise of arrogance.   15
But underneath our masks, are we not one?
Do not all wish for love, and joy, and peace?
And whether rebel or Imperial,
Do not our hearts all beat in time to make
The pounding rhythm of the galaxy?   20
So while Darth Vader's mask keeps him alive,
And sits upon his face for all to see,

'Tis possible he is more honest than
A man who wears no mask, but hides his self.
But come, Piett, now still thy prating tongue—   25
His private time is done, his mask back on.

VADER   Yes, Admiral?

PIETT   —Our ships have found the swift
Millenn'um Falcon, Lord. However, it
Hath ventur'd deep into an ast'roid field.
It seems unsafe to make pursuit therein: 30
To follow it is far too great a risk.

VADER   Thy fear of asteroids concerns me not.
I want the ship, not thy most weak dismay.

PIETT   I understand, my Lord, and shall obey.

                                        [Exeunt.

SCENE 7.
The Dagobah system.

Enter LUKE SKYWALKER *and* R2-D2.

LUKE   What misadventure I have seen today!
Our sensors spied no cities or machines
Within this system desolate, but life
Forms plenty. As we made our way unto
The planet's atmosphere, all went awry: 5
My X-wing ship began to shake and groan.
My scopes had fail'd, and I did blindly spin
Into a landing doom'd to end with strife.
'Tis almost fortunate that I did land
Within this swampy bog where now the ship   10

Is partway sunk, for had I hit the ground
My ship and droid and even my own self
Might have been crush'd, and ev'rything destroy'd.
But now my ship is fixèd in the mire,
And how it shall come out I cannot tell.   15
Was this first trouble all I would endure?
Nay, nay! It seemeth Fate did not see fit
To send pain singular, but multiple!
Fate hath provided pains abundantly,
For this is not the end of our distress.   20
As R2 and I headed for the shore
He fell into the water, wheels to scope,
And was assaulted by a mighty beast—
Aye, swallow'd whole and disappear'd from sight.
For seeming ages I did search for him,   25
To no avail. And then, with frightful scream,
He was ejected from the swamp as fast
As proton-fill'd torpedoes from their shaft.
Above my head he sail'd, well o'er the ground,
And landed in a heap of dirt and grime.   30
'Twas only for his metal-tasting shell
This little droid shall live to see tomorrow.
So much misfortune! After all this pain
I should feel grateful still to have my life.
But now we are maroon'd within a place   35
Where neither friend nor contact may be found.
I should have listen'd to the wise R2
When he said coming here would work us woe.
Our camp is now set up, our food prepar'd,
My faithful R2 chargeth up his pow'r,   40
The semblance of good order we present—

But I have neither stomach nor desire
To sit down to a hale and hearty feast.
More pressing, too, I must this Yoda find,
Indeed, if that good man doth e'en exist.   45
Look 'round about, R2: is this place not
Unlikely for a Jedi master's home?
'Tis strange, 'tis passing strange, 'tis pitiful.

R2-D2   Beep, squeak?

Enter YODA, *hidden behind.*

LUKE   —I know not what it is, dear friend.
'Tis like some thing appearing from a dream,   50
Some midnight reverie I cannot shake.
For neither does this circumstance seem real,
Nor do I slumber here—aye, that I know.
It seems the place is but a walking shadow—
Not dream, not wake, but something in between.   55
The strangeness of the scene creeps in my bones,
Yet also do I feel familiar pangs.

R2-D2   Beep, whistle, meep?

LUKE   —I know not. I do feel—
                         [Yoda reveals himself.

YODA   What dost thou feel, hmm?
Prithee, I would truly know   60
What is it thou feel'st?
                         [Luke points his blaster at Yoda.

LUKE   That odd, familiar sense that we are watch'd!

R2-D2   Beep, beep, meep, whistle, beep, squeak, whistle, nee!

YODA   Away with weapons!
I mean no harm, but wonder   65

	Why thou hast come here.
LUKE	Thou sneaking imp! I look for someone here.
YODA	Looking, are you, hmm?
	Found someone you have, it seems!
	Is that not correct? 70
LUKE	'Tis true, I may suppose—I've someone found,
	Though such a one as this did not expect.
YODA	Help you I can, aye.
	[*Aside:*] I, indeed, more help shall be
	Than he imagines. 75
LUKE	Nay, I think not. My search is for a great
	And mighty warrior, a man of strength!
YODA	O, great warrior!
	A great warrior you seek?
	Wars not make one great. 80

But soft, no more of
Talking, for my appetite
Dinner demandeth.

Thus shall I explore
The food thou hast here prepar'd.   85
Mmm, and I shall taste.

LUKE	Nay, nay, unhand my supper, little one!
YODA	How dost grow so big
	When the food of thy diet
	Is of this strange kind? 90
LUKE	Attend, my friend, thou must leave this alone.
	My food I shall have need of, as we strive
	To free our ship. I did not try to land
	Inside that puddle drear, and if we could

Our ship remove, we would. But we cannot—   95
At least, I know not how it shall be done.

    [Yoda rummages through Luke's supplies,
        discarding them to the ground.

YODA   Unfortunate ship . . .
Thou canst not get it out, hmm?
O, what merry light!

    [Yoda removes a light from Luke's supplies.

LUKE   A mess thou now hast made! Give me that light!   100
YODA   'Tis mine, it is mine!
I shall the pretty thing have
Or I help you not.

LUKE   I need not thine assistance, nay! I need
My lamp, for it shall guide me out of this   105
Most slimy and disgusting hole of mud!

YODA   What slimy, what mud?
Thou speak'st indeed of my home.

    [R2-D2 reaches out and grabs the lamp.

Alas, naughty droid!

    [R2-D2 and Yoda fight for the lamp.

LUKE   O R2, let the creature have it now.   110

    [R2-D2 releases the lamp.

Now move along, good fellow. We have much
To do. Thou art small in both size and help.

YODA   Nay, nay, I shall stay.
For I shall stay and help thee
Find thy long lost friend.   115

LUKE   Thou dost not understand, thou useless scamp.
I search not for a friend in this damp place,
But for a Jedi master wise in skill!

YODA   O Jedi master!

Yoda that you seek it is.   120
'Tis truly Yoda!

LUKE   [*aside:*] A strange turn of events! This tiny sprite
May yet prove useful if he knows the man.
[*To Yoda:*] Attend: thou know'st of Yoda, little one?

YODA   I'll take thee to him.   125
Aye, but first, let us eat food.
Come, I good food have!

LUKE   I follow. R2, stay and watch the camp—
Mayhap some hope still lives within this damp.

                          [*Exeunt, Luke following Yoda.*

ACT III

SCENE 1.

Aboard the Millennium Falcon, *inside the asteroid.*

Enter HAN SOLO, PRINCESS LEIA, CHEWBACCA, *and* C-3PO.

HAN   Now shall I shut down ev'rything except
               The ship's emergency pow'r systems.

C-3PO   —Sir,
               I am almost afraid to ask, but doth
               This mean that I shall be shut down as well?

HAN   Nay, nay, good droid, for thou shalt speak unto   5
               The *Falcon* to determine wherefore doth
               The hyperdrive not operate aright.
               For once I find thee useful, goldenrod.
                    [The ship shakes and all are rocked from side to side.

C-3PO   Sir, it is possible this ast'roid may
               Not be entirely stable.

HAN   —Dost thou think?   10
               O droid of wisdom, skill, and excellence—
               Howe'er would I survive if I did not
               Have thee here to reveal such mysteries?
               From usefulness to obvious within
               A single stroke. I pray, Chewbacca, take   15
               This scholar made of wires and metal to
               The back and plug him in the hyperdrive!

C-3PO   Sometimes I do not comprehend the strange
               And varied ways of human beings. True
               It is that I did only try to help!   20
                    *[Exeunt Chewbacca and C-3PO. The ship
                    shakes again and Leia falls into Han's arms.*

LEIA   [*aside:*] O happy accident! O fall most fair!
Now in his arms, where I have long'd to be,
I know not whether 'tis the ship or if
It is my heart that I feel quaking. Yet,
Alas, this moment not befits our love.   25
The situation is too strain'd. I wish,
With all my being, to be in this place—
But not like this. [*To Han:*] Pray, let me go.

HAN   —Tut, tut!

LEIA   I prithee, let me go.

HAN   [*aside:*]   —O small request
That tears apart my soul! [*To Leia:*] Indeed, indeed,   30
Be not with such excitement overcome.

LEIA   My captain, being held by you is far
Too plain a thing to e'er excite my mood.

HAN   I crave your kindly pardon, sweetheart fierce,
But we have little time for something else—   35
I'll leave thee here alone and then, mayhap,
The time apart shall heighten thy desire.

                                   [*Exit Han Solo.*

LEIA   O man of pride and will most obstinate!
However can I love thee, being as
You are? But being other than you are,   40
I would not love thee. How this pirate hath
Laid claim upon the bounty of my soul!
O, wherefore did I speak so testily?
Why is it that whenever he is near
My wit is turn'd to unto a laser beam   45
With Han plac'd firmly in its sights? I tear
His heart in twain with words too cruel and harsh,
Then wonder why he is so full of pride.

'Tis now quite clear that he with arrogance
Doth speak so that he may his heart protect.   50
Forsooth, was e'er a woman placèd in
So delicate a situation yet?

                              [*Exit Princess Leia.*

                    Enter C-3PO.

C-3PO   O, where is that knave R2 now? For when
          I need him most, then is he far away.
          Perhaps on some adventure, which will serve   55
          To puff him up most mightily, and leave
          Him ever bragging o'er his exploits. Pish!
          The scrawny, errant scamp perplexes me,
          For he is both my nuisance and delight—
          The thorn deep in my side and, stranger still,   60
          The very object of my happiness.

              Enter HAN SOLO *and* CHEWBACCA.

          Now, Captain Solo, pray, a word with thee.
HAN   [*aside:*] A word from thee belike means hundreds more.
C-3PO   I know not where your ship did learn to speak—
          It hath a most peculiar dialect.   65
          It is as though 'twere programm'd by a thief,
          And spends its days with smugglers, thugs, and crooks.
          But now, no more of that; my point is made.
          It doth report the power coupling on
          The axis negative is polariz'd,   70
          And must replacèd be to operate.
HAN   'Tis plain it must replacèd be. Presume

Thou not to tell a pilot—one so grand
As me, at least—the bus'ness of his ship.

                                   [Exit C-3PO.

[*To Chewbacca:*] Good Chewie?

CHEWBAC.   —Egh?

HAN   —It seems we must replace   75
The power coupling negative, yes?

CHEWBAC.   —Grrm.

                                [Exit Chewbacca.

       Enter PRINCESS LEIA, *aside, working.*

HAN   [*aside:*] We are alone. Yet ev'ry time I have
Approach'd her recently I've been rebuff'd.
This should not be a nut I cannot crack—
I am not ignorant in women's ways.   80
Although, by troth, most often when I speak
Of "she" or "her," I indicate my ship.
And yet, I am a man of many strengths:
I pilot ships with talent, skill, and grace,
In battles or in races hard to best,   85
My swift maneuvers legendary are
And through the galaxy my ship is known.
But with this princess, all my skill is naught.
My tongue is tied, and I resort to barbs
And witticisms sloppily convey'd.   90
How shall I show this princess my true heart?
How set aside my ego and be kind?
Here, in this moment, I shall undertake
To set my pathway not toward my pride,
But through the smoother course that runs to love.   95

        [He approaches to help her and is shoved away.

        [*To Leia:*] Pray patience, Worship, I but try to help!

LEIA   Couldst thou forswear thy pompous attitude

        And promise thou shalt ne'er call me that name?

HAN   Aye, Leia.

LEIA   [*aside:*]   —Prithee, give me patience now!

        To make him thine, respond thou not with fire.   100

        [*To Han:*] You do not make it simple.

HAN   —Yes, 'tis true.

        But 'tis not I alone who is to blame,

        For thou couldst softer and more gentle be.

        O Princess, may we end these pointless games?

        May we two souls of flame extinguish'd be   105

        Just long enough to drink of love's rewards?

        I ask thee, truly, dost thou sometimes think

        That certain virtues may be found in me?

        Canst thou imagine ever looking deep

        Into my soul to see the man within?   110

        [Leia stops working and rubs her sore hands.

LEIA   Occasionally, mayhap, when you are

        Not acting in the manner of a scoundrel.

        [Han Solo takes Leia's hands in his.

HAN   A scoundrel? "Scoundrel" is the word you choose?

        I like that word, when spoken from your lips.

LEIA   Pray cease that touch, it doth my heart confuse.   115

HAN   But wherefore cease? What reason shall eclipse

        The greater reason of my heart's intent?

LEIA   But lo, my hands are dirtied by my work.

HAN   My hands are likewise dirty. Pray, assent

        Unto this moment. What fear makes you shirk?   120

LEIA   What fear? I tell thee, I am not afraid.

HAN   Did I imagine that your hands did shake?
             Thou likest that I am of scoundrel made.
             For thy life could more scoundrel gladly take.
             If thou wouldst cast my suit off, think again—   125
             I would that thou within me deeper look.
LEIA   I tell thee true, that I do like nice men.
HAN   I too am nice.

                                                  [They kiss.

                           Enter C-3PO.

LEIA   [*aside:*]   —He kisses by the book.
C-3PO   Sir, Sir, I've isolated the reverse
             Flux power coupling. Have I done thee proud?   130
                                          [Exit Princess Leia.

HAN	O thank you, 3PO, thank you so much.
C-3PO	But speak none of it, Sir—I have a touch.

[Exeunt.

SCENE 2.

Aboard the Empire's Super Star Destroyer.

Enter DARTH VADER *and* CAPTAIN NEEDA *(in beam).*

NEEDA   The swift *Millenn'um Falcon* made its way
                Unto the field of asteroids and that,
                My great Lord Vader, was the last that they
                Within our scopes did e'er appear. They must
                Have been destroy'd, if one considers all   5
                The damage we have tolerated here.
VADER   Your answer's insufficient, Captain, for
                I know they are alive. Thy scanners are
                Poor proxies for the Force. Now listen well
                To my command: I tell thee ev'ry ship   10
                That hath some power left to give shall search
                The ast'roid field until they have been found.
NEEDA   I shall with haste fulfill thy shrewd decree.

[Exit Captain Needa from beam.

Enter ADMIRAL PIETT.

PIETT   My Lord?
VADER   —Yes, Admiral?
PIETT   —The Emperor
                Commands that thou do contact him at once.   15

VADER   Then, move the ship out of the ast'roid field
               That I may with my master clearly speak.
PIETT   We will, my Lord.

                                        [*Exit Admiral Piett.*

VADER   —Now shall I speak with my
               Dread Emperor. The man who gave me life
               When all was lost. The man to whom I owe   20
               All that I am, and e'er shall be. The man,
               Indeed, who like a father is to me.
               His plans for pow'r and schemes most excellent
               I do obey and carry out with pride.
               Though people fear my aspect bleak and dark,   25
               They should, more surely, fear what I will do
               When answering his perfect, flawless will.
               For sooner would I sacrifice my life
               Than disobey the word of this great man.

               Enter EMPEROR PALPATINE, *in beam.*

               What is thy bidding, master pure and true?   30
EMPEROR   There is a great disturbance in the Force.
VADER   I too have felt it.
EMPEROR   —A new enemy
               Arises, e'en the rebel who destroy'd
               The Death Star—and I have no doubt this boy
               Is kin to Anakin Skywalker.
VADER   [*aside:*]   —O,   35
               Profoundest revelation! I knew he
               Was powerful and bore Skywalker's name,
               Yet that the boy is kin to Anakin
               I did not see. [*To the Emperor:*] How is this possible?

EMPEROR   You only must within your feelings search,   40
           Lord Vader. Then shalt thou too know 'tis true.
           He could destroy us.

VADER   —He is but a boy,
           And Obi-Wan no longer is his help.

EMPEROR   The Force is strong with him, and mark me well:
           The son of Skywalker must ne'er become   45
           A Jedi. Dost thou comprehend my words?

VADER   [*aside:*] I do his meaning understand, and yet
           Another future for this boy I'll write.
           Not death, but something even greater still.
           It may be that this young Skywalker will   50
           Still prove to be most worthy of the name.
           [*To the Emperor:*] If he could but be turn'd, an ally

                                                    strong
           He could become.

EMPEROR   —Indeed, thou speakest true.
           The boy may prove himself an asset sure.
           Can it be done? What is thy true reply?   55

VADER   The boy shall surely join us, or shall die.

                                            [*Exeunt.*

SCENE 3.

Inside Yoda's homestead.

Enter LUKE SKYWALKER.

LUKE   This creature I have follow'd to his home,
           But still no further answers are reveal'd.
           It seemeth that he stalls in bringing me

Unto the one I truly hope to see.
With all that hath befallen in this place   5
My patience runneth thin. I'll press the point.

Enter YODA.

Thy generosity is truly rare,
I'll warrant that thy food delicious is.
Yet neither rhyme nor reason have I heard
Of wherefore we may not go, even now,   10
To see good Master Yoda where he lives.

YODA   Pray, patience, young one.
For Jedi too must eat—thus
My good food, eat now.

LUKE   How many leagues away is Yoda? Shall   15
The journey to him long and per'lous be?

YODA   Not far is Yoda.
Aye, soon thou shalt be with him.
First, eat of rootleaf.

Feast for a Jedi—   20
Food that enlivens the mind
Should thy repast be.

And now, a question:
What drives the young man's heart to
Learn the Jedi way?   25

LUKE   This is an inquiry perceptive, friend,
For I am driv'n by force unto the Force:
My noble father doth inform my steps.

YODA   Thy father, indeed.

Powerful Jedi was he.   30
Powerful Jedi.

LUKE   Avaunt, thou silly creature, how canst thou
              My father know? For surely thou dost not
              E'en know who I am. Fie! I know not what
              Or who or why or when or where or how   35
              Hath brought about this meeting! Time is short;
              Each minute pass'd with thee hath gone to waste!

YODA   [speaking to the air:] I cannot teach him.
              The boy hath none of patience.
              How shall he be taught?   40

The voice of the GHOST OF OBI-WAN KENOBI *is heard.*

OBI-WAN   He patience lacks, but patience can be learn'd.

YODA   Much anger in him.
              Sudden and quick in quarrel:
              Too like his father.

OBI-WAN   Was I then diff'rent when thou didst teach me?   45

YODA   He is not ready.
              'Tis now the thing that I see:
              This one's unprepar'd.

LUKE   'Tis Yoda! Nay, but Ben, pray argue for
              My cause, for verily prepar'd am I!   50
              I can and shall a Jedi be. True, Ben?

YODA   Ready are you, hmm?
              What know you yet of ready?
              Say naught of "ready."

              For eight hundred years   55
              Have I the Jedi trainèd,

So say not "ready."

I my own counsel
Shall keep on who's to be trained!
A Jedi is wise.   60

A strong commitment
And a most serious mind
Are necessary.

Long have I watch'd him.
All his life looking away   65
To the future, hmm,

To the horizon.
Ne'er his mind on where he was,
What he was doing!

Ventures, excitement: 70
A Jedi craveth not these.
Thou art reckless, aye!

OBI-WAN   And so was I, if thou dost think on it.
YODA   And he is too old
            The training to begin now.   75
            Certain, he's too old.
LUKE   But Master Yoda, I have learn'd so much.
YODA   And will he finish
            The thing he doth begin here?
            I prithee, tell me.   80
LUKE   I shall not fail thee: 'tis my promise true,
            For I am not afraid of anything.

YODA   Thou shalt be yet, Luke.
              My words most carefully heed:
              Thou shalt be, indeed.   85

                                          [Exeunt.

SCENE 4.

Aboard the Millennium Falcon, *inside the asteroid.*

Enter HAN SOLO, CHEWBACCA, *and* C-3PO.

C-3PO   Good Sir, if I may venture my belief—
HAN   I tell thee honestly, C-3PO,
              That neither appetite nor inclination
              Have I to feast upon your odd beliefs.
              Do thou thy work but keep opinion out,   5
              And we shall feast together on the silence.

Enter PRINCESS LEIA, *in fear.*

LEIA   O Han, a horrid sight I have just seen!
              Whilst I did in the cockpit sit and think—
HAN   On what? Pray tell: what didst thou think upon?
LEIA   'Tis not the time for jokes and parries, please! 10
              As I did sit there, suddenly a jolt
              Went through me as I heard a sound upon
              The window. Looking closer, I espied
              A second beast outside that hard upon
              The window fell. There's something out there,
                                          Han—   15
              Beyond the ship, abiding in the cave.

          [A great sound is heard and the ship shakes.

CHEWBAC.   Auugh!

C-3PO   —Listen!

HAN   —I shall venture out to see.

LEIA   Nay, art thou mad? It is not wise or safe
           To go without when there are creatures we
           Know nothing of.

HAN   —This bucket is just fix'd,   20
           Wouldst thou I let some thing tear it apart?

LEIA   I see thy reason, and shall go with thee.

C-3PO   I shall with courage and with honor stay
           Behind to bravely guard the ship.

                          [Another sound is heard.
                            O dear!
            [Exit C-3PO as the others go outside the ship.

LEIA   What is this ground that we do walk upon?   25
           'Tis strange—it doth not feel at all like rock.

HAN   Indeed, with thine assessment I agree:
           It seems there is much moisture in this place.

LEIA   I have a feeling bad about this cave.
           What odd new situation find we here?   30
           Do not these signs and portents give thee fear?

HAN   Aye.

                       [Han sees something move.
           Take thou cover!

                           [He shoots.
         'Tis all right.

LEIA   —What is't?

HAN   'Tis what I did suspect: some mynocks. They
           Are fasten'd to the ship, a'chewing on
           The power cables.

LEIA   —Mynocks? O what beasts!   35

HAN   Return inside, and we shall search for more.

> *[Several mynocks fly by. Han shoots,*
> *and the cave walls shake.*

But hold one moment, something seems awry,
For blaster fire should not cause walls to shake.

> *[Han shoots the cave wall,*
> *and the ground shakes mightily.*

O, horror, for I now do understand:
The cave doth quake whenever it is shot.   40
But what knows rock of pain, or stone of hurt?
Whenever did a cave feel anything?
Impossible it is, unless this cave
Is much more than a cave. [*To Leia and Chewbacca:*]

> Pray, go inside!
> *[They run into the* Millennium Falcon.

With speed now, Chewie, let us fly away!   45

LEIA   *[following Han to the cockpit:]* The Empire is without,
                       we should not go—

HAN   We've no time to discuss this in committee.

LEIA   O, fie! Thou scoundrel, I am no committee!

> *[They arrive in the cockpit and start the ship.*

See reason! For thou canst not make the jump
To lightspeed midst this field of asteroids.   50

HAN   Make sure thy back end finds a seat—we go!

> *[They begin to leave the cave, which is actually an*
> *exogorth, or space slug. Its mouth begins to close.*

Enter C-3PO.

C-3PO   Observe! We are destroy'd!

HAN	—I see it plain.
C-3PO	O, we are doom'd!
LEIA	—The cave, it doth collapse!
HAN	This is no cave, and I am not its food.
	Now we do fly—another close escape! 55

> [Exeunt C-3PO, Han Solo, Princess Leia, and
> Chewbacca in the Milennium Falcon, flying out
> of exogorth's mouth and leaving it alone on stage.

EXOGOR.	Alas, another meal hath fled and gone,
	And in the process I am sorely hurt.
	These travelers who have escap'd my reach
	Us'd me past the endurance of a block!
	My stomach they did injure mightily 60
	With jabs and pricks, as though a needle were

A'bouncing in my belly. O cruel Fate!
To be a space slug is a lonely lot,
With no one on this rock to share my life,
No true companion here to mark my days.   65
And now my meals do from my body fly—
Was e'er a beast by supper so abus'd?
Was e'er a creature's case so pitiful?
Was e'er an exogorth as sad as I?
Was e'er a tragedy as deep as mine?   70
I shall with weeping crawl back to my cave,
Which shall, sans food, belike become my grave.

                                              [*Exit.*

SCENE 5.
The Dagobah system.

Enter YODA, R2-D2, *and* LUKE SKYWALKER, *training.*

LUKE   [*aside:*] This Yoda is indeed a teacher wise,
              And hath agreed to train me in the way
              Of Jedi. Strong and quick I show myself—
              With leaps and flips I train my body and
              Instill within a Jedi's discipline.   5
              Aye, with the Force I like a sand bat fly.
              My spirit feeleth free, my muscles strong,
              My mind is calm inside, my heart is still.
              What gratitude I feel toward this new
              And treasur'd mentor. Thus I train my best—   10
              His expectations I'll not disappoint.
YODA   Now run, indeed, run!

A Jedi's strength doth surely
Come from the Force, Luke.

But mind the dark side.   15
Anger, fear, aggression—from
The dark side are they.

Easily they flow,
Quick to join you in a fight.
Aye, they do not fail!   20

Once on the dark path,
Forever shall it control
Thy destiny, Luke.

It shall consume thee,
As it did the apprentice   25
Of good Obi-Wan.

LUKE   Darth Vader: legendary is his pow'r.
    But Master, hath the dark side greater strength?

YODA   Nay, nay—forsooth: nay.
    'Tis quicker, easier, more   30
    Seductive only.

LUKE   But how, good master, shall I know the good
    Side from the bad, the darkness from the light?

YODA   Thou shalt know, my lad,
    When thou art calm and passive.   35
    [*Aside:*] I hope thou shalt know.

When fac'd with terror,
And with thy father's grim fate,

I hope thou shalt know.

[*To Luke:*] A Jedi uses   40
The Force only for knowledge
And defense. Is't clear?

The Force is no club,
Neither is it a weapon
Us'd for attacking.   45

LUKE   Yet it is still a weapon for defense.
              So wherefore may I not the Force employ—
YODA   Nay, there's no wherefore.
              Nothing more shall come today.
              From thy questions, rest.   50
LUKE   [*aside:*] Reliev'd am I this training to complete,
              If only for this day, which hath been years.
              But is this not a strange and troubling thing?
              Where only moments past I felt at ease,
              Now there's some sprite within that troubles me—   55
              A chill, a solemn aura in my bones.
              I would not much ado o'er nothing make,
              But still shall I ask Yoda what it is.
              [*To Yoda:*] I feel a cold, a presage here of death.
              What is it that I sense within this place?   60
                        [*Yoda points to the opening of a cave.*
YODA   With the Force's dark side
              Is that place yonder quite strong.
              A place of evil.

              Discover thou shalt

That wherever good is found,   65
Evil is nearby.

Here on Dagobah
'Tis also so. For e'en here
That evil place is.

Bound thou art now, Luke,   70
To enter it, and face its
Deepest darknesses.

LUKE   But Sir, I prithee, tell me: what's within?

YODA   Only that which thou
Shalt take away with thee, Luke.   75

[Luke begins to enter the cave,
carrying his weapons.

Take not thy weapons.

R2-D2   Beep, meep, meep, squeak, beep, whistle, meep,
beep, nee!

[Luke enters, bringing his weapons,
as Yoda and R2-D2 remain outside.

LUKE   What twists of knotted vines and tangl'd fates
Await me in this hole? I shall go in,
And prove that I am not afraid of it,   80
Nor any task or misadventure here.
What evil can await I have not seen?
For I have facèd evil enemies
Who kill'd my mentor and my family.
What evil in this place can greater be?   85
Now doth time seem to slowly beat its pace.
And all is like a thick and restless dream.
But wait, who comes unto this deep, dark place?

It moves with grace—is it my father good?

Enter shadow of DARTH VADER.

Nay, nay, how I have been deceiv'd, abus'd!   90
For it is Vader here, my greatest foe,
The cruel defiler of my father's youth.
I stand preparèd to do battle as
A Jedi, full of rage and righteous hate.
Now up, lightsaber, light my keen revenge!   95
Lay on, Darth Vader, damnèd henchman vile.
And now we fight! Yet seems it that my limbs
Are made of stone—but he is slower still!
I see my chance to strike, and let it fall—
The blow that shall release my father's soul.   100
Now Vader's head doth fall onto the ground
And I feel no relief, but only pain.
The mask doth split, his visage to reveal!
O, I shall see the face that kill'd a man,
That kill'd a thousand fathers like my own.   105
But wait, what is this here—and can it be?
This is no face of Vader: 'tis my face!
The horror, O the horror! Darker yet
That e'er I had imagin'd possible.
The greatest evil I may face—myself!   110

                              [*Exit Luke, in fear.*

YODA   Now hath he seen it,
              And he shall ever see it
              Till he sees it through.

                              [*Exit Yoda.*

R2-D2   O strange and somber night that falleth here—

My master Luke all out of sorts from what   115
He spies inside this hole. What lesson is
It Yoda hath reveal'd to him inside?
I would that I my master could protect,
But such is not the role I have to play.
And thus, since I may not protector be,   120
My path shall be to play the fool and watch:
I shall maintain my droidlike silence and
Bear witness as the boy becomes the man,
The learner doth become the Jedi true.
Content yourself with this, R2, and rest,   125
For other times than these require your best.

[*Exit.*

SCENE 6.

*Space, aboard the Empire's Super Star Destroyer
and the* Millennium Falcon.

Enter ADMIRAL PIETT *and* IMPERIAL CONTROLLER, *with* DARTH VADER
and BOUNTY HUNTERS, *including* BOBA FETT, *aside,
aboard the Super Star Destroyer.*

PIETT   These bounty hunters, O they reek! We have
          No need for their most wretched scum.
CONTROL.   —Aye, Sir.
PIETT   The rebels surely shall not 'scape us now.
CONTROL.   We have been hail'd by the *Avenger* ship.
PIETT   Now let us hear it.
VADER   —There shall be rewards   5
          Aplenty for the one who finds the swift

Millenn'um Falcon. Ye may use whate'er
Approaches, weapons, means, or what ye will,
But mark ye well: I want them all alive.
[*To Boba Fett:*] There shall be no disintegrations.
                                              Clear?   10

FETT   As you wish. [*Aside:*] The darkest Sith that e'er
did live, and I am his choice to find those he cannot.
Yet who am I? A mere bounty hunter like the others
here? Nay, far more. I am Boba Fett, the vilest,
fiercest, most deadly hunter in the galaxy. More   15
than that, Darth Vader knows that I shall serve
him well and faithfully in the pursuit of Solo. He
knoweth well that Boba Fett doth worship at sweet
compensation's throne, and would happily
betray my own kin to earn the great reward   20
that hath been promis'd. I would kill Solo
without a thought, for what is he to me?

Disintegrations, indeed. I would disintegrate,
disembowel, dismember, destroy utterly Han Solo,
for I know him not nor care what he hath done   25
to earn Darth Vader's ire and the scorn of Jabba
of the Hutt. I shall play my bounty hunter's part,
obey the dark lord, take my prize from the Empire,
and receive a second prize on the dunes of Tatooine.
A double prize—'tis wonderful a bounty hunter to be.   30

PIETT   [*to Darth Vader:*] My Lord, the ship hath been
                              discoverèd!

          [*Exeunt Darth Vader, Boba Fett, other bounty hunters,*
               Admiral Piett, and Imperial Controller.

          Enter HAN SOLO, CHEWBACCA, PRINCESS LEIA,
          and C-3PO *aboard the* Millennium Falcon.

C-3PO   O, praise the maker! We are venturing
           Out of the ast'roid field, and are alive—
           Miraculous! [*Aside:*] I almost am convinc'd
           That Captain Solo bears a hero's air.   35

HAN   Now let us hence. Chewbacca, art prepar'd
           For lightspeed?

CHEWBAC.   —Auugh!

HAN   —Now one, two, three, and go!
               [*The* Millennium Falcon *makes a sound and fails.*

CHEWBAC.   Egh.

HAN   —'Tis not fair. I say, it is not just!

C-3PO   [*aside:*] A hero, did I say? O man of folly!

CHEWBAC.   Auugh, auugh!

HAN   —The transfer circuits do not work   40
           'Tis not my fault!

LEIA   —No lightspeed once again?

HAN   'Tis not my fault. In troth, 'tis not my fault!

C-3PO   The rear deflector shield is compromis'd,
             And if we do sustain another hit
             Upon the ship's back quarter, 'tis our end.   45

HAN   [*aside:*] 'Tis madness, this maneuver I'll attempt.
             But desp'rate times for desp'rate measures call.
             [*To Chewbacca:*] Turn thou this ship around.

CHEWBAC.   —Egh?

HAN   —Turn it 'round!
             I shall put all our pow'r to shields in front.

LEIA   Thou wilt attack a Star Destroyer?

C-3PO   —Sir!   50
             The odds of our success in a direct
             Attack upon a Star Destroyer—

LEIA   —Tut!
                         [*Exeunt, flying toward the Star Destroyer.*

             Enter Captain Needa, Tracking Officer,
                   and Communications Officer.

NEEDA   They move into attack position—shields!
             But now, where are they gone? Pray, track them straight.

TRACK.   The ship's no longer shown in any scopes.   55

NEEDA   That is impossible. No ship that small
             Hath any ways or means to cloak itself.
             Nay, they cannot, as magic, disappear.

COMM.   Good Captain Needa, our Lord Vader doth
             Demand an update of our keen pursuit.   60

NEEDA   [*aside:*] O dreaded moment. This shall mean my death.
             Farewell now, for my life's gone with the ship.

[*To Communications Officer:*] Prepare a shuttle for me.

                                                 I'll accept

The full responsibility for their

Escape, and shall apologize unto

Lord Vader. Keep thy watch most vigilant.   65

COMM.   Aye, Captain Needa.

                [Exit Tracking and Communications officers.

      Enter DARTH VADER, *as Captain Needa*
      makes his way toward him.

NEEDA   —On thy mercy great

I throw myself and all my hopes, dear lord.

The great *Millenn'um Falcon* now is fled.

It hath evaded even our vast fleet.   70

Take my apology—

VADER   —The ship is lost?

And thus thy life—dead for a ducat, dead!

        [Darth Vader chokes Captain
        Needa with the Force, killing him.

The necks of fools deserve a crushing Force.

Let this serve as thy dying lesson, Needa.

With that last breath thy recompense is done   75

And all apologies accepted.

      Enter ADMIRAL PIETT.

PIETT   —Lord,

Our scan of the surrounding area

Is now complete, but has, alas, found naught.

Lord, if the swift *Millenn'um Falcon* hath

    Made good the jump to lightspeed, it may be   80
    Beyond the far end of the galaxy.
VADER   Alert thou every Imperi'l post,
    And calculate the ship's most likely course
    From its trajectory as it did flee.
PIETT   Aye, Lord, I'll warrant we shall find them soon. 85

            [Exit Admiral Piett.

VADER   O ancestors, pray save me from these fools
    Who with their instruments and scanners could
    Not find a bantha in a womp rat's hole.
    But calm thyself now, Vader, be at ease.
    This momentary failure may yet prove   90
    Most beneficial, and I'll warrant that
    The time shall not go dully by us, for
    It shall be us'd to finalize my plans
    And think upon the moment when I shall
    Both meet and then defeat the Skywalker 95
    Who dares to call the Empire enemy.
    So let these rebels go for now, my soul,
    And ponder how to make their downfall whole.

               [Exit.

SCENE 7.

The Dagobah system.

Enter YODA, R2-D2, *and* LUKE SKYWALKER, *who practices*
lifting things with the Force.

YODA   Use the Force, Luke, yes.
    Now, lift thou the stone. Feel it.

The Force within flows.
                    [*R2-D2 begins to beep as Luke's ship sinks.*
Nay, listen thou not
To the droid and all his beeps.   5
Do thou concentrate!
                    [*Everything that was lifted falls.*

R2-D2   Nee, nee, beep, meep, beep, squeak, squeak,
                                        whistle, squeak!

LUKE   Fie! We shall never extricate the ship.

YODA   So certain are you?
        Always with you, my pupil,   10
        It cannot be done.

        What have we done here—
        Hear'st thou nothing that I say?
        Dost thou attend, Luke?

        If depend upon   15
        The Force thou shalt, anything
        Possible shall be.

LUKE   But Master, moving stones with the great Force
        I do admit may be achiev'd. But this,
        This ship—to lift its hulk, its mass, its size—   20
        'Tis different, aye, wholly different!

YODA   Nay! No different.
        Only within thy mind, Luke,
        Different it is.

        Thou must unlearn all   25
        Those things that thou hast learnèd.
        Dost thou understand?

LUKE   In troth, I understand, and I shall try.
YODA   Nay, nay! Try thou not.
         But do thou or do thou not,   30
         For there is no "try."
LUKE   [*aside:*] I shall stretch out my mind, and shall attempt,
         But this is madness—lifting e'en a ship?
         The greatest Jedi still cannot achieve
         That which is patently impossible.   35
         Methinks no Force can move this ship, and thus
         I certain am I never shall do this.
                         [*Luke tries to lift the ship with the Force,*
                                 but the ship sinks lower.
R2-D2   Beep, hoo.
LUKE   —Nay, I cannot. 'Tis much too big.
YODA   Nay, size matters not.
         Look thou at me, I prithee.   40
         Judge me by my size?

         And where you should not.
         For my ally 'tis the Force.
         A pow'rful ally.

         Life doth create it.   45
         Its energy surrounds us,
         Binds us together.

         Luminous beings
         We are, not this crude matter.
         You must feel the Force.   50

         All around thee, here—

        Between thou and me, tree, rock:
        Ev'rywhere it is.

        E'en between the land
        And your ever-sinking ship,   55
        The Force is there, too.

LUKE   I know now thou dost ask th'impossible.
                   [Luke sits aside, as Yoda lifts his hands.

YODA   *[aside:]* Be mindful, young one,
        And watch what inner strength great
        May come from small size.   60
             [Yoda moves the ship out of the swamp
                            using the Force.

LUKE   The ship! It cometh out—thou hast done it!
        I ne'er imagin'd it was possible.
        With eyes I see, but mind does not believe.

YODA   Thus is your error.
        Against the Force you do rail;   65
        That is why you fail.
                        [Exeunt.

ACT IV

SCENE 1.

Aboard the Millennium Falcon, *moored to a Star Destroyer.*

Enter CHORUS.

CHORUS   With such deep wit Han hath the Empire trick'd
          That now the Falcon hides within its fleet!
          With skill he doth the Empire's moves predict,
          And bravely plans to make his move discreet.

                                                        [Exit.

Enter HAN SOLO, PRINCESS LEIA, CHEWBACCA, *and* C-3PO.

C-3PO   I tell thee, Captain Solo, thou hast gone   5
          Beyond all measure with this reckless move.
          Thou hast put all aboard in danger grave,
          And yet thou seem'st to have but little care.
CHEWBAC. Auugh!
C-3PO   —Nay, I'll not be silent! Wherefore am
          I never listen'd to?
HAN   —The fleet doth break   10
          Itself up into pieces. [*To Chewbacca:*] Go thee now,
          Chewbacca; stand aside the manual
          Release to liberate the landing claw.
CHEWBAC. Egh.
                                          [Exit Chewbacca.
C-3PO   —Truly, I see not how that shall help.
          Surrender is, in circumstances such   15
          As these, a fair alternative. Perhaps
          The Empire may yet reasonable be.
                                    [Leia turns off C-3PO.

HAN	Great thanks I give thee for the gift of peace.
LEIA	Brave soul, what dost thou think thou next shalt do?
HAN	Before these ships do from the fleet release, 20
	They should their garbage dump ere they pursue
	A jump to lightspeed. Then we'll float away.
LEIA	Thy ship with all the garbage, eh? Well said.
	And what then?
HAN	—We shall haply find our way
	Unto a port where safety makes its bed. 25
	Pray, dost thou know of any port like such?
LEIA	Mayhap I might, if I knew where we were.
HAN	Anoat system, but doth that help much?
LEIA	O, the Anoat system? I aver:
	'Tis bleak.
HAN	—But hark! An interesting name 30
	My ship's computer showeth: Lando!
LEIA	—Han?
	What Lando system?
HAN	—"System," you exclaim?
	He is not system: Lando is a man.
	As Lando of Calrissian he's known.
	The man doth deal in cards, in gambling and 35
	In scoundreling—thou wouldst his type condone.
LEIA	[*aside:*] He jests with me as one in love's command!
HAN	He is in Bespin—rather far, but we
	May make it there.
LEIA	[*reading from screen:*] —A colony? A mine?
HAN	Tibanna gas mine—I would wager he 40
	Hath ta'en the mine that someone did call "mine."
	This Lando hath a hist'ry long with me.
LEIA	But dost thou trust him?

HAN   —Nay, thou'rt right. But I
                    Believe we have no need of fear, for he
                    No love doth harbor for the Empire, aye.   45
                                        [*The ship shakes.*
                    [*Into comlink:*] Prepare now, Chewie, 'tis the time.
                                                Detach!
                                        [*The* Millennium Falcon *detaches*
                                                from the Star Destroyer.

LEIA   Thou hast these moments that are unsurpass'd—
                    Aye, when thou hast them, they are without match.
                    Not numerous are they, but aye: thou hast.
                                        [*Leia kisses Han and exits with* C-3PO.

HAN   'Tis said that sometimes those who knew us in   50
                    Our youth did know us best. From them we have
                    No secrets and cannot pretend to be
                    Another thing than what we are. They keep
                    Our living honest, for they know who we
                    Have been. And such a man is Lando. He   55
                    And I have known each other many years,
                    So he doth know me from my smuggling past,
                    The days when I did gamble, cheat, and fight—
                    And often in that order, too. He knew
                    Me ere I was with the Rebellion join'd,   60
                    And knoweth what Han Solo once hath been.
                    Thus is he prim'd uniquely to give aid
                    Unto a friend who now hath found a cause:
                    A cause to join, a cause e'en to defend.
                    O Lando, all our hopes are pinn'd on thee.   65
                    What shall it be, old friend? I here take all
                    I have—my ship, my mates, my one true love—
                    And stake it all on thee and on our past.

How shalt thou answer, O Calrissian?
Will this, my wager, prove a foolish bet?   70
How shall the deck unfold, the players end?
And is the dealing in my favor stack'd?
The playing of the game is yet to be,
But Lando: I do seek to win with thee.

[Exit.

Enter BOBA FETT.

FETT   A smuggler's ways are e'er unchanging and   75
            predictable. Thou hast let the *Millennium Falcon*
            go out with the refuse, Solo, but I refuse to let
            thee play a jade's trick and go thy merry way.
            Thy course shall I pursue, and e'en best, for my
            ship is swift of flight unlike thy tir'd and agèd   80
            Falcon. To the last I'll grapple with thee, and
            in the heart of Bespin make thee cold with fright.
            The Fett doth promise it, and it shall be.

[*Exit Boba Fett.*

SCENE 2.
The Dagobah system.

Enter YODA, R2-D2, *and* LUKE SKYWALKER,
doing a handstand and lifting things with the Force.

YODA   Now, concentrate, Luke.
            Feel the Force, how it doth flow.
            Be calm, at peace, yes.

When you use the Force,
The Force, in your soul, begins   5
New paths to open.

Through the Force, your mind
Shall see future things, things past.
Friends nearer and yon.

LUKE   Alas, my mind doth see—'tis Leia, Han!   10
          [Everything drops as Luke's concentration breaks.

YODA   Nay, be in control!
      Thou must, beyond all else, Luke,
      Have control entire.

LUKE   O vision most horrendous and most drear.
      A city in the clouds most beautiful,   15
      Beneath a golden sun—as though 'twere heav'n.
      But hidden just beneath its luster doth
      A harsh and painful nightmare lurk. I saw,
      Beneath a sky of orange hues array'd,
      Dear Leia weeping at some cruel, dark thing—   20
      She will not be consol'd from her great loss.
      And Han, his screams do echo in mine ears,
      Such cries of suffering I ne'er have heard.
      What signs are these, what ghosts of future hurt?
      What doth the Force attempt to show to me?   25
      O tell me, Master, tell me plain, I pray:
      Shall Han and Leia die, is that their fate?

YODA   A future sight, this.
      Hard to see is the future—
      'Tis e'er in motion.   30

LUKE   I understand 'tis hard for thee to see,
      But harder yet the vision echoes in

My head, and reaches deep within my soul.
If thou canst not give reassurance they
Are safe, and shall be safe, 'tis I who must   35
Ensure the same. I will not idly stand
By whilst they suffer many agonies.
My mind is settl'd: I must thither go.

YODA   Decide thou must, how
            Thou shalt truly serve them best.   40
            Mayhap you may help.

            But also shalt thou
            Sacrifice all for which they
            Shall fight and suffer.

LUKE   But Master, tell me what then I should do?   45
            Wouldst thou allow thy friends to suffer thus?
            Wouldst thou accept the future's "hard to see"?
            Wouldst thou ignore the screams within thy brain?

YODA   [aside:] The boy doth not hear—
            His friends' fates I cannot see,   50
            But his looketh bleak.

            Convince him I must,
            Else he shall suffer greatly
            And lost is our hope.

            [To Luke:] Go not, I prithee.   55
            The training must thou complete.
            To my words listen!

LUKE   The vision shall not, will not, leave my head.
            E'en now I witness Leia in her torment,
            And Han, alone, as if upon some isle.   60

E'en brave Chewbacca cries for what is lost—
These signs can only equal tragedy.
They are my friends, and I must fly with haste.
Or else, I'll warrant, all of them may die.

Enter GHOST OF OBI-WAN KENOBI.

OBI-WAN   Thou canst not know this, Luke. E'en Yoda doth   65
               Not have the pow'r, their final fate to see.
LUKE   But I may help them now; I feel the Force!
OBI-WAN   To see is one thing—to control is yet
               Another. Dangerous this moment is
               For thee, for thou shalt be sore tempted, in   70
               Thy rage, toward the dark side of the Force.

YODA   Yes, to Obi-Wan
              Thou must listen. The cave, Luke:
              Recall thy failure!

LUKE   But truly, I have learn'd so much since then.   75
              I know what I must watch for and beware,
              I know how tempted by the dark I'll be,
              I know this and shall, therefore, guard my soul.
              I tell thee, Master Yoda, I'll return
              And finish all my training. This I vow.   80

OBI-WAN   Pray, open up thine eyes. 'Tis thee and thine
              Abilities the Emperor desires.
              They are the bait, and thou the colo claw—
              Thou art the fish the Emperor would catch.
              Thy friends do suffer only for thy sake,   85
              So that, through them, thou mayst be easily
              Drawn in.

LUKE   —And that is why I have to go.
              Present unto the Emperor the fish,
              And rest assur'd the bait is off the hook.

OBI-WAN   O Luke, I would not lose thee as I lost   90
              Darth Vader. His betrayal made my life
              A bleak and tragic thing. Thy loss unto
              The dark would make my death a hellish, cold
              Eternity.

LUKE   —I shall return, dear Ben.
              My training thus far shall suffice, it is   95
              Enough; I stand prepar'd to face the dark.

YODA   Stoppèd they must be;
              On this depends ev'ry thing.
              But pray, attend me:

Only a fully   100
Trainèd Jedi may defeat
Vader and his Lord.

If thou leavest now,
And here do end thy training,
Thou art choosing ease.   105

And once on the path
Of ease and haste, like Vader
Thou mayst become, Luke.

OBI-WAN   Attend to Yoda's wisdom, Luke, and stay.
             O, exercise thy patience, worthy lad.   110

LUKE   And in the waiting sacrifice my friends?
             Is that the choice that ye would have me make?

YODA   This hard indeed is.
             But if thou honor the thing
             For which they fight: yes.   115

OBI-WAN   If thou dost choose to face Darth Vader, thou
             Shalt be alone; I cannot interfere.

LUKE   I understand, and have been fully warn'd.
             My mind is set; good R2, do prepare.
             Fire up the ship's converters: we depart.   120

OBI-WAN   O, do not give in unto hate, dear Luke,
             In doing so the dark side shalt thou find.
             [*Aside:*] Indeed, I once did see it happen thus.

YODA   Strong is Darth Vader.
             Remember what thou hast learn'd,   125
             For save thee it can.

LUKE   I shall, and shall return: you have my word.
                                 [*Exeunt Luke and R2-D2.*

YODA   Warnèd thee I have—
            He a reckless spirit hath.
            Now matters are worse.   130
OBI-WAN   That boy is our first, last, and greatest hope.
                        [Exit Ghost of Obi-Wan Kenobi.
YODA   But nay, 'tis not so.
            For another yet there is:
            One more hope for us.

            O how this plagues me!   135
            The boy for training hath come,
            But too soon is fled.

            A young bird he is,
            Too eager the nest to leave,
            Yet trying to fly.   140

            But young birds fly not—
            Their wings still too fragile are.
            Instead, they do fall.

            And fall this one shall.
            But how far, how fast, how long?   145
            Time only shall tell.

            Little bird, be safe.
            If thou the nest seest again
            I shall meet thee then.
                                        [Exit Yoda.

SCENE 3.

Bespin, the cloud city.

Enter HAN SOLO, CHEWBACCA, PRINCESS LEIA, *and* C-3PO,
attempting to land the Millennium Falcon *in the city,*
speaking with GUARD 1 *in comlink.*

HAN   Nay, nay, good Sir, as I have said before:
             I have no permit that shall let me pass,
             But Lando of Calrissian I seek.

GUARD 1   [*through comlink:*] Thou shalt not enter unto Bespin,
                                                              nay.

HAN   Why dost thou fire at me and my good ship?   5
             Be not so quick to turn to blasters, Sir—
             I prithee, grant me time but to explain . . .

GUARD 1   [*through comlink:*] Make thou no deviation from
                                               thy course.

C-3PO   These Bespinites are rather petulant—
             They've nothing of my disposition sweet.   10

LEIA   [*to Han:*] I thought that thou didst say thou knowest this
             Man Lando.

CHEWBAC.   —Auugh!

HAN   —But 'twas so long ago.
             Nay, surely he doth hold no grudge by now.

GUARD 1   [*through comlink:*] Thou hast permission now to
                                               land upon
             The platform three–two–seven.

HAN   —Many thanks.   15
             Now do ye see, ye doubters all? I tell
             Ye truly: Lando is a friend, indeed.

LEIA   Nay, who hath worri'd? [*Aside:*] Verily, there is

A something here that seemeth not aright:
This welcome hath been less than welcoming.   20
Yet Han with brave nobility hath led
Our troubl'd quest—I shall not doubt him now.
   [*The* Millennium Falcon *lands and Han Solo,*
   Chewbacca, Princess Leia, and C-3PO disembark.

CHEWBAC. Egh.

C-3PO   —O, there is no one to meet us here.

LEIA I do not like this, Han.

HAN   —What wouldst thou like?

C-3PO At least we are no more upon the ship— 25
Enough of space I've seen to last a life.
'Twas kind of them to let us land.

HAN [*to Princess Leia:*] —Be calm
And trust me, all things shall end well.

  Enter LANDO *with* LOBOT *and* GUARDS.

    My friend!
[*To Chewbacca:*] But keep thou watch now, Chewie,
        just in case.

LANDO [*aside:*] How shall I play this? Shall I distant be? 30
Nay, then he shall become suspicious and
May have some cause to fear ere Vader comes.
I shall be jovial and shine with joy—
A colt is ridden best by kindly rider.
I know 'tis true: it worketh ev'ry time.   35
Thus, to deceive I shall employ a jest.
[*Walking to Han:*] Thou slimy, double-crossing,
        no-good swine!
Thou hast a nerve to show thy cheating face,

    Since thou hast prov'n thyself a lying thief.

HAN   Is't possible? Is friendship's mem'ry slain?   40

LANDO   Heigh-ho, I mock at thee, my goodly friend!

    How art thou, pirate? 'Tis a joy to see

    Thee here.

C-3PO   [*to Princess Leia:*] —He doth seem full of

              friendship's mirth.

LEIA   Aye, truly, he seems full of it indeed.

LANDO   What brings thee here to Bespin?

HAN   —Ship repairs.   45

    Methought thou couldst some kind assistance grant.

LANDO   What hast thou done unto my ship?

HAN   —Thy ship?

    Remember thou didst lose her o'er to me

    As fairly as the day is long.

LANDO   —And how

    Dost thou, Chewbacca? Hang'st thou still around 50

    This aging renegade?

CHEWBAC.   —Egh!

LANDO   [*to Princess Leia:*]   —O, what light

    Doth break upon mine eyes? What beauty's this?

    I give thee welcome, gentle lady. I

    Am Lando of Calrissian, and do

    Administer this great facility.   55

    And who, pray tell, art thou? Eh?

LEIA   —Leia, I.

LANDO   [*kissing her hand:*] Most welcome, Leia.

HAN   —Aye, 'tis well, 'tis well.

    Thou ever wert a lover of fair things.

C-3PO   C-3PO am I, and at your service . . .

            [Lando turns his back.

	[*Aside:*] I wonder that I still am talking here:	60
	Nobody marks me.	
LANDO	[*to Han:*] —What doth ail the ship?	
HAN	The hyperdrive.	
LANDO	—My people shall begin	
	Work on't immediately. I tell thee,	
	That ship in many cases sav'd my life!	
	What stories of adventure I could tell	65
	In which the ship doth play the central part.	
	She is the fastest heap of scrap in all	
	The galaxy!	
LEIA	[*aside:*] —He loveth this old ship	
	Almost as much as Han! This love of ships,	
	'Tis like an illness wild within these men.	70
HAN	Now tell me of thy life and bus'ness, friend—	
	How doth the gas mine for thee? Doth it pay?	
LANDO	'Tis credits in and credits out, but more,	

I fear, of out than in. We are but small,
An outpost minor. Thus have I supply   75
Dilemmas, labor difficulties, too.

HAN   Ha, ha!

LANDO   —Why say'st thou "Ha"? And wherefore twice?

HAN   'Tis thou. Pray, hearken unto thine own voice.
So rife with deep responsibility,
So serious, experienc'd, mature,   80
And bus'nesslike. 'Twas not my expectation.

LANDO   [*aside:*] O weep, my heart, to see him brings such joy,
And pains me more to seal his awful fate.
[*To Han:*] Pray, hear me truly, Han. Whatever else
May happen, hear these words: this moment doth   85
Recall for me our past together, which
Is sweetness in my memory.

HAN   —Indeed.
'Tis well to see thee thriving so, my friend.

LANDO   And thou hast hit the mark: I duties bear,
And grave responsibilities are mine.   90
'Tis but the price of one's success, I s'pose.

                    [*Exeunt Han Solo, Chewbacca,*
                          Princess Leia, and Lando.

                Enter another 3PO DROID.

C-3PO   What joy to see a kind, familiar face.

DROID   E chu ta!

                              [*Exit 3PO droid.*

C-3PO   —O, how rude! But pray, what's here?

                          [*C-3PO enters another room.*

Was that an R2 unit's sound I heard?

Is't possible that R2-D2's here?   95
Hello, who is herein?

          Enter a SHADOWY FIGURE.

FIGURE   —Say, who art thou?
C-3PO   Alas, this is my end! An enemy—
               If only I could others tell. O me!
                         [Exeunt as C-3PO is shot into pieces.

          Enter PRINCESS LEIA.

LEIA   Time's passage hath not sooth'd my mind's distress.
               Full many moments we have waited here   100

Within this lovely city in the clouds,
Yet I am neither rested nor relax'd.
Foreboding doth creep o'er me like a plague—
My mind is sore afeard, my hands do shake,
And nowhere can my troubl'd soul find peace.   105
The quick permission given us to land,
The too-familiar welcome Lando gave,
A small apartment offer'd for our use—
It seems as though we were expected here,
Though how this could have happen'd, I know not.   110
For surely when th'Imperi'l fleet broke up,
We in the opposite direction flew.
But e'en beyond that worry there is more,
For though I do not love the prating droid
C-3PO has not been seen since our   115
Arrival here. We have too much of quiet—
I almost miss his constant chattering.

Enter Han Solo.

HAN   All shall be well. The ship is fix'd with care.
             There are but two or three things more, then will
             We make our swift departure hence. 'Tis fair?   120
LEIA   The swiftest shall be best. Some thing is still
             Awry. Where is C-3PO? He hath
             Not seen us or been seen for many hours,
             And no one knows about his way or path.
             Hath he lost all his faithful, droidly sense?   125
             Most happ'ly would I by him be annoy'd,
             If it did mean that he, at least, were near.
HAN   I shall inquire of Lando 'bout the droid.

But in the meantime, Leia, have no fear.

LEIA   I trust not Lando.

HAN   —Neither, sweet, do I,   130

Yet he's my friend who helpeth us, dost see?

I'll warrant that we soon from here shall fly.

LEIA   Then thou shalt take thy flight as well—from me.

HAN   The future has its own time yet to write,

And wheth'r or not we worry, my good lass,   135

It comes as sure as day doth follow night.

So, think not of it till it come to pass.

                   [Exeunt Han Solo and Princess Leia.

Enter a merry band of UGNAUGHTS,
singing as they pass around parts of C-3PO's body.

UGN. 1   O pass me that!

UGN. 2   O give me this!

UGN. 3   We Ugnaughts are a'working!   140

UGN. 2   O pass the head!

UGN. 3   Give me the chest!

UGN. 1   Our duties never shirking!

UGN. 3   Thou naughty droid—

UGN. 1   Thou hast been caught!   145

UGN. 2   Thy prying never ceases!

UGN. 1   Your lesson learn'd—

UGN. 2   Our treasures earn'd—

UGN. 3   For now thou art in pieces!

Enter CHEWBACCA.

CHEWBAC.   Auugh!   150

[Chewbacca begins collecting pieces of C-3PO.

UGN. 2	Take not the arms!	
UGN. 3	Pray, leave the legs!	
UGN. 1	Thy greed thou art revealing!	
UGN. 3	But naught shall last!	
UGN. 1	For nothing doth!	155
UGN. 2	Our treasures thou art stealing!	
UGN. 1	So shall we speak—	
UGN. 2	Our proverb true—	
UGN. 3	With voices loudly ringing—	
UGN. 2	It easy came—	160
UGN. 3	And easy goes—	
UGN. 1	But still we keep on singing!	

[Exeunt Ugnaughts, singing.

Enter HAN SOLO *and* PRINCESS LEIA.

LEIA   I see, Chewbacca, thou hast found the droid,
              At least some small and varied parts of him.
              O, what hath happen'd?

CHEWBAC.   —Auugh!

HAN   —Thou hast found him   165
              Upon a junk pile, what? How can that be?
              C-3PO was fine when we arriv'd.
              But now, I fear, he is more dread than droid.

LEIA   'Tis such a mess. Canst thou repair him, good
              Chewbacca?

CHEWBAC.   —Egh, auugh.

HAN   —Lando's people can   170
              Provide the cure.

LEIA   —Nay, thank you: I'd not hav't.

Enter LANDO.

LANDO   Forgive me, worthy guests. Do I intrude?

LEIA   Nay, verily.

LANDO   —O, but thou art a beauty.

I prithee, never leave—thou dost belong

With us in our great city in the clouds.   175

Thy loveliness doth put the sun to shame,

Thy brightness of your cheek would shame the stars.

LEIA   [*aside:*] This scoundrel too familiar is. Now do

I see that though I once thought Han uncouth,

He is the sweetest smuggler ever liv'd.   180

[*To Lando:*] Thou hast my thanks.

LANDO   —Now come, will ye join me

For some repast?

CHEWBAC.   —Auugh.

LANDO   —Chewie, fear thou not!

Be sure I meant that all invited are.

[*Seeing C-3PO:*] Is there some matter with your droid?

HAN   —Nay, I

Know not of any matter.

                        [*They walk, leaving C-3PO's parts.*

                Tell me, though,   185

As we proceed to supper: art thou an

Accepted member of the mining guild?

LANDO   Nay, we are none. Our operation is

Still small enough that we may be discreet.

'Tis advantageous to our customers,   190

For they are anxious to escape attention.

LEIA   [*aside:*] O, all this talk of bus'ness, mines and stealth!

My mind cannot abide it, for I sense
That terrible events shall soon befall.
Within my mind a vision of some pain   195
Begins to form, but still is indistinct.
Would that I had some time to clear my thoughts!

HAN   [to Lando:] But art thou not afraid the Empire shall
Find out about your operation and
Then drive you out of business, or e'en worse?   200

LANDO   'Tis e'er a danger that looms over us
And all that we have built in Bespin's walls.
But things have just develop'd which shall make
Our future safe and well-secur'd. A deal
I've with the Empire made that shall keep them   205
Far distant from our operations.

                    [They arrive at a door and open it.

Enter DARTH VADER and BOBA FETT, revealed inside.

CHEWBAC.   —Auugh!

HAN   [aside:] But what is this? Betrayal! Hands, take flight—
My blaster shall I use, and save us yet!
                    [Han fires, but Vader deflects the blast
                    and uses the Force to takes Han's blaster.

VADER   We would be honor'd should ye join us here.

LANDO   I am most sorry, worthy friend. They did   210
Arrive in Bespin ere thou here didst fly.

HAN   No sorrier, I do expect, than I.

                              [Exeunt.

SCENE 4.

Bespin, the cloud city.

Enter GUARDS 1 *and* 2.

GUARD 1   Oi! Well met, worthy friend. What dost thou here?
GUARD 2   I have been poring o'er our city's plans.
GUARD 1   What's this? A newfound interest? Shalt thou
            Turn architect?
GUARD 2   —Nay, nay, and yet I have
            Found something curious.
GUARD 1   —Indeed?
GUARD 2   —Indeed.   5
GUARD 1   Pray tell!
GUARD 2   —The city hath been built within
            The Empire's strict specifications for
            Design and building standards.
GUARD 1   —Aye, 'twas wise,
            Thus may the Bespin council never have
            A reason for to fear the Empire's sharp   10
            Inspectors.
GUARD 2   —Verily, but follow on:
            That they unto the code this city built
            Is not the thing that I found strange. Instead,
            It was the code's requirements I did mark.
            For didst thou know the Empire doth require   15
            That any major structure shall include
            At least one chasm that's deep and long and dark?
            Not only shall these chasms exist: the code
            Doth further specify that they shall be
            Abutting pathways where pedestrians   20

May walk. The Death Star that was built some years
Ago had, evidently, sev'ral of
These holes, and our Cloud City has them, too.
Is not this strange?

GUARD 1   —I know them well, and did
Go walking past just such a gaping hole   25
That led to nothingness but yesterday.
But wherefore dost thou say 'tis strange, I pray?

GUARD 2   It simply maketh little sense to put
Such vast, deep holes in ev'ry structure next
To well-worn paths. Could not a person, by   30
Some simple misstep, fall most easily ·
Down one of these great chasms? So wherefore place
Such hazards into ev'ry structure built?

GUARD 1   I see your reasoning, but shall rebut:
The Empire is the greatest strength e'er known,   35
'Tis true?

GUARD 2   —Of course. I'd not say otherwise.

GUARD 1   And any great thing—person, beast, or realm—
Doth put its greatness on display, agreed?

GUARD 2   'Tis natural, I'll warrant. Pray, say on.

GUARD 1   I posit that the Empire doth command   40
That structures have these chasms immense because
It is through their immensity that our
Great Empire's strength is shown. And since they are
Vast holes that deadly are, should one fall in,
They send a message strong and clear to all: 45
The Empire is a proud and mighty pow'r
And doth not fear sure death, but laughs at it.
I' faith, we are so full of life that we
Walk by our certain passing daily—it

GUARD 2   Is but quotidian for us—and yet   50
                                 We have no fear.

GUARD 2   —Thy point is clearly made.
                                 But still, I think it strange that this is true:
                                 A structure is not whole till it hath holes.
                                 Such things lie far beyond my understanding,
                                 Yet do I trust there is a master plan.   55

GUARD 1   Shall we to supper, friend?

GUARD 2   —Forsooth, lead on!

                                                [Exeunt Guards 1 and 2.

                                 Enter LANDO.

LANDO   O what is this dire sound I just have heard?
                                 My friend Han Solo screaming in great pain,
                                 The shrieks of man turn'd victim through my fault—
                                 My quick decision to protect myself.   60
                                 Yet what choice had I? Could I else have done?
                                 No person in my place would diff'rently
                                 Behave. No choice had I but one: to save
                                 Myself, my interests, and my belov'd
                                 Cloud City from a dark and awful fate.   65
                                 Yet ever shall my soul be haunted by
                                 These dismal howls of my old friend, unless
                                 I can find some way to make recompense.
                                 But how shall that e'er be whilst Vader's threats
                                 Do cast their shadows o'er my ev'ry move?   70
                                 I know not how, but yet it must be so.
                                 I shall—belike with loyal Lobot's help—
                                 Discover yet a way to make this right,
                                 And save myself from a betrayer's name!

Enter LOBOT, DARTH VADER, *and* BOBA FETT.

VADER	[*to Boba Fett:*] Thou mayst take Captain Solo
	and transport 75
	Him unto Jabba once Skywalker has
	Arriv'd and captur'd been. Say, is this clear?
FETT	'Tis, my Lord. But Solo is no good to me, should
	he be dead upon delivery. He hath been tortur'd
	severely in this last hour. 'Tis well, but I prithee do 80
	not kill the man ere I deliver him to Jabba.
VADER	No harm beyond undoing shall he bear.
LANDO	Lord Vader, do I comprehend this fully—
	Thou shalt surrender Han unto this man,
	This bounty hunter here? So what is next? 85
	I prithee, tell me: what shall happen to
	Both Leia and the Wookiee?
VADER	—Never shall
	They leave this city.
LANDO	—This doth push the bounds
	Too far! Imprisonment was never a
	Condition of the bargain we did make, 90
	And 'twas not in the plan to hand o'er Han
	Unto this bounty hunter!
VADER	—Mayhap thou
	Dost think thou hast unfairly treated been?
LANDO	[*aside:*] A threat is in his voice and aspect. [*To Vader:*]
	Nay,
	For I shall model flexibility. 95
VADER	'Tis well. 'Twould be a pity should I feel
	It necessary to retain a full
	And armor'd garrison in Bespin. [*To Boba Fett:*] Come!

                                  [*Exeunt Darth Vader and Boba Fett.*

LANDO   He orders what he will sans sense or rhyme—
             This deal is worse becoming all the time!   100

LOBOT   . . .

                                              [*Exeunt.*

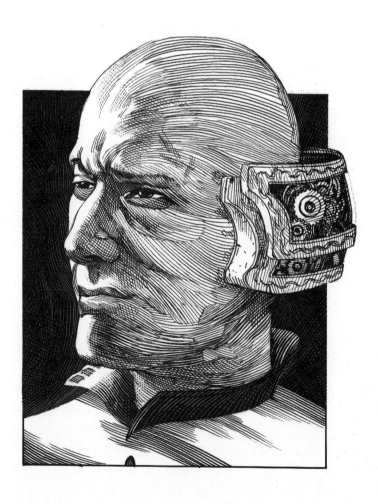

SCENE 5.

Bespin, the cloud city.

Enter CHEWBACCA, *with* C-3PO's *parts.*

CHEWBAC. Auugh.

C-3PO [*being reconnected:*] —Stormtroopers? In Bespin?

                      I am shot!

              [*Chewbacca disconnects C-3PO and*
                  tries to reconnect him again.

CHEWBAC. Egh!

C-3PO   —O, 'tis better! That is quite improv'd.

But hold, for something is not right: my eyes—

I cannot see.

                 [*Chewbacca adjusts C-3PO.*

         Now that is mended, aye.

Yet wait, I now am backward—head is back   5

And front's reverse and all has gone awry!

Is this a Wookiee's notion of a joke?

Thou stupid, senseless beast!

CHEWBAC. [*laughing:*]   —Gihut, gihut!

C-3PO Thou furball wretched! Mophead ignorant!

              [*Chewbacca switches off C-3PO.*

Enter HAN SOLO, *carried by* STORMTROOPERS,
who drop him and exit.

CHEWBAC. Auugh, auugh!

HAN   —O, Chewie, I'm in agony—   10

My ev'ry bone and sinew cries with pain.

Enter PRINCESS LEIA.

LEIA   What have they done to you, my noble man?
     And what can be their purpose, dost thou know?

HAN   'Twas torture unlike any I have known,
     For never any questions did they ask.   15
     Instead, with silent mouths and darting eyes
     They fix'd me solidly unto a seat
     And lower'd me unto a mechanism.
     At first 'twas like a searing heat that rac'd
     From skin to bone and back again. Then sparks   20
     Flew out, upon my chest and neck and face,
     Such fire as though a hundred blasters spread
     Their shots across my body or, perhaps,
     As though a million tiny lightsabers
     Did prick and dance their way about my skin.   25
     All this they did, but ne'er made inquiry,
     Ne'er ask'd me whence we came or where we go,
     Ne'er ask'd about the rebels' rendezvous.
     No information they did seek to know,
     It only seem'd they wish'd to bring me pain.   30
     I tell thee, 'twas far worse and terrible
     Than if they had sought answers from my blood.
     But this demented evil shakes my soul,
     For wherefore torture without questioning?

Enter LANDO, *with* GUARDS.

CHEWBAC.   Auugh, egh, auugh!
HAN   —Get thee hence now, Lando.
LANDO   —Tut!   35

Attend my voice, for this ye both should hear:
Darth Vader hath giv'n word that he will turn
Both Leia and Chewbacca o'er to me.

HAN   What dost thou mean by "o'er to me"? Thou knave!
          I would not turn a rival o'er to thee,   40
          Much less the ones belovèd by my heart.

LANDO   They must stay here, but will, at least, be safe.
          'Twas not my choice—I have no say in this.
          'Tis Vader who doth pull the strings, and we
          Are but the puppets with which he doth play.   45

LEIA   And what of Han?

LANDO   —Darth Vader shall give him
          O'er to the bounty hunter.

LEIA   —Vader doth
          Desire that all of us are dead.

LANDO   —He wants
          You not at all. He searches for someone
          Called Skywalker.

HAN   —Aye, Luke—thou meanest Luke!   50

LANDO   Lord Vader set a trap for him to fall.

LEIA   And we are but the bait by which he's caught.

LANDO   The trap shall soon be sprung, for Skywalker
          Is on his way, e'en now.

HAN   —This villainy
          Thou hast arrang'd is all too perfect. Fie!   55

                    [Han Solo strikes Lando but is
                        quickly restrained by guards.

CHEWBAC. Auugh!

LANDO   —Cease! I have done all that I may do.
          For certain I am sorry I could not
          Do better yet than this, but I do have

Enough vexations here.

HAN   —O, thou great man!
Thou art a hero, and thy tale shall e'er   60
Upon the lips of lesser folk be told.
Throughout all history it shall be writ:
"Behold, great Lando of Calrissian,
A man who ever serv'd his comrades well."

LANDO   [*aside:*] This stings my soul, yet no more can I do   65
Than hold my head up high, and plan what's next.

                              [*Exeunt Lando and guards.*

LEIA   My soldier, O my heart, thy fire doth blaze!
Thy skill with others ne'er doth cease t'amaze.

                                   [*Exeunt.*

ACT V

SCENE 1.

Bespin, the cloud city.

Enter UGNAUGHTS 1, 2, *and* 3, *singing.*

UGN. 3	The time is ripe!
UGN. 1	His time is nigh!
UGN. 2	And soon he will be frozen!
UGN. 1	We've never done—
UGN. 2	This on a man—
UGN. 3	But someone's now been chosen!
UGN. 2	A merry prank!
UGN. 3	O shall it work?
UGN. 1	Or will the man be dying?
UGN. 3	What'er befall—
UGN. 1	One thing is sure—
UGN. 2	The pleasure's in the trying!

5

10

[Exeunt Ugnaughts.

Enter LANDO, LOBOT, DARTH VADER, *and* BOBA FETT.

VADER   A perfect touch this is, to freeze Skywalker.
The plan is perfect—he who hath destroy'd
The Death Star shall be packag'd as a gift.   15
But now, let us inspect the details. Aye,
This crude contraption should be adequate
To put this vexing Skywalker on ice
Ere his deliv'ry to the Emperor.

Enter IMPERIAL SOLDIER.

SOLDIER   Lord Vader—there's a ship that doth approach,   20
                   An X-wing class.

VADER   —'Tis well. Watch Skywalker,
                   Allow his landing, let him hither come.

                            [Exit Imperial soldier.

LANDO   Lord Vader, this facility has ne'er
                   Been us'd for humans, only carbon freezing.
                   If thou dost put him in this vast machine   25
                   It may not freeze him, but may mean his death.

VADER   This is a point that I consider'd not.
                   It seems, Calrissian, that thou dost learn
                   To be obedient unto thy Lord.
                   'Tis well, and it is in thine interest.   30
                   I do not wish him harm'd; the Emperor
                   Shall not enjoy a damag'd prize. So shall
                   Another stand for him to be a test—
                   We shall make Captain Solo undergo
                   The freezing process first, to test its pow'r.   35

FETT   My Lord, although his death would bring me
                   joy, it doth not pay. Jabba, like thine Emperor,
                   giveth no fees for damag'd goods. I prithee,
                   what shall happen if the man doth die? What
                   then, for Boba Fett?   40

VADER   Fear not, thy hunt shall have its bounty still.
                   Thou shalt be compensated if he dies.

       Enter HAN SOLO, CHEWBACCA, PRINCESS LEIA, *and*
       C-3PO *(attached to Chewbacca's back), all guarded.*

C-3PO   *[to Chewbacca:]* I almost fully am restor'd to my
                   Old self, except thy work is not complete.

	If thou had but attach'd my legs, I would	45
	Not yet remain in this position rare!	
	I prithee, good Chewbacca, do recall	
	That I am thy responsibility—	
	Do not in any instance foolish be!	
HAN	[*to Lando:*] Pray tell, O dearest friend, what is at hand?	50
LANDO	Thou shalt be plac'd in total carbon freeze.	
HAN	[*aside:*] The news of my grim fate doth chill my blood.	
	O, how I once thought Hoth was cold and bleak,	
	Yet now I pine for all its balmy plains.	
VADER	Now, put him in!	
CHEWBAC.	—Auugh!	

[Chewbacca fights guards and
slays three of them.

HAN	—Chewie, stop, I pray!	55
C-3PO	Alas, yes, stop! I am not set to die!	
HAN	This cannot help me, brave Chewbacca, nay.	
	I prithee, save thy strength to fight again.	
	Attend me now: the princess—thou must be	
	Her strength, her stay, her guard, her confidence:	60
	These things that I no longer can bestow.	
LEIA	O, I do love thee wholly, Han.	
HAN	—I know.	

[Han is placed into the machine and
emerges in a frozen block.

C-3PO	Pray, turn around, Chewbacca, let me see.	
	O, he in carbonite hath been encas'd—	
	He should be well protected, if he hath	65
	Surviv'd the freezing process.	
VADER	—Make report,	
	Calrissian, is he alive?	

LANDO   —He is,
               And rests in perfect hibernation here.
VADER   The prize is thine now, bounty hunter Fett.
               Take him to Jabba, with my gratitude.   70
FETT   [*aside:*] Aye, prize, indeed, and worthy of
               the wait. To Tatooine I fly, with expectation
               of payment great.
VADER   Reset the chamber for young Skywalker—
               He shall the next a'freezing undergo.   75

               Enter IMPERIAL SOLDIER.

SOLDIER   Skywalker's ship hath just made landing, Lord.
VADER   'Tis well, and be thou sure he hither comes—
               Put him upon the path that leads him here.
                                        [Exit Imperial soldier.
               Calrissian, take thou the princess and
               The Wookiee to my ship, and there remain.   80
LANDO   Nay, thou didst say they would in Bespin dwell—
               With me, under my supervision keen.
               How canst thou bargain thus? 'Tis always thy
               Side of the deal that doth improve. What shalt
               Thou give to me to make this deal worthwhile?   85
VADER   Seek not to deal thyself a winning hand.
               The Empire shall not e'er play by thy rules.
               By my command, the deal is alterèd.
               In all thy orisons thou mayst yet plead
               The deal no further alterèd will be.   90
                       [Exeunt Darth Vader and Boba Fett. Chewbacca
                            and Princess Leia sing a song of lament.
CHEWBAC.   [*sings:*] Auugh, egh, auugh, auugh egh. Auugh,

                                                            muh, muh,

              Egh, egh, auugh, egh, egh, muh, muh.

              Auugh, auugh, egh, auugh, muh, egh, muh, muh,

              Muh, wroshyr, wroshyr, wroshyr.

LEIA   [*sings:*] Full fathom five my lover lies,   95

              Within an icy tomb,

              They say he lives, yet my heart dies,

              Sing wroshyr, wroshyr, wroshyr.

CHEWBAC.   [*sings:*] Egh, auugh, auugh, auugh, egh, egh,

                                            muh, muh,

              Auugh, egh, egh, auugh, auugh, muh, muh.   100

              Egh, auugh, auugh, grrm, auugh, egh, muh, muh,

              Muh, wroshyr, wroshyr, wroshyr.

LEIA   [*sings:*] Now he is gone, and so's my life,

              All frozen in a moment.

              He my seiz'd lov'd one, I his strife,   105

              Sing wroshyr, wroshyr, wroshyr.

                                          [Exeunt.

SCENE 2.

Bespin, the cloud city.

Enter LUKE SKYWALKER, *with* R2-D2 *behind.*

LUKE   Yes, now am I in Bespin—more fool I,

              For though my feelings say this is the place,

              I know not yet for certain if it be.

              My friends I have not heard from, hide nor hair,

              And yet the Force doth call in clearest tones   5

              As if to say: "Here lies thy destiny!"

[Luke sees Bespin guards carrying Han Solo.
But wait, what's this? Procession most sincere,
And with such maimèd rites? This doth betoken
The corpse they follow was an enemy.
These Bespin guards do make odd pallbearers;   10
This scene is verily a sign of ill.

Enter BOBA FETT, *shooting at Luke. Luke shoots back.*
Exit Boba Fett.

Aha! It seems that I expected am—
This then must be the place my vision saw.
The Force hath led me here by prophet's hand—
I shall pursue the fiend most ardently,   15
Belike he shall lead me unto my mates.
                    [Exeunt Luke and R2-D2.

Enter CHEWBACCA, PRINCESS LEIA, *and* LANDO,
with GUARDS *and* BOBA FETT.

LANDO   These blasts and great commotion indicate
             Skywalker's recent advent unto Bespin.
             This great upheaval his arrival makes
             Doth grant me the diversion that I seek   20
             To call upon my man-at-arms for help.
                        [Lando presses buttons on
                        his wrist communicator.

Enter LUKE SKYWALKER *and* R2-D2.
Boba Fett shoots again.

LEIA   O Luke, pray fly! 'Tis but a trap! A trap!
         Flee now, dear friend, ere thou art captur'd too.

LUKE   But what is this? 'Tis Leia in distress!
         Yet here, beset by blasts, I'll not prevail.   25

             [Exit Luke Skywalker under fire, with R2-D2
                    behind him. Exit Boba Fett.

       Enter LOBOT *with* ARMED BATTALION.

CHEWBAC.   Auugh!

LANDO   —Aye, well done, my aide! Pray, put them in
         The tower most secure, and be ye quiet!

LOBOT   . . .
          [Exeunt Lobot with battalion and Imperial guards.

LEIA   *[aside:]* O, will he play the hero now? A fig!
         [To Lando:] What is in thy imagination, man?   30

LANDO   We shall depart at once.
         [He releases the bands from Chewbacca's hands.

C-3PO   *[aside:]*   —I knew 'twas thus,
         A regular misunderstanding.
             [Chewbacca begins to choke Lando.

CHEWBAC.   —Auugh!

LANDO   *[choking:]* I had no choice!

C-3PO   —What is this foolishness?
         Pray, trust him!

LEIA   —Aye, we understand, thou knave,
         Thou didst have neither choice nor will to act.   35
         Thou brute! Imperi'l officers act by
         Their Lord's command and blind obedience,
         The bounty hunter is well paid for his
         Nefari'us actions, e'en Darth Vader and

	The Emperor are fully driven by	40

The Emperor are fully driven by   40
Their power, aye! But shalt thou say thou hadst
No choice? What lily-liver'd weak excuse
Is this? At least assume thy stature as
A man, and here confess thy shameful deeds!
We'll give thee opportunity to 'fess   45
Thy wrongs before thou diest at Chewie's hand.

LANDO   [*choking:*] I did but try to help.

LEIA   —We do not need
Thy help, thou whoreson, senseless villain!

LANDO   [*choking:*]   —Han!

LEIA   What didst thou say?

C-3PO   —It sounded like a "Han!"

LANDO   [*choking:*] There may yet be a chance we can save

                                             Han.   50

The bounty hunter's ship, the platform east.

LEIA   Pray, Chewie, let him go.

          [*Chewbacca releases Lando. He and Princess Leia*
              begin to walk away, followed by Lando.

C-3PO   —My ferventest
Apologies for this, good Sir. See, he
Is but a Wookiee, ignorant and plain.

          Enter BOBA FETT *on balcony, with* GUARDS
              and the frozen body of HAN SOLO.

FETT   Now put him in the cargo hold. Who now   55
hath been victorious, Solo? Who is the winner
clear? And as the victor, so go the spoils. Jabba's
bounty and his great pleasure shall I enjoy when
I arrive with thee on Tatooine. I shall become a

courtier in the palace of the Hutts ere this is   60
through. Boba Fett triumphant!

                [Exeunt Boba Fett and guards.

             Enter R2-D2.

R2-D2   *[aside:]* I have been separated from my master.
        Yet happy circumstance, for here I see
        The others, and may now rejoin them.

                  [To C-3PO:] Squeak!

C-3PO   O R2, R2, say, where hast thou been?   65
        It does me well to see thee, little droid.
        Yet prithee, haste thee, for we all now strive
        To save our captain from the clutches of
        The bounty hunter!

R2-D2   —Meep, beep, whistle, squeak!

C-3PO   At least thou art still in one piece—observe   70
        My sad fragmented fate!

               [They arrive at the east platform to
                 see Boba Fett's ship flying away.

LEIA   *[aside:]*   —O flown, alack!
        My Han—his body flown and fled. Now break
        My heart, and weep mine eyes. A princess I
        May be, but first and foremost human with
        Emotions that betray my higher sense.   75
        O gracious Han, forgive that I did come
        To love thee late, and only then to lose thee.
        I'll find thee in the stars, my Han—I'll search
        The galaxy until I find thee.

C-3PO   —O!
        [To Chewbacca:] Pray, Chewie, look, they come
                    behind thee!

CHEWBAC.   —Egh!   80

Enter STORMTROOPERS *from behind, who battle with*
CHEWBACCA, PRINCESS LEIA, *and* LANDO.
The stormtroopers are slain.

LEIA   The soldiers are dispatch'd; now let us go.
              A princess doth command thee, Lando: make
              Thy choice once and for all whom thou shalt serve.
              Wilt thou remain the Empire's stooge, or shalt
              Thou go with us to serve rebellion's cause?   85
LANDO   Good lady, this demand is fairly made.
              Forgive me of the things I've done, I pray,
              And I shall fly with thee and serve thee true.
              But first, let me a final action take
              To serve the Bespinites I love so well—   90
              One moment for the greater good. [*Into comlink:*]
                                        Hear ye,
              'Tis Lando of Calrissian who speaks.
              The Empire doth control the city now—
              I do advise ye all: evacuate
              At once, before more troops arrive within.   95
                        [*Lando tries to open a door and fails.*
              [*To Princess Leia:*] This door shall lead us to the
                                        Falcon, but
              The codes have chang'd. I know not how!
C-3PO   —R2,
              Thou canst o'erride the door's security.
              Pray, R2, speed thee!
                        [*R2-D2 tries to plug into the computer
                        and gets shocked.*

R2-D2	—Beep, meep, whistle, beep!	
C-3PO	O blame me not, I am interpreter,	100
	And know not power socket from computer!	

        [More stormtroopers enter and begin to
        shoot at Chewbacca, Princess Leia, and Lando.

LANDO   Now under siege again! O, let us hence
               Away unto the *Falcon*. Droid, canst thou
               Release these doors that we may pass and fly?

LEIA   If ever droid were worthy, R2 is.   105
               Go to it, R2, make our good escape!

R2-D2   Beep, meep, beep, beep, squeak, whistle, beep, meep,
                                    meep!

C-3PO   We do not care about the hyperdrive—
               The great *Millenn'um Falcon* is repair'd!

R2-D2   *[aside:]* Fie! This computer tells me all's not well, 110
               But how shall I convey this 'midst these blasts?
               The doorway first; the hyperdrive shall wait.
               [To C-3PO:] Beep, meep!

C-3PO   —Pray, ope' the door, thou stupid lump!

                               [The door opens.

               O, R2, never did I doubt thee, thou
               Art wonderful!

                    [Exeunt R2-D2, Lando, and Chewbacca
                    with C-3PO, into the Millennium Falcon.

LEIA   —I know that I should fly,   115
               And yet for Han's sake would I stay and slay
               Each enemy that cometh from within.
               Love unfulfill'd turns quickly into spite,
               And vengefulness doth fill the empty place
               Within my heart. O die a thousand times, 120
               Ye basest beasts who fed upon my love.

O brutes, ye think not of the lives ye take—
You are but senseless minions who fulfill
The sordid whims of your Imperi'l lords.
Belike 'tis not your fault, for you are by   125
A merciless, vile Emperor controll'd.
Yet I shall strike at ye till you do fall
For ev'ry pain that you have giv'n to me:
The loss of Alderaan, of my great friends,
And now the loss of my belovèd one.   130
O die, ye mindless men of Empire cruel!
I shall upon the Empire be reveng'd
Until my gallant Han hath been aveng'd.

                                        [Exit Princess Leia.

SCENE 3.

Bespin, the cloud city.

Enter LUKE SKYWALKER.

LUKE   Where am I now, and where are all my friends?
Some wrong turn have I ta'en, and now am lost
Within a cavern, dark and fill'd with mist.
R2 is left behind; I am alone.
What evil lurks within this passage bleak?   5
What fate shall I discover in this place?
What pow'r hath brought me here—is it the Force?
If not, what messenger of darkness vile
Hath giv'n me up unto this realm of fear?
The cold I feel is as on Dagobah,   10
When in the cave my darkest self I fac'd.

The thoughts I thought therein do now return,
The questions that did rise and give me pause:
O, what is life, and what our purpose here?
Are living creatures made for pain and strife,   15
Do we but walk our days upon the ground
To perish without memory or fame?
If so, what shall we seek whilst we yet live?
Is brave adventure worthy of our time,
Or should we seek the principle of pleasure?   20
Are family and children noble aims,
Or is the Force itself our holy goal?
Is life a quest or is it but a farce—
A splendid journey or a fool's crusade?
Such questions plague my soul, and make me doubt.   25
They draw my mind toward the darkest thoughts
That e'er I've known since I became a man.
And here, away from Dagobah, I have
No firm assurance of my safety, nor
The comfort of my master being here.   30
Thus shall I face my fortune by myself,
Without my mentors great to give me help.
The thought doth bring me trepidation, for
I have relie'd upon their counsel wise.
Be with me here in spirit, if not form,   35
Good Obi-Wan and Yoda—masters true.
O life, O Fate! I would I knew my place,
My time, my end, my destiny complete—
But I cannot see why or how life is.
Because the past is not a perfect guide,   40
And since the future still remains unknown:
My fate shall I meet in the present tense.

                                              [A sound is heard.

But soft, I hear slow footsteps drawing near.

Enter DARTH VADER.

VADER   The Force is with thee now, young Skywalker,

             In troth—but thou art not a Jedi yet.   45

LUKE   [*aside:*] 'Tis Vader, and 'tis Fate. Let it begin.

                                                   [They duel.

Enter CHORUS.

CHORUS   O mighty duel, O action ne'er surpass'd:

             The lightsabers do clash and glow like fire.

             Darth Vader in the villain's role is cast,

             While Luke's young temper turneth soon to ire.   50

             They flash and fly like dancers in a set,

             Yet never dance did know such deadly mood.

             Luke tires, and soon his brow begins to sweat,

             Whilst Vader doth attack with strength renew'd.

VADER   Forsooth, young one, 'tis plain thou hast learn'd much.   55

LUKE   Thou shalt find me full of surprises yet!

VADER   Thy destiny doth lie with me, Skywalker.

             Your teacher Obi-Wan did know 'twas true.

LUKE   Thou liest, O thou villain cruel and cold.

                     [They duel, and Luke falls into the carbon

                                        freezing machine.

VADER   [*aside:*] 'Twas far too simple, trapping him within.   60

             Perhaps the boy is not as powerful

             As my great Emperor and I did think.

                 [Luke leaps out of the carbon freezing machine.

LUKE   I am not captur'd yet, thou lord of hate.
            Thou must another evil scheme derive
            To catch me in thy snares. For I am quick,   65
            And move with all the power of the Force.
VADER   Impressive, most impressive, worthy lad,
            Thine Obi-Wan hath taught thee well, and thou
            Hast master'd all thy fears. Now, go! Release
            Thine anger, for thy hate alone can strike   70
            Me down! [*Aside:*] Now 'tis the moment to provoke
            His inner rage. Come walls, machines, and parts
            And come at him from ev'ry side. He'll be
            Made weak, and in his weakness darkness find!

                          [*Darth Vader uses the Force to strike
                                  Luke with nearby objects.*

LUKE   Alas, I fall—O Fate, be on my side!   75

                                  [*Luke falls out a window.*

VADER   The battle goes exactly as foreseen.
            The boy is powerful and skill'd, 'tis true,
            But his young powers are no match for mine.
            It seems that Obi-Wan was weak with age,
            For this boy's training still is incomplete.   80
            He shall be turnèd yet, for I still hold
            The news that shall undo him utterly.
            He thinks the speed of my lightsaber and
            My power to send objects hurtling at
            Him are the worst that I can muster, but   85
            My greatest weapon yet shall break his soul,
            Not touch his body. He shall know the truth.
            But even as I plan to share with him
            The story of his father, I must pause.
            The strange confusion I before have felt   90

Hath come again into my mind. What is't?
I know no better Fate for him and me
Than to be join'd in service to my Lord
And Emperor. So why am I confus'd?
Enough of this now, Vader: finish it.   95
The boy shall turn or he shall be destroy'd.

> *[Exit Darth Vader. Luke begins to*
> *climb through the window.*

LUKE   O pain, O bitter weariness. I did
Not know the power of the Force till now—
Till it, to purpose rank, was turn'd on me!
Now for my very life I grasp and hold   100
Unto the precipice whereon I cling.
Be with me now, O Ben, restore my strength.
I see that Vader hath ta'en flight, yet it
Is plain he doth but wait for his next chance.
Some hope remains, e'en now, amidst my fear—   105
He may yet be defeated, all's not lost.
I have regain'd my footing, and may rest
Until the fight must be resum'd. Now quick:
Look deep within your heart, Luke, and recall
The teachings of your gentle master Yoda.   110
Breathe deeply and call on the Force, that it
May show to thee the path that thou must take.
O, give me strength to win this battle now
Or, if not win, maintain my sense of right.
But lo, Darth Vader cometh once again!   115

Enter DARTH VADER. *They duel, and Luke*
is forced to the edge of a deep cavern.

VADER   This is the end for thee, Skywalker. See,
           Thou art defeated now; resistance would
           Be futile. Let yourself not be destroy'd
           As Obi-Wan did, weak old man he was.
                    [They duel. Darth Vader cuts off Luke's
                              right hand with his lightsaber.

LUKE   O horror! O vast pain exceeding words!   120
VADER   Thou shalt find no escape. Do not make me
           Destroy thee. Great importance shalt thou have
           Within the Empire's power, and thine own
           Shall only grow with time. I prithee, join
           With me, and I your training shall complete.   125
           When our strength is combin'd, we shall conclude
           This bitter conflict and bring order to
           The galaxy entire.
LUKE   —I never shall
           Join with thee; I would rather be destroy'd.
VADER   [*aside:*] The boy doth admirably keep his head, 130
           But now I shall unleash the final blow.
           [*To Luke:*] If thou but knewest all the power of
           The dark side. Obi-Wan hath never told
           Thee of what happen'd to thy father, Luke.
LUKE   O, he hath spoken much. And he hath told   135
           Me of the truth—that thou didst slay him, aye,
           And without cause or mercy, murderer
           Most vile and wretched!
VADER   —No, I am thy father.
LUKE   Nay, 'tis not true! It is impossible!
VADER   Pray, search thy feelings, Luke. Thou knowest it 140
           Is true.
LUKE   —Nay!

VADER   —Luke, thou mayst the Emperor
                Destroy; he hath foreseen what thou wouldst do.
                It is thy destiny, come join with me—
                Together we shall rule the galaxy
                As son and father. Come now, Luke, it is   145
                The only way: the dark side is thy path.
                O join with me, and we shall be as one.
                        [Luke looks down and drops into the cavern.

LUKE   I fall, and yet no death's upon me yet.
                I fall, for 'tis a better path than hate.

VADER   He falls, and welcomes death instead of pow'r.   150
                He falls, but I can sense he liveth still.

LUKE   I have not died—but pass into this shaft.
                I have not died—though I may wish it so.

VADER   He hath not died—his heart screams in its fear.
                He hath not died—so may he yet be turn'd.   155
                        *[Luke falls onto a weather vane at
                                the bottom of the shaft.*

LUKE   I am held fast by this vane o'er the clouds.
                I am held fast by some mirac'lous pow'r.

VADER   He is held fast within the dark side's grasp.
                He is held fast by his own clouded mind.
                                        [Exit Darth Vader.

LUKE   O Ben, I call to thee, but wilt thou hear?   160
                I do remember thou didst say thou couldst
                Not interfere in this, but O Ben, hear!
                Alas, my mentor's gone fore'er, and gives
                No answer—e'en deserted by the dead.
                If he cannot appear and rescue me,   165
                Then I shall try the living: Leia, next
                I call to thee. I prithee, Leia, hear!

Enter CHEWBACCA, PRINCESS LEIA, *and* LANDO,
aside in the Millennium Falcon.

LEIA   [*aside:*] What is this voice that echoes in mine ears?
                'Tis Luke, I know it is. Yet how is it
                That I do hear him when he is not nigh?   170
                No matter—more important 'tis that I
                Respond unto his call. [*To Lando:*] We must go back.
LANDO   What didst thou say?
LEIA   —I know where Luke is!
LANDO   —What
                About the fighters drawing near?
CHEWBAC.   —Egh, auugh!
LEIA   I prithee, Chewie: Han we could not save,   175
                But may yet rescue Luke, if we make haste.
LANDO   But what about the fighters, Princess?
CHEWBAC.   —Auugh!
LANDO   Pray, peace, good Wookiee, thou shalt have thy way.
                        [*They approach Luke in the ship. Lando
                        breaks off from the others to let Luke in.*
                What ties most deep do bind these souls as one!
                In all my workings as a bus'nessman,   180
                In all my making deals and earning more,
                I have forgotten what doth make life rich:
                'Tis friendship, love, and sacrifice that make
                A life, and I too long have not liv'd well!
                Farewell, the former Lando, lonely man!   185
                Farewell to selfish pride and high ambition!
                Farewell to scoundrelhood and avarice!
                Farewell to all the things my life has been!
                From now, I shall the great Rebellion serve,

And join myself unto this band of friends   190
Whate'er befall—pain, injury, or death.

[Lando opens the hatch.
Luke drops from the weather vane
into the ship.

Now come, brave Luke, whose mates to thee are dear,
I have not met thee, but do call thee brother.
Give me your hand, good Sir, if we be friends,
And Lando shall, in time, restore amends.   195
[To Leia:] Good Princess, let us fly, for all is well!

LEIA   O Luke, my heart doth swell to see thee safe!
Thou hast been caught within Darth Vader's trap,
But now thou art deliver'd and restor'd.

[Luke and Leia embrace while Lando
returns to the cockpit.

Now go with me unto the cot, and rest.   200
In time, we shall trade tales of grief and woe.

LANDO   The man is sav'd, but now the battle's on,
For by TIE fighters is our ship pursu'd!

LEIA   The *Falcon* is attack'd, Luke. Lie thou back,
I shall anon return to give thee aid.   205

[Leia goes to the cockpit.

[To Lando:] Behold, a Star Destroyer doth approach.

LANDO   Make ready, Chewie, for the lightspeed jump.

LEIA   Aye, if thy people fix'd the hyperdrive,
Coordinates are set—'tis time we flew.

LANDO   Now make it so!

[The Millennium Falcon *makes a sound and fails.*

CHEWBAC.   —Auugh!

LANDO   —I was told 'twas fix'd!   210
My trust I gave them, to repair the ship.

Some treachery and villainy lie here.
Forgive me, I know not what hath transpir'd.
'Tis not my fault. In troth, 'tis not my fault!

Enter DARTH VADER *and* ADMIRAL PIETT *on balcony.*

PIETT   The ship shall be in tractor beaming range   215
             Before thou canst say "aye."
VADER   —Thy trusty men
             Disab'd the swift *Falcon*'s hyperdrive?
PIETT   They did, my Lord.
VADER   —'Tis well. Prepare to board
             Their ship, and set all weapons onto stun.
             They have not made escape for long, and soon   220
             Skywalker shall be in my hand again,
             And I shall bring him to the Emperor.
PIETT   Indeed, my Lord, I shall with joy comply.
             The rebels shall be in our grasp anon.
             [Exit Admiral Piett, while Darth Vader stares into space.

Enter C-3PO *and* R2-D2, *who is repairing* C-3PO.

C-3PO   Why have we not to lightspeed flown?
R2-D2   —Beep, squeak!   225
C-3PO   What dost thou mean that we cannot? How canst
             Thou know the hyperdrive disabl'd is?
R2-D2   Beep, meep, meep, beep, squeak, whistle, nee, beep,
                                                          hoo!
C-3PO   The city's central processor hath told
             Thee so? O, R2-D2, how have I   230
             Oft warnèd thee of talking to a strange

Computer? Now, attend to my repair!

          [R2-D2 continues to repair C-3PO.

VADER   [*to Luke:*] Luke, well I know that thou canst sense

                                   my call.

LUKE   My father! Word most strange upon my lips.

VADER   My son.

LUKE   —O Ben, why didst thou tell me not?   235

                        [Luke walks to the cockpit.

LANDO   Chewbacca, we must fly or we shall be

Destroy'd!

LUKE   —It is Darth Vader on that ship.

We are in danger here. When shall we fly?

VADER   Luke, come with me, fulfill thy destiny!

LUKE   [*aside:*] O Ben, I ask, why didst thou tell me not?   240

What anguish and disorder fill my mind!

                    [R2-D2 goes to the control panel.

R2-D2   [*aside:*] It falls to me again to win the day,

And rescue the Rebellion from dire loss.

I shall reactivate the hyperdrive,

Thus we shall fly, to fight another time!   245

C-3PO   O clever droid, great R2, rescuer!

             [R2-D2 adjusts the control panel and the

                Millennium Falcon flies into lightspeed.

                    Exeunt all but Darth Vader.

VADER   Fie, fie! Yet once again the ship escapes.

I shall devise brave punishments for those

Who put upon our state this grievous blight.

Then shall I seek my son, the Jedi Knight.   250

                          [Exit Darth Vader.

SCENE 4.

Aboard a rebel cruiser.

Enter LUKE SKYWALKER.

LUKE   The medic droid hath fix'd my hand with care,
            Though never shall it fully be repair'd.
            For though I can this hand use as before,
            It shall ne'er truly be a hand of mine.
            For now I am machine, though partly so,   5
            Now have I ta'en a step toward the man
            Who saith he is my father, yet is wires
            And bolts. O hand, I find thee yet so dear.
            Pray, serve me well, and prick my memory
            That I did once the dark side briefly know—   10
            And fac'd, and fought, and ultimately fail'd.
            Then rise once more with me, my true right hand—
            Thy rightful place thou shalt take at my side
            To right the wrongs that we have sufferèd,
            And right now thou and I begin to work   15
            T'ward righteousness in great rebellion's cause.

Enter CHEWBACCA, PRINCESS LEIA, *and* LANDO.

            Now Lando, shalt thou go?
LANDO   —Aye, Luke, for all
            Hath been prepar'd. When we find Jabba and
            The bounty hunter, we shall tell thee all.
LUKE   I'll meet thee where we plann'd—on Tatooine—   20
            My homeland that is now estrang'd from me.
LANDO   Good princess, now farewell. Apologies

	Most earnest I convey again, and with	
	Them come a vow: we shall find Han, I swear.	
LUKE	Dear Chewie, I'll await thy signal.	
CHEWBAC.	—Auugh!	25
LUKE	Now take thou care—the Force be with ye both.	

                          [They move to separate parts of the stage.

LANDO	Now ends this troubl'd time of Empire's rise,	
	Our time of harsh betrayal, painful loss.	
	Now have we learn'd what friendship truly costs,	
	And in the learning lost a comrade strong.	30
LEIA	Along the way, our hearts were movèd much:	
	By sacred love, most wondrous to behold,	
	By bravery that shall outlive the times,	
	By sacrifice of our most precious friends.	
LUKE	Encounters unexpected we did meet	35
	With masters wise and persons unforeseen.	
	These are the star wars, yet they are not done—	
	For sure, the final chapter's just begun.	

Enter CHORUS *as epilogue.*

CHORUS	A glooming peace this morning with it brings,	
	No shine of starry light or planet's glow.	40
	For though our heroes 'scape the Empire's slings,	
	The great rebellion ne'er has been so low.	
	Brave Han is for the Empire's gain betray'd,	
	Which doth leave Princess Leia's heart full sore.	
	Young Luke hath had his hand repair'd, remade—	45
	The man is whole, but shaken to the core.	
	Forgive us, gentles, for this brutal play,	
	This tale of sorrow, strife, and deepest woes.	

Ye must leave empty, sighing lack-a-day,
Till we, by George, a brighter play compose.   50
Our story endeth, though your hearts do burn,
And shall until the Jedi doth return.

[Exeunt omnes.

E N D .

AFTERWORD.

A Winter's Tale, indeed: *William Shakespeare's The Empire Striketh Back*. Let me lift the curtain a bit to tell you about four aspects of what you've just read.

First of all: what does Yoda sound like in a galaxy filled with Elizabethan speech? This was the question that gnawed at me as I began to write this second *Star Wars* book. Yoda is famous for his inverted phrase order, but many people who read *William Shakespeare's Star Wars* commented that every character in it sounds a little like Yoda. So what to do? Originally, I had four different ideas:

- Do a complete reversal and have Yoda talk like a modern person: "Stop it. Don't try, just either do it or don't do it. Seriously."
- Have Yoda talk in something like Old English, approximating Chaucer: "Nee, do ye nae trie, aber due it oder due it not." (My Chaucer admittedly isn't great.)
- Don't do anything special, and have Yoda talk like the other characters.
- Repeat Yoda's lines verbatim from the movie, nodding to the fact that Yoda already sounds a little Shakespearean.

In the end, as you've read, I had a fifth idea, which I hope was better than any of these. Yoda is a wise teacher, almost like a *sensei*—he has something of an eastern sensibility about him. Why not express that by making all of his lines haiku? Yes, I know: Shakespeare never wrote in haiku. But he did break from iambic pentameter in certain cases—Puck from *A Midsummer Night's Dream* speaks in iambic tetrameter, songs in several Shakespearean works break meter, and so on. And yes, I know: the five–seven–five syllable pattern I adhere to in Yoda's haiku is a modern constraint, not part of the original Japanese poetic form. Most haiku are simpler than Yoda's lines and do not express complete sentences as Yoda's haiku do—I know, I know! Remember, this isn't scholarship; it's fun. For you purists:

> If these haiku have offended,
> Think but this, and all is mended:
> That you have but slumber'd here
> While these haiku did appear . . .

Second, *William Shakespeare's The Empire Striketh Back* introduces us to the first character in my Shakespearean adaptations who speaks in prose rather than meter: Boba Fett. Shakespeare often used prose to separate the lower classes from the elite—kings spoke in iambic pentameter while porters and gravediggers spoke in prose. In writing *William Shakespeare's Star Wars,* I did not want to be accused of being lazy about writing iambic pentameter, but with this book it was time to introduce some prose. Who better to speak in base prose than the basest of bounty hunters?

Third, one criticism of *William Shakespeare's Star Wars* I heard several times—and took to heart—was that I overused the chorus to explain the action sequences. Some argued that I shouldn't have used a chorus at all, which I disagree with; when I began writing the first book, the chorus seemed like a logical way to "show" the action scenes without actually showing them, and there was precedent in Shakespeare's *Henry V.* However, by leaning heavily on the chorus, I neglected another Shakespearean device, of having a character describe action that the audience can't see. Here's an example from *Hamlet*, Act IV, scene 7, in which Gertrude describes what happened to Ophelia:

> There is a willow grows aslant a brook,
> That shows his hoar leaves in the glassy stream;
> There with fantastic garlands did she come
> Of crow-flowers, nettles, daisies, and long purples
> That liberal shepherds give a grosser name,
> But our cold maids do dead men's fingers call them:
> There, on the pendant boughs her coronet weeds
> Clambering to hang, an envious sliver broke;
> When down her weedy trophies and herself
> Fell in the weeping brook. Her clothes spread wide;
> And, mermaid-like, awhile they bore her up:
> Which time she chanted snatches of old tunes;
> As one incapable of her own distress,
> Or like a creature native and indued
> Unto that element: but long it could not be
> Till that her garments, heavy with their drink,
> Pull'd the poor wretch from her melodious lay
> To muddy death.

This device is called on more frequently in *William Shakespeare's The Empire Striketh Back*, giving the chorus a needed break.

Fourth, Lando. As much as I like Billy Dee Williams, and as smooth as he was in 1980, in my opinion his character isn't fleshed out very well. We never know what he was thinking when he was forced to betray his friend, or what made him decide to help Leia and Chewbacca in the end. Filling in some of Lando's story with asides and soliloquies that show how conflicted he feels hopefully gives him some depth and makes him even more compelling than in the movie.

Once again, writing *William Shakespeare's The Empire Striketh Back* was a delight. Most *Star Wars* fans agree that *Empire* is the best of the original trilogy, and I hope I've done it justice. I say "most *Star Wars* fans" because in fact, *Empire* is not my personal favorite. I prefer *Return of the Jedi*, thanks in large part to two things. First, it is the first *Star Wars* movie I saw in the theater (I was six). Second, when I was growing up we owned a VHS tape of *From Star Wars to Jedi: The Making of a Saga*, and I loved hearing about the seven puppeteers who made Jabba move, seeing how the rancor came to life, learning how the speeder bike sequences were done, and so on.

That said, of the three movies, *Empire* has the most Shakespearean themes—betrayal, love, battles, destiny, teachers, and pupils. All of those, plus the shocking father–son relationship. In some ways, *Empire* follows an ancient story form that Shakespeare used: a classic tragedy, with Luke Skywalker as the tragic hero. He is like the Greek tragic hero Oedipus, who learns only too late that his mother is his wife and tears out his eyes after she hangs herself. Luke discovers that Darth Vader is his father just after losing a hand—close enough, right? Luke also demonstrates some serious hubris, just like Oedipus: he faces Darth Vader before being truly ready, despite the objections of the two remaining Jedi in the entire galaxy. And he pays the tragic price for it. Along the way, Han Solo is put on ice and Leia's and Chewbacca's hearts are broken. All the heroes will, of course, live on, and the tragedy will turn toward Darth Vader's redemption in *Return of the Jedi*, but when you take *Empire* as a single unit, the tragedy is Luke's, and the rebels see the worst of things by far.

Thank you for continuing this adventure with me. I hope *William Shakespeare's The Empire Striketh Back* offers plenty for both *Star Wars* fans and Shakespeare fans to appreciate. For instance, I hope talking wampas, AT-ATs, and space slugs (to say nothing of singing Ugnaughts) bring a smile to your face. And did you notice whom Han and Leia sound like once they start getting romantic? (Hint: look at the line endings.)

The positive response to *William Shakespeare's Star Wars* was a gift to me as a writer; I hope my retelling of *Empire* (and *Return of the Jedi,* coming soon) is a fitting thank-you.

ACKNOWLEDGMENTS.

So many people provided love, support, and encouragement for the release of *William Shakespeare's Star Wars* and the writing of *William Shakespeare's The Empire Striketh Back* that this book would be twice as long if I tried to name them all.

Thank you to the amazing people at Quirk Books who make the *Shakespeare's Star Wars* world go round: Jason Rekulak and Rick Chillot (the best editors a guy could ask for), publicity manager extraordinaire Nicole De Jackmo, the epic Eric Smith, and everyone else at Quirk. Thank you to my agent, Adriann Ranta, for hearing every idea—even the crazy ones—and responding to them gracefully—even the crazy ones. Thanks to Jennifer Heddle at Lucasfilm and, once again, to incredible illustrator Nicolas Delort.

Unending thanks to my college professor and friend, Murray Biggs, who once again reviewed my manuscript to improve the Shakespearean elements of the book. He confessed to me, after reading *William Shakespeare's Star Wars*, that he has never seen the *Star Wars* movies but said, "I have a feeling about that Luke and Leia." I hope *Empire* hasn't crushed that romantic hope too harshly. (And wait until he reads *Jedi*—gasp!) Huge thanks are also due to my friend Josh Hicks, who has been my confidant for ideas about these books ever since I had the inspiration for *William Shakespeare's Star Wars*. Josh and I have spent endless hours watching and discussing the *Star Wars* movies (like all true geeks), and he has been a constant encouragement. Thank you, Josh—now let's finish that children's book.

My parents, Beth and Bob Doescher, are my biggest fans and let me know how proud they are every time I see them. I know how rare it is to have parents who love you deeply and let you know it, and I don't take it for granted. To my brother Erik Doescher, my aunt Holly

Havens, and my dear college friends Heidi Altman, Chris Martin, Naomi Walcott, and Ethan Youngerman: thank you for continuing to show your love and support as one turned to three.

I have been blessed throughout my life by wonderful teachers and mentors: Jane Bidwell, Betsy Deines, Doree Jarboe, Chris Knab, Bruce McDonald, Janice Morgan, and Larry Rothe top the list. Thank you all so, so much for the lessons in school and life.

A big thank-you to the *Star Wars* fans who embraced *William Shakespeare's Star Wars* (and me) so warmly. You are an amazing group of people. Special shout-out to the worldwide members of the 501st Legion, and especially the 501st's Cloud City Garrison in Portland, Oregon.

Thank you also to so many who offered their kindness and assistance: Audu Besmer, Travis Boeh, Chris Buehler, Erin Buehler, Nathan Buehler, Jeff and Caryl Creswell, Katie Downing, Ken Evers-Hood, Mark Fordice, Chris Frimoth, Alana Garrigues, Marian Hammond, Brian Heron, Jim and Nancy Hicks, Apricot and David Irving, Alexis Kaushansky, Rebecca Lessem, Andrea Martin, Joan and Grady Miller, Jim Moiso, Michael Morrill, Dave Nieuwstraten, Julia Rodriguez-O'Donnell, Scott Roehm, Tara Schuster, Ryan Wilmot, Ben Wire, and Sarah Woodburn.

Last but never least, thank you to my spouse, Jennifer Creswell, and our children, Liam and Graham. Jennifer continues to be incredibly encouraging, even though this endeavor has taken much of my time and energy. Liam stops everyone he can, even complete strangers, and tells them I am the author of *William Shakespeare's Star Wars*. Graham shows his support through the biggest, strongest hugs an eight-year-old can give, which are the best cure for just about anything. Thank you, Jennifer, Liam, and Graham: you are my high every day.

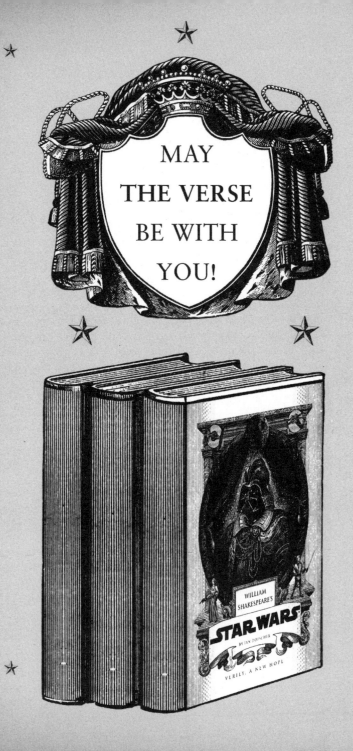

COLLECT

ALL THREE VOLUMES

IN THE

WILLIAM SHAKESPEARE'S
STAR WARS TRILOGY.

SONNET 3720-2-1
"To Thine Own Site Be True"

Thus far, with rough and all-unable Mac,
Our bending author hath pursu'd the flicks.
As thou hast read, the Empire hath struck back,
With grim Darth Vader up to his old tricks.
The tale is finish'd, but there is much more
That thou canst find within a website near:
A treasure trove of *Shakespeare's Star Wars* lore
From this book and the first that did appear:
A **trailer** for the world to share and see,
An **educator's guide** for those who learn,
An **interview** with author Ian D.—,
And **teasers** for *The Jedi Doth Return*.
As Hamlet to Ophelia did say,
"Get thee unto the Quirk Books site today!"

quirkbooks.com/empirestrikethback